Recall

The Eli Carver Supernatural Thrillers

Alan Baxter

Sobelo Books

Book Cover by Wendy Saber Core

Designed and published by Sobelo Books

ISBN (paperback) 978-1-965389-07-2
ISBN (hardback) 978-1-965389-12-6
ISBN (ebook) 978-1-965389-06-5

Omnibus first edition 2025

Contents

"The souls that throng the flood
Are those to whom, by fate, are other bodies ow'd:
In Lethe's lake they long oblivion taste,
Of future life secure, forgetful of the past."
***The Aeneid (Book VI)**, Virgil, 19 BCE*

Part I

Manifest Recall

Chapter 1

I bought a used car off a woman as thin as her hand-rolled cigarettes. "It's a good price," I told her. "Why are you selling?"

"Last year," she said, beginning to tremble, "I had a business and a husband. Now I have neither. I can't wake up in the middle of the night anymore, unable to breathe, panicking about debt."

I remember that clearly. Her wide, bloodshot eyes, her stained teeth and rat-tail hair. I feel it like a weight on me, my sympathy for that terrible, mundane predicament. It's indelible that memory. So I know exactly who I got this car from, even if I have no idea where it happened. Or when. Or where I am now.

Or who the hell this shivering girl beside me might be.

Her knees are pulled up to her chest, dirty bare feet on the seat, arms wrapped around her shins. She's wearing her seat belt, and black plastic cable ties secure her hands at the wrists. All that I see from the corner of my eye. I dare not turn to look directly at her. Not yet. She stares ahead through the windshield, unmoving. Her face is almost as dirty as her feet and she's wearing an oversized T-shirt. Whether she has on shorts or only underwear underneath, or even nothing at all, I can't tell.

The road ahead is dark, no streetlights, only the car's headlights spiking onto the gray, dirty asphalt. Trees flicker by on either side, occasionally a glimpse of stars in the night sky when the canopy over the road briefly breaks.

Where the hell am I?

I feel as though I've just been switched on, like a light in an old house, flooding a room with illumination for the first time in years. Or ever. A flicker of a story from Greek mythology comes to me. Lethe. One of five rivers in the underworld of Hades, the river of unmindfulness. The shades of the dead were required to drink its waters to forget their earthly life. Maybe I've died and drunk a gutful of Lethe and this is some strange hell.

I need to take it back a bit. Instead of trying to figure out why I can't remember all this stuff, let's see what I *can* remember. Can I remember anything?

My name is Eli Carver.

I'm twenty-eight years old.

I killed a man in New Orleans and it made me vomit.

Jesus fuck, I put that gun against his ear and pulled the trigger and his head exploded like a fucking watermelon. I can still see my hand trembling as I did it, recall the wash of terror and disgust. I didn't want to do it, but something made me. Some*one* made me. It was a hot night, a warm breeze blowing gently across that balcony overlooking Bourbon Street, carrying the aromas of fried food and cigar smoke. My knees were knocking like saplings in a gale. But I did it. I killed him.

"You back, you fucking weirdo?"

Her voice startles me out of my thoughts and the car weaves slightly left and right.

"Don't drive off the fucking road and kill us now, you dick."

She's still staring straight ahead, still clutching her knees. Her voice is hard, hateful.

I glance across at her. She can't be more than eighteen or nineteen. "Back?"

"You've been a robot since Vernon's, man. You gotta pull it together."

She clearly knows more than I do, but I can hardly ask her to fill me in. Can I? She's the one tied up and filthy. I'm driving. Have I kidnapped her? I suck a long breath in through my nose and try to stay calm, act like I'm not a blank page in an empty notebook. Vernon's, she said. Do I know any Vernons?

"Can you at least turn the damn heater on?"

It is cold in the car and I'm wearing jeans and boots and a short denim jacket over a black T-shirt. No wonder she's shivering. I crank up the heat and it blasts from the vents in an instant, warm and musty, stinking of burned oil. Maybe this car isn't what it used to be. In the memory of buying it, the thing was almost new, smelled of air freshener and the seats were clean. That must have been a long time ago and I obviously had some money back then. I'm not sure what's in my pocket now.

And it's cold, but the night I shot that guy was warm. How much time has passed? He was the first, I realize, long ago. But not the last. He was the catalyst, the one who changed me. Here and now, this night, this dark road, was kick-started *that* night as I turned and vomited into a potted palm on that sweaty balcony. Someone laughing, saying, "Damn, kid, I didn't think you had it in you. Thought we'd be burying two bodies tonight."

And through the haze of my vomit tears I see the broad back of a man with a bald head, trailing acrid cigar smoke, walking back through double leadlight doors into the house. His shoulders move as he's still laughing to himself. Vernon. Vernon Sykes, mobster extraordinaire. Of course. That's him, but I can't see his face. Still can't remember that. Two burly guys clap me on the back, one says, "That puking will stop. You'll get used to it."

It's not something I ever want to get used to.

"We got this," the other says. "You're done for tonight. Go and get drunk, get laid. We'll see you tomorrow."

The first one leans in, dark skin glittering with a sheen of sweat. "But this is your virgin special. After this you take care of your own stiffs, you get me?"

I just nod, catch a glimpse of the dead guy's head smeared up the wall, his neck leaking ichor onto the white deck, half his face staring back at me with a blank eye, and I turn and puke again.

Michael. His name was Michael Privedi. He was a rat and Vernon had me take care of it, because he thought I was a rat too. But I wasn't.

"We need to stop before I piss my pants," the girl says.

So she's wearing pants then. "You just want to run away."

"Fucking right, I do!" she spits. "You're gonna get us both wasted! But out here in nothing but a T-shirt and panties? I'd be dead before morning. How about you stand beside me and hold my fucking hair while I squat? That work for you? I just need to piss."

She is so angry, and I can't blame her. But she's clearly terrified too. Not even twenty years old. Something jolts through me. Twenty years old. That's how old I was when I shot Michael in New Orleans. I don't know how, but I know I'm twenty-eight now. Why do I remember that and so little else? Eight years ago. No wonder the car looks crappy. I pull over to the shoulder and get out, go around to her side, and open the door. She looks at me and then tips her head towards my hands.

"I don't want to hold your hair. Just stay nearby."

She makes a hissing sound of disgust and moves a yard away to the edge of the trees. It's awkward for her to pull her underwear down with her hands bound up in front, but she does it, sits, and a stream of steaming piss hits the dirt. She really needed to go. It makes me want to go too, so I move away and piss into the trees with my back to her.

"You really know how to take a girl on a date, Eli," she says, and there's a tone of amusement in her voice, the anger a little dissipated.

I can't help laughing a little. "I bring all my girls to this stretch of highway for a piss."

She huffs, half a laugh, and I hear her scuffling around as I zip up. I expect her to be hightailing it into the woods as I turn back, but she's already back in her seat, pulling the car door closed. I get back into the driver's seat, start the engine, and pull away again, the dark highway sliding by. As dark as my still empty mind.

"Where do you think we're going?" she says.

I don't even know her name. "North."

"North? How much further north can we go? There's nowhere you can go to outrun Vernon."

Michael leans through the gap between the front seats, one side of his head and half his face a ragged, bloody mess. "She's right, man. You know she's right."

I scream and the car swerves, gravel sprays from the tires. The girl slams her hands to the dashboard to brace herself. "What the fuck, Eli?"

My heart is hammering, my throat feels swollen with it. In the rearview mirror, the back seat is empty. I twist around to see and there's no one there.

"The fuck is wrong with you?" She glances back too, smooth brow creased in a frown.

Man, she's beautiful. It's like I'm only just noticing that, but I've known it for a long time. I've known her since she was a child, ten years old, maybe less. As she got towards thirteen and fourteen, I hated myself for the carnal thoughts I had. Then she got to sixteen and seventeen, started looking like a grown woman, and everyone agreed she was a stunner. Long, black hair with a soft wave, startling green eyes, smooth skin. The body of a dancer and a heart-shaped face with full lips.

Her name rises like a bubble through tar. Carly. Oh shit. Carly Sykes.

I've got Vernon's daughter.

"If you hadn't smashed my phone, we could find out where the nearest motel is," she says after a few miles of silent driving.

"Motel?"

She looks at me, her gaze searing as I drive, and I refuse to take my eyes off the road. "You blanked out for a long time, Eli. You really scared me."

"How long?"

"You don't remember?"

"It's a little blurry." Understatement of a lifetime.

"Fucking *days*, man. You remember driving for two days with me in the trunk?"

I can't help looking at her and my shock must be written across my face, because her own hard gaze softens.

"You really don't, do you? You were like a zombie. You didn't even feed me for the first day and a half or give me any water."

I lick my lips, shame burning my cheeks. "I'm sorry, Carly."

She shakes her head, stares down into her lap. I catch the glint of a tear reflecting the dashboard lights as it falls to her thigh, soaks into the dirty T-shirt. "I thought you were going to kill me, too."

Who else did I kill?

"I guess there's a part of me that wouldn't blame you."

I remember I have a bag behind the passenger seat with a couple of changes of clothes, some cash, a few other survival bits and pieces. For whenever I found myself out on the road for a day or two, unexpectedly, sent on some mission for Vernon. Maybe I could give Carly something else to wear from there. I get a flash of her standing in that oversized T-shirt, clean but shocked, the room around me drenched in blood. I gasp and my brain shuts down on the recollection.

"Hey! Hey, asshole!"

I blink and shake my head, turn to look at her.

"Don't you blank on me again, man. I need you to hold it together. I'm so hungry and so tired, and so fucking filthy. We have to rest. Find a motel, get ourselves sorted out. You stink, man. You need a shower, too."

I let my eyes roam over my hands, realize I'm dirty as hell. There's dried blood on my pale knuckles and jammed under my nails. A sidelong look at the rearview mirror shows my face is smeared with dirt like hers. More blood there, too. Pretty sure none of it's mine. My green eyes are hooded, my dark, curly dark hair matted and greasy. I have a hell of a bruise across my right cheekbone, swollen and yellowing around the edges of a midnight blue lump.

"Okay." I know she's right. We've been driving like this for two days? Surely there's enough space and time for me to catch up, figure shit out. "No names, no credit cards." The words come to me as easily as breathing. I know I'm good at this stuff.

"Like I've got those any more than I still have my phone." She leans back, gestures at herself with both hands. "Maybe I can at least get some fucking shoes?"

I grind my teeth. I have to stay in control of this. "No phone calls. You stay in the room."

Her eyes flash fury, she opens her mouth to speak. But I interrupt before she can get going.

"You give me your sizes. I'll get us both new clothes and whatever else we need. Meanwhile, I might have something here you can use."

She presses her lips together, staring daggers at me, but I keep my eyes on the road. Eventually she subsides, slumps back down into her seat, staring balefully out at the night.

Chapter 2

We don't speak for over an hour and the whole time I'm searching the blank cavern of my brain, but all I come up against are dark walls. Except for one thing. My second kill.

Now, I know Vernon made me kill Michael Privedi. He was my first and made me puke. We'd come up together, Michael and me, both making good at Vern's heel. But Michael had always been a little unstable. I remember Vernon took me under his wing when I was eighteen. That memory is clear enough now. My parents died at the hands of a drunk driver when I was five. I remember that too. Well, I remember being told about it. In all honesty, I have precious few recollections of any kind until I was into my teens and in state care. I guess I've always had this propensity for lost memories. I recall hundreds of books, though. Giant fantasy romps and science fiction space operas. Thrillers and mystery novels, Tarzan, and Sherlock Holmes. I've been mocked my whole life for being a bookworm, but I'm a big guy too and learned early on how to fight, so I've never really taken too much shit off anyone. And I'd always retreat into books to hide from the pain of real life.

When I was fifteen or sixteen, I used to skip out from school by hanging around in Privedi's Workshop with Michael. He'd skip classes too. His dad owned the garage. His old man didn't give a crap whether his son went to school or not. He let us both hang around and talk shit with the mechanics, drink beer and smoke cigarettes while they fixed cars, or chopped them. When you think about it, Michael's dad was an asshole. But he was connected too, a wingman in Vernon's crew. And soon enough, Vern started showing an interest in me and Michael. Brought us both in when we turned eighteen, after grooming us for a good year or so.

Then, only two years later, a jack mysteriously failed and dropped a '97 Buick right on Michael's dad. Except it was only a mystery to the police. We all knew Vernon made it happen because Mr. Privedi had been into the Colombian cartel for about fifty large and face had to be saved. The fool was playing around with all kinds of gamblers, and one of Vern's made men owing that kind of cash to the Colombians? Unforgiveable. These memories are flooding back now.

But Michael couldn't forgive Vernon. He kept raving about how come Vern couldn't make some other retribution, save face some other way? Why did his dad have to die? Michael knew the truth. He just didn't want to accept it. And so he started looking for a way out and that kingshit detective, Rob Bradon, got his claws in. Made Michael give stuff up. Of course, Vern had considered that possibility and was watching closely. As soon as Michael cracked, Vern called a meeting at the house on Bourbon Street.

"I wanna make things right between you and me, about your dad," Vern had said to Michael.

Right then I got chills. I could tell something was up. So could Michael. He started looking left and right like a cat that's forgotten to check a room for exits. Vern's main wingmen, big black Charles and equally big, white and red-haired Peter, shifted up to either side of Michael and led him by the elbows.

"Let's go on the balcony for some air," Vern had said. "Eli, come on."

Trembling set in as I wondered what the hell was up. Me and Michael, we were close like brothers, everyone knew that. If Michael had done something fucking stupid, was he going to take me down with him? At that point I'd no idea he was giving intel to Bradon, but I was getting concerned about him, wondering if he might do something unforgiveable. I was so damn young and naïve then.

When we walked into that sticky night, out of the cooling comfort of the fans and AC, Vernon dabbed his sweating forehead with a white handkerchief and passed me a gun with the other hand. Now I can see him, square-faced, granite jaw, eyes a little too close together, dark and penetrating. Skin like cement, always a little gray. But he was strong and healthy too.

"We all know why we're here," he said, almost like he was too tired to even bother.

"You got this wrong, Vern," Michael said. His teeth were chattering like he was cold, and his eyes darted left and right, tears sitting on his lashes. "You know I wouldn't rat you out. You know I wouldn't cause you any grief, Vern. You know I'm not like my old man."

Vernon shook his head. "Seems I know a lot of stuff. I'll tell you the only thing I don't know." He looked at me and the weight of his gaze was like a punch.

The gun seemed to weigh a ton in my hand, but it was only a revolver. A thirty-two with six bullets. I already knew it would only spit one tonight. I had no choice.

Vern's face was blank. "I don't know whether it's just you or you and your buddy here."

His eyes didn't leave mine, so I straightened up and met his gaze. I'd suspected Michael might crack, but I'd also ignored it, distanced myself a little since Mr. Privedi got flattened by a Buick, waiting to see how Michael would shape up. Self-preservation is a strong instinct. I had nothing to hide, nothing to be guilty about.

"I don't know what he's done wrong, Mr. Sykes. But whatever it is, it hasn't been with me."

Vern had smiled. "You only call me Mr. Sykes when you're nervous, Eli."

"Damn straight I'm fucking nervous now, Mr. Sykes."

"So prove to me you're not a rat. I know for a fact that he is. He dies tonight."

Michael was gibbering and gabbling, crying and wiping at the snot flooding his top lip. Charles cuffed him into silence and he quietly hitched breaths while Vern stared at me.

"He dies tonight by your hand, to prove you're with me," Vern said. "Or he dies by Charles's hand and Peter kills you."

I shook my head, mind spinning, feeling like I was about to explode from the sheer pulse of nerves. "Mr. Sykes, I'm for you all the way, but please don't make me kill Michael. He's my friend. I've never killed a man before."

"It was bound to happen sometime."

"Sure, I figured that, but not my best friend."

Vern's eyes narrowed and a cold wave broke over me. "Your best friend?"

"Mr. Sykes. Vernon! I'm not a rat!"

And Michael's sobs grew louder.

Vern gestured to the gun hanging loose in my hand. "Prove it, Mr. Carver."

So I put that gun to Michael's ear and I pulled the trigger, before I could stop to think about it any more, because I knew I was a dead man otherwise. And I couldn't bear to hear another second of Michael's panic and distress.

And then I puked in a potted palm.

And Charles said to me, "But this is your virgin special. After this you take care of your own stiffs, you get me?"

Seems I remember more than I thought.

But that was my first kill. It's directly connected to my second. A guy called Alvin Crake, who used to be a mechanic at Mr. Privedi's and talked a lot of shit about the man after Vernon dropped that Buick on him.

Vernon had taken control of the workshop, of course, and technically Alvin worked for him. I used to spend a lot of time there. Still, the office out back was a place I conducted a lot of business for Vern. One day, after hearing just one line too much about Mr. Privedi and his shitheel son, I asked Alvin to join me in that office. He'd scowled at me but came along. I'd closed the door behind him, turned around, and shot him in the face. I didn't puke that time. It was easy. I hated that guy. And I took care of my own stiff.

Told Vern that Alvin had been making trouble and the big man slapped me on the shoulder and said, "Well done for taking care of business. I never did trust that asshole." Which was fortunate for me. Then he'd gone about his day like nothing was out of the ordinary. I suppose it wasn't for him.

But that was another turning point for me. When I became a willing killer. There's been a few more since then, but they've all deserved it. Haven't they? I know there have been more, though I can't remember right now who they are or why they died. Everything's so goddamned hazy.

"Town up ahead," Carly says, leaning forward in her seat. "You have to stop, okay?"

"Yeah, okay."

A scattering of properties mark the start of the locality. Streetlights up ahead and then a sign saying Palm Tree Motel, 1 Mile. Carly looks at me pointedly and I nod. She's right, we badly need to rest and clean up. And we need food. My gut rumbles and I realize I'm starving. I've barely fed her, apparently. Maybe I've hardly fed myself either.

The sign for the motel is bright white and blue neon, glowing out over the dark road like a fake moon. I pull into the parking lot and brake to a halt, heart hammering. A police cruiser sits there on the asphalt, along with three or four other cars, presumably belonging to motel guests.

Carly shakes her head. "Don't you dare pull out again. We have to stop."

"Cops," I say stupidly.

"Yeah, no shit, cowboy. But we're not in trouble with the cops, remember? Quite the fucking opposite."

"But...look at us."

She holds up her hands. The cable ties have rubbed red raw lines into her skin, even made it bleed in places. "Maybe you should cut these off."

I lick my lips, look out the window. The motel office is lit up like a fish tank with venetian blinds on the inside and a cop has parted two with his fingers, stares out at us.

"Put your fucking hands down!"

I slap her hands into her lap and pull forward again, park across the lot from the cruiser and kill the engine.

"Let me preempt all your concerns," Carly says. "I'm not gonna run away because I'll be raped and killed by local rednecks before dawn running around like this. I'm not going to the police, because they'll ask way more questions than I can answer, and we both know Vernon has too many connections in the police, anyway."

I frown at her. "You're not desperate to get back to Vernon? Surely turning me in is your best bet."

She frowns back at me, shakes her head. "I just need to be clean and get something to eat, Eli. Please. You cut these off, then I'll sit here like a good girl while you check us in. Then we'll take care of cleaning ourselves up."

"I'm looking pretty beat up myself," I say. "They might ask me questions."

"So tell 'em you got in a fight. Miles back, yesterday, whatever. What do they care?"

I take a deep breath, thinking of all the things that might get me hooked. I think the car is clean and legal. I'm pretty sure there's no contraband inside, nothing incriminating. But then, there's so much I don't remember. How the fuck do I know what's there? I've carried kilos of cocaine, weed, and smack for Vernon before, so who's to say there's not a life sentence sitting in the trunk?

"Get moving!" Carly says. "I'm getting cold again."

With the engine off, the nighttime chill is biting down quickly.

"Okay."

Chapter 3

Fucking cops. It's not like I've ever cared what they think before. I've had my run-ins with them often enough and they're all the same, looking out for themselves. Just as bent as the rest of us, except they do their crime from behind a badge and get paid by the fucking government for it.

There's a rush of warm air as I push open the office door and two people turn to look at me. A cop in front of the desk and an old man in a stained T-shirt behind it. The cop moves only a little to one side of the small space, so I have to step right next to him to approach the old man. Bastard.

I give a nod and half a smile as the old man says, "I'm Clarence. Help ya?"

"Need a twin room for me and my sister."

"No problem. Just tonight?"

"Yeah."

Clarence names a price and my heart thumps. I pat my jacket for my wallet, feel the square lump of it and hope there's money inside. When I open it up, I'm relieved to see quite a few hundred. Good for a little while, at least. I remember I have bank accounts. I have a vague memory of several stashes here and there too, cash tucked away. And other stuff, lot of little bolt holes. After what happened to Michael... After what I did to him, I've always been careful to have quick ways out.

"Sir, you okay?"

I snap back to the present, shake my head and the cop is staring hard into my eyes. He's got a sharp nose and a pointed chin. Looks like a giant fucking rat.

"Yeah, sorry. Just really tired. That's why I've stopped."

"You look a little worse for wear."

"Got in a fight. Yesterday. Outside a truck stop."

"That right?"

The best lies are the simple ones. The more complicated you make a lie, the bigger it gets, the more easily you trip over it. "Yeah. No big thing."

The cop nods, mouth twisted in thought. I hold his eye for a moment more, then turn back to the motel clerk, hand him the bills.

Clarence hands me a key with a ridiculously large wooden fob swinging off it. "You parked all the way over there outside number twelve, so you may as well take that room. It's a twin and we're quiet right now."

"Thanks."

I nod to him, then to the cop, and suddenly feel like an imbecile, waggling my fucking head around at everyone. Jesus, but I am tired. I could sleep right here on my feet. How long since I last slept? Something occurs to me and I turn back.

"Say, is there anywhere to get something to eat this late?" I don't even know how late it is, but spot a clock above the old man. Ten thirty-five. Not too bad.

"There's a diner one block down on the other side. It's called Noah's Place. There's a number in your room and they'll deliver for an extra ten bucks."

"Ten bucks for a single fucking block?"

The cop laughs and says, "Old Noah knows how to turn a profit. You're gonna pay it though, right? Save yourself a walk?"

I'm annoyed to admit he's right, but he is. "Ten fucking bucks. You should be over there arresting that thief instead of shooting shit here."

They both laugh and I grin at them, the tension in the air gone like it was never there. Maybe that didn't work out so badly.

I'm relieved to see Carly's silhouette still in the car as I trudge back across the parking lot. There's one tall halogen casting a pool of light into the middle of the lot, everything around it in blacks and grays, lost shadows. As I get near the disc of brightness, Alvin Crake falls into step beside me. His face has a half-inch-wide hole right between the eyebrows, the back of his head opened up like a bony flower blooming, the result of that casual shot in Privedi's office. I yelp, but swallow down panic as he says, "You'll never get away."

I suck fast, deep breaths in through my nose. I killed this fucker nearly eight years ago. He's not here. He can't be here.

He slaps my shoulder with one meaty palm and I feel it and hear the *thwack*. "You know it. You'll never get away. Vernon has too many connections, too many eyes, too many fucking people!"

I turn and swing a fist, aiming to crack him across his stupid square jaw, but my arm sweeps through air and there's no one there. Carly is looking at me with a frown through the passenger window. I glance back and that cop has his fingers in the blind again, watching me. I sweep my hand again, like I'm batting at a fucking moth or something, then swipe the other hand too. Have I overdone it now? Do I look more or less like a madman?

Carly pushes the door open, still frowning. "The fuck?"

"Don't worry about it."

"Where are we?"

I nod at number twelve, directly in front of the car.

"Good. Stay between me and the office, so they don't see I'm hardly fucking dressed."

I do as she says. It's a good idea. I hand her the key and she opens the door, goes inside. As I close the door behind me, she turns, holds her hands out. "I really want to wash. Please, cut these?"

With pursed lips, I look around. She's being okay with me, didn't run or scream at the cops. I guess I have to trust her. How much she's biding her time though, that's a mystery. Still, what can I do? I just need a knife.

"Use the one in your pocket." She's staring at my jeans.

Of course, I've always got a Swiss Army Knife on me. The blade is sharp, bright, and clean, shining silver. I slit the tie and she virtually sprints into the bathroom, slams the door, and locks it.

A moment of panic passes over me, and I head back outside. The cop is gone from the window of the office, but the cruiser is still there. Our room is the last in the row, so it's easy to slip around the back and check. The bathroom window is tiny and barred. I hear the shower rushing inside. No way she's getting out of there. The only way in or out is the front door.

I go back to the car and start searching the trunk. Nothing but some old oil stains. The back lights both have metal sheets bolted over the inside, to stop anyone in the trunk from punching out the light unit and waving out of the hole for help. If ever anyone throws you in the trunk of their car, that's the best thing to do. Wait until the car is moving, punch out the lights and wave frantically. Hope like hell someone sees you and calls the cops. So, of course, people like me, who routinely put fuckers in the trunk, we make sure no one can do that. And that's probably why there's nothing else in here. If I had Carly there for a couple of days, I'd make sure she had nothing to use, no means of escape. Jesus, poor Carly, I feel bad for what I've done to her, but there must be a good reason.

I get another wave of panic and rush back into the motel room. The shower is still going, the bathroom door shut. With a breath of relief, I pull the cord of the phone from the wall, rip the wires clean out. Clarence can bill me later if he wants to, but at least Carly can't call for help now. I should have thought of that right away. I'm so fucking tired.

I return to the car and get my bag from behind the seat. Clothes, toi-letries, toothbrush, all that shit. The zip is open and there's a nine-millimeter semi-automatic lying on the top. Just as well, the cop never got a look at that. I don't expect it's legally mine. But good to know I'm armed.

As I head back to the room, the cop is returning to his cruiser. The rat-looking fucker raises one hand in a wave. "Take care now."

I nod. "You too."

I watch from the window, the room door closed and locked, as he backs up and pulls away into the night. The place is quiet and still except for the continuing rush of the shower. Then I realize I fucked up the phone before I called for some food. Goddamn it.

When Carly comes out of the bathroom, she's transformed. She seems taller, stronger than the beaten-down little girl in my beaten-up old car. Why am I driving that car, anyway? I've had a dozen since I bought that from the chain-smoking woman who lost her husband and business in the same year. Something else to think about. I really drank a bellyful of Lethe.

Carly has a towel wrapped around herself, her fine legs bare from the knees down. She is a stunning figure of a woman. Her hair is wet, hanging loose all around her face, laying over her firm shoulders. There's a muscular strength about her. She's not skinny, but not bullish either. Graceful. Lithe.

"I'm not putting that damn T-shirt on again."

I can't blame her for that. From my bag I take another T-shirt, hand it over. "I'll get you some better clothes soon, but right now, all I have is my own stuff."

"And what are you, six two and two hundred twenty pounds? Like anything is gonna fit me any better than that last shirt."

I dig around and find a pair of baggy track pants. "Can you roll these up or something?"

She shakes her head and takes the clothes back into the bathroom. A few minutes later she emerges with the track pants cut off at the ankle, rolled up at her hips and cinched tight. The T-shirt is pulled around and knotted at the waist.

"Your pants gave up their life for me," she says, eyes daring me to be annoyed.

I shrug. It's fair enough. She looks faintly ridiculous, but kinda hot too. All baggy like some eighties throwback. "You need some Reebok Pumps and a boom box."

She looks at me, one eyebrow raised. "You're feeling better, clearly. Making jokes now?"

I shrug again, because I really don't feel any better. Then again, before now, I wasn't feeling anything at all. "The phone is broken. I have to order food at the office."

"I'm not going anywhere."

I take the phone and go to Clarence. He frowns at me as I walk in. "Some idiot ripped the phone cord clean out of the wall," I tell him.

"Damn thing was fine when I cleaned up in there this morning."

I put the phone on his desk, make a face like I don't know what to tell him. Honestly, I really don't. "I don't need a phone except to order food, so it's no big thing to me. If I can order from here?"

Clarence's face is dark as he pushes the office phone across the counter. He points to a menu tacked on the wall beside his laptop, Noah's Place. The number is big and bold right across the top. "Better hurry. He closes at eleven."

According to the clock, it's ten minutes to. I ring up and the kid on the other end sounds bored as hell as he takes my order for two burgers with everything, large fries with each, and a big bottle of soda. Tells me it'll be about fifteen minutes, so I tell him room twelve, and to make sure he knocks loud.

"Thanks, Clarence." I give the old man a smile and walk away, leaving our busted phone on his desk.

Chapter 4

Carly is watching some late night talk show on the TV when I get back to the room. "I hope you ordered for ten people."

"I ordered enough."

She wrinkles her nose at me. "Seriously, go wash. You fucking reek."

As I get undressed, I realize my shirt is stiff with dried blood. Just as well it's black, so it only looks like dirt. And what must that cop have thought, me looking and smelling like this? The hot shower is like a benediction, washing away more than the dirt and blood. But it doesn't seem to wash in any more memories. When I push the shower curtain aside, step out into clouds of steam, a shape in the mist makes me jump, drop into a fighting stance.

"You've made a terrible fucking mistake, bro," Michael says. He's sitting on the closed toilet seat, half his face gone, smoking a cigarette like nothing's wrong. The sharp scent of the Marlboro is strong in the small bathroom.

"The fuck are you doing here, man?"

"Looking out for you. Aren't I the best example that you don't cross Vernon Sykes?"

"There have been many other examples, Michael. Some of them better than you."

"Well. Even still. You've made a big fucking mistake. And taking Carly?"

"You thinking about fuckin' that sweet thang?" Alvin says, leaning back against the sink.

Michael looks over at him with a frown. "What the fuck are you doing here, asshole?"

"Just tryin'a help."

I bark a laugh. "What fucking help are either of you two dead fuckers?"

"Seriously," Alvin says. "You're already in as much trouble with Vernon as you can possibly be. So fuck that hot bitch out there. I mean, man, she's fine. That body! And that mouth, tell me you don't wanna drive your cock into that sweet mouth."

I swing a punch at Alvin again, the second time I've tried to punch the same dead asshole in half an hour, but I only hit air and steam. I turn back to Michael, but he's gone, too. A banging startles me, then I hear Carly opening the door, taking the food from the delivery boy.

"Hey," she calls out. "We need to pay this guy."

I pull on clean jeans and a T-shirt from my sports bag and go out to find my wallet and hand over the bills. I tip him heavily, wave him away and shut the door, then we both fall on the food like lions on a gazelle. I don't think anything has ever tasted so damn good.

Fatigue hits me like a truck once we've devoured the food, my body finally admitting that I've been pushing too hard for too long. All I want to do is sleep when I see Michael at the window, lifting the curtain aside to look out at the lot. A glance at Carly shows she's not seeing him, or choosing to ignore him. Given that there's no way she could ignore a guy with half a face who wasn't there five seconds ago, I can only assume I'm hallucinating.

Then Michael, still holding the curtain aside, looks around at me and says, "He's back."

Ice runs through my gut and I jump up, run to the window. Michael's not there by the time I've cleared the end of the bed, but I'm too preoccupied to care. The police cruiser *is* there, pulled up across the back of my car. The rat-faced fucker who tried to make conversation shines a flashlight out of his window, checking out the plate. He nods and says something into his radio, then gets out.

"Get your shoes on."

Carly looks up from the bed, where she's laying flat out and almost asleep. "What?"

"Shoes, now. Grab the bag. We're leaving."

"What the fuck, Eli, I need to…"

"*Now!*" I yell and it's like my voice physically lifts her to her feet, because she's standing by the bed, reaching for the bag in an instant.

"I don't have any fucking shoes," she says, tears in her eyes. She looks really spooked again, watching me like a cow watches the farmer with a bolt gun in his hand.

I pull on my boots as the cop slowly approaches our door. Carly comes to stand beside me and I stuff my hand into the top of the bag and pull out the automatic.

"What the fuck, Eli?"

She seems to ask me that a lot. I push her back behind me and say, "This is gonna be messy."

"Who is it?"

"Cops."

Her voice is a strained and panicked whisper. "You're gonna waste some cops?"

"Just one. No choice." Then I look at her, one last glimmer of hope fading as I ask, "They can't help us, right?"

"Of course not."

I move to the side of the door, looking out the small window beside it. The cop is on the sidewalk right outside.

"Vern would get us anywhere," Carly says. "But especially in police custody. We can't trust cops any more than strangers."

That last hope stutters out and as the rat-faced cop reaches up to knock on the door, I put the muzzle of the automatic against the weak plywood and fire three times. He staggers backwards, his chest and throat bursting out bright crimson in the weak glow of that tall halogen over the parking lot. I pull open the door, but he's already dead, staring at the dark sky. Steam is curling from the police cruiser's tailpipe, so I grab Carly by the arm and haul her along. We jump over the dead cop and into the cruiser, then I'm flooring it, the tires spraying gravel as we fishtail out of the lot and onto the main road.

Chapter 5

Adrenaline has slammed my fatigue away for now, my focus tight, my vision sharper than a bird of prey. Carly is muttering and sobbing and clutching her knees again. The police radio is crackling, then a voice comes over, but I can't make out the words for the blood pounding in my ears. In the mirror I see movement in the back seat, behind the cage, and bite down a gasp. Michael and Alvin are both there, twisting around to see out the back window.

"That old man Clarence is on his knees out there," Michael says.

"Old fucker is howlin' like a whipped dog!" Alvin says, laughing like that's the funniest thing he's ever seen.

"They can trace this car easy."

Carly's voice cuts through my pulse and the voices of those dead fuckers. "What?"

"The police. They can trace their own cars. GPS and shit. We gotta dump it."

She's right. I nod tightly, looking around. The town is small, the streetlights far apart. Most everything else is dark, but for a few shops with illuminated window displays. The place is a ghost town. Noah's Place shoots by on the right, all closed up and dark but for its neon sign.

"Jesus, Eli, you're in some shit here. You ever wasted cops before?"

I look over, wondering how much to tell her. Because I don't fucking know. I'm sure I've killed plenty more than Michael and Alvin, but any cops? Any real people? I just don't know. My hands are shaking on the wheel, so I grip it tighter before she can see.

She jabs a thumb back over her shoulder. "I mean, you left your car right there. He made it, obviously. Tell me it's not in your real name, Eli."

I swallow, thinking hard. I bought that car so long ago, but I don't think I've used it in years. That skinny woman with the broken life and narrow cigarettes, she wanted cash. I didn't even register the damn thing when I bought it. Maybe it's still in her name.

Oh wait, I used it in a job that went bad. I remember now. Had to get away fast. Ran right into a cop standing on the corner outside the bar. He had his gun leveled at the car, squeezed off one shot, then I swerved and clipped him. Didn't kill him, I remember that, sent him sprawling and he came up onto his knees, holding one arm against his chest like it was broken, his face twisted in pain. And I bolted, managed to not get followed, and I took the car to Vernon's place. It had stolen plates over the real ones for that job. Vern kept an eye on things and, after a few days, announced that neither we or the car had been made, but best not to drive it around anymore. He said to leave it on his property. He had someone come out and fix the ding in the wing and the bullet hole in the hood, get rid of the fake plates. Then he let his teenage kids drive it around for fun. No wonder it's so beat up. It's been a private joy ride for six or seven years.

And that was my third kill.

Not the cop, but in the bar right before. Vern had sent me to whack a guy by the name of Sylvester Barclay. Sly Barclay. He was a small-time hood, worked for the Jamaicans. I guess he was Jamaican too, I don't know. But there was some balance to be redressed. One of our boys got killed in a drug deal with those guys that went bad, and Vernon told me we had to even the slate.

"We gotta waste one of theirs," he said. "Go down to Maloney's and see if that Sly Barclay is there. I know him and some pals drink there all the time."

"And bring him in?" I'd asked.

Vernon laughed. "Fuck no, son. Put a bullet between his fucking eyes. Public execution. And say, 'We're even now.' And walk out."

Bold as brass and twice as hard, that's how Vernon liked to do business. So I put on a balaclava, walked into Maloney's, and there was Sly right there. But he was already standing, had a gun pointed right at the door. Somehow, someone inside had tipped him off. I hit the deck and rolled as the place burst into mayhem. Sly had three others with him and they started moving, fanning out to find me and finish me. I was alone. It couldn't have been worse. Thankfully, the regular patrons all panicked and ran or hit the deck themselves, so the only feet moving towards me were Sly's goons. From the floor, I shot under the table and took out two of them at the knees. They went down screaming and I leaped up and rolled, made the gap behind the bar. There was a barman crouched down there, reaching for a shotgun. Without pause, I swung my gun butt into his jaw and he dropped like a sack of rocks. I grabbed the shotgun and came up pumping. That was the first time I got shot. Sly fucking Barclay put a bullet in my shoulder, then I put a hole right through his torso. His other buddy was about to lean over the bar looking for me and I leveled the gun at him. He rose up, real slow, like he was underwater.

"I only came for Barclay," I told him, muffled by my balaclava and because my teeth were gritted in pain. My shoulder felt like it was on fire. "Let's not make this worse." Then I remembered Vernon's orders. "We're even now."

The two mooks on the floor, still howling in pain and clutching their ruined knees, were not dead, at least. I hoped the Jamaicans would accept the situation and call it even. Surely they didn't want a war. The one at the bar nodded, dropped his piece and backed away. I kept the shotgun sweeping the room, trying not to get dizzy at the pain, ignoring the blood soaking into the sleeve of my jacket.

My car was outside, and I jumped in, but that cop must have heard the shooting and was creeping up the sidewalk. He squeezed off a shot, I knocked him down, and then I was out of there. I've still got the scar from that bullet wound, but Vernon's in-house doc pulled the slug, stitched me up neat.

All of which means the car has been out of action for years, so I must have taken it from Vernon's place when I went on the run. Did I run from Vernon's? Is that where I got Carly? And what was that cop looking for? Whatever, it was enough to make him come knocking to ask questions. Maybe I could have talked my way out, no big deal. Perhaps I just fucked up back there, but it's too late to worry about it now. What's done is done.

"You coming back?"

I suck in a long breath again, realize I'd been phased out for a while. The street's dark. We've driven right out of town and onto country roads again.

"I'm here."

"You haven't been for the last twenty minutes. You gotta stop doing that, Eli."

At least it wasn't two days this time. "I'm here now."

"So what are we gonna do about this car?"

As we round a bend onto a straight, two pinpoint red taillights appear in front, a few hundred yards ahead. I accelerate and catch up, see it's a small Toyota, pretty nondescript, in decent condition. A quick scan of the dashboard and I find the switch and blip the lights and sirens. A woman's face, lit up red and blue, appears wide-eyed in the rearview mirror of the Toyota. She signals, pulls over.

"I suppose that'll do it," Carly says.

"Bring the bag."

We get out and I go straight to the driver's door, haul it open and drag the woman out. She's screaming and thrashing, but I throw her away, make her stumble across the road well out of reach, then get in. My knees crack the steering wheel and I grab the bar, scoot the seat back. Carly's already in the passenger side, my bag on her knees. Our doors slam almost simultaneously and I'm accelerating away.

"Neat and easy," Carly says.

"For now. This'll be reported stolen in no time."

"Yeah, but at least it can't be traced like the cruiser. We need to find something else, but we can make some distance first."

I'm so confused by what's happening here. I just wasted a cop because I'm clearly on the run, but why isn't Carly against me? "You're being very helpful."

She laughs and shakes her head. "I want to stay alive."

"I won't hurt you."

"Any more? I know that. At least, I think I know that now."

She seems so small and vulnerable. "Why aren't you mad at me?"

She laughs again, but it's bitter. "Oh, I'm mad as fucking hell, Eli. You hurt me, you scared me, you kept me in the fucking trunk for two days. But there's more happening here, right?"

"Is there?"

She looks over, then leans forward to look more closely. "Do you remember?"

My gut clenches. Is it really that obvious? "Remember what?"

"Oh man, she got you now!"

I press my lips together at the sight of Sly Barclay in the back seat. His dark face is all shadows in the mirror, but his eyes are bright. I know if I could see lower, there'd be a gaping hole where his chest should be. I catch his eye and shake my head.

"Oh yeah, she got you, man. She knows you faking all o' this shit."

Michael leans in from Sly's left. "It's true. You gotta remember, dude. But what might happen if you do?"

"What might happen, motherfucker?" Alvin says from Sly's other side.

The rat-faced cop leans in. How the fuck do they all fit back there? His name badge glitters in the dim dashboard light and I see Officer Graneystitched above it. There's a wet, dripping hole where his throat should be. "What might happen, Mr. Carver?" he asks, his voice gravelly. How does he know my fucking name?

The four of them rock back in the seat and laugh, their eyes and teeth white in the darkness, blood bright red all over them. The space they occupy is like a cave, an uncannily wide seat with room for them all, and I can see it all in the mirror every time I glimpse away from the road, space contorted out of true to accommodate them.

"Eli?" Carly's eyes are wide too, but in concern, her full lips down-turned. She's dropping into fear again, the flashes of confidence she'd been showing washing away like dust in a rainstorm.

"I've always got an out," Carly says. "If I did escape from you, I could spin any yarn I like to Vernon and he'd believe it. He saw you take me. But it's not that simple. I can see a chance here, though I'm beginning to doubt it."

What is she talking about? A chance for what? I stare at the road, searching my memories. It's all black once more, my head as empty as the night ahead of us.

"Do you remember?" she asks again.

I breathe deep and even, steadying my nerves like I do on a job, controlling the effects of adrenaline that's surging.

"Eli? About Caitlyn?"

And something electric pulses through me, heaving up though I try to press it down, but it's unstoppable and her face swims into my mind.

Caitlyn, with her blue eyes and copper red hair. Caitlyn with her musical laugh and furious Scottish temper.

Chapter 6

C aitlyn Carver.

My wife.

She wasn't in the life until I brought her in and even then, I did my best to keep her out of it. That was always going to be dangerous, but Vernon was obliging.

"You're like a son to me," he said. "You watch her and I'll let it lie."

The implicit threat was clear, but I knew I could handle things. My god, Caitlyn was beautiful, and powerful, and funny. I saw her first only about a year after the botched Sly Barclay job. But not so botched after all, so Vernon had decided. Despite the additional two kneecappings, the Jamaicans had called it even, things had gone back to normal there for a while. Vernon told me I'd done well under trying circumstances and that was to be applauded.

"Adapt and survive, son. That's the mark of a great man."

So he thought I was a great man? I swelled with pride and let that small compliment fuel me for months. And maybe that's why I was so filled with confidence that day when I went into Maloney's about a year later. It was still called Maloney's, even though old Maloney himself had sold and moved on after I'd knocked him out with a gun butt. He knew the place was getting too popular with made men and other gangsters, he wanted no part of that. Fair enough. So, of course, Vernon bought it and used it as one of his many legitimate fronts. We didn't do much business there, but I liked to go in for social reasons. Have a few beers with the guys, play pool, sometimes watch a band. Maloney's had a good stage up the back and a decent sound system. After Vernon took over, it developed a reputation as a good blues joint and the weekends got extra busy. They had to take on new staff and one of the new girls was Caitlyn Lans ing.

I went swaggering into the place one Friday night feeling like a fucking giant for no particular reason, except maybe Vernon thought I was a great man. Or maybe simply because it was the site of one of my proudest moments, even though I'd originally thought the whole thing a debacle. I went up to the bar and this stunning redhead smiled at me and we locked eyes. Copper hair and blue eyes are a rare combination, so I'm told. It mesmerized me for a moment. She grinned, knowing she'd bowled me over, and that grin seemed to say that in this case she didn't mind at all.

"New girl?" I asked.

"Aye, started last week. You regular?"

"I am, but I have a feeling I'm going to be a lot more regular from now on."

She laughed, that magical music, and then the band had hit the opening strains of a twelve-bar beat and talking became difficult. I pointed to the pump. She smiled and pulled me a beer. We made plenty of eye contact for the rest of the night. I didn't hang around the bar like a loser but went to watch the band, hung out with some pals, but every time I needed another beer, I'd wait until she was between customers and pin her with my gaze. She'd lift a glass, I'd give her a thumbs up, and she'd pour. Right off the bat, we just got along.

I wanted her so much, but I felt something else there too. Something beyond desire, maybe even something spiritual. I agonized over whether or not I'd stay until closing, try to take her home. Then decided to play the long game.

As the band took a break, I put my empty beer glass on the bar. She raised a fresh one, lips split in a sweet smile, and I shook my head. "I gotta jet, sorry."

"Aw, I was hoping you'd stick around." She twisted to look at the clock above the bar, her fine body on display in tight jeans and white tee. "I get off in a little under two hours."

My blood pulsed, but I knew I didn't want to fuck this up, so I gave her my most winning smile and said, "I would love nothing more, really. But business is pressing. You on tomorrow?"

"Sure am. Will I see you?"

"Most definitely." And I walked out, my cock heavy in my jeans, partly unable to believe what I'd done. But it felt like the right decision. I went home and masturbated furiously and had to drink a flask of whiskey to sleep, despite the beers.

The next night I went back, not too early so as not to seem desperate, I showed up a little after ten and she lit up when she saw me.

"You weren't lying!"

"I was not. And tonight I plan to stick around until you get off. When's that?"

"Hopefully about an hour or so after you take me home?"

And that was it. We fucked all that night and I'd never experienced anything hotter in my life. Of course, Vernon knew all about it within a couple of days. He called me into his office at the estate and asked me about her.

"She's special, boss. Really."

He nodded. "Well, she works for me, but in a legit capacity. You keep her away from our business and it's all good."

"You got it, Vern. No problem."

"It might be better if she didn't work for me," he said, one eyebrow arched.

I knew he was right. Distance was essential. "Don't sack her. Not yet. I'll sort it out."

It took a few weeks, but she was talking about going back to school, she wanted to be a real estate agent but could never afford the courses. I convinced her I could afford it, she should quit the bar, move in with me, go to school. We were so hot for each other, fell in love hard and fast right away, and never shied away from telling each other so. It was perfect. She knew my income wasn't entirely above board, but that was as far as she pursued it. She was happy to accept the things I wouldn't tell her, and I assured her there was nothing really bad involved.

"You don't, like, kill people, do you?" she'd asked, laughing nervously, uncertain.

I laughed right back. "No, baby! Nothing like that!"

It was the only time I ever directly lied to her. As she slowly got her first qualifications and then a job as an assistant realtor downtown, she also came around a little more to the idea of what I did. It's funny how people ease into the life gently, and after a few years they don't balk at stuff that would have horrified them before.

She would come to Vern's estate sometimes, for the big social events. She knew Vernon Sykes was my boss, but never asked in too much detail about what I did for him. The estate parties were always fantastic fun, barbeques and drinks and playing in the huge pool. It was at one of Vernon's parties, right after I turned twenty-five, almost two years to the day since we'd met, that Caitlyn told me she was pregnant. Man, I went over the moon. We were going to be a family.

Vernon's parties.

Where's Caitlyn now?

Pregnant, right after I turned twenty-five. That was three years ago.

"Eli? Eli, don't you fucking blank on me!"

Vernon's parties.

Red washes over my eyes, I see four tiny limbs all pointing in the same direction.

Darkness closes in on the red.

Chapter 7

The road ahead is awash with wan light, a peach and gray dawn rising through the trees to the right. Darkness like indigo ink to the left. A girl is in the passenger seat, sobbing quietly. She has a dark bruise around one eye, a cut just above the eyebrow that's dried up, beginning to scab over. She's wearing track pants and a T-shirt that are both way too big for her, the pants cut off at the bottom of the legs. Her knees are drawn up to her chest, arms clutched around them, her feet are bare. She has her face pressed to her knees, muffling her weeping. Her black hair hangs like a shroud over her head.

Carly.

It's Carly Sykes, Vernon's daughter.

Something stutters deep inside me, I remember a different car, a motel, gunfire.

Fuck, I shot a cop. We took the cruiser, then a Toyota. The badge in the middle of this steering wheel isn't a Toyota logo. We're in a different car, but I don't remember switching.

It was night, now the dawn is rising. I must have blanked out for a few hours.

"How long?" My voice is low and gritty, like morning voice when you haven't spoken for hours.

Her head snaps up, tears standing in her red raw eyes. "You're fucking back, you piece of shit?"

"How long? A few hours? It's nearly morning."

"A few hours? Fuck you, Eli. Fuck. You."

I take a deep breath. "How long?"

"Today is Saturday, Eli. You shot that cop on Thursday night. You remember murdering a fucking cop?"

"Yeah, I remember that." Something nags at the side of my brain, like a dog scratching at a screen door to get in. Something about red, and small people. Nausea ripples across my gut and I push that thought away. I can't let that in again yet, I think that might be where I went last time. I owe Carly better.

"What else happened?"

She sighs, tips her head back against the headrest. "I'll give you the short version. You went dark on me again. I'm not bringing up what we talked about, but you gotta get your shit together, man. This is the first time you've said a single word since then. We drove for hours in that stolen Toyota, then as the sun came up you found a truck stop. You parked, and just left. Went inside. There was some shouting, some crashes like breaking plates and glasses. I thought about taking the car and clearing out, right there and then, and I really should have, Eli." She starts crying again, tears rolling over her cheeks. "I really fucking should have, I don't know why I'm still here. Maybe it's some kind of fucking guilt, though God knows none of this is my fault. None of it!" she yells, then breaks down sobbing again.

I give her a minute, then ask, "What happened?"

She sniffs, drags a forearm across her face, takes a shuddering breath. "You came back out with handfuls of fucking cash. Like about three grand or something. You handed it to me and then you drove on. We got to another town and you parked outside a used car dealership and just sat there waiting. So I took the money inside and I bought us this car. Because I figured that's probably what you wanted. I let the guy see down this baggy-ass T-shirt and I batted my eyes and I got the car no questions asked. Signed fake names without him asking for ID or anything, because he was a sleazy fucker. You sat outside in that Toyota. So I drove away in the new car. And you followed. Once we got out of town, you flashed your lights, I pulled over, and you took over driving, just left the Toyota sitting there. I asked you something and you did this, you asshole." She points to her eye, her cut brow.

"I did that?"

She doesn't say anything, just glares.

"What did you ask me?"

"I'm not fucking telling you, man. You are unstable."

"I'm really sorry, Carly. I don't know why I did that. I can't imagine doing it now. I...I wasn't myself, I guess."

"That's no fucking excuse!"

"No, it's not. But it is the reason. I'm sorry."

We lapse into silence again. We're in a legit car at last, bought for cash, not hot. With any luck the cops won't zero in on that dealership any time soon, which means we're mostly under the radar again. Maybe we can stay that way and I won't have to kill any more of them.

"Where the fuck are we?" We've been driving for days, half of them I can't even remember.

Carly doesn't take her eyes off the road ahead. I can't blame her for not wanting to look at me. "Somewhere west of Philadelphia. You've been avoiding cities, passing around shitbox towns, sometimes driving in circles."

Where do I think I'm going? Away from Vernon Sykes, sure. But with his daughter kidnapped, am I just trying to get away or is there some kind of plan? My brain feels like high country desert, cold and barren, full of dust and pretty much fuck all else.

"We have to stop, Eli. You need to get your shit together."

"Yeah. I do."

The back seat of the car is half lit by the rising dawn. Shadows shift and move there, but I'm expecting them this time. I wait to see what smartass things they've got to say. Nothing helpful, I'm sure.

Michael leans forward first. "It all started with me, huh? Can you remember your life before you fucking killed me? Before you wasted your brother from another mother?"

"You made that happen," I tell him. "You're the rat."

Carly frowns at me. "What?"

Michael laughs. "Like I had a choice!"

"You always were a fuckin' weak little shit," Alvin Crake says, leaning right close to Michael's broken face. I can see the bony flower at the back of Alvin's head catching the first rays of the morning sun. "You an' your dad were both shitheels an' deserved to die."

Michael wheels around on him, snarling, and they tumble backwards in a mess of thrashing limbs, rolling through that uncannily large space that makes the back of the car.

Smoke swirls up, weed, the aroma thick and cloying suddenly in the enclosed space. "So they no help," Sly Barclay says, then draws heavily on the thick joint. His face disappears in a cloud of smoke as he exhales, but I still hear him. "What you gonna do, man? Where you think you're going?"

Officer Graney leans in, takes the joint from Sly and sucks deeply. A smile spreads across his face and smoke roils out of the hole that is his ragged throat. "You're going down, Eli. One way or another. We'll get you, or Vern will. Or we'll get you and *then* Vern will." He smiles, hands the joint back to Sly. "That's good stuff."

The smoke is drifting all around Carly and me. She doesn't seem to notice, stares at me with confused eyes. But I can taste it, feel the effects of it pushing a little more cotton wool into my brain. The last thing I need now is to be stoned.

"Give me a hit on that." A skinny, pale face appears between Sly and Graney and they shift over, make room for him.

Who the fuck is this?

"You need a plan, *cocheeese*." The southern drawl in his voice is strong.

Now I remember this racist sack of shit. It's the weed that's brought him back. We used to buy off him and his redneck idiot friends, transport it to dealers in the cities: Atlanta, Birmingham, Knoxville, Charlotte, Nashville. That was one of my regular jobs, to pick up big vacuum-packed bricks of weed from this asshole and drive them to one of those places, make the second deal and deliver the cash to Vern's banker. Easy money.

Except this racist asshole always rubbed me up the wrong way. Dwight Ramsey. Yeah, that's right. Fucking Dwight. And then Dwight gets in a little trouble trying to rip people off, starts thinking he's a big player, not some shithead grower, and Vernon says to me, "I think our friend Mr. Ramsey has outlived his usefulness."

I didn't need any more instruction than that and drove right down into the swamps west of Jacksonville that very night. For a bunch of fucking idiots, Dwight's operation was pretty tight, but he was so used to me his goons opened the gate and I drove up the hill to his place without any trouble. I parked outside his wooden house and he came out onto the veranda and lifted a beer can in greeting.

"Hey, cocheese, can you believe what that fucking nigger in the White House done now?" he asked, like we were right in the middle of a conversation.

I still had one foot in the car when I raised my automatic and put a slug right between his eyes. I've always been a crack shot, no idea where I learned to be such a good shooter, but it's always served me well. I've always felt like I was a natural, Vernon said I was born to it. But I practiced diligently too, still do. Natural talent is only the start, the rest is continuous hard work.

I was back in the car before Dwight's corpse hit the deck and back down the hill before his people even knew what happened. I waved as I drove through the gate and his goons frowned at me, must have realized right then something was up because they turned tail and started sprinting back to the house.

"What the fuck do you know about anything?" I ask.

"Are you talking to me?" Carly says. "Eli, the fuck is going on here?"

"I know plenty, cocheese."

He always called me that, one of so many things about him that just pissed me off.

"Like, I know you ain't ever gonna outrun Vernon Sykes. He's got a hunnerd guys just like you, all of 'em fucking better than you, and they'll soon *do* to you what you did to me. 'Less you think you can get out of the country. You reckon you can do that, cocheese? Days on end drivin' around and around aren't going to help. When was the last time you slept?" He jabs the joint at Carly. "She's been getting a few hours here and there while you drove, but you ain't. What's it been? Four days without a wink? Five? You're losin' your fucking mind, cocheese."

He leans back, hands the joint to Sly who takes a big hit. "Racist fuckwit here is right, man."

"You have to sleep," Graney says, taking the joint from Sly. "You have to sleep and get your head together. You need a plan."

They're right. They keep passing that joint around, the smoke getting thicker and thicker, filling the car like storm clouds. It's sweet and strong and my mind is swimming and I can't see.

The car swerves and Carly is yelling at me, grabbing the wheel. "Wake up! Pull the fuck over before you kill us! Wake up, Eli!"

I manage to get the car to the curb and she jumps out, runs around to open the driver's door. She pushes at me. "Get over. Sit there, wind the seat back and sleep. I'll keep driving, okay? I'll just drive us around and I'll only stop for gas and I'll pay cash. You sit there and sleep, Eli, please."

I can hardly see her, let alone argue. She leans over me, I feel her breasts against my chest as she struggles with something, then the seat is tipping into the back and I go with it and all I want to do is sleep forever.

Chapter 8

I t's dark when I wake up, every part of my body aches. I open my mouth and it's dry as a lizard's ass. Carly glances over from the driver's seat.

"Finally! Here." She hands me an open can of Coke.

It's a little warm, but does wonderful things to my mouth. I wind the seat up and look out, see trees going by, ghostly in the headlights, long empty road ahead. Seems like it's been a long empty road ahead forever.

"Epic sleeping."

I rub my eyes. "How long?"

"About fourteen hours straight. I stopped for gas about two hours ago, otherwise I've just been cruising, going nowhere. Parked up a few times and just looked at the view."

"Where are we?"

"Somewhere west of Martinsburg, I think. I had to circle around or we'd be going to fucking Canada."

I remember something that racist Dwight said. "Might not be such a bad idea. Get out of the country."

"Depends how much they know about you killing that cop. Bound to be cameras at the motel." She looks over, her eyes worried. "They must know you killed him, Eli. If you want to leave the country, you'd only manage it with the help of someone like Vernon. You know any other Vernons?"

"Kinda, but maybe not well enough to ask for that kind of help." I start to think about it, all the ID men I know. Maybe I could organize something, though it might be hard to do without Vernon finding out. My head is clearer than it's been in days, but I still need time and space to think about this stuff.

"We need to hole up somewhere and figure shit out," Carly says. "We can't just keep driving aimlessly around."

"Why are you helping me? I kidnapped you and you've had ample chance to run."

She looks over, nervous, then back at the road.

"What?"

She frowns, lips tight. Then, "I'm scared of saying anything to you. Scared of what I might trigger. You hurt me when you blank."

"All the more reason to get the fuck out, no?"

She laughs bitterly. "Yeah, maybe it is."

We lapse into silence again as the night darkens further around us, the last of the indigo leaving the sky behind.

"Seriously though, you should be turning me in." And even as I say it, I know there's been something else there all along. Something that's made me okay with trusting her, but that I'm not letting myself think about too much. "I mean, you're his daughter."

She looks at me, horrified, her eyes flashing fury. "I was never his fucking daughter! He married my mom when I was a kid, that's all. And when I turned eighteen, he killed her to have me."

"He killed her? Had you?" Memories swim like sharks in the blackness of my empty head. They're stirring down there, agitated, about ready to come surging up to feed.

Carly clams up, stares at the road.

"Tell me, Carly."

"I'm scared you'll go under again."

"I won't."

"You can't promise me that! You can't stop it."

I sigh, shake my head. "That's true. But I have to know, Carly."

She drives in silence for a while, then, "You think that hit-and-run was really random? My mom taken out like an annoying mole, excised from Vern's life so neatly, so he could have me? She died, and he made it clear he would look after me. He also made it clear I wasn't a little girl any more. He took me whether I wanted it or not, had done for years anyway. You lot all knew and didn't do a thing."

The memories swim upwards, snapping their teeth. She's right. We all turned a blind eye, let Vernon replace his wife with his wife's daughter, because what could we do? "I never thought he killed her," I say, and I'm not lying. "I remember him taking you as his new wife after she died, I thought that was creepy, but it never occurred to me he had your mom killed for that."

"You naïve fucking idiot." Tears are on her lashes again, but they don't fall, tethered there by her rage.

"Yeah. I guess so. How long ago?" My brain is skidding without purchase, trying to place events.

"Two years."

"So you're twenty now?"

She glances across again, brow creased. There's something else here, something she's not telling me. Something massive.

"Why didn't you leave him?"

"Oh, like it's that easy?" She's really hurting inside, using anger as a shield. "He controlled everything about our lives, Eli! Everything. My mother had no agency at all, so I sure as hell had none. After he killed her and took me I had literally nothing. He's had me under his wing me since I was eight years old. He's been fucking me since I was thirteen. I've got no money, never had any ID, nothing."

"I'm sorry." She's been in an effective jail all this time. I imagine her running away anyway, even being on the streets is better than what she's describing. But is it really? She'd still be raped, no doubt, probably killed. At least with Vernon she had a roof, food, all the toys she wanted. It was prison, but she's right, what else could she possibly do?

"Oh, you're sorry? Now? You know what, you're a far better guy when you can't remember shit. You're a far more decent fucking guy right now than you've ever been before." I open my mouth to say something, I don't know what, but she plows right on. "I couldn't believe it when you took me after... After what happened." Memories surge and gnash their teeth and I force them down. Not yet. She looks over at me, checks I'm still engaged, I guess, not blanking on her again. She sniffs, still angry, but refusing to cry. "I suddenly thought maybe this was a chance I'd never imagined before. After all that horrible shit happening so suddenly, maybe something good would come of it, for me. You'd have to run and hide, and you had me with you. I thought it was my out. You'd take me along, protect me, at least for a little while, until I found a new life, got some money. But I didn't expect you to blank out. To tie me up and throw me in the fucking trunk, Eli! To kill cops. But despite all that, I still thought maybe there's a chance. Is there? Eli? Is there?"

No wonder she's helping me, trying to stay with me. Maybe I did kidnap her, but if I took her away from Vernon's enforced life of rape and helplessness, perhaps she's right and there is a way out with me. And like she said before, she can still turn back at any time, turn me in to Vernon, go back to that life. It's better than death or destitution.

"You still think I can help you." It's not a question, seems like such a dumb, pointless thing to say. Her desperation claws at me, drags at my heart. But those other recollections are swarming and churning down there in the dark.

She sighs heavily. "Maybe."

"If I can only get my shit together, right?"

"Right. Can you?"

"I'm trying."

We pass a large billboard advertising Green Hills Motel, 2 Miles. She points at it. "That's gonna be our new home for a little while. We gotta stop driving around."

"Okay."

"And when we get there, I'm going to tell you something. And you have to do your fucking best not to blank out on me again."

"Okay."

"Maybe start trying to brace yourself or something."

"I'll try."

They're all lined up in the back seat. Alvin, Sly, Michael, Dwight and Officer Graney, shoulder to shoulder, grinning at me. Another joint is traveling slowly back and forth.

"This is gonna be good," Alvin says.

"I'll bet you twenty he cracks and goes bananas," Dwight says.

Michael looks at me hard. "Brother, you've got one chance. You think hard and you make it work, okay?"

Sly's laughing, shaking his head.

"We'll get you first," Graney says, wagging one index finger. "Oh, we'll get you, some PD, somewhere. And shall we hand you over to Vernon? Hmm? Maybe!"

Alvin cackles, rubs his hands together. "Oh man, he's gonna lose it! I reckon he won't blank this time, he'll go ballistic instead. That right, Eli? Do it for me! Fuck that li'l bitch. Fuck her in every hole she's got, then kill her an' fuck her again."

"Jesus, man." Sly's looking at Alvin like the man is literally made of shit, and he's not far wrong.

"What do you think?" Graney says. "You going to rape and kill her? Or just kill her? Who else are you going to kill? Maybe some more cops will come to this motel and you'll kill them too. You're just racking up the life sentences, boy. We'll get you."

"One chance," Michael says, squeezing my shoulder so hard that his fingertips dig in and make me wince.

"I don't think you'll survive much longer, cocheese," Dwight says. He snorts, hocks up something brown and sticky, tobacco distending his cheek. He spits on the ground, then looks back up at me. "I hope a fucking nigger kills you. The most undignified death. You deserve nothing less."

Sly leans forward in the seat. "You got a problem with me, redneck?"

"You a nigger, ain't ya? Course I got a fuckin' problem with you. Subhuman piece of shit."

Sly launches right across Alvin's lap and starts raining punches down on Dwight's face. I see Dwight's nose burst in a shower of blood, and Alvin's leaning back clapping his hands and laughing like a hyena. Officer Graney leans away from one side, shaking his head. Michael catches my eye again. "One chance, brother. Hold. It. Together."

"Here it is," Carly says, and the tires crunch gravel as we pull into the lot.

The motel is green and cream, surrounded on three sides by tall trees, a few spotlights in the parking lot cast pools of light. We get out of the car and walk together towards the office. I look Carly up and down, suddenly see she's wearing jeans and a T-shirt that fit, a short leather jacket and bright new sneakers.

She grins crookedly. "Yeah, so when I stopped for gas it was in a small town and there was a store right opposite. You were sleeping so hard, I couldn't wake you, so I locked you in the car and bought clothes. I used some of that money you stole from the truck stop. Where you'll also be on security footage, by the way."

I frown at her.

"I was only in the store for five or ten minutes! You slept right through it, didn't notice a thing. I couldn't go any more without clothes or shoes, man."

"No, no. That's fine, of course. I'm thinking about the footage you're talking about. Might be there's my face all over TV and whatever, from the cop thing at the motel, the robbery at the truck stop. My face must be everywhere, right?"

She purses her lips. "Yeah, you're probably right. It's been a couple days, easily enough time for people to take notice, watching out for the cop killer on the run. Maybe you should stop shaving. Get some bleach for your hair."

"You still have some cash on you?"

"Yeah."

"Then you book us in. I'll wait in the car."

"I'll be on CCTV too, from the motel, at least."

"I guess we'll have to chance it. You've done a lot less than me. Here." I hand her a trucker's cap from the back and she pulls it low over her eyebrows.

Chapter 9

I sit in the shadows of the car and watch her in the office, chatting and laughing. There's an old woman behind the counter with a face more wrinkled than my ball sack, but she's all smiles and open body language. Looks like Carly is charming the shit out of her.

The motel is two-story and Carly secures us a room upstairs on the end of the row. I'd rather be on the ground floor, but it'll do. Can't expect her to know stuff like that. I'll have to school her a little. When we unlock the door and walk in, they're all lined up on one of the beds: Michael, Alvin, Sly, Dwight and Officer Graney. They're grinning like idiots.

"Oh, we ain't gonna miss this show!" Alvin says, his eyes alive with excitement.

Along with the bullet hole between his eyes, Dwight's face is puffy with bruises, his lip split, his nose bleeding. Sly really beat the shit out of him. They're at opposite ends of the bed, but seem to have settled their differences for now. Dwight is grinning, showing off bloody teeth. Sly is casually smoking another reefer, smiling crookedly, his eyes hooded, smoke curling out of the huge ragged hole in his chest. Organs hang in there, glistening and pulsing. Graney wags that index finger again and Michael raises a finger of his own. Yeah, one chance, I know. I need to not lose it here. Not let the blanking thing happen and not let these circling memories eat me alive. I'm more than a little scared, I feel like a child. Something throbs in my gut at that thought and I bite it down.

Michael is serious-faced, his voice little more than a whisper. "Hold it together, brother."

Carly takes my gun from the bag and holds it loosely in her hand while she shuts the door. "Go sit over there." She points to the bed with all those dead bastards lined up along it.

I look from her back to the bed, start to gesture and say it's occupied, but it's empty now. There's muffled sniggering and they're all in the bathroom, crowding around each other to look at us through the door. All in various states of entertained, except Michael, still serious as hell.

Carly has one hand on the front door handle, the other holding my gun. "We really have to get focused here, okay?"

I sit on the bed, as far across the room from her as I can be, clench my hands together in my lap. "Okay."

"I'm going to say a name. You have to try to focus. It's gonna hurt like hell, but you gotta get your shit together, Eli Carver."

I take a deep breath. "Okay."

She frowns, purses her lips. Then she takes a deep breath of her own and says, "Caitlyn."

My body shudders. Beautiful red hair and glittering blue eyes. Oh man, my wonderful Caitlyn. Red starts to swamp my vision, Carly receding into it like a car powering away along a foggy highway.

"Hold it together!" Carly shouts, and she's crying again. "Please, stay with me. You have to *face* this!"

I grind my teeth, biting down on a howl that wants to burst out of me and split the night wide open.

"I'm going to say more, but don't you lose it, Eli! Don't make me shoot you and have to go back to him!"

"Tell me," I growl, but it's already coming up anyway, unbidden like irrepressible vomit, impossible to hold back.

"My birthday party," Carly says, sobbing openly now. "And Caitlyn. And Scottie."

And my brain explodes in fire and hate and fury.

Vernon's place is huge, a sprawling estate with the main house like something from a fairy tale, all towers and gables and crenelated edges. Several other buildings are dotted around the grounds and pools, with a stepped lawn out back that can hold a thousand summer barbecue goers and still seem spacious. But those events were always business. Carly's birthday was just family. And by family, that meant the closest members of the crew too, so I was there with *my* family.

Vern had been drinking, which was not all that common for him. A big deal had gone south, he had the DEA on his ass, people were being killed. Business was at a low, but that happened from time to time. I guess that's why he took the excuse of the party to have a drink, but it never did sit well with him. Lots of others had been drinking too. Carly's twentieth birthday, for some reason, seemed to bring out the rager in half the crew and their partners, and by eight in the evening people were raucous. Except Carly herself. She spent the whole afternoon and early part of the night looking stressed and put out. I couldn't figure why. Vernon had bought her the most amazing diamond necklace thing, and there was a new Corvette on the gravel drive that had to be worth a mint. When he'd handed her the keys she had just shaken her head. "Maybe later," she said, and Vern grimaced, his left eye twitching.

I knew that sign. We all did. When Vern's left eye started to go, some-one was going to get it. So the crew were a little on edge, but most of the partners had no idea. And the drink kept flowing and the edges began to round off. Or so I thought. But it turned out Vern was still pissed.

Carly made it clear she was at the party under duress. She made it equally clear she kinda hated her husband right then, when usually she was quiet and resigned about it. Of course I knew the whole thing was a fucking mess, Vernon marrying her less than a year after her mother died. He was more than thirty years her senior and there'd never been anything between them beyond a strained stepfather to reluctant stepdaughter thing. But then they'd got married, she'd seemed glassy-eyed during the ceremony, but accepting, and we all just went along with it the same as she did. You don't cross the boss, after all.

Except Caitlyn. Oh, Caitlyn, why couldn't you have just sucked it up like everyone else? Like even Carly did. But Caitlyn was adamant that she would show her disgust. Maybe she knew about the rapes since Carly was thirteen. Perhaps the women talked about that stuff. But I kept my word to Vern and kept Caitlyn as much at a distance from the business as I could. Of course, family stuff was different.

And by around nine o'clock on the night of the party, Carly must have decided she'd put on enough of a show. She disappeared for a few minutes, I suppose none of us thought anything of it. Bathroom break or something. Then she came back wearing a long T-shirt like a nightgown, and nothing else, bare feet, hair down, face defiant.

"The fuck is this?" Vernon asked.

"I'm going to bed."

The air thickened, tension building from a strange root of rebellion.

"It's early," Vernon said. "You can't leave your own party yet!"

"I can," Carly said, lips twitching like she was trying to not cry. "I'm tired, it's been a big, exciting day." Then she'd cast a look at him that was saturated in hate. "I want to be well rested so I can drive my new Corvette tomorrow. Did you buy me lessons too?"

We all knew the car was more of a symbol than anything else, but she could have driven it all over Vernon's sixty acres.

Vern wasn't having it, and he'd been drinking, was uncharacteristically drunk. Unusually stressed. His regular shield of iron control was crooked and he backhanded Carly across the cheek. So sudden and unexpected, despite anything else we might have suspected, we'd never seen him hit her before. The room froze, a thick silence filling the place up like water. Carly looked at him, eyes wide, tears rolling over her cheeks and a single trickle of red tracking from one corner of her mouth. She just stared at him.

Eventually Vernon said, "Don't sass me, you little bitch. Go and get dressed." And he raised his hand to hit her again.

Carly just thrust her chin forward, daring him to do it. No one else in the room moved a muscle, and then Caitlyn said, so quietly, "Don't you dare." Her Scottish accent was soft, but always in evidence. It was a beautiful sound. But right then it was strong and menacing.

She was right beside me and I put a hand on her arm, opened my mouth to tell her to quiet down, not her business, when she looked at me and said, "Don't you dare, either. Not one of you fuckers."

"Pardon me?" Vernon's voice was ice cold.

"You all stand here and don't raise a word to defend her, let alone a hand," Caitlyn said, eyes scanning the room. "And you, you fucker." She pointed at Vernon. The silence became almost solid, tension in the air like molasses. "Bad enough you hold her here and fuck her whether she likes it or not. You don't get to hit her too."

Caitlyn had been swallowing a few drinks of her own, that's all I can think of to explain why she suddenly felt she could challenge Vernon like that. He turned to her, one hand in the pocket of his expensive linen jacket, the other still half raised where he had been going to hit Carly for the second time. Carly's eyes flicked between Caitlyn and Vernon and there was something in there, something lost and pleading.

"Pardon me?" Vernon said again.

"You fucking heard me."

I put a hand out, took Caitlyn's forearm and I wasn't gentle, tried to turn her towards me. "That's enough," I said, but it's all I got out before she shook me off.

She pushed me away from her, eyes furious, red hair flashing in the chandelier light like fire. "Oh, that is not fucking enough. That is not nearly enough. Bad enough that your business is whatever it is, but at least here, with these people, you should show some respect to each other.”

"Five seconds to rein your bitch in," Vernon said to me, his voice level.

I stepped towards her. "Caitlyn, please, we need to go now. This isn't—"

"Fuck you!" she screamed at me. "You can't all stand around here and let this happen to Carly. Why are none of you fuckers standing up for her? Against this fucking rapist piece of…"

And Vernon showed her why no one did. His hand came out of the jacket pocket holding a nine millimeter and I yelled and dove towards Caitlyn, but Vern was quick and nearly as good a shot as me. *Bang! Bang! Bang!* And three red spots in a triangle dead center of her chest. She staggered back, blood bubbling as she opened her mouth to scream, but it was a gargle. And she dropped. That was it. Gone. Dead.

My mind started spinning, others in the room were backing away, Carly had her hands over her mouth, sobbing, eyes wide. Vernon turned his gaze back to me, the gun still in his hand. "I warned you on day one she was trouble. I am not best pleased I had to take care of that trouble myself."

Fury roiled in me, my muscles spasmed in a kind of tautness that paralyzed me. I wanted to kill him, I wanted to wrap my hands around his throat and squeeze until his fucking eyes burst. And he saw that in me. He tipped his head to one side, eyebrows high.

"Yeah, Eli? Really? You wanna run at me? Have a fucking go, I dare you."

And then movement in the doorway far to my left. Strawberry blond hair from his mom, curls from me. He had my green eyes and broad face and shoulders. Scottie, my rough-and-tumble little bruiser. Just over two years old, we'd celebrated his party here only two months before. "What's the noises?" he asked, rubbing puffy eyes, woken from the silk sofa in the room next door where we'd put him down hours before, peaked on sugary cake and excitement.

And Vernon had looked at him, then back at me, his eyes red from drink and rage. "I think our relationship is at an end, no?" Vernon said.

And I mouthed something, some words, I don't know what. My mouth opened, my body shook, and all I managed was, "No, no, no."

And Vernon fired. One shot. Scottie's chest turned red and he flew back through the door he'd just entered by, all four limbs pointing back accusingly at Vernon Sykes. His tiny, round face and equally round mouth, an O of utter surprise as he vanished from sight.

And I was moving, and Carly was screaming, and crew members were running, grabbing partners, some trying to get out, others trying to get between Vernon and me. I had a knife in my hand and I opened the throat of Pauly Brand and he collapsed in a waterfall of red, staring at me in disbelief. Then my hand found my own nine millimeter and I started firing, left and right, almost randomly, but I'm a good shot. My mind was lost in a scarlet haze of grief and raging fury and all I wanted to do was kill everybody, destroy everything.

Chapter 10

I can't remember how it all went down, but I know there was slaughter. And then I found myself momentarily still and Carly had run in front of me, Vernon was ducked behind a huge mahogany cabinet full of awful porcelain statuary and Carly was screaming, "Stop it! Stop it!"

And several guns were on me. I was well outnumbered, by skilled men, and though I'd killed a few, I never had a chance. I froze and Vernon reappeared, face twisted in rage.

"Fuck me, Eli. What a mess."

He wasn't wrong. And I was a dead man standing. Unless...

I grabbed Carly and slammed her back against my chest before anyone could move, pressed my gun against her temple. I count bullets subconsciously, it's a habit we all have, and we all knew I had two left. And another clip in my pocket.

"Nobody move!" Vern yelled.

I backed out of the room, Vernon staring at me and I could tell he was deciding whether or not to sacrifice Carly to have me, but there must be something real inside him after all, because he paused.

"I'll fucking kill you," he said, and I continued back, didn't answer.

I had no chance to get away, not really. Vern's estate was huge, he had guards everywhere, it would only be moments before they had the jump on me again. Except right outside the front door was the old car I'd bought off the skinny woman with the hand-rolled cigarettes all that time ago. The one the teens used for joyrides around the estate. Right there with the keys in it. We were in and gone in seconds, slewing left and right on the gravel driveway as I powered dangerously fast for the gates. They were closing automatically, an order from the house, but I squeezed through, the metalwork on one side squealing as sparks flew, and I was out. I needed to grab one of my emergency bags. I kept a few around the place, with a change of clothes, stuff like that. I sped a mile down the road, then grabbed a cable tie from my pocket, bound up Carly's wrists and threw her in the trunk. She was screaming and yelling at me, but I was already shutting down, already blanking out. I needed her for security, couldn't risk her running away, I had no idea what I was going to do, and then I was driving again and my brain locked down and down and down and everything went dark.

"Eli! Please, Eli!"

Carly is pressed back against the door, trembling all over, crying. My gun in her hand is wavering, tracking left and right over me as I sit on the bed, my muscles locked tight all over as the incandescent fury blisters through me. Blackness creeps in and pulses out at the edges of my vision, my heart is pounding.

"Eli, come back! I *need* you!"

Carly's voice is like an anchor, hauling against me every time I try to let the black take me. I don't want to remember. I don't want to see little Scottie flying back from the room, so surprised. I don't want to see that triangle of red spots appear on Caitlyn's chest. I can't live with that. I can't live with the guilt, the knowledge that my life led to theirs and their lives led to that. Blackness swallows and Carly screams.

The five fuckers are lined up near the bathroom door, all leaning forward, like they're expecting me to actually explode. Officer Graney, neck and chest blood-soaked, is wagging his finger again. Dwight and Alvin are laughing, almost dancing a jig.

"Cocheese gonna go apeshit!" Dwight says.

Sly is grinning, sucking on a reefer the size of a Cuban cigar, it's cloying stink filling the room. "You deserve all o' this, you fuck."

And Michael, shaking his head, turning it further one side to show me the blown-out skull and teeth, the ragged wet hole where his ear should be. Like he's reminding me what I did, what Vernon made me do. Like he's telling me, "You expected anything less after this? You thought you were fucking special somehow?"

And their presence has anchored me a little further, ironically given me a moment to hold the blackness away.

Carly is leaning forward, the gun hanging at her thigh. "You back, Eli? You with me?"

I draw a ragged breath, look up to meet her eyes.

"Oh, Jesus," she says. "Are you really? You're really still here?"

And I'm sobbing like a child, my chest heaving, my face flooded with tears and snot. "They're dead," I manage between gasps. "They're both dead."

Carly nods, tears of her own spilling but she's still not game to come near me. The hand without the gun reaches out, like she wants to hold me, console me, but I'm a caged tiger and she's not putting her hand between these bars, not yet.

"Jesus fucking kee-rist," Dwight says. "The fucker is crying!"

"You weak fucking shitweasel," Alvin says, his face twisted in disgust. "Don't cry! Fuckin' rape this bitch, then kill this bitch, then go and kill Vernon!"

And part of me wants to. Part of me wants to do nothing but hurt and kill and desecrate everyone I've ever known because my Caitlyn and my little Scottie have been torn away from me and the world is fucked. There is nothing good, nothing wholesome in the life of humans. We're broken fucking animals, eating each other alive, and I want to stand atop a pile of bones and blood, and scream my fucking defiance at the heavens, and then spill my own life out at my feet and let the blackness take me forever.

"Yeah, fucker, that's more like it!" Alvin says.

Dwight's dancing again. "Hoo-ee, now you're acting like a man!"

"One chance," Michael says and his voice is calm enough to make me look him in the eye. "You break now, you're broken forever," he says. "This is it. One chance."

"Please, Eli," Carly says. "Come on. Hang in there. We can do something."

"Do what?" I manage to growl, and Dwight and Alvin exchange a look of disgust.

"We can finish this," Carly says.

I turn my gaze to her, drag breath in through my nose, fast and shallow, my heart hammering a pulse in my throat I can almost taste.

"Finish it?"

She nods, holding my eyes with her own, still streaming tears, but intense. Focused. "Vernon lost men in that deal, he's got the feds on him, his shit is messed up. You took out Pauly and Kirk and Peter. Maybe others. I know for sure Charles survived, but no idea who else. It's been a few days, but Vern's weakened, right? If you give him time to recover, to gather a new crew, you'll never get near him. And once he's found balance again, he'll come for you and you'll never get away. I'll have to go back to him, to protect myself, I'll have to and I won't be able to help you. But now, if we move quickly, we can move against *him*. Kill the shit-eating motherfucker. Let some other crews fill whatever gaps we leave and then we'll both be free and clear."

And I realize she's right. I can never outrun him, I'll always be watching my back. My other crimes, Officer Graney, the truck stop, notwithstanding, I'll never outrun Vernon Sykes. And I can't live anyway, not without my Caitlyn and Scottie, not while Vernon is still breathing too. All I can do is take him out. Or die trying. Carly says she'll help. She's scared, maybe she'll turn me in to save herself anyway, but what other choice do I have?

"So how do we do it?" I ask, and the blackness has receded from my vision. My gut is a seething lava pit of grief and anger, but maybe it can fuel me, not consume me.

I look over at the bathroom and all five are standing there, looking disappointed. Except Michael. He simply looks resigned, and he nods once.

"You're swaying where you sit," Carly says. "Lie down. Sleep again, let your brain settle. We're safe here."

"Safe?" But I think she's right, for now at least. I fall onto my side, pull my feet up. Grief chews holes through me, I can't get their faces out of my mind. I roll over, turn my face to the wall and let the pain come again. I hear the other bed creak as Carly sits while I quietly sob and at some point a new blackness steals in and I sleep, deep and dreamless.

Chapter 11

I wake to total blackness and the sound of soft snoring behind me. I'm still facing the wall, haven't moved a muscle in hours and my body aches like I've been beaten up. My knees pop as I stretch and slowly sit up, my head pounds.

They're really gone.

The tearing grief is a ragged hole in me, sucking away light and goodness, hauling against me like a vortex, but it's somehow dulled. Maybe I'm too broken down to feel it like before. Maybe it's just not possible to feel that wrenching pain continuously and survive. My mind is closing doors here and there, blocking up corridors of thought to protect me. But one is wide open. One has a light at the end, and it's the face of Vernon fucking Sykes. I remember him as I last saw him, watching me back out of that door, Carly pressed against me. He was scowling, narrow-eyed, hate and murder in that gaze. But there was some resigned loss, too. Maybe, just maybe, the breakdown of his deal, the trouble he was in, the loss of control at Carly's party, all in such quick succession, made him see his empire crumbling. Perhaps Carly is right and if we move fast, he might be ruined enough that we can finish him.

I walk to the bathroom, feet silent on the cheap motel carpet, and don't turn on the light until I'm inside and the door is shut. Cold water on my face washes away some of the pain and some of the fogginess. Helps me find some sharper focus. Who will I have to get through?

Carly said I killed Peter, that big red-headed bastard. I remember dropping Pauly with the knife, but he was only ever a runner, a bootlicker. She said I dropped Kirk as well, so that's a bonus. He was a fucking psychopath and too dangerous for even Vernon to keep too close by, but he was loyal as a dog. I'm glad he's out of the picture. Short of a handful of regular guys that Vern can call in, it's only big Charles with his shiny bald head and ebony skin I have to worry about. And Vern himself, of course. So if I know Vernon Sykes, and I do know him well, he will have gone to ground somewhere, keeping Charles right at his shoulder. He'll be gathering whatever men and resources he can, trying to rebuild. I need to figure out where he's gone to ground, take him and Charles before they regain that strength of numbers.

"You think it's going to be as easy as finding him?" Michael says behind me.

They're all there, lined up in the mirror.

I shake my head. Of course it's not as simple as that, but I have to start there.

"You gonna have to shake down a whole bunch of people, cocheese" Dwight says. "Start liftin' rocks and shouting at cockroaches, see if you can't find information."

"People ain't gonna give up information easy," Alvin says.

"And as soon as you ask," Officer Graney puts in, "word will get back to Vernon very quickly that you're asking around. How will you stop him from being one step ahead all the way?"

"Why the hell are you all helping me?" I ask, watching their faces float in the mirror.

Sly holds out a joint, like he's offering it to me.

"We all buddies now, all of a sudden?"

Sly laughs, shakes his head. "We just wan' see you try, motherfucker. And die horribly for your efforts."

I suppose that makes a kind of sense.

There's a light tap on the door.

"Who are you taking to?" Carly asks, her voice small and frightened.

I turn and open the door. The five amigos are nowhere to be seen. "Just myself."

"You still here? Still okay?"

"Not okay, no."

She looks down, unable to hold my eye. "Yeah, sorry. But not blanking. You're talking, so that's a good sign, whether it's to yourself or anyone else."

"I didn't talk before?"

"Not when you blanked, no. You'd go hard, like a statue. It was terrifying. And you hit me if I didn't comply, whether I understood or not."

Now it's my turn to look down. "I'm sorry."

She puts a finger under my chin, lifts my face gently. "You really are, huh?"

"I know I'm not a good guy. I've done more than questionable things, but I've always had some kind of code. I've always tried to do right by people. Not hitting women has been high on that list. I should have done more to protect you from Vernon. Omission is still guilt, I guess. I'm not proud of that."

She frowns. "You're a better guy now than I've ever known you before. Code or not, you were a hardass, nasty piece of work all the time you worked for Vern. This... Well, I guess it's no surprise it's changed you."

"I feel like all my shields and shells have shattered. When I had Caitlyn and Scottie, for the first time ever I felt like I had a life to look forward to. We even talked, Caitlyn and me, about getting out of the life. Moving somewhere, me getting a regular job. We were gonna have more kids, were already trying." A sharp, barbed hook hitches in my chest. "And he took all that away."

She squeezes my hand, just nods, lost for words. We stand like that for a moment, then I say. "So where do we start?"

"It's the middle of the night."

"So?"

She turns and goes back to the bed, falls flat on her back staring at the ceiling. Her eyes glitter in the soft light from a red LED bedside clock that reads 3:04. "Vernon will have gone to ground."

I sit on the other bed, elbows on my knees, staring at my hands hanging above the hard-wearing carpet, almost lost in shadow. "I was thinking the same thing. Do you know how bad it was with the deal that went south right before your birthday?"

She's still staring at the ceiling, like maybe there are answers up there. "Worse than any of us realized, I'm guessing. I think that's why he went so...so uncharacteristically..."

I nod, still watching my hands as I pick at my fingernails. Grief is welling up again, a tide that threatens to swallow me whole. "Yeah, he was obviously stretched far beyond taut. He was using your birthday as an excuse to forget about things for a while."

"He hardly ever drinks, and never that much. I watched him sinking bourbon after bourbon and I wondered why. I know it made me push harder than I might have otherwise."

I look up, but she's still staring above into nowhere. "You poked the bear while he was vulnerable?"

Her gaze snaps to me. "Don't try to make this my fault!"

"I'm not, that's not what I mean. But it contributed. And then Caitlyn." I hitch a breath, her name like a blade in my throat. "Then Caitlyn really pushed too hard and he snapped."

"Any one of those things might have passed without too much drama. But all together..."

"Yeah. So the deal that went bad. What do you know?"

"You don't know?"

"I'd been on another job, hadn't been in for a few days. Your party was my first time back at Vern's for nearly a week, I was planning to catch up the next day."

She settles back, looking up at the ceiling again. "Well, I don't know much. You know how it is, I was the plaything at home, never in on the business. But I heard plenty, always tried to stay informed where I could, in case it was ever useful. And because my life was fucking boring otherwise. Anyway, the details are beyond me, but the big picture is this. Vernon had a deal set up for a lot of cocaine. It was coming from some Colombians, but Vern refused to deal directly with them. Some bullshit about one of the main guys there having disrespected him once before."

I sigh. "He's done that before. Uses intermediaries to make the other party feel like losers, not important enough to deal with Big Vern himself."

"That's it. But the intermediary he uses this time is in trouble. Charles and Peter were in charge, but that Tweezer guy was making the collection and dropping the cash."

"The biker? Seriously, Vern put a Desert Ghost nobody in charge of a deal like that?"

"No, he put Charles and Peter in charge, but told them to use Tweezer. He thought it was funny, having this wasted, grizzled old biker turn up with the cash and leave with the cases of coke."

"So what happened?"

"Tweezer had no idea, but he had a police tail. Had it for a couple of weeks, apparently. He'd run some guns over from Texas two weeks before, made a deal that nearly got him picked up, so he'd aborted the run. The police assumed he still had the guns and was laying low, waiting to make the delivery at a later date, so they were watching. They see him heading off with a big case, in a car instead of on his bike."

I'm nodding, hands rubbing slowly together as I see it take shape. "So the cops think he's making another run at delivering the guns?"

"Right. Except he's still putting that off for the time being and fulfilling his little job for Charles and Peter in the meantime, completely unaware that he's surveilled."

"What a fucking idiot. If the original gun deal went bad, he should have known the cops would be watching."

Carly laughs softly. "Sure. But this is Tweezer we're talking about."

"Right. And the deal gets busted?"

"Yep. A couple of Colombians die in the gunfight, Tweezer took a hit in the leg, apparently, whether from the cops or the Colombians I don't know, but it makes no real difference. Charles and Peter got away, obviously."

Now I can see the whole picture. "So the deal is busted, the money and the drugs are in police custody, as is Tweezer, and Vernon doesn't know whether the fucking loser will squeal or not."

"Exactly. As soon as the DEA realize what they've stumbled onto they start following leads. So of course, Vernon gets a call. 'Anything you want to tell us?' they ask him. 'Go fuck yourself, talk to my lawyer,' says Vernon. But that's where it stands. So when my party came around, Vernon was stressed, unsure how much the Feds knew, unsure how likely Tweezer is to cave."

I let a soft laugh out, shake my head. "He'll fold up like a tissue paper house in a tornado. I can't imagine how many priors he's got, but regardless, they've got him dead to rights on this deal. If he takes it on his own, he's solely responsible for what I imagine is a big amount of coke. That's a life sentence, right?"

"Almost certainly."

"He'll definitely cut a deal."

Carly sits up, crosses her legs atop the mattress. "However!"

I raise an eyebrow, smile. "There's a twist?"

"Kinda. Naturally Vernon isn't taking any chances. He wants Tweezer dead. So he organizes a hit in the hope he's soon enough to get Tweezer before he blabs. The morning of my party, he hears that the hit went bad and Tweezer is still alive in there, still liable to talk."

"So surely Vernon organizes another hit right away?"

"And *that's* what he was waiting on at my party. That's why he was drinking. The longer it takes to kill Tweezer, the more likely it is that Tweezer will crack and get Vernon in the shit. He still hadn't heard yet when everything went...you know. Meanwhile, Vern's lawyers are working overtime, shoring up against any chance of Tweezer saying something that'll stick."

I sit there staring at my hands again, breathing deeply and slowly through my nose. This is good. Talking and planning like this, it stops me thinking too much about Caitlyn and Scottie. Maybe if we keep talking, I might get their dead faces out of my mind for at least a few moments at a time. "So that's where we start," I say eventually.

"Where?"

"Find out if Tweezer went toes up or not. And either way, find out who's been contracted with that hit. Whoever that is will have a way to let Vernon know the state of play, so if we find the hitman, we might find where Vernon is hiding out."

"*If* Vernon is hiding out," Carly says.

"If?"

"Yeah. I mean, if the hit was successful and Tweezer died before fingering Vernon, then the cops have nothing on him and he can go back to business as usual."

"Which is gathering his remaining crew and coming after me?"

"I assume so. Coming after me, more specifically, with a plan to kill you. I'm abducted, don't forget."

"Yeah. Right."

"And that depends on whether Vernon has managed to get people around him again. It might take a while, so maybe we still have a few days, maybe not. But if Tweezer is still alive, then Vernon is almost certainly in some shit right now and will still be lying low." Carly raises both palms up, shrugs. "Right now we have no idea about any of it. We can't know anything beyond the state of play at my birthday. After that, it's all dark."

"How long has it been?" All those blanked out moments, those periods where I shut down, did horrible things to Carly. How much might Vernon have accomplished while I floundered?

"My birthday was Saturday. It's nearly Sunday now."

I'm stunned, silent for a moment, then, "A week."

"Yeah."

"So Vernon has had a week to get organized."

She nods, lips pursed. "If Tweezer is dead, we might be in trouble. But if the hit hasn't been made, Vern may still be struggling."

"Or of the hit was successful, but Tweezer had already given up some dirt," I say. "We may find that Vernon is fighting off the DEA right now."

"We can only hope."

Another thought strikes me. "Or if Tweezer is dead, but Vernon is still weak for manpower, he might still be lying low anyway, regathering his strength."

"Maybe."

"We need to know and not waste any more time."

She gives me a sarcastic *You think?* look.

I stand up, pace back and forth as I try to figure out a plan. "So if we need info on all of this, that means we need to know what state Tweezer is in. And what he may or may not have said before finding himself in said state. Which means we have to find a way to chat to some Desert Ghosts."

Carly twists her mouth in disdain. "Fucking biker gangs. Great."

"But first, we need to not look like us. The car we have is safe for now. How attached are you to your long hair?"

"Seriously, you want me to cut it all off?"

"And bleach it? How do you fancy a peroxide pixie cut?"

She laughs, shakes her head. "Guess I'm game to try it. And you?"

"I've got a week's worth of stubble here. I'll shave my head and maybe cut this into a goatee. Reckon that'll make us both look different enough to casual observers?"

"What choice do we have?"

"Okay. I'm going shopping. You'll stay here?"

She gives me a crooked smile. "Still so convinced I'm going to run out on you."

"I guess the life makes a man paranoid."

She moves to sit next to me, puts one hand on my knee. "Everything here is beyond fucked up, Eli. But I know you'll do what you can and I know I'm only going to be safe from Vernon when he's a fucking corpse. So yeah, I'll stay here. I'll help you. If it goes really bad, I'll tell anyone who will listen that everything happened against my will. You abducted me, you made me do stuff. And I'll have to go back to Vern and maybe I'll get another chance to get away. I won't lie to you, I'll drop you like a hot rock if I have to. But I don't want to and I will help you all I can."

"I appreciate the honesty." I'm not lying. Truth like this is worth far more than some line of bullshit and she's smart enough to know that.

She just nods.

"So I'm going shopping."

"You can't wait till morning?"

"Quieter now. There'll be somewhere open."

Without a backward glance I pull on my cap and drag out an old hooded top from my bag, pull the hood up over the cap and make sure the peak is down low. If I hunch my shoulders, keep my face in shadow, I should be okay.

Chapter 12

I find an all-night pharmacy not too far from the motel and the walk through dark and quiet streets has done me good. Given me time to think. But I try not to think of too much. I'm pretty sure I'm not going to blank again, but every time the memories rise up, I choose to push them aside. I won't bury them again, where they can eat me from down deep. But I won't think too hard on them either. The images, red blooms, tiny limbs, are burned into my mind like brands on a steer, but I won't look right at them, won't obsess over them. I need to focus here and two things will keep me on track. One is the sure need that Vernon Sykes needs to die. The other is that I have to protect Carly and make it as right for her as I can. There is a chance for her here. Maybe I can see some tiny bit of atonement in giving her back her life. I'll let the grief out after that.

The woman behind the counter in the pharmacy is nervous when I put the stuff on the counter. I can't blame her, really. I'm not looking up much, avoiding all the CCTV cameras, shoving cash at her with grunts and gestures. I've bought the most suspicious things possible, really. Peroxide, razors, scissors. So I've added a toothbrush and paste for Carly, and grab some gum from the little display on the desk.

She rings it all in. "This everything?"

"Yeah."

There's a pause and I wonder for a moment if she's going to try to be a hero. Tell me she needs the manager, or she just needs to make a call or something. I'm tense as hell, and my hand creeps around to my back where the gun is jammed in the waistband of my jeans. I don't want to shoot anyone else. Ever. Except Vernon Sykes. I want to shoot that fucker until there's nothing left of him.

I can tell the clerk is looking at me, trying to decide something. Don't do it, lady.

She draws a deep breath. "You okay, honey?"

"What?"

"You okay? You hurt? You need help?"

Jesus fuck, she's a good Samaritan. "Fine. Really tired."

"That's all?"

"Just finished a double shift."

"Okay, honey."

I slide money over the counter and she lets her fingers linger on mine as she takes it. "I'm here all night, don't finish until eight a.m. If you decide you need anything... Even if it's only to talk."

I grab the paper bag and nod. "Thanks."

I can't stop thinking about her all the way back to the motel. What a bizarre world this is, really.

Carly is fast asleep in bed, an inviting line of curves under the covers as she lies on her side. I creep around the room, bemused that she can sleep through my return. I know I'd wake if I was in a strange room and someone came in, even if I was expecting them back. I guess that's the difference in our lives though. She's always been safe except from her captor and there's nothing she can do about that. Her long, even breaths trigger a wave of fatigue over me and I know I'm ready to crash too. I hope I don't dream. Once the room is locked up and a straight-backed chair from the little desk in one corner is jammed up under the door handle, I shower, piss, and fall into bed. Blackness swallows me like a whale.

I wake up to the sound of running water. The room is bright, curtains wide letting in the day. It doesn't feel early. My body protests when I push myself up on one elbow. The clock beside the bed Carly slept in says 11:39. Nearly noon, fucking hell.

The bathroom door opens, steam curling out, and Carly emerges like something from a movie. She's wrapped in a towel, legs and shoulders bare, and my heart thumps. But she looks so different, her hair hacked into a punky short cut, bleached platinum.

"Oh, you're finally up." She pops one hip, looks left and right. "You like?"

I try to ignore the things her body is doing to me and concentrate on the new look. "Actually, it really suits you."

"Yeah, I think so too." She points to the table I took the chair from last night. The chair is back and there are paper sacks on the desk. "Bagels, pastries, some ham and cheese and shit."

"You went out before you changed your look?"

"I was starving, man. Don't worry, I borrowed your cap and hoodie. Eat, then I'll fix your hair."

I raise an eyebrow but choose not to argue. She's taking to all this pretty well. Maybe she's enjoying the freedom. Ironic that for her freedom is being on the run. The food is good and there's coffee, long since gone cold, but I gulp it down, anyway. She goes back to the bathroom with more new clothes, comes out dressed in tight black jeans, a white T-shirt and short leather boots. She looks hot. The leather jacket she bought before is on the bed, along with a small sports bag with her other stuff. She's taking good care of herself, and I'm happy if she's using my cash for that. A paranoid part of me wonders if she isn't maybe getting ready to run, but if she is, there's really not much I can do about that. I have to trust her.

When I've eaten, she guides me to the bathroom and sits me on the edge of the bath. The scissors make short work of my hair, then she lathers and shaves my head. It feels weird, I've never been bald before.

"You look really different already." Her head is tipped to one side.

"Better?"

She snuffs a little, lips pressed together then, "Not really for me to say."

Something bites deep inside. Caitlyn used to do that, the little non-laugh through the nose. Carly and Caitlyn couldn't really be more different, but right then she let out a mannerism that felt like a knife in the guts.

Something stings my cheek and I'm looking into Carly's wide eyes under that new white hair. "Don't you fucking dare!" she yells, and I realize she slapped me.

"What?"

"I saw it in your eyes. Do not blank on me again, Eli. I can't take it any more."

She's right, I was going under. I need to avoid that more than anything else, and that means not thinking about the little stuff, the details, the minutiae. Caitlyn and Scottie are dead. That punch in the heart is all I can allow, all I can use to drive me towards Vernon Sykes.

Carly raises her hand to strike again, but I gently take her wrist. "It's okay. I'm okay."

"Really?"

"Yeah. Just getting used to things, you know? Got to find a new normal."

She stares with narrow eyes for a moment, then nods once. "Shave your face. Then we should maybe go."

They're standing behind me as I shave, once Carly has left and shut the bathroom door. I try to ignore them in the mirror, but they keep ducking left and right, leering at me, mocking me.

"You think that's going to help?" Officer Graney asks. "There's facial recognition software now, you know. You'll get picked up easy."

"That right?" Dwight asks. "Goddamn, the po-lice sure are cheating on every aspect of fightin' crime."

"*You* such a fucking loser, they don't even need technology," Sly says and Dwight rounds on him.

"Oh yeah? They didn't bust me! I was cruisin' until this shithead showed up and fuckin' shot me."

Graney laughs. "You have a rap sheet longer than an elephant's erect dick, Ramsey, you redneck fuckwit."

Alvin barks a laugh and shoves Dwight away. Sly, on the other side of Alvin, sticks his chest out. "You want another go? Didn't I whip your ass once already?"

I stare in the mirror trying to zone it all out, concentrate on getting neat lines to this new goatee. It's not something I've ever done before. How much do I leave under my chin?

Michael is still and I realize he's staring hard at me. I can't help pausing as I catch his eye.

"You ready for this?" he asks.

"Ready for what?"

"Anything. Everything. Whatever comes next."

"Sounds like maybe you don't think I am."

The others have stilled, quietened to hear.

"You want me to fail?" I ask Michael.

"You fucking killed me, man. We were brothers."

"You fucked up. You crossed Vernon. You know it was kill you or both die."

Michael shakes his head sadly. "I would have died before I killed you."

I swallow, something about his tone betraying the truth of that. "Really?" I ask eventually.

"What kind of man are you, really?" Michael's eyes are hurt.

Something hardens in me, I know the truth of what *I* did. "You're the one who fucked up. Why should I let you get me killed?"

"You shot me in the fucking head."

"Yeah, and I lived to tell the tale. Now it comes all the way around and I plan to shoot Vernon Sykes in the head."

"You think that'll make things right?"

I look away from his hurt gaze. "It'll make things over."

Carly bangs on the door. "How long does it take?"

"I'm done." It's a pretty neat job as far as I can tell. It'll have to do, anyway. Within minutes, we're in the car and gone.

I look like a badass with a bald head and goatee. I think it suits me, but it's not really the way I want to look. Though given the mop of curly hair I used to have, it makes a stark difference, and that's all that matters.

"Watch the road."

I pull my eyes from the rearview mirror and straighten up in the lane.

Carly's grin is a little crooked. "Can't stop looking at yourself."

"I've never looked like this before."

She pulls down the sun visor, checks herself in its mirror, then flicks it back up. "Yeah, it's a bit weird. Best to ignore it."

"You're probably right."

We drive in silence for a while as I find my way to the interstate.

"So where are we going?" Carly asks as I floor it up to the speed limit and sit in the right-hand lane.

"Charlotte. We need to head back south, but not all the way to New Orleans. Not yet. I know there's a Desert Ghosts clubhouse in Charlotte."

"That's a long way from Tweezer's club though, isn't it?"

"Yeah, but he's known there. I used to do weed runs for Vern and one of the buyers was the Desert Ghosts up in Charlotte. I would sell to Tweezer and he'd take it up there. He blabbed a lot about all the people he sold to."

Carly frowns. "You don't think that's too close to Vern, do you?"

"No, that's the beauty of it. None of the guys in Charlotte know jack about me or Vern. They only know Tweezer. I'm just a name as far as they're concerned, assuming Tweezer blabbed about me too. They've never seen me. But I know it's a place where we can ask after him. We'll have to wait and see what happens."

"Long drive."

"About six hours."

We lapse into silence, and I try to ignore the five assholes lined up in the over-sized cavern of the back seat.

"Shoot me in the fuckin' head then use my contacts, cocheese," Dwight says, and spits.

As if they're his contacts. His connection to the club, to Tweezer, is vague at best. I don't think he's ever even met them. Just because I'm talking about the weed he grew, he thinks he has some stake in it. Jesus, to think I was deeply entwined with people like this my whole life until now. Makes me sick. I turn on the radio, find a blues station and crank it. Carly looks at me sidelong, so I flick up one eyebrow at her. She chooses not to say anything.

Chapter 13

We stop for drink, food, and piss breaks but don't say much all the way down. I think we're both happy to be moving forward instead of running in circles. It's difficult not to think too much, but I refuse to blank on her again and so I train myself to focus on other things. By the time we've hit Charlotte, I think I've fantasized just about every possible outcome of this meeting and everything that may follow, but I'm no more prepared for it than I was when I woke up this morning.

It's dark, nearly 9:00 p.m., when we cruise past the clubhouse and case the place.

"We can't just walk in there," Carly says. "Not like biker clubhouses are open bars."

"No, but they'll go out, I expect, head somewhere. We'll follow someone."

On our third pass, the chain-link fence is sliding open and three black and chrome Harleys thunder out and power up the street. I fall into place behind them, letting a few other cars separate us. It's a fairly easy tail.

"What if they're just going out for milk or something?"

I shake my head. "Carly, you need to learn patience. Play the odds. All this stuff, it's like a game. Or a sport. Think about fishing. You don't expect to haul a fish in every time you throw a line. It takes a few tries, maybe a few places. It takes patience."

She huffs, slumps down into her seat.

After a few minutes, one of the bikes peels off with a wave and the other two head on, making their way towards the outskirts of the city.

"Traffic's getting thinner," Carly says, and she's right.

I drop back a little further, start to guess at the occasional junction. But I've done this a lot, I'm pretty good at it. As I make a left in an industrial backwater, the two bikes are parked against the curb and the bikers stand on the footpath, one lighting a cigarette. Without pause I keep going.

"Don't look out the window," I tell Carly. "Count out loud one to ten."

"Seriously?"

"Just do it."

As she gets to four, we're passing the bikers, both staring straight ahead. They glance up as we pass, I see them in the side mirror, but their eyes don't linger.

"Why did you have me counting?"

"So your mouth was moving as we passed like we were having a normal conversation. If I'd asked you to talk, make it look like a conversation, you'd probably have clammed up wondering what to say and we'd have looked suspicious."

She scowls at me and I shrug. I know I'm right. After a minute, she knows it too.

I make a right half a block down and pull up on the other side of the road in deep shadows between two streetlights. I can just see the bikes parked back there. Carly's smart enough not to ask what now. She knows we have to wait. My fishing analogy is holding up.

After half an hour, she says, "Starting to get old."

"Yeah. We'll give it a bit longer."

Another fifteen minutes and the two of them emerge again, laughing at some shared joke. The one has another cigarette while the other makes a phone call. He talks with his hands a lot, gesturing up and down, left and right, but it all seems good natured. He hangs up, slaps his buddy on the shoulder. That one drops his cigarette, grinds it under a scruffy black boot heel and they get on their bikes and head back the way they came.

It's not long before they're back in the clubhouse and we've learned nothing. I can feel Carly's frustration, but she's not talking. "Hungry?" I ask her.

"Yeah."

We go to a McDonald's, eat our fill, use the bathroom, and head back out. It's nearly eleven when the gates open again. We're parked up across one corner, masked by shadows. Another group of bikes roars out, five of them this time, and head into town. Ten minutes later and we're at the back of a parking lot, the bikes lined up at the front under the neon of a sign advertising Jem's Bar. They're laughing and bumping fists with others already there.

"Hooked a fish on our second cast."

Carly glances at my smug grin and shakes her head. "Now what?"

"This is obviously a place they hang out, so we act like we just wanna hang out here too. You okay to play my girlfriend? It'll stop people sleazing onto you."

"Fucking sucks that I have to be your property to be left alone. Can't I just say I'm not interested?"

I stare at her till she subsides. "Hey, I agree, society is fucked. But right now we have other crusades."

"Fine, I'm your bitch."

"They aren't rappers, they're bikers. You're my old lady. Just hang on me, fawn a little, make it obvious, and it won't be a thing."

She scowls. "I can do what's needed. What do we do inside?"

"I'll case it out a bit first, but I'll just find a good time to ask if any of those guys have seen Tweezer. Tell them I have a deal going with him, spin some shit. See what we learn."

It's loud inside, a rock band playing covers on a stage on the far side of the wide open space. There're hundreds of people, the lights low but not too low. The stink of beer, perfume and aftershave permeates the air. The music isn't quite enough to cover the hum of conversation and the rattle of glasses, at least not up the back near the bar. The bikers are all gathered in a knot around two tables in one corner, about as far from the stage as they can get. A few of their old ladies are lounging around with them, some other young girls who look like maybe they'd like to become attached are flitting about like moths around flames. A lot of beer, hair, beards, tattoos, and laughter are on display. It's all about as amiable as I can imagine given the context.

Carly holds my hand, her fingers soft and warm, but her grip strong. She leans into me as we stand at the bar, runs her free hand over my shoulder possessively. She's good at this stuff. Part of me feels a thrill at her touch, the rest of me trembles inside, refusing to let memories of Caitlyn surface. Among it all is guilt. Caitlyn would rip the face off any girl she saw acting like this. But Caitlyn is dead, Carly can do what she likes, what does it even matter?

I grunt as pain whines into my thigh, a sharp knee from Carly. She's looking up at me with hard eyes. "Bar girl wants your money, honey." Her voice is singsong, but her gaze is ice. I was starting to blank again.

I hand over cash and we pick up our beers. "You gonna lose it here?" she asks me.

"No, I got it." I hope I sound more confident than I feel.

I lean back against the bar, make a show of enjoying the band a little. Halfway through my beer, I draw a long breath.

"Okay, let's do it."

Snaking my fingers to entwine with Carly's again, I pull her over to the tables in the corner. My stride is confident, but not arrogant, my face open but not weak. Several bearded Desert Ghosts look up at our approach, and the general conversation among them all dwindles.

"You got the wrong tables," one of them says, his beard down almost to his navel. He's that frightening combination of fat and muscle, maybe fifty years old but looks like he'd still win a wrestling match with a bear.

"Just wanted to ask a quick question."

"Wrong fucking tables, man." The tension ratchets up.

I notice the guy speaking has the Sergeant-At-Arms badge on his leather, putting him up there in the top of his chapter. Only the President and Vice-president of his club would rank higher. I hold his eye. "I don't want any drama, just a quick chat. I'm looking for a friend of mine. Friend of yours, too."

"That right?"

Carly's fingers tighten around mine, her eyes are a little wide, fear setting in.

Some young punk leans forward in his seat, drags a palm from Carly's shoulder to her elbow. "This one's pretty!"

He's drunk, stupid. As he twists to leer at his boss, I can see his back patches. He hasn't earned all his colors yet. Desperate to please, a Prospect trying to boost himself up.

Without looking at him, I say, "Touch my woman again and you'll be shitting teeth for a week."

Sergeant-At-Arms barks a laugh, others around the two tables look amused or annoyed in equal measure. This is the test, this is the establishment of a temporary pecking order. Here's where they'll decide to talk to me, or destroy us.

"The fuck you say?" Young Punk demands. He stands up, all chicken chest and furious eyes.

Sergeant-At-Arms looks from me to him and back again.

Still not deigning to look at the fool, I say it again. "Touch her once more, you shit teeth. If you're so stupid you can't understand that, just try. Now about my friend."

Sergeant-At-Arms grins. Young Punk pulls Carly aside, tries to step between us. He's decided his boys will have his back, too stupid to realize he's the meat in this hierarchy sandwich, I almost feel sorry for him.

"I'll touch whoever—"

That's as far as he gets before my fist slams into his face.

He makes a strange surprised cough, staggers back. Not wanting to seem uncommitted, I finally turn to look at him. He's staring, blood pouring from split lips. He starts to look towards his Sergeant-At-Arms but I punch him again, lead two knuckles aimed right at his mouth. It'll cost me, but I'm a man who keeps promises.

I feel his teeth snap and crack, they bite into the flesh of my hand. I hope this fucker doesn't have hepatitis or anything. But his eyes roll, he collapses back into the lap of another, who grunts and pushes the hapless fucker to the floor. Young Punk is rolling and howling, both hands clapped over his mouth, blood pouring between his fingers.

I turn back to Sergeant-At-Arms. "You guys have a good dental plan?"

"I guess we'll take care of him."

The tension is still high, twanging in the air like a tripwire, everyone waiting to see which way Sergeant-At-Arms will play it. I hope I made the right choice. Carly's frozen like a statue.

"I did warn him," I say, amiably enough, even though my blood is rushing and my heart thumps in my throat. Carly presses back against me like I can hide her from sight.

Sergeant-At-Arms nods. "You did at that." There's a heavy pause, pregnant with every flavor of violence. Then he says, "Who you looking for?"

Stress drains from the area like rainwater down a drain. Several around return to their beers and conversation, no longer interested. Some relax but keep paying attention. No one even looks at Young Punk as he gasps, sobs, tries to pull himself back into his chair. I watch from the corner of one eye, but he's subdued now. As long as he doesn't follow us when we leave, we'll never have to worry about him again.

"I'm looking for a pal who's with your chapter down in New Orleans, goes by the name Tweezer."

Sergeant-At-Arms purses his lips. "Tweezer, eh?"

"Yeah. I assume his mother gave him another name, but I wouldn't know what it is. He and I have done business quite a bit over the years, but the last week or two I've been trying to reach him and getting no answer. That's not like him."

"And you just happened to come by here?"

I gesture vaguely back over one shoulder. "We're on the road back south, stopped in for a beer and a rest. When I saw your colors, I thought I'd ask. I know Tweezer came up to Charlotte pretty regularly. He talked about it."

Sergeant-At-Arms's face darkens. "Tweezer talked altogether too fucking much."

I make a point of looking surprised, concerned. "Oh, really? He never told me about any of y'all's business or anything. Just that he would regularly run to Charlotte, Atlanta, some other places."

Sergeant-At-Arms nods again, sniffs. "Yeah, well, he won't be running anywhere again."

"Is he inside?"

"Inside a pine fucking box, yeah."

My heart thumps once, so hard I think maybe he could see it through my jacket. That's potentially bad for us. "What happened?"

"Why do you care so fucking much, man?"

"Just that we were kinda friends, you know. Not close, but I've known him a long time."

"And what was your name again?"

"Gary. Gary Baker." No idea where that came from. "I used to run around some stuff that Dwight Ramsey grew, if you know what I mean."

Sergeant-At-Arms frowns. "You think name-dropping some bunch of fucking losers will help your case? I never heard of no Dwight Ramsey."

"I don't have any case. Just looking out for a friend, you tell me he's dead. That's a surprise, you know?"

Sergeant-At-Arms rubs a hand over his long beard, takes a slow, casual gulp of beer. "Our mutual friend Tweezer got himself entangled in something that put him in New Orleans jail. While he was in there, a white supremacist asshole by the name of Carl Hildebrand whacked him. Dispute about tobacco is what I heard. Who cares? He's gone. Now it's time you got gone, I'm running out of goodwill towards strangers who make my Prospects swallow their teeth."

"He was warned," I remind him.

"He was. And now you've been warned. Fuck off."

"Fair enough. I'm sorry for your loss."

There are barks and guffaws around the two tables, much shaking of heads.

"Find somewhere else to drink tonight," Sergeant-At-Arms says.

"Okay. Thanks." I pull on Carly's hand and haul her away. "Let's go, baby."

As we go, I whisper, "Glance back, look scared, but see if any of them get up to follow us. If I look back, it'll seem weak."

Her hand is still trembling in mine, but she says, "Okay."

After a few more paces, as I put my glass on the bar and head for the door, she turns to look around. I yank her towards me for effect, eliciting a genuine, "Hey!"

Before she can berate me, I ask, "Anything?"

"Yeah. Looked like he was giving two of them the nod to follow us. They've got up and are strolling behind."

"They might jump us in the parking lot. Prepare for that. If I let go of your hand, you dive away from me instantly, understand? It means I'll need room."

"Okay. Jesus."

Chapter 14

The night outside is cold, an icy bite to the breeze. The lot is well-lit, but not many people around. After the first couple rows of cars, heading for ours at the back, I turn around. The two Desert Ghosts are sitting astride their bikes, watching us. I tip my head, give them a "What?" expression. They don't even blink.

"Looks like they plan to follow us, not jump us here," I say to Carly. "Let's go."

As I start the car, I hear the roar of the two Harleys firing up. As I leave the lot, they pull in behind, making no attempt to hide the fact.

"What do we do?" Carly asks.

I sigh. "I'm a little offended he only sent two."

She looks at me, but doesn't say anything.

The five idiots are lined up in that oversized back seat again when I next check the mirror.

"More deaths on your hands?" Officer Graney asks. Smoke curls from the hole in his throat as he hands a joint back along the row.

"I hope these guys fuck you up, cocheese," Dwight says. He draws deep on the joint, then holds one finger up. "In fact," he says, voice tight as he holds in the smoke, "I hope they fuck you, *then* fuck you up."

Alvin takes the joint. "You're a twisted freak," he says to Dwight.

"But do you disagree with me?"

"I don't want to watch anyone fucking anyone, but I would gladly watch this fucker die."

"Me too." Sly takes his hit, offers the joint to Michael.

Michael sighs, shakes his head. He looks at me with a questioning gaze.

"Yeah, I may have to kill them to save myself," I say.

Graney laughs, shakes his head. "You're racking up a real body count here."

"I get the feeling I've barely started."

Carly's brows are knitted. "What?"

I snap my attention back to her, back to the road ahead. "Nothing, just thinking out loud."

"Kill them?" she asks.

The back seat is empty, the two Harleys large in the rear window, staying close. I put my foot down a little, pushing to the top of the speed limit, and make a turn to lead us out of town.

"What if they're armed?"

I shrug. "I'm sure they are. Shouldn't matter."

"Was all this worth it? Did we learn anything? I mean, we know Tweezer is dead and that's maybe bad for us, but what else?"

"We know that Carl Hildebrand killed Tweezer. I know that name. Neo-Nazi fucker Vernon has used before to take out someone in New Orleans Parish Prison. It's one of the worst jails in the country, a real shit pit. Vern has some influence there. So we've learned that someone got word to Carl Hildebrand that Tweezer needed to die, and Carl Hildebrand fulfilled the request. Argument over tobacco, my ass. Whatever Carl got from Vern must have been worth it, but that evil fucker may well have done it for fun once the order came down. Regardless, if we can find whoever got word to Carl Hildebrand, we should be able to find Vern, right?"

Carly shakes her head, lips pursed. "But not Vern himself, maybe. He would have used someone else."

"Sure, but we're getting closer. It's like unraveling a knot, you have to take it one thread at a time."

"And as Tweezer is dead, Vernon is free to build up his strength again. We probably don't have much time."

"We may already be facing a back-to-strength Vernon. But does that change anything?"

She shrugs.

Finally the town falls behind and the road ahead stretches long and dark, the last lights of Charlotte fading. No other traffic shares the tarmac except the two Harleys on my tail. Maybe this is where they'll make a move. I won't chance it. I press the accelerator harder, roaring away to make a run for it, see if they're just watching me out of town. The engine note of the Harleys goes up to match me, sticking close. No way I can outrun two powerful bikes like that. But that's okay.

"Put your hands on the dash, Carly?"

"What?" Confused, but she complies all the same.

I stand on the brake, tires howling as we slide on the asphalt, the nose of the car diving. Then the crunching impact and shattering glass as the two bikes slam into the back of us. One goes under, disappears from the view. The other flips up, the rider punching back-first into the rear window, bowing it in. Before he can fall through, I stand on the accelerator again and the car lurches forward, bumps over something. The biker on the trunk rolls off to sprawl in the road, bikes and broken glass all over. The trunk of our car stands up like a crooked flag, the back window hanging in like a hammock.

"Fucking hell, Eli!"

"I don't have time to fuck around."

"They dead?"

"Don't know. Don't really care."

"What if they were just following to make sure we left town?"

I pin her with my eyes. "I don't care, Carly."

She watches me, licks her lips, draws breath to speak, then pauses.

I look back to the road ahead, the wreckage of the Desert Ghosts already lost in the darkness. All I want is to find my way to Vernon Sykes and woe betide any fucker who does anything to interfere with that. My wife and my son will be avenged.

"Don't go," Carly says quietly.

"What?"

"Don't go. Don't blank on me."

I suck a long, deep breath in, push images of Caitlyn and Scottie from my mind. A gathering darkness I hadn't noticed quivers and recedes from the edges of my vision.

"You still here?" She sounds like a little girl.

"Yeah, I'm here. You keep doing that. You think I'm going under, talk me out of it."

"I'll try."

"And so will I."

We drive in silence for a long time, even the five dead amigos are conspicuous by their absence.

Eventually, Carly says, "Still here?"

"Yeah."

"So what's the plan?"

"We have to change cars again. We'll get pulled over for sure, the way this one's banged up now."

She nods. "Let's take a look."

I pull over and we climb out. The damage is pretty extensive, the rear quarter panels are all folded in, the trunk concertinaed up into the shattered mess of the back window. All the taillights on both sides are destroyed except for one bulb, glaring defiantly white in the night.

"If we steal another car, we'll be at risk again," Carly says. There's a low level of accusation in her tone.

"I know. This car was good, it was clean."

"Now it's not."

I sigh, rub my head. I'm beginning to tire of all this, frustration gaining ground on determination. It doesn't mean I'll give up going after Vernon, but it does mean I might fuck up. Like this, now, a good car wrecked. That's a fuck up. I can't let myself slip. But I did need to lose those bikers.

"We got money for another car?" Carly asks.

"Yeah, maybe. If we can find some piece of shit for a grand or something."

"We gonna drive through the night in the meantime?"

"No. Let's not. Come on."

It takes another half hour to see a sign for a motel and I park a half mile away from it, wipe down the car as well as I can for prints. It's a half-hearted effort, really. With the bag slung over my shoulder, Carly carrying hers the same, we walk to the motel, check in and crash out without another word passing between us.

Chapter 15

I'm woken by the sound of the shower again, and I take one myself after Carly emerges, dressed and ready. There's a fire in her eyes, she looks at me sidelong, but I don't question it. After the way I took out those bikes, I guess she's wondering how far I'm willing to go, how many risks I'm willing to take. I'm willing to take them all. But hopefully she'll know, above everything else, that I plan to kill Vernon Sykes. And then she'll be free. But I have to stop fucking up.

When I come out of the bathroom, she holds up a local paper, points to an ad. We pack up and go to a public phone, call the number. It's just what we need. An hour later and we're driving a beat-up old Dodge that we bought for the last of my cash, but we're back on the road again. Clean again. For now.

"We going to need more money?"

I shrug, shake my head. "I guess so, just to eat and sleep if nothing else. But it's okay, we're heading back south. I've got a few bolt holes and stashes around we can raid."

"You said you knew about this Carl Hildebrand guy? What do you know?"

"Part of a pack of white supremacist fuckwits in Baton Rouge, that's it. And I have a good stash in Baton Rouge. We go and get some money first, then we'll talk to Hildebrand's friends."

She thinks about this for a while, then, "Is it a risk? Will they know you?"

"No. I only know Hildebrand and his crew by name and reputation. We've never met. I'm not sure how we'll find them, but I guess we ask around."

"Ask around for a white supremacist group? In Baton Rouge?"

There's a *hyuck* from the back seat. "Y'all gonna get shot to death, cocheese," Dwight says, idiot face twisted in glee. If anyone knew about other racist shitbags, it would be him.

"I should kill you myself," Sly says.

Dwight flips him off. "Can't kill what's already dead."

"I can have fun trying."

"Don't start again, you two," Officer Graney says.

"You know where I can find 'em?" I ask Dwight.

"What?" Carly says.

Dwight howls laughter. "Oh, cocheese, you really want to go right to 'em? Yeah, I do know Carl Hildebrand. We've rallied together. His crew hangs out at a vehicle spray shop called Carl's Paints, somewhere on the outskirts of the city. Can't wait to see what happens there!" He sits back, rubbing his hands together.

Now he's mentioned it, it does ring a bell, somewhere back in my memory.

"Who are you talking to?" Carly asks. She looks at me, at the mirror, turns to look into the empty back seat.

"Just thinking out loud. I've remembered where I can look for Hildebrand's people. But we'll have to be careful what we ask and how."

My stash in Baton Rouge is a locker in the back of a comic store, owned by an old school pal. We stayed kind of close for a while, though I slowly dropped out of that circle. Most importantly, he's got nothing to do with the life, no connections to Vernon Sykes. I hope my stash is still there. His eyebrows raise as I enter the shop, he takes a moment to recognize me.

"Goddamn, I thought maybe I'd never see you again, man!"

He comes around the counter and we go from a tentative handshake to a brief hug. "Sorry it's been so long Jeff."

Jeff grins. "Life, right? I know how it is. You look different with a bald head! Suits you. I'm glad you're not dead."

"Me too. How are things?"

We make small talk for a while, I introduce Carly as my girlfriend, Clare. Jeff nods approval and she stays mostly quiet. After a few minutes I make a rueful face. "I'm sorry I can't stick around for long right now, but I'll come back soon and we'll catch up properly, yeah?"

"Sounds good, man."

"Meanwhile, you still got that stuff I left here?"

Jeff nods, bites his lower lip. "I was tempted to open it up after it had been so long. Over two years, now."

"Did you?"

"Open it? Nah. You know where it is."

I tell Carly to wait for me and go through to the back. The locker isn't locked, just standing half open beside a small fridge. My bag is in there, like an overnight bag for traveling, a padlock holding the zipper closed. I sling it over my shoulder and head back out.

"Thanks, Jeff."

"You really gonna come back and catch up properly?" he asks.

I pause before answering. We go back a long way, Jeff and me, we have history. He was a good pal, and he's right, I've ignored him for over two years. "I'm really gonna try," I say eventually.

He nods. "You okay, dude?"

"Right now? Not really. But I hope to be soon."

"Always cold beers in the fridge."

I clap his shoulder. "Thanks, man. I'm looking forward to those." I mean it, but he can see the doubt in my eyes.

Back in the car, I check the bag before we pull away. No idea where the key might be, so I use my pocket knife to slice it open alongside the zipper. A couple of changes of clothes, a pair of sneakers, toothbrush and other toiletries, a snub-nosed .38 and five grand in cash.

Carly whistles low. "Handy."

"Yeah. I've got a few of these around the area, but only this one had a decent amount of money in it. It'll see us right for now." I pocket the cash, leave everything else in the bag and drop it behind the passenger seat. "Let's go. I'm hungry."

"Lunch first, then white supremacists?"

"Sounds like fun."

After lunch I look up Carl's Paints and we drive over there. Plenty of people around in various businesses, junkyards and delivery warehouses, all with wide concrete aprons out front. Trucks and cars move in and out between chain-link fences. Carl's is at the end of a row, a big sign with the name in airbrushed chrome and red fire. A few cars sit out front waiting, a Harley with a skull and mist design on the tank right by the door. A young skinhead with a white-collared shirt and jeans sits in a chair leaned back against the wall of the office. The shirt sleeves are rolled down and closed at the wrists, no doubt concealing swastika tattoos from the general public. He's taking in the sun, though the day is cool, and smoking a cigarette. No one else seems to be around.

"A white supremacist getting a tan," Carly says. "The irony."

I park the car and the kid tips his chair forward, looks disdainfully at the crappy Dodge we're driving.

"How do we do this?" Carly asks.

I grin at her. "Reckon my new haircut might help me out?"

She huffs that humorless laugh. "Good luck with that."

"Play it by ear, see how it goes."

The roll-up front of the paint shop is closed, no one else visible in the office. As we get out of the car, I see the five ghosts lined up along the chain-link, like an audience at a show. Michael and Officer Graney look bored, their bloody wounds glistening in the sun. Sly is staring at the paint shop kid with undisguised hatred.

"You kill this fucker for me," he says. "Consider it a payback."

"I don't owe you anything," I mutter as I pass.

Carly frowns at me, but says nothing.

Alvin Crake and Dwight Ramsey are the two most interested, Dwight almost slavering like a dog.

"You gonna fuck this up and get killed right here, cocheese!" he says.

I ignore him.

"Help ya?" The kid has a strangely high voice, like it never really broke, though he must be at least seventeen or eighteen.

"Maybe. Who's in charge here?"

"Me."

"No, seriously."

He bristles and Dwight *hyucks*. If he wasn't already dead, I'd kill him again right now. My gun is tucked in the back of my jeans, under my jacket, but it'll stay there unless this kid causes trouble. I swallow, realize I'm angry and ready to kill. I need to not fuck up.

"I think that piece of shit needs more than a paint job," the kid says, jutting his chin at my car.

"I'm not here for paint."

"What you want then?"

"You really here alone right now?"

The kid sneers. "Yeah, I'm holding the shop. The others are...out."

"When are they back?"

He stands up, decides to act hard. "What do you care?"

Big mistake. My hand clamps around this throat and I slam him back against the white brick wall. He grunts and fear widens his eyes. Carly turns to watch the driveway and the road, ready to warn me if anyone comes, I figure. Good girl.

"Fuckin' hell," Dwight says, the wind gone from his sails. "Couldn't be timed worse!"

I grin. Couldn't be timed better in my opinion.

"What are you smiling at, man?" the kid asks. I can see the top of an Iron Cross tattoo on his neck where I'm stretching it out of his collar.

"I'll ask the questions, you answer."

"Fuck you!"

My free hand finds my gun and I jam the barrel up under his chin. His jeans stain instantly with piss. "You will answer me."

"Okay, man, okay. What do you need?"

"What's your name?"

"Kevin!"

"Okay, Kevin. A friend of mine, you don't need to know who, has to get some information to Carl Hildebrand." Kevin's eyes betray his recognition. "Yeah, you know Carl. So do I. See how we're all friends here? So stop acting like a prick. Now here's the thing. I need to get word to Carl about something too, so who among you lot would I see about that? Unofficial word, obviously, so don't suggest I just go up to New Orleans Parish like a common visitor."

Kevin swallows hard against my palm, I feel his Adam's apple bob desperately. "I don't know, man. I only know Carl's name by conversation." I squeeze harder, he yelps. "But Gene will know."

"Gene?"

"Yeah, yeah. Gene. He'll help you get word to Carl, for sure. I know he's done that stuff before."

"And where is Gene?"

Kevin starts to grin just as Carly says, "Hey, Eli. Trouble."

I turn to see a white van pull into the small lot. Three dudes with bald heads and lots of tattoos are lined up all along the front seat, faces twisted in hate at the sight of me holding young Kevin by the neck. Dwight starts dancing from foot to foot, laughing and saying how this is more like it.

I drop Kevin and slip the gun back into my jeans, hopefully before they feel the need to pull theirs. This was going so well. The three pile out and two more leap from a sliding door at the side. They line up across the concrete looking at me and Kevin runs to join them. Six of them in a line, the paint shop at our backs, the road out front empty. This has turned very bad indeed.

"The fuck is happening here?" the one in the middle demands. He glances at Kevin's wet jeans, sneers.

Kevin leans forward. "Gene, this guy threatened to kill me, says he knows Carl Hildebrand."

Gene doesn't take his eyes from me this time. "Shut up, Kevin." At least now I know which one is Gene. He's the only one I need to talk to.

Gene's fingers flex at his side. I know a draw tell when I see one, the guy is itching to grab the gun in his waistband. The others are looking from him to me and back again, waiting for orders.

"Why don't we all go inside?" Gene says.

I don't like that idea at all, out of sight and heavily outnumbered. "I just need to know how—"

"I don't give a fuck what you need! Turn around and walk in that office door now."

The door next to where Kevin was sitting when we arrived is ajar. There's a desk and filing cabinets in there, another door, wide open, leading directly to the paint shop, which only has one car in it, though room for three or four. A closed off spray room fills one back quarter.

"Eli," Carly says, her voice thin.

"Come on." I turn and walk in, taking her hand as I go. "First chance you get, you run. The keys are in the ignition. Understand?"

"Eli..."

"Understand?"

"Yes."

Chapter 16

"Go through," Gene says and we enter the big space and turn to face them.

"We got off to a bad start, Kevin and I. Let's maybe try again."

"One kid and you've got an attitude and a gun, now you want to play nice?"

I raise my hands, palms up. "The kid has a mouth, pissed me off."

They all laugh at that and Gene nods. "He's a pain in the ass, but little brothers, eh? What can you do?" He holds out a hand. "Now how about you give me that gun?"

There's no way I can let that happen, and I know there's going to be blood. I can see it in Gene's eyes, he doesn't give a fuck about us. He plans to hurt us, probably rape Carly, there's no negotiating here. I know bad people when I see them. I fucked up again. Truth is, now I can either fuck up completely, or get lucky.

I reach slowly behind my back, watching the twitch of the others here. "Carly, run."

I pull the gun quickly and dive to one side. Surprise is my only advantage. Dwight whoops, Alvin laughs like a hyena. Sly coughs on his joint smoke.

I'm firing as I roll to the cement, two of the fuckers dead with holes between their eyes, but then the others are drawing. Gene is fast and furious, Kevin drops and cowers, unarmed and terrified. The two remaining neo-Nazi fuckers both leap in opposite directions, both pulling hand cannons. Death or glory now.

I try to draw a bead on one, but my peripheral vision picks up their movement and I can't fire, have to keep rolling. Cement chips spit up from where I just was. Carly is running, but not for the door. She's leaping for the cover of the one car in here. Fuck it! If nothing else, she was supposed to get away, to survive.

Gene is yelling something I can't make out over the booming gunshots, then fire sears along my right calf. I fire twice, miss once, but kneecap one of the fuckers with my second shot. He screams like a schoolgirl on a rollercoaster, the sounds is staggeringly surreal.

But Gene and the other one have got me in their sights, I'm out of time, out of options. The ultimate fuck up. For fuck's sake, Carly, run. But then she pops up from behind the car and one neo-Nazi looks suddenly stunned with a bullet hole right over his heart. A rivulet of scarlet runs down his shirt and he collapses. Carly has the .38 from the bag I picked up at Jeff's and she's a damn fine shot.

My gun tracks to Gene, and so does hers. Suddenly he's outgunned, teeth bared as he was about to murder me. Now he pauses. The kneecapped one is squirming on the cement, howling like a whipped dog, blood spreading in a fast-growing pool. Kevin is still huddled against one wall, hands clasped over the back of his head, shivering violently. The rest, bar Gene, are dead. Goddamn. Way to go, Carly.

There's a tense pause but for Kneecap's howling, then he slowly winds down. He tries to sit up, sees the mess his leg has become, and passes out. The silence is sudden and physical. Gene, Carly and me, we're locked in a Mexican standoff. He's outgunned two to one, I can tell he's trying to decide whether he should pull the trigger or not. I'm dead if he does, no way he'll miss. I'll fire too and hopefully I won't miss. But Carly will also fire, and judging by her last shot, she definitely won't.

I draw a shaky breath, my calf throbbing with pain. I dare not look at it yet. "If you shoot me, you die. She'll get you. Lower your gun and we'll talk."

He growls, low in his throat like a cornered dog. Then hisses and drops his gun to clatter onto the cement. "This is fucking insane!"

From the corner of my eye, I can see that Carly is starting to shake. Shock and adrenaline rushing through. I wonder if she's ever shot someone before. I'm going to have to find out where she learned to shoot, but targets and humans elicit a very different response. I need to give her something to do.

I keep my gun on Gene. "Carly, go staunch his blood loss. And get Kevin over there in the corner, keep an eye on him."

She nods, Kevin puts himself in the corner, eyes wild, while Carly grabs some rags from a bench and ties up the poor bastard's knee. He's weak and slurry, moaning and crying. I stand up, ignoring my own hurt, glance around. "Three of your boys are down and done," I say. "That one will never walk the same again, but he'll live if you're quick."

Gene is literally shaking with rage, his face is red like he's sunburned. He'll have a heart attack or aneurysm the way he's going. "The fuck *are* you?"

"Your worst nightmare. You shouldn't have acted so tough and brought us in here." I gesture at the dead and injured. "This is all your fault, I got nothing to lose. So tell me what I need to know and you can maybe save that one."

He growls again. "What if I don't care about him?"

I swing my arm around to level my gun at Kevin. "Little brothers, eh? What are you gonna do?"

His eyes widen. "You fuck!"

"Talk or he dies."

"What do you want?"

I already know how all this will go down, I don't have time for niceties. "I know you got word to Carl Hildebrand in the Parish to kill Tweezer, the Desert Ghost."

His anger turns to confusion. "That's what this is? You a biker? The fuck that have to do with you?"

"Who told you to tell Carl to kill Tweezer?"

He tips his chin up. "You really avenging some piece of shit, two-bit, fucking loser biker?"

"No. I don't care about him."

Realization dawns. "Oh, you're after whoever wanted Tweezer dead. I honestly can't help you. I don't know who sent the order down."

"Sure, you maybe don't know who it was, but someone passed on that message. Someone came to you and said Tweezer needs to die, and they told you to tell Hildebrand to do it. They're the next link in the chain. Who is that?"

"I tell you that, I'm dead."

I gesture with my gun at Kevin. "You don't tell me, he's dead."

He stares at me and he sees where this is going. Sees the only place it can go. A strange calm descends over him. "You'll let Kevin go?"

"Tell me what I need and he lives. But I'll be taking him with me, so if your information turns out to be bullshit, he dies after all."

I watch the last of his defiance drain out. He looks past me. "Kevin. Kevin!" The kid looks up, face the color of ash. Gene smiles. "You do whatever this guy says, okay? And then you'll be okay."

"Gene?" Kevin's voice sounds more like he's seven than seventeen.

Carly looks up from where she's trying to stop the blood flowing out of that ruined knee. Her mouth falls open and she steps away, makes like she's going to say something then shakes her head and moves to a sink to wash the blood off her hands.

"You hear me, Kevin?" Gene says. "Do exactly what he says."

"Okay, Gene."

He looks back to me. "You promise me. He's too young to know better. You let him live."

"If what you tell me is true."

He nods, swallows. "Kevin, you take this guy to see Simon Clarke."

"The retard?"

"Don't call him that. But yeah. You can do that?"

"Sure, I can do that. You'll be okay?"

"Yeah, little brother. I'll be okay. You just take this guy to Simon."

"Okay."

Kevin stands, his legs flapping together like flags in a storm.

I catch Carly's eye. "Take Kevin out to the car, start it running. Keep your gun on him."

She stares at me hard for a beat, then drops her gaze. She hooks the little .38 at Kevin. "Come on."

When they've gone, Gene looks at me with undisguised venom. "Fuck you, you piece of shit."

I know he's told me the truth. As the car outside roars into life, I jam my gun barrel into his chest to muffle it as much as possible and shoot his heart out. He drops with hate still burning in his eyes. The kneecapped guy on the floor has passed out again. I crouch and hold his nose and mouth closed for a count of one hundred, watch the pulse in his neck slow down and stop. Officer Graney was goddamned right about a rising body count, but these guys would be too good at getting word out ahead of me. Besides, they started this. I collect up their guns before I leave, five variations on nine-millimeter semi-autos, all with full clips of ammo. The bullet wound in my calf is thankfully superficial, despite the roaring pain of it. I strap it up with a clean rag and leave.

Carly is in the front passenger seat of the Dodge, twisted around to keep her gun on Kevin. Exhaust curls up from the tailpipe. I drop into the driver's seat and say, "So, where do we find Simon?"

"Gene's okay?" Kevin asks.

"He'll be right in there waiting for you to get back. Now which way?"

"Head out to the main road and hang a right."

All his attitude and bravado are gone, but I'm more worried about Carly. How long can she hold it together before what she did in there catches up with her? I glance over and she catches my eye, nods once, teeth pressed hard together. Muscles twitch in her cheeks. Damn, she's strong. She's not happy, far fucking from it, but she's strong. I head for the main road.

"Where'd you learn to shoot like that?"

She grimaces. "Vern used to let me shoot targets out back all the time. I enjoyed the sense of power, played with all kinds of guns. He said it never hurt for a girl to know how to defend herself. Always a little nervous too, like maybe he was teaching me something I might use against him one day. But he knew it was important to keep me from getting bored, and I wanted to know how to shoot."

"You're good."

"I didn't know for sure until just then." She gulps, half laugh, half sob.

There's a heavy silence in the car for a while as we drive, except for the occasional direction from Kevin. His voice is small, all that audacity from outside the paint shop shattered like thin ice under a boot heel.

"How old are you, Kevin?" I ask eventually.

"Nearly sixteen."

Fucking hell. He really is a kid.

"Okay, Kev, now here's how it's going to go. Things got really messy back there, didn't they?"

"Are they really dead? Dylan and Sam and—"

"Don't think about that now, okay? There's business to take care of. I need your help, then you can go back and see about all that."

"They were going to hurt us, weren't they?" Carly says. "Be honest, Kevin."

In the mirror I watch tears well up in his eyes. Eventually he nods. "They've done it before."

Carly slumps a little, some measure of relief, I guess.

Chapter 17

"Kevin!" His eyes snap to mine in the mirror. "Tell me about Simon Clarke."

"He's a retar... He's a mentally disabled guy that Gene knows. Used to be Carl Hildebrand would get work via Simon, now Gene does, since Carl got locked up. There's a few people, a few networks, you know? I don't know how it all breaks down, but there are a few trusted connections who act as intermim...inteminn..."

"Intermediaries."

"Yeah, that. Right. So one of those is Simon. He shows up now and then with instructions for Gene. Once Gene does whatever it is he's been asked to do, he lets Simon know, then Simon shows up with some money."

"And that way Gene never knows who actually contracted him for the work."

"Exactly."

"Bit of a risk, isn't it? Using someone mentally disabled for a job like that?"

"No, Simon's not an idiot or anything. I shouldn't call him a retard, Gene doesn't like it when I do. Simon's got the autistic, only he has it pretty bad. Can't touch people, never looks you in the eye, has to count fucking everything and shit like that. But he absolutely will get things done."

"But what if Gene got fingered by the cops and he turned Simon in? He wouldn't hold up much under interrogation would he?"

"I guess it depends how much he knows, right? How much he'd have to tell. He might not know who it is that gives him the information."

"Layers like a rotten fucking onion," Carly mutters.

I can only nod. "One step at a time," I tell her. I catch Kevin's eye again, then turn my attention back to the road as I say, "So here's how it goes. When we get to Simon, you're going to take him a message. You tell him it's from Gene."

"Is it? Turn left here."

"Yeah, it is. Me and Gene talked about it while you waited in the car. Simon does everything face to face, right? No discussions on the phone?"

"That's what he does with Gene. Just calls and asks to catch up. I don't know where."

"Okay. So you tell Simon that Gene talked with Carl Hildebrand. Carl knows some stuff about Tweezer and thinks it's worth something. Tell him Gene wants to meet, and it's really urgent."

"Who's Tweezer?"

"You don't need to know the details. You tell Simon to meet his contact and say that, then you come back and tell me what's what. You understand?"

"Yeah, I got it. Go left up ahead."

We turn into a fairly quiet-looking suburban street on the south side of Baton Rouge.

"We going to Simon's house?"

"His mom's house. Simon lives with her."

"He your age?"

"Nah, in his twenties or something."

"You fucking dumb, man?" Michael's voice is strange, it's the first time he's spoken to me in ages. I'm seeing double, Kevin in the real back seat, but that wide open space with the ghosts in it overlaid, coexisting.

I blink and look away. "What?"

Carly frowns at me, but I ignore her.

"In his twenties," Kevin repeats.

"Simon Clarke, man," Michael says. "Pauly Brand's nephew?"

A flood of realization hits me, but I don't say anything.

"You remember Pauly Brand," Michael says. "You opened his neck with a knife when everything went bad. Fiona Clarke is Pauly Brand's sister, she has an autistic son. That's too much of a coincidence to be random. Vernon is using Pauly's nephew as a runner."

"We're only one step away," I say, and the ghosts flutter and disintegrate, their mouths twisting, angry faces fading, annoyed they didn't get a chance to harangue me this time.

Carly is still frowning. "Are we?"

"I'll explain later."

"Here," Kevin says, pointing at a big house on a nice lawn.

"You remember what I said?"

"Yeah."

"Then go and come right back."

After a minute, Kevin is standing at the door talking to a young man with a dark bowl cut and Pokémon T-shirt. It must be Simon, he's starring at his shoes, nodding short, sharp nods, hands clenching and unclenching at his thighs.

"This gonna work?" Carly asks.

"Hopefully. Simon sets up the meet, we follow whoever turns up when they leave."

"And after this," she gestures at the front step, "we don't need Kevin any more." Her eyes are challenging.

I look away, see Simon go back inside, close the door without looking up. Kevin comes back to the car.

"Simon says he'll call his contact and pass it on. But he says the contact will not be happy about Gene wanting to meet."

"What did you say?"

"Told him that's all I knew and they'd have to work it out."

"Good. You did well."

Kevin licks his lips, gaze darting between me and Carly. He's not stupid. "So can I go now? Will you take me back to Gene?"

"Not just yet."

I drive away, go around the block and pull up on an opposite corner to watch Simon's house obliquely from afar.

"We could be here a while," I say. "If you're quiet and well-behaved, Kevin, I'll let you go soon, okay?"

"Okay."

We sit without talking, staring at the house. I ignore the harassment of the ghosts in the back seat, refuse to even look in the mirror. I can't figure out why it's these five fools who plague me, I've killed many more men than them. Then a thought occurs to me: perhaps it's guilt. Of all the men I've killed, these five weren't trying to kill me. Weren't even planning to kill me. They may be far from innocent, but did I take their lives unjustly perhaps, by some strange metric? Is that it? I cast a glance in the mirror and they're still and calm. Michael raises one eyebrow, as to s ay, *You think?* Graney toasts me with a bottle, Sly with his joint. Alvin and Dwight sneer. What does it really matter?

Thinking I'm staring at him, Kevin slumps against the door and closes his eyes. Carly alternately stares at the house and then her hands. Stillness envelopes us for a time.

"I've never done that before," she mutters after a while.

"I know." She's talking about killing someone. It never affects two people the same way. It had to come up in conversation sooner or later. "You wanna talk about it?"

She nods towards the back seat. "Not now."

"If it's any consolation, you're doing really well."

"Feel like I might crack into pieces."

"There'll be time for that later. You can wait?"

"Guess I'll have to."

I give her a soft smile. "It's okay to fall apart a bit. Normal." I remember vomiting into that potted palm. "But if you can hold it together for a while, that's good."

She takes a long shuddering breath and stares at her hands again.

It's over an hour before the front door opens and Simon steps out.

He's wearing a tweed jacket over his Pokémon shirt and shiny leather shoes below straight jeans. He's skinny and nervous, taking short, rapid steps off up the sidewalk. When he turns the corner, I cruise up to watch him standing at a bus stop. After a few minutes, he boards a bus and I follow. A sense of finality begins to descend, like we're heading into an endgame.

It's only a ten-minute bus ride for Simon, then he gets off and goes into a doughnut shop. I pull up on the opposite curb, wondering where the best place to see will be. I catch my breath when a car door opens in the doughnut shop parking lot and big, black Charles gets out. Vernon Sykes's right-hand man.

Carly gasps and I nod.

"Now we just have to follow him when he leaves." I quickly maneuver the car into a side street from where we can watch Charles's car.

"Once he comes back out, can I go?" Kevin asks.

"We'll see."

Carly flicks me a glance, face pained. Kevin just nods, frightened but smart enough to stay silent.

We wait.

It's not too long before Charles and Simon emerge together. Charles has a face like thunder, rage and frustration clear in his eyes, the set of his mouth. Simon seems just like he was outside his house. They exchange another couple of words and then Simon walks off across the parking lot, towards a bus stop to go back home.

Charles stands by his car, hands on top of his head, fingers laced together. He stares off into nowhere and I have a tight pulse of panic, think he's going to look right at us. But even if he sees this car, surely he can't recognize the occupants from this distance. He gives a quick shake of the head and gets in, slams the door.

"Can I go?" Kevin asks, a waver in his voice.

"Not yet." I start the engine, watch Charles pull out and turn south. I join the traffic flow to follow him, several cars behind. This is going to sorely test my tailing skills, I know how good Charles is at spotting a tail, because he taught me how he spots them. He taught me a lot, but maybe I can use that against him and do things differently. With any luck, he's not expecting to be followed.

"You're in deep shit now, cocheese." Dwight's drawl is worse than ever, his cheek distended with tobacco, a quart of Jack Daniels in one grimy fist. Where do ghosts get liquor? Where do they get joints?

"He's right," Alvin says, swigging from his own bottle. "You're gonna walk right into a hornet's nest and get stung all to fuck."

I ignore them, but maybe they're right. I have no way of knowing how well-protected Vernon is now, how much of a force he's gathered.

"You know how the man works," Sly says, eschewing bourbon for his ubiquitous spliff. Blue smoke clouds around his head, snagging tendrils in his afro. "He has connections, man. Even if he not operating at full strength again, he'll have a contingent of fucking soldiers. They'll be ready and willing to smoke you!" He gestures with the joint, takes a long draw and blows a cloud over me.

It's thick and pungent, makes me cough. I wave a hand to waft it away.

Carly frowns. "You okay?"

"You can't see that?"

"See what?"

I watch her for a second then look back at the road. "Nothing."

"What's happening, Eli?"

"There'll be a gunfight at the end of this."

"Yeah, I figured as much."

"You should wait it out, don't get involved."

"Fuck you, Eli."

I sigh.

"Dragging more people to early graves, eh?" Officer Graney says. He takes a swig from Dwight's bourbon, grimaces, hands it back. "That body count going up and up. How long before it's you? Or her?"

I shake my head, refusing to answer.

"He's right, dude." Michael's face is pained. "So many deaths."

Better if we're all dead and gone, I think. Not like the world will miss us.

Chapter 18

We join Interstate 10 heading southeast and I realize where we might be going. About halfway between Baton Rouge and New Orleans is Lake Maurepas and the Maurepas Swamp Wildlife area. I10 runs right between the lake and the Mississippi River, through a small town called Laplace. North of Laplace, in the middle of nowhere, Vernon Sykes has a house with about ten acres of land around it. Old colonial place, hardly anyone knows about it except a few of his closest associates. He's not aware that I know about it, but I do, through a little gossip, a little adding two and two together and coming up with Laplace.

"I can't imagine we're going back to New Orleans, are we?" Carly says. "I mean, if Vern is back in town, that would mean he feels back up to strength."

I shake my head. "The place near the lake."

She looks over at me. "How do you know about that?"

I shrug. "Just do. I bet he's holed up there."

"With a fuckin' army!" Dwight says, then spits and cackles.

"I'd really like to get out," Kevin says. He looks pale, sick. "Just here on the highway, no problem. I'll hitch back."

"Sorry, Kev. You have to stay here just a while longer yet." I can't risk him maybe calling the wrong person, dropping us in it.

"What can you tell me about the place?" I ask Carly.

She purses her lips for a moment, then, "It's a big old house, like something out of *Gone with the Wind*. White balconies and columns and shit. It's got a fence all 'round, high gate at the front that's controlled from inside the house. Long driveway, kinda twists its way up to the house, nice gardens close by, then nothing else except a bunch of cypress trees and grass."

"Any outbuildings?"

"Got a big-ass barn on one side, a three-car garage on the other, both detached from the house, but nearby. That's all. The gardens around the house itself are managed, all flowerbeds, a fountain, bushes and shit. There's a gardener's shed about two hundred yards from the back of the house."

"What's the fence like?"

"About six feet high, wooden palings."

"Easy to scale?"

"Sure. But the house has security lights all around, motion sensors, cameras, you know? It's not Fort Knox, you can get in easily, but you won't get close without being seen."

I think about that for a while. I guess maybe being seen is the least of my concerns. I just need to get in. And hope the odds against me aren't too ridiculous. I have a righteous need for vengeance and surely that will get me a long way on its own. Stupidity might get me the rest of the way. Or get me dead. Either way, I'm on a collision course I can't change now.

Sure enough, Charles heads north off I10 just before Laplace.

"You know how to get to the house from here?"

Carly nods. "Yeah, I've been there plenty. I remember the way."

I pull up and let Charles drive away. No point in risking him seeing us now we don't need to tail him. If he isn't going to that house, we might be in the shit again, but I feel pretty confident we're on the right track.

"We can't wait long," Carly says. "Once Charles reports back, Vernon will get angry about Gene and start proceedings. Won't take him long to find out what's happened."

She's right. I'd like to wait for night, but that's not an option. I'll be doing this in broad daylight. "We'll give Charles ten minutes to get ahead of us and get inside."

Carly nods, but says nothing. Kevin is equally quiet, the ghosts absent.

Restless, ignoring the throb of the bullet burn across my calf, I give it eight minutes then pull away. Carly directs me and it's not long before she says, "About another mile up there, you'll see the gates on the left."

I don't slow down, cruise right by. She points as we pass, high white metal gates set in a couple of brick columns. Wooden fence like she described stretching away to either side. Numerous trees overhang the fence, fill the garden. Twisted branches of bald cypress trees, long beards of Spanish moss. The grass is a deep emerald green. It all looks so calm and peaceful, but it will run red before this day is done.

And I have to protect Carly from all of this. If nothing else, she needs to remain safe.

There's a small road a few hundred yards past the house and I pull in, park up in the shadow of some trees off the asphalt.

"So what's the plan?" Carly asks.

I stare straight ahead, knuckles white on the wheel.

"Eli? Eli, what are..? Oh no, come on, Eli! Not now!"

Without looking at her, I get out and pull open the back door. Kevin looks up at my face, sees something he really doesn't like and tries to scramble back, but I'm too fast. I grab his arm and haul him out. The ghosts are lined up by the trees, faces alive with glee.

"Oh yeah, let's have some fuckin' mayhem!" Alvin says.

Officer Graney and Michael are off to one side, both looking on with hooded eyes.

"What's happening," Kevin says, voice high and panicked. Piss stains the front of his jeans again, spreading like a blossoming flower. Poor kid. But this is for the best.

I hit him, not too hard, but right across the point of the chin, and he crumples like tissue paper, silent.

Carly is out of the car, screaming at me, not daring to come near.

I crouch, pull cable ties from my pocket. I've always got a whole bunch of them, tools of the trade. I secure Kevin's hands behind his back, then fix his ankles together. He seems to weigh nothing as I pick him up and dump him into the spacious trunk. Thankfully there's room for two in there.

Carly scrabbles in her pocket as I walk around the car for her, not looking at her, but past her. "No, Eli! No!" She manages to pull the .38 from her pocket, but I cuff her hand aside and the small gun flies off into the underbrush. It passes right through Sly and he laughs, deep and booming.

"Eli, no!"

It's hard, so hard, to show no emotion as I raise my other hand, this state of mind so hard to fake. But it's for the best. I want to apologize to her first, tell her this is for her own good, but it's all pointless. No time, and I can't trust myself to say anything right. Her eyes go wide and she opens her mouth to say something else, but I can't let her. Suppressing a grimace, I knock her out and tie her up too. Once she's in the trunk next to Kevin, I close it up, then unlatch the back of the rear seat. She won't find it right away, but if she thrashes around enough, she'll knock it open and find her way out. I haven't tied her feet, so maybe she'll be able to go for help. Hopefully I can come back and set them both free myself, apologize, put myself at their mercy. But right now, I have one focus.

Chapter 19

I collect the five nine-millimeters I took off Gene and his crew, stuff two into my waistband, one into the top of each boot, carry the fifth. It takes only a minute to push through the trees and scrub and find my way to the side fence of Vern's house. Another minute and I've found the gardener's shed Carly told me about.

There's a fair amount of cover between the fence and that shed, maybe I can use the trees and shrubbery to get close. Maybe not. Who cares? Here goes.

I'm over the fence and into some dense shrubbery in no time at all. Carly said there were motion sensors, who knows what else, so I can expect company any time. I just need to make sure Vernon digs in and doesn't make a run for it under cover of their fire.

A quick sprint, crouched low, takes me past a bed of rose bushes and into the shadow of the gardener's shed. As I peek around the side of it, the back door of the house slams back and three guys come bursting out. I don't recognize any of them. I was hoping to get a bit closer than this. Perhaps I've made the worst fuck-up of all. But there was no time to plan, no opportunity for subtlety and stealth. Oh well.

Game on.

The three fan out from the door, pistols gripped double-handed, raised to eye level like FBI recruits on a practical exam. The one in the middle yells, "It's broad daylight, there's nowhere to hide!" and I put a bullet between his eyes. His face is more surprised than anything else as he falls, but I'm already rolling to the rose garden, firing again.

I'm a damn good shot, but rolling and shooting is a low-success maneuver. Even still, one of the other guys screams and spins to one side, his left arm a flood of blood.

"Keep moving!" the other one shouts.

I take his advice, roll again. Coming up onto one knee, I pause long enough to shoot him, then I'm up and running. His jaw disintegrates, and he howls and mewls as he stumbles and falls to his knees, hands trying to hold back a crimson waterfall, his gun dropped, forgotten. Shit, that was an ugly shot. The one with the arm wound is tracking me and he starts squeezing off shots. I hear them tear through the air by my face, but he's not quite good enough. A concrete fountain offers me cover and I take it. I count a beat of three then pop up and rapid-fire three holes into his heart.

I'm distracted by the one with his face shot off, sobbing and staring in disbelief at his red palms. Thankfully my peripheral vision catches a glint of light and I'm moving before I realize what it is. Then I'm scanning for it, see an upstairs window swinging open, two silhouettes moving inside. I empty the clip of the gun, destroying glass and frame alike before they can aim and fire.

The next gun comes free of my waistband as I run to the cover of the house and quickly put Jawless out of his misery. There's hate and relief in his eyes. That's a look that'll haunt me if I survive this.

Someone appears at the back door and would have got the drop on me but there's a crash to the other side. A steel wheelbarrow rocks on its side, Michael standing there beside it. Did he just kick that over? Regardless, the man emerging from the house spins toward it, unaware of me, and I shoot him point-blank.

Now I get to go inside. More cover, but more chance of ambush too. I pause for one long, deep breath, then duck in, my gun held before me, playing left and right across a big kitchen. Brass and copper pans hang from the ceiling, an old black iron stove dominates one corner. Otherwise it's all modern, brushed aluminum and bright white. As white as the weatherboards cladding the outside and the balustrades of the balconies.

I pause, listen. Everything is eerily still. Surely that wasn't all of them? Only four. And no Charles yet. He'll be close to Vernon, that's his job. He's not a smart man, but he's strong as a bear and loyal as a dog. Vernon never keeps the really smart guys so close.

Dwight strolls across the hall outside the kitchen, points upwards. I shift to see a staircase curving up one wall, wide and ostentatious. The kind of thing a well-dressed lady might slowly descend to greet a party full of guests. Alvin steps up next to Dwight and whispers something, and they both giggle like schoolboys. I shake my head. I can't afford these distractions.

"Proceed with caution," Michael says from behind me, standing in the open back door, silhouetted by the sunshine outside.

I ignore him too.

My feet are silent on the tile floor as I stalk to the kitchen door, look past Dwight and Alvin. The hallway is dominated by the large staircase on one side, huge white double doors leading into a large reception room on the other. I can see fancy furniture inside, a ridiculous chandelier glittering. Edging around I see that it's empty. Light pours in through glass panels in the ostentatious front entrance dead ahead, dust motes dance and gleam.

"Up, fool," Sly says, sitting in a gold and satin chair by the front door. Marijuana smoke wreathes his head, jets from his nostrils in two thick streams.

I narrow my eyes at him, at Dwight and Alvin.

"You wondering why they're helping you?" Officer Graney asks from the bottom stair. "It's because they love the mayhem. The blood and the violence. And be honest, you love it too. It fuels you. Fulfills you. You thrive on it."

Fuck Graney and his philosophizing. I push by him and edge up the stairs, leaning back against the wall to point my gun at the landing above. I'm nearly at the top when something tickles in my hindbrain.

"Duck," Michael says casually.

I flinch to one side as rapid pistol fire breaches the silence. A tall vase beside me shatters into a million shards, chunks of plaster and wood spit out of the wall where I'd been standing a second before. I saw two muzzle flashes, some ten feet apart. I can't respond to both, so I pump shots at one as I dive up another five stairs. A bark of pain makes me smile and then the corner of a wall protects me from the firing angle of the other. For now. The first one is down, his feet toes up in the doorway of a bedroom.

I feel the smile still on my face, remember Graney's words, and it fades.

The other shooter is breathing hard, the kind of rasp that accompanies a lot of weight. Nervous fat men can never hide once they're out of breath. Maybe this guy ran upstairs when the shooting started. By the sound, I judge distance and angle. The muzzle flash was low, so he must be crouching. Assuming he hasn't moved, which makes him an idiot, I tuck my gun around the corner and fire three shots.

He screeches like a little girl, then his panting rapidly increases and he's muttering, "Oh god, oh god, oh god!"

I chance a look and he's clutching his chest, running bright with blood. He is a big guy, morbidly so, and his jowls wobble with his panic. He looks up, startles, tries to raise his weapon at me, but he's dead before his fat ass slaps into the floorboards.

Everything is still and quiet again. I listen hard, can only hear birdsong outside, the soft sough of the breeze. The house makes tiny creaks and moans of age and settlement, something downstairs pings quietly. A clock ticks, unnaturally loud, in the bedroom now blocked off by the fat man's corpse.

That's six of them. More like it. Could there be more? This pistol has four more shots, then I have three more fully loaded. And I'm not scratched yet. Doing pretty well. Maybe I didn't fuck up.

Crouching on the top step, protected from the large part of the house by the corner of the wall, I feel reluctant to move again. There are two doors in view in front of me, one with Toes Up lying half in and half out, the other closed. Could be a cupboard, a bathroom. Could be a room with a dozen armed men in it. And I have no idea what lies the other w ay.

Michael is sitting on the step below me, looking up. "Gonna chance it?"

"You could help me."

He smiles sadly, shakes his head. I take a deep breath, lie low to the floor of the upstairs landing, and quickly look around the corner. Gunfire booms, the wall and carpet kick and splinter as I whip back into cover. Something burns above my left eyebrow and hot blood is running in rivulets over my cheek, dripping onto my shoulder. Fuck, that was close. Someone up there is a good shot.

But I saw the layout. The landing extends along with two doors on either side and double glass doors at the end opening out onto a small veranda. I remember that from the outside, just a semicircle with a white railing fence, big enough for a small table and two chairs, maybe. Somewhere for a quiet breakfast or afternoon tea.

Of the two doors nearest on either side, one is closed, the other filled with the obese corpse. The next two are both open and shooters sit in both, at least one on either side. The guy who nearly killed me is crouched on that tiny balcony, aiming through the glass doors. So three of them. At least. Still Charles and Vernon himself unaccounted for. But three others fanned out with complete coverage of my course, one of them an excellent shot. Presumably Vernon is in one or other of those open rooms, cowering but well-protected.

Maybe my luck just ran out.

Chapter 20

M ichael is gone, and Officer Graney is leaning against the closed door I can see from where I'm sitting. "You wanna know the odds?" he asks me.

I try to ignore him, but he goes on.

"Most gun battles, like this, it's momentum that keeps a shooter successful. Once they stop to think, to hunker down and regroup, that's usually when it's all over. They eventually try to move again and then they get shot. We train that way, to put ourselves in a position that makes the shooter stop and think, then we've got him. So. What are you thinking about?"

I shake my head, look away from him. Adrenaline surges in my system, blood thrums through my veins. My breathing is calm and measured, but my heart vibrates like a jackhammer. If I pop out again, that sharpshooter on the balcony will get me for sure. He's only about twenty feet away. As I shift on the stair, shattered ceramic grinds under my feet. Another of those tall vases stands a little further down the stairs, about three feet high, maybe a foot in diameter. As carefully as possible, not taking my eyes from the landing above, I shift step to step down to it and test its weight. Not too heavy at all.

Without stopping to think about it, I switch out to a fresh, fully-loaded pistol and carry the vase back up, my shoulder pressed to wall. I close my eyes, think about the distance, the angle, the width of the corridor up there. I'll only get one chance and I have to kill that fucker and hope the other two don't get a drop on me in the moments between.

The bullet wound across my forehead burns and my head is starting to pound, feels like my skull is swelling fit to crack. I breathe it down, mentally run through once more, then move.

My left hand launches the vase around the corner and it sails, spinning horizontally as I duck out behind it. Sharpshooter's eyes are wide as he both fires and raises his arm to block the incoming missile. It's enough, pulling his shot wide and I pump the trigger. My shots shatter the vase at the moment it collides with him. He staggers back, crying out as his arm and chest explode with blood. There's a crash as he backs into the small table, it tips, his legs flip up and he's gone, over the railing.

I'm already ducking back into cover before I hear his body hit the patio paving below, but it's masked anyway by gunfire from the doors either side. Two flares of pain makes me yelp, one in my left upper arm, one in my hip. I fire randomly left and right as I duck back behind the wall, then grit my teeth against the burning pain, gasping for breath, forcing down the adrenaline that narrows my vision and makes my hands shake.

The shot to my hip is a graze, hurts like fuck, but barely even bleeding. The arm is a different matter, the bullet punched right through the muscle of my triceps, my sleeve already soaked in blood. It hurts like hell to move that arm even slightly. I tear off my T-shirt from under my jacket, use the adrenaline and fury to wrap up the wound tight, stem the blood loss as best I can for now. Sharpshooter is down, but those other two are still there and I'm running out of time and blood. I wipe my head, my hand comes away red and dripping. At least it's to one side, not flooding my eye.

I tuck my injured left arm into my jacket to immobilize it. Thank fuck I'm right-handed. I take a deep breath. This has to end.

"He down?" a voice says from above.

"Did you get him?"

"Yeah, definitely. But I don't know if it was well enough to kill him. You?"

"Dunno."

Might be I can use this. I groan weakly, gather saliva in my mouth and cough wetly. I've heard enough dying men to know the sounds they make. Hopefully these goons have too.

There's a soft laugh. "That sounds promising."

"You go, I'll cover."

"*You* fucking go!"

"Jesus. All right."

Idiots. I cough and groan again, weaker this time, barely enough for them to hear. But just enough.

There's a shuffle of feet on the runner rug that covers the center of the hallway, a shadow appears on the wall opposite. I press myself hard against the wall at my back. As the shadow moves almost close enough to see, going slow as a nervous tortoise, I pop around the wall and empty three shots, gut, chest, head. His face is anger and shock, then I'm grabbing his falling corpse with my left hand, screaming at the pain in my arm, and holding him against me as a shield. He bucks and shifts as bullets from his pal riddle him, then I twist and empty my clip into the open door now I know which one it is. He dies with a furious, "*Fuck!*" and then everything is still and silent again.

Breathing hard, willing myself not to pass out from the pain, I tuck my injured left arm back into my jacket and stand there with a fresh gun held out before me. Slowly the blackness recedes a little from my eyes, my ragged breath the only sound. Even the birds outside have fallen silent, probably flown far away from the racket of explosions in the house.

So was that eight or nine? I've lost count, but it feels like enough. How many men could Vernon have gathered in the past week? How many would be here?

"Just you and me now, Vernon?" I say loudly. "And good old Charles, with his tongue up your ass."

There's a soft bark of laughter from the room on the left. "Fuck me, Eli. You're still alive? Again you decimate my associates in my own home."

Red attempts to replace the black in the edges of my vision and I gasp a deep breath before saying, "No number is enough to account for what you took from me." I move towards the open door. A study begins to reveal itself, shelves of leather-bound books, a red leather wing-backed chair, standard lamp. One end of a dark wood desk. I imagine Vernon is sitting or standing behind the desk, a weapon leveled at the doorway. Charles is probably tucked close to the wall near the door, at an oblique angle to ambush me as I enter.

"I was having a bad day," Vernon says.

"You fucking cunt."

"One thing you have proven beyond any doubt, Eli, is what an asset you'd be to anyone. I'd be a fool to keep you as an enemy. What is it you want?"

"I want you dead."

"Come now. There's better than killing. I'm on the back foot right now, I don't deny it. I have some...spot fires to put out from that idiot Tweezer blabbing. But I'm getting things organized. And I still have enormous wealth, Eli. I can give you virtually anything. Name your price."

"Walk to the doorway of this office, your empty hands held out in front."

"But why would I do that unless you can convince me you won't simply execute me?"

"Then we appear to be in a stand-off, as I'm sure you're armed."

His façade cracks. "Of course I'm armed, you pissant piece of shit!"

Movement catches my eye. The doors to the small balcony open in-wards, panels of smooth glass. I can see him, reflected faintly, ghost-like, as the lowering sun lights his study. He is behind his desk, standing slightly to one side, a pistol leveled at the door. I shift ever so slightly left and right, wincing against pain and adrenaline, fighting the dizziness of blood loss. I can't see anyone else. It's a fifty-fifty guess which side of the door Charles will be on. Best guess is behind the door itself.

I relax, let my mind operate autonomous of thought, reversing angles, estimating distance. "Tell you what," I say. "How about..." then I'm moving.

I duck around the doorframe and fire. Vernon yells as my shot takes the gun clean out of his hand, even as it goes off. Plaster falls from the ceiling as his shot goes wild, then he's cradling a bloody hand and snarling at me as I body-check the door back to slam Charles. But the door bounces off the wall, Charles nowhere else to be seen.

"Fuck you, Eli!" Vernon growls.

I'm an idiot.

I step away from the door, turning back to the hallway, but I'm too late. Light flares in my left eye, closely followed by a blast of pain and shock, as Charles flies across the hall from the room opposite and hits me. On instinct, as I spin away I pump my right elbow that way, feel it crack satisfyingly into a nose. Charles grunts and staggers back. What a fucking fool I am, hurting and hopped up on the action, but I should have known to check the other rooms as I went. I assumed Charles would stay close to Vernon. Assumptions get people killed. After all this, one ultimate fuck-up to end it all.

But Charles is a fool too. Following my elbow, my arm opens out, the pistol tracking to Charles's wide-eyed face. He expected his hit to knock me out. He should have shot me. Last mistake he'll make, I'm tougher than old boots when it comes to being KO'd. My vision is crossing, vertigo makes the walls tilt, but at point-blank range I blow his face into mincemeat then spin back to Vernon before Charles hits the floor.

But it's too late.

Vernon has another gun drawn and it booms. He's holding it left-handed, his right hand ruined and bleeding from my shot to his previous weapon, but even wrong-handed he's good enough to tag me. Pain flares again, this time in my right arm, near the shoulder. My gun drops from nerveless fingers.

Fuck it, so close! I slide down the wall, scrabbling for one of the guns in my boots despite the searing pain. I dare not look at the damage, but the agony makes my vision cross, my fingers aren't working properly, then Vernon is over the desk and aiming down at my head from only a yard away. Just beyond my reach.

His face is a mask of fury. "Even Charles? He was my best man."

I grunt, force a laugh. "Looks like I was your best man, fucker." Then I'm yelling at him. *"Maybe you shouldn't have murdered my family!"*

He smiles, shakes his head. "It didn't have to be this way, Eli. Are we not civilized beings?"

I'm incredulous, despite impending death. "No, we are clearly not. We're animals who wear clothes and pretend at some purpose, some perceived higher calling, when our brutality makes liars of us time and again." I have no idea where it's coming from, but the words pour out of me. "I mean, sure, some individuals can be virtuous, even civilized, but humanity, en masse, is no better than a well-dressed pack of hyenas, chattering excitedly around whatever carcass it's managed to subjugate this time. And that's the best of people, even those only concerned with themselves, ignoring so much suffering. And people like us? We are *far* from the best of humanity. We're among the worst, lying all the time to conceal our true natures even from ourselves."

Vernon tilts his head to one side. "So eloquent all of a sudden? And so cynical."

"But no less true."

"And all so pointless, now that you're going to die. A fucking mess you've made here, but I'll rise again, as I always do. You can't finish me, Eli. I'm untouchable. Immortal."

"You really believe that, don't you?"

He gestures loosely around. "See for yourself." He raises the weapon and lines it up to my face, taking his time to aim well left-handed.

As I brace for the final shot, I see the ghosts lined up along one side, all five of them, grinning.

"Ask him about the time he was raped in the can when he was a teenager," Alvin says. "A skinny con, drunk on moonshine, called him sweet honey."

Alvin is older than the others, been around a while. As he says this, I remember that he knew Vernon's father, the previous generation of this messed up family.

"Untouchable?" I ask Vernon. He raises an eyebrow at me. "Like that time you got fucked in the ass by a scrawny fucker who stank of jail-brewed moonshine and called you his sweet honey?"

Vernon's mouth drops open a fraction. "How can you know that?"

"I know Vernon tried to fuck my mom and she kicked him in the balls and ran away as he screamed like a little girl," Michael says with a laugh. They're enjoying Vernon's discomfort now, maybe given that my death is guaranteed.

"Or that time Mrs. Privedi made you think your nuts had burst when she kicked them?" I ask Vernon, hoping my embellishments ring true.

His brow creases. "How much did you fuckers all gossip? Is that how loose information is in my crew?"

"He came to my place once and raped an eleven-year-old girl," Dwight says, and even he seems disgusted by that. It surprises me, but maybe they were related. Would that be enough to cause Dwight distress?

Ignoring the roaring pain in both arms, my head, my leg, I creep my fingers towards my right foot, tucked up underneath me where I collapsed against the wall. My right foot, and the gun tucked in that boot. "What about the child you raped just outside Jacksonville?"

Vernon's face creases, and I can see even he regrets that one. His left hand shudders as trembling set in.

"Yeah, not even a teenager, so tight and crying out in pain, but you saw it through anyway, didn't you." My fingers inch nearer the gun, almost touching it now.

"No one knows about that!" he roars. "Tell me! Before I fucking kill you, tell me how you know that!"

"You'd be amazed what I know."

"That piece of shit Dwight is long dead, he can't have told you! Can he?"

I shrug my left shoulder to draw his eye, ignoring the flare of pain in that arm, and my fingers close over the gun in my boot.

"I can see you reaching for that weapon!" Vernon screams, and kicks my right arm, where his bullet hit me.

Pain howls from fingertips to neck, I choke out a sob of agony, my hand numb and throbbing. Vernon jams his gun barrel hard against my temple.

"Well, fuck you and whoever leaked this shit about me! It's all over, time for a new chapter. I'm glad I'll get to start again."

Fuck it all. I squeeze my eyes shut, my body as tense as racquet strings.

"Hey, Vern," Carly says.

My eyes pop open and there she is in the doorway, the .38 in her hand, the cable tie nowhere to be seen. Vernon stares agape.

"Eat shit and die, Vernon."

She fires and Vernon's eye bursts in a spray of scarlet. The back of his head opens out, bright white shards of skull and gobs of pink brain spatter back across the room. I dive to one side, anticipating his reflex shot. It's deafeningly loud and plaster showers over me in a white cloud, then I'm scrambling away.

I back up against the wing-backed chair, fighting off the blackness of pain. Carly stands in the doorway, staring down at Vernon, the .38 hanging forgotten at her thigh in a trembling hand.

"Ah, fuck me!" Dwight says, disgust plain. "You're gonna survive this after all, you suck-ass piece of shit?"

I manage to raise a middle finger at him and he fades.

"So unsatisfying," Alvin says, and he fades too.

Sly makes a disappointed tutting sound, blows out a huge cloud of joint smoke and disappears into it.

"Vernon may be dead," Officer Graney says. "But we'll catch up to you, eventually." He points at me, pins me with one long index finger. "You can count on that."

Then he's gone, and only Michael is left. He walks over, crouches beside me, puts one hand on my shoulder. He smiles thinly, gently kisses my forehead. Is that forgiveness? When I open my eyes again, he's gone.

"It's done," Carly whispers, still staring at Vernon.

It's only her and I now, and a house full of corpses. I can't speak. I swallow hard, wait. Eventually she turns her eyes to me.

"You were faking it," she says.

"What?"

"Fucking blanking out! You faked it. After everything, all we'd done, you still didn't think I was strong enough." There's a slight bruise on her chin from where I hit her.

"I just wanted to protect you from—"

"Fuck you! You would have died here and I'd be left to go back to him. Could you not tell I had the strength to be here? Surely I'd proven that."

I look at the floor, ashamed. She's right. "I'm glad you came."

"Fortunately, I kept a small knife in my sock ever since I first got a chance to shop, just in case you went weird and tied me up again. I cut the tie easily enough, took a while to stop feeling sick from being knocked the fuck out!" I wince. "Then I banged on the trunk for ages until the seat behind Kevin shifted and I realized I could get out there."

"In case I didn't come back." It sounds so lame now. "And Kevin?"

"I cut him free and told him to go home. He was going to walk to the highway and hitch back." She crouches and starts checking me over, dressing my wounds with Vernon's shirt, Charles's shirt, torn into strips. "Fucking hell, Eli."

"I got pretty close."

"It's a massacre out there, but you would have fucked up at the last minute. Fallen at the last hurdle."

I hiss between my teeth. "Story of my fucking life."

She keeps glancing back at Vernon as she fixes me up.

"You did it," I say after the fourth or fifth time. "He's not getting up again."

She looks at me with tears in her eyes. "You should have trusted me, and you did fuck up, but I would never have had that chance if it wasn't for you. You cleared the way here."

I smile weakly, unsure what to say.

Her tears breach, as much from the relief of finality as anything else, I imagine. "But now what will happen? A life on the run?"

I pick up the .38 from the floor beside her leg, put it in my jacket pocket. "You were never a willing accomplice. Tell them that. Keep telling them that."

"What?"

"When they find you here, you tell them I brought you along to get to Vernon, I killed everyone. It's almost entirely true. The whole time we were on the run, this past week, I've kept you tied up. Your bruises, those were from a couple of times you tried to escape, to come back to your husband."

"Eli..."

"And once I'd got him, I left you here and you don't know where I went. Which will be true."

"Eli, no. There must be something else."

"I've been a fuck-up my whole life. Even when I started making something good with my time, it was tied up inextricably with this fucker and this life. And it got them killed." I sniff, swallow hard. "Caitlyn and Scottie. They died because of me. I can't fix that." The pain of their loss roars louder than the bullet holes riddling me.

"So what will you do?"

"No idea. Something. Hide, drift, do what I can, where I can, try to atone for my myriad sins. And when they eventually catch me, I'll back up your story. You're safe from all this now. You're free. If nothing else, I've done that much."

I haul myself to my feet, blinking against the pain, the exhaustion, the dreggy comedown of fading adrenaline. Carly jumps up, grabs my arm but I shake her off.

"You're too hurt!"

"I'm tougher than you think. I know a guy in New Orleans, he'll fix me up, no questions asked. And he's not associated with Vernon. An independent guy."

She starts to speak again and I hold up my hand to stop her. "Don't follow me. Give it fifteen minutes, then call the police. Get them out here, tell them our story. You'll be free once all the bullshit gets worked through, you know you will."

"Eli, please."

"Seriously, don't follow. Okay?"

She stares at me hard for several moments, like she's trying to commit every line of me to her memory. Eventually she nods once. "Okay. Thank you." She leans up on tiptoes and kisses my cheek, comes away with blood-stained lips.

I huff a soft laugh. "You're welcome."

I don't look back as I stagger off through the house. It's a struggle to get back over the fence, but I manage, and the relief of falling into the driver's seat of the car is almost enough to finish me. Refusing to pass out, I start the engine and head towards New Orleans. I wasn't lying about the doctor there.

Chapter 21

I'm sitting in a bar in Ottawa, slowly drinking a cold beer, when I next hear Carly Sykes's name. It's been eighteen months since I left Vernon's house near Lake Maurepas. I'm used to the heavy ponytail of hair brushing my back, dyed jet black, and the thick beard that comes past my collar line now. Not yet used to the holes in my life where Caitlyn and Scottie used to be, but coping. I'd been ignoring the TV set burbling away in the corner until I heard, "Carly Sykes, infamous for being central in the botched kidnapping massacre in Louisiana a year and a half ago, and heir to the Sykes fortune, was upbeat when she left court this afternoon."

I turn on my stool, and there she is: radiant, powerful. She looks stronger than ever, hair grown out again, back to her natural color. "It's a great relief to put all this behind me," she says, and my eyes narrow at the practiced voice, the familiar turn of phrase. "I'll be glad to get back to business as usual. Thank you. No further comment."

She breezes past the flashing cameras and microphones being thrust at her, a soft smile fixed in place, and ducks into a waiting limo.

The newscaster's voice drones over the top. "The so-called fresh power in organized crime in the American south, Carly Sykes maintained her innocence throughout proceedings. The case was thrown out for lack of evidence, fallen apart, some say, after the sudden car crash death of a key witness."

I tune it all out again. I've tried not to think about her for a year and a half, and I don't plan to start now. She's a pro, I'll give her that. I've seen Vernon do the same thing half a dozen times in the past. Looks like she's inherited Vernon's empire along with his fortune. I'd hoped for better, can't help wondering if she's the abuser now. Was it all for nothing? Maybe she's going to be as bad as Vernon ever was. Or perhaps she'll be a new breed, a benevolent dictator. I guess it doesn't really matter. It's all just people feeding off each other, no better than a well-dressed pack of hyenas.

Part II

Recall Night

Chapter 22

My name is Eli Carver and I am not a good man.

My hands are soaked in blood that will never wash off, but it's like the blood of an abattoir worker—obtained while providing a service. People can survive without meat, but a lot of people wouldn't survive if the assholes I killed were left alive. So maybe it was even a good service. But that's rationalization.

I knew I was never one of the good guys, but I didn't realize how bad I was until my world fell apart. When Vernon Sykes, the boss I'd served my whole adult life, murdered my wife and child, I had what can only be described as a breakdown. I found my way back through seas of blood, the body count higher than I ever thought possible, and all but Vernon's daughter Carly are dead. She was his victim too, and now Carly runs the old man's business.

So the wheel turns, nothing changes. And I'm still a bad guy, I guess. I just didn't realize how bad until that blood washed the shit from my eyes. But I'm not the kind to wallow. I did what I did, can't change it.

I'm trying to be better. I have a new code now. I still have no faith in people and I still have no idea what I'm supposed to do with my life, but I must have some atonement still to make, because the ghosts are back. And the ghosts are telling me I'm about to be up to my neck in blood again. They're not usually wrong.

Maybe some things never change.

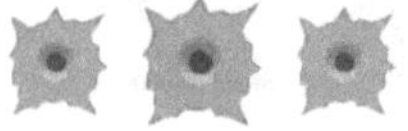

Then

It's bizarre how I ended up in this mess. Quite the re-entry to life.

After the massacre at Vernon's place, I survived under the radar in Canada for nearly two years. Rebuilding a life after my breakdown, stealing sometimes, sure, but working too. Taking cash-in-hand laboring jobs, doing some less-than-honest work for less-than-honest people here and there. I don't really know how to do anything else. But I tried, hiding out after the debacle with Vernon, a long way from the scene of those crimes. In a way it was peaceful for a while, but always looking over your shoulder takes its toll. Then these shithead ghosts started cropping up again. I guess they weren't part of the breakdown after all. Or maybe I'm lining up to lose it again. That's an ongoing concern.

"Probably wanna pay attention up here, dude."

Those words marked their return. Michael Privedi, my best friend. I shot him in the head when we were about twenty years old, to save my skin. It was his fault, he'd crossed Vern, but I guess he still thinks it's unjust that I took him out. I was following Vernon's orders or I'd be dead now too. Perhaps that would have been better. Maybe that would be justice. Who knows?

I tried not to look at him on the barstool next to mine, half his head blown away, flesh and bone hanging wet, teeth a rictus grin where his cheek was torn free by the bullet I put in his other ear. His collar burgundy from the blood soaked into it.

"Up where?" I asked quietly. I didn't want to draw attention to myself, talking to someone I knew no one else could see or hear.

Michael nodded upwards, at the big-screen TV above the bar. Following his gaze I was startled to see Carly Sykes, looking hotter than ever, so settled into her role as a matriarch of organized crime. She's only twenty-two, but hell, she's a queen. Frowning, I tried to figure out where she was and realized it was a courthouse. That's where I'd last seen her, maybe six months ago, on the news. Now she's at it again.

A scrum of reporters surrounded her. Carly smiled like a movie star.

"Miss Sykes, would you care to comment on the verdict?"

"It's exactly as I always said it would be, I'm innocent and my associates are innocent. This has been nothing but police harassment from the beginning. I know Vernon was a bad man, but look what happened to him! I'm not about to follow in those footsteps."

A *hyuck* of a laugh on my other side and that a racist sack of shit called Dwight Ramsey, a weed grower who pushed us too far so I put a hole between his eyes, was staring up at the screen too. "She's good, ain't she, *cocheese*!"

Fuck, I hate it when he calls me that. And he always calls me that. He glanced at me, then turned back to look up at the screen and the bone flower of an exit wound in the back of his head glistened and dripped. I ignored him.

"And that case was never solved, right?" another reporter calls out. "The police still don't know who was responsible for the bloodbath?"

That would be me.

Then Carly turned, looked right down the camera, like she was looking right at me. Into me. "I told you guys then, like I told the police, I have no idea who it was. I was kidnapped, kept blindfolded, spent most of the time in the trunk of a car. I only managed to get out once it had been parked at the Lake Maurepas house for hours. I went inside to find the..." She hitched a breath, suppressed a sob. It was almost convincing. "The massacre. I don't think I'll ever know who it was. I guess no one will." She stared hard at the camera a moment longer, then one eyebrow hitched, then she looked away.

"The fuck is she on about?" Dwight asked and hawked a wad of tobacco spit.

"You're a fucking idiot." Perhaps the only person who hates Dwight Ramsey more than me, Sylvester Barclay, was standing right by the bar. I put a shotgun hole through his torso in Maloney's bar, on Vernon's orders. His organs hang in there, shiny. Calls himself Sly, a Jamaican gangbanger and drug dealer, always stoned, but smart as hell.

"What?" Dwight demanded.

Sly tipped his head toward me. "She's talking to him."

"Why?"

"Because," said Officer Graney, "she needs him to know he's in the clear."

Graney is a sharp-nosed, rat-faced fucking cop I wasted in a motel parking lot during my breakdown. His voice is rough, no doubt from the big hole in his throat, two more in his chest. He's maybe the only one who genuinely didn't deserve to die, but how good is any cop, really? I guess there are good ones somewhere. Something tells me Graney would never fit in that group, anyway.

"How can he be in the clear?" Dwight asked.

Graney shrugged. "She's done something, pulled strings. Probably takes every public opportunity to drop him a hint and he's finally noticed one."

Could they be right? And perhaps the more pressing questions rose again: Are these assholes really ghosts? Really here? Or is this my psychosis coming back, talking to itself? Regardless, right then, they made sense. But how could I be in the clear? Maybe I needed to reach out to Carly to see if I could learn anything.

"Might be worth a call to one or two of the redline numbers."

And there was the last of my ghosts, my peanut gallery of mockery and hate. Why these five I'm still not sure, but now the gang was all there with the arrival of Alvin Crake, a shitheel employee at Michael's dad's garage. I wasted him for talking shit about the dead, Michael and his father. Of course, Michael and Alvin share the pleasure of haunting me, but they hate each other. Like Sly and Dwight hate each other. Like Graney is full of disdain for everyone, the self-righteous prick. And I pretty much hate them all, except Michael. And he annoys the shit out of me more often than not. What a fucking circus.

But perhaps Alvin was right. Vernon kept a handful of what he called redline numbers that we all had to commit to memory. Landlines mostly, that we could call in emergencies, speak in code. I wondered if Carly kept them up. She knew about them. She knew everything about his business.

If they were right, and I was off the hook, I could go back to the US, return to a normal life. Whatever the fuck that might be. But I was curious if nothing else. Part of me wanted to ignore the whole thing, leave Carly out of my life and stay in Canada, stay incognito.

"You know you have to find out," Michael said. "You won't rest until you do."

Pissing me off again. I stood quickly from the barstool and waved my arms through the insubstantial smoke of all five assholes. "Get out of my way."

A few confused faces, belonging to real people in the bar, turned to me, but I ignored them and walked out into the cool spring air. I needed to find a pay phone.

I tried the Bourbon Street redline first. No answer. No idea if the place is even still part of Carly's empire. It's where I shot Michael in the ear, on the second-floor balcony on a hot, sticky night. Better not to linger on thoughts like that. Michael leaned against the other side of the pay phone glass, looking at me with hooded eyes. Did he forgive me back then, after Vernon was dead at Carly's hand? How could he? It was his own damned fault, I have to remember that. He fucked up and I wasn't going to let him get me killed too. He pointed pistol fingers at me through the glass and fired.

I tried the Maurepas Lake house redline next and it was answered after three rings. "Yeah?"

"I need to talk to Carly Sykes."

"Wrong number, pal." But he didn't hang up.

I let the silence drag out for a few moments. I could hear him breathing. "You gonna put her on or what?"

"Why should I? Who the fuck is this?"

"Just tell her it's the guy with the cable ties."

There was a moment of silence, then the scuffling of the handset being handed around.

"You finally checked in." Her voice was smooth velvet, soft and confident.

A thrill tickled through me. If I'm honest, a large part of why I'd avoided even thinking about her as much as possible over the last two years is because of what stirs deep down when I remember her. We went through some major stuff together, after all. Dwight stood outside in the spring sun, thrusting his hips and slapping an imaginary butt. Sly looked on disdainfully, half obscured by a thick cloud of joint smoke. I turned my back on them. "I had no idea you were waiting to hear from me."

"You saw the courthouse footage from this morning?" she asked.

"I guess so."

"I figured you'd catch one of my appearances, eventually. Right from the outset, I told them I had no idea who it was. And you'd left no one alive to contradict me."

"But the truck stop while I was out of it. The thing in the motel parking lot." Graney shot me with pistol fingers that time, mouthing *Asshole!*

"Yeah, that was the harder stuff to deal with. Took an awfully long time, but all the evidence, CCTV footage, witness statements, it's all gone. I figured I owed you that."

Holy shit, that was some powerful string pulling. I stayed silent while I considered it all. Eventually I said, "I don't want back in. If you did it to get me—"

"I did it because you deserve a second chance. I don't expect you to come to me, I don't expect anything. You gave me a new life. I wanted to return the favor."

"That's a big thing."

"Ain't no big thing." She laughed softly. "I won't lie, it would be nice to see you again. I miss you, believe it or not. But if I never do, I get it. And we can't talk any longer. Just know you're all clear. Okay?"

I missed her too, still do, I can't deny that. "Thank you." And I meant it. Felt like a yoke had been lifted off the back of my neck.

"Good luck." I heard a gentle smack of a kiss being blown down the line and then the dial tone.

I kept the handset pressed to my ear for several seconds, a tide of emotions crashing against me. Eventually I hung up and stepped out into the cool, sunny day. Holy hell. Eli Carver was back. Now what the hell should I do with myself?

Chapter 23

Now

Turns out, I get myself right into trouble.

"Miss Carlson, so good to see you again. And right on time."

The guy talking is a long, thin drink of water in a dark suit, maybe fifties, slicked black hair over a pointed face and eyes shaped from a lifetime of narrowed suspicion. But his smile seems genuine enough. He looks directly at me over Bridget's shoulder.

"And who's this large gentleman?"

"Just a friend of mine," Bridget says. "We're going out after I drop off your money, so excuse him hanging around, yeah?"

"Certainly, I don't see why not."

I hear their conversation, but I'm on auto, clocking the layout, checking for exits. Two mooks are hanging behind either shoulder of the tall man, who's sitting at a table, elbows on the checkered cloth. Dark wood chairs, small gaps, but only two other tables in the small restaurant are occupied. Both by another pair of mooks. So that's the boss and six heavies. No customers. I guess it's late enough for that to be normal.

In fact, a third table is occupied. Officer Graney, Sly Barclay, Dwight Ramsey, and Alvin Crake sit around it, lounging back in the chairs, casually passing a joint. Then Michael Privedi catches my eye, leaning up against the back wall under a giant photo of Vesuvius. That's all five of my ghosts accounted for. I can ignore them.

Michael nods toward the corner. A guy in chef's whites is looking through the glass panel in the swing door to the kitchen, so that makes seven heavies, potentially. Might be others in the kitchen. There's another two doors in the back, one marked Restrooms, the other plain. Could be people there too. No idea if the plain door is an office or a back way out, maybe both. But despite the numbers and unknowns, everything seems chill.

"You have the money then?"

"I do, Mr. Lombardi."

"With the interest as discussed?"

"Yep, 40K, just like we talked about. I'm sorry it all went down this way, but I pay my debts."

Lombardi nods. "Let me have it. And all this will be done with. Of course, if you ever want to play again, you're welcome by the club any time. Assuming the money you claim to have is correct."

"It is." Bridget pulls a large, thick envelope from her bag, walks quickly to Lombardi's table and slaps it down, then hurries back to my side. She gives me a tight smile on the way back.

She's smart, getting back close to the door, and her exterior is cool, but it's a shell. Close up I can see her hands shaking.

"Stevie," Lombardi says, not even looking at the envelope. One of the two standing behind him moves around and takes a seat, starts counting the cash. Lombardi is still smiling at Bridget. "We have to check, of course."

She shrugs. "Of course. Take your time, there's no rush."

And then the shit hits the fan.

I see Michael's face drop, his eyes and mouth go wide looking behind me and I react instinctively, pulling Bridget aside into the corner. Graney, Alvin, and Sly rock back in their chairs laughing, and Dwight is suddenly right there.

"You're a dead fucker now, cocheese!" He dances a jig like an idiot.

The restaurant door slams back and two dudes with submachine guns fill the space. The roar is deafening as they open fire. Lombardi is fast, dropping behind the table, and I don't know if he's hit or not. The top of Stevie's head vaporizes in a red mist that spatters over the payment of Bridget's debt and he keels over. The other heavy beside that table gets one hand into his jacket before his chest erupts in red and he staggers back, limbs hectic and loose. Already the gunmen are tracking across the restaurant. I see the chef duck out of sight, the other four heavies are rising and drawing.

"Stay down!" I yell at Bridget, shoving her away from me, then remember she has a gun and I don't.

The two machine-gunners have stepped in, either side of the door, and another man comes through. He has automatic pistols, one in each hand, and starts assisting their fire. The next two heavies are blood-soaked and falling by the time the last two have finally drawn and start to return fire. But the attackers haven't seen me yet, tight by the side of the door as I was.

I step across and bring one arm up underneath the elbow of the shooter closest to me, my other forearm slamming down across his wrist. I feel the heat of the barrel through my jacket as the gun bucks up, but the pop and snap of the guy's elbow joint is louder. He screams but it's already too late for him. I grab the weapon from his suddenly useless fingers, reverse it and find the trigger, turn his face to paste and he flies back out of the door.

The guy with the pistols turns to me as the other machine-gunner dives for cover in the opposite direction. Lombardi is still out of sight, the remaining two heavies are moving and firing. I have to leap away and hope like hell Bridget stays in the corner.

I roll over a table, flipping it up behind me as I land, then pop up for another burst of fire, make the attackers duck. As they all react, I move again, trying to get around the restaurant, draw everything away from

Bridget. This gig might only be for seven-fifty, but it's the principle of the thing. I have a new code now. I've agreed to do a job and I plan to keep her alive. Anyone else can get fucked.

And if I'm honest, this is the most fun I've had in ages.

As I move around, the guy with the pistols drops for cover right where Bridget was hiding. Shit. The other one is using the corner of the door and the front window for a modicum of cover, squeezing off bursts at Lombardi's last two. He clips one, sends the guy spinning to the floor with a yelp of pain, then I get a bead on him and squeeze two short bursts. He drops, chest and throat jetting blood, the skin at the side of his neck flapping open like a saloon door.

What the fuck were these guys thinking? Did they expect much less resistance? Even without me here, three against six on home turf is bad odds. Then again, they nearly had them all down before I stepped in. I start to line up on the last guy, with the pistols, when he does a crazy twist that a gymnast would be proud of and slips behind a table. My burst of bullets shreds the window frame right where he'd been crouching, then Bridget is screaming as he hauls up and drags her with him. It takes me a second to realize he's trying to drag her in front of himself like a shield, but he's grabbed her bag, not her body, with one hand, firing randomly at me and Lombardi's remaining heavy with the other. Bridget has the bag strap, still over her shoulder but held tight with both hands, and she's pulling back against him. She doesn't want to be a shield, but she's not letting go of that bag either. No surprise, her whole life is in it, in used bills from Jerry Slovak's stash.

Pistols is panicking, his face twisted in effort, and I line up to reduce his head to mince, but Lombardi's boy clips him low on the thigh and he goes down to one knee. My burst misses and, as he falls, the bag strap gives up its hold on life. The gunman rolls backward, still holding the bag. In another feat of gymnastic prowess, he lets the roll take him all the way over, flipping his feet behind him out the door, then he's up and limp-running, heading north back along 7th Avenue. Still with Bridget's bag.

Her scream of, "*NO!*" is punctuated with a couple of last-ditch shots through the window from Lombardi's boy, but his aim is off and the man is gone. Ignoring the moans and cries of pain, the patter of raining glass, I run back across the restaurant, knowing damn well Bridget is going to chase her bag. Sure enough, she's out the door a few steps ahead of me.

"He's still armed!" I yell, just as the sharp cracks of two shots sound over the traffic noise, and brick chips fly right beside Bridget. She ducks and skids to a stop and I grab her.

"My fucking money!"

"I know!"

We're looking, but can't see the guy anywhere. There's a screech of tires and a dark blue Lincoln SUV tears away from the curb. A yellow cab blares its horn and barely misses the car beside it, then they're gone. I see the attacker briefly through the window as they tear off. The road is busy despite the hour, people on the sidewalks are crouched in panic or running away from the mayhem that erupted inside Gino's. The whole thing only took about ten seconds and some folks are still standing wide-mouthed, trying to figure out what the hell is going on.

"Where the fuck is he?" I hear the sob in Bridget's voice.

She didn't spot the getaway. "He had a car waiting. He's gone."

"My life went with him!"

"I know. I'm sorry. Jesus fuck, what a mess." I realize I'm still holding the submachine gun, people are staring, some have started screaming. "Let's get back inside."

"We can't let him go!"

"We already have. He's gone. That was nothing to do with us, it was a hit on Lombardi. So if anyone's gonna know who it was, therefore who we have to squeeze to get your money back, it's him. So let's get back inside and hope he survived."

Chapter 24

Then

I couldn't stop thinking about Carly's call. I always thought I'd have to stay in Canada, but if the way really was open to go back to the US, I wanted to take it. I have no home, I have no life, but I decided that whatever I built from here on needed to be in the country I was used to. I'd always felt like an interloper, those two years in Canada. Treading water.

I realized I was excited again. When Vernon wasted Caitlyn and Scottie, he killed me too. He killed the Eli Carver I was, but I resurrected myself, baptized in a sea of blood. I never saw anything beyond that. It turned out Canada had been a waiting room. Thanks to the bastard's daughter, I could finally begin to live again. Not that I was suddenly full of rainbows and unicorns. Any life I built would still be populated by the human animal, feeding on itself, but at least I wouldn't be hiding anymore.

It took a few days, but I finally got my stuff in order. I had a couple of extant fake IDs I'd managed to slip away with, and I used one to get back into the States. Carly may have swept up the evidence, but that didn't mean the authorities just forget. They might not be able to nab me for those crimes, but the name of Eli Carver will likely still trigger red flags somewhere. Better to stay incognito across the border. So I left Canada via Cornwall in a beat-up old Ford Taurus I'd had for twelve months, and re-entered the US via Rooseveltown, New York, as Steve Johns. It's an alias I never used much before. I decided it would be my fall back ID from there on.

My nerves ratcheted up at the border, but it all went smoothly. I guess I'm a white guy and that privilege gave me easy passage. "You've been in Canada a while," the border officer said, his voice bored.

"Work contract," I told him. "All done now and glad to be heading home."

He nodded, barely sparing me a glance, and that was it.

And then I felt lost, like I was floating in open ocean. What the hell did I do now? No way I was going back south, too many memories, too many ghosts, real or imagined.

And of course, as soon as I thought of ghosts, the furious five materialized in the back seat, faces leering into my rearview mirror.

"Fuck off," I said, before they could talk, but I knew it wouldn't help.

"You really think you'll be okay here?" Graney asked, leaning forward between the front seats. Blood dripped from the ragged hole in his throat, I heard it patter on the armrest next to me.

"Okay?"

"You may be grease when it comes to evidence, but we'll find you. We'll get you for something else."

"Even if you have to plant new evidence? You're a bunch of corrupt fucks, every bit as criminal as anyone I ever knew."

He bubbled soft laughter and sat back, accepted a fat joint from Sly and fragrant smoke filled the car.

"What are you going to do?" Michael asked. "Where are you going?"

"I don't know."

"Better look out, cocheese!"

"For what?"

A loud bang startled me and I hit the brakes. The car coughed and lurched, then cut out, steam and smoke billowing from either side of the hood. Dwight's laughter was brittle and only annoyed me further. How did he know that was going to happen? Or did I hear something and my brain gave me the thought through the psychosis I've named Dwight Ramsey? Every time I try to unravel this mania, I get a headache, and a stabbing behind my eye means the start of another, so I let the thoughts go.

"Sounds pretty fatal," Alvin said, and he's a mechanic so I had to accept he probably knew what he was talking about.

"Make yourself useful and help me fix it then," I said as I popped the hood and climbed out. When I opened it up, more smoke roiled out.

Alvin stood next to me, thumbs in his belt loops. He leaned forward and blood dripped from the hole between his eyes, sizzled and steamed on the hot metal of the valve cover. "Yep, pretty fucked."

"Gonna tell me how I can get it going again?" I asked.

He used his middle finger to point to the bullet hole between his eyes, then slowly tipped his hand down to flip me the bird. With a short bark of a laugh, he walked away.

"Leave it," Michael said from my other side. "You got a few grand in savings, right? Walk away from this and from everything else. Really start again. Get to a city and find work."

"Work?"

"Guy like you? You're resourceful. You got skills."

I took his advice. I hitched to Syracuse with a trucker who thankfully didn't talk much and figured I'd take Amtrak to New York City. I don't have many friends, but there was an associate there who'd give me a couch and a hot meal. Tony Moretto. Made guy, nasty piece of work, always trying to make up for his short stature with meanness, when really no one else gives a fuck he's only five foot six. Not a great associate, but it's a start. If he was still there, of course. I had no number for him, but remembered his address. It was the start of a plan.

The train was busy when I got on board and I sat opposite a woman in a neat skirt and suit jacket, a large leather bag on the table in front her. She kept one hand on it like someone might try to snatch it any minute. Maybe they would. She should put it on her lap. She had another bag, one of those small rolling suitcases like people use for airline carry-on, between her feet. My only luggage was a large gym bag I could carry over one shoulder, a few changes of clothes and a handful of essentials. The previous couple of years had taught me to stay light.

I ignored Dwight and Alvin, pulling idiot faces that were probably meant to signify some kind of sex act. I mean, the woman was hot, probably around my age, definitely not over thirty. She had black hair, it glistened like a raven's wing, and fine bone structure, cheekbones you could carve with. Her eyes were deep brown like fresh-tilled earth. I wondered if she was Japanese, maybe? She looked like a femme fatale from a Dashiell Hammett novel in her sharp suit. I gave her a smile and a nod, tried to make sure I looked as non-threatening as possible. She returned the nod and I looked away, hoping to make her feel at ease. Five minutes later, the train eased out of Syracuse.

I realized Graney was sitting next to me, his police uniform neat as a pin. "Better look out!" he said, eyes narrowed and feral.

I glanced up and two police officers were walking through the car, looking left and right. My heart thumped an extra beat then I told myself to chill. I had nothing to fear, I'd done nothing wrong. Technically. Officially, anyway.

I realized the woman opposite had seen me tense up and it seemed infectious. She glanced back, spotted the cops, and whipped her eyes front again. Her knuckles whitened on the bag and she dragged it into her lap. My tension eased as curiosity took its place. I wondered what she'd done.

The cops stopped and talked quietly to a guy a couple of rows from us. I could only see the back of his head, but he seemed relaxed enough. They moved on and the one on the left eyeballed me and his face hardened. Fuck it. I'm an easy target, I guess, at around six foot two and two-twenty pounds. With my full beard and long black ponytailed hair, I suppose I looked like trouble. I was in jeans and a canvas jacket, so it's not as if I was dressed like a biker or a thug, but perhaps it was time to clean up my head a bit. A haircut and a shave might be in the cards, since Carly had cleared me. I'd never liked the damn beard, anyway.

"Where you going?" the cop asked me. I noticed the woman opposite tense even more. She needed to chill out. As if she read my mind, she sucked in a deep breath and relaxed her face. She immediately locked down a façade of calm. Impressive.

"New York City," I told the cop.

"What for?"

"Catching up with an old friend." What the fuck business was it of theirs? This was harassment.

"Be cool!" Michael said in a harsh whisper beside me, his face all blood and bone and hanging flesh. I saw it from the corner of my eye, but refused to look at him. I was already cool, fuck ya.

The cop stared at me a while, then turned quickly to the woman. To her credit, she didn't flinch. I decided these two were just a couple of king-shits, enjoying their power. Assholes.

"You?" he asked her.

"Me what?" She smiled. She was suddenly all smooth and confident calm.

The cop twisted his mouth in a grimace of annoyance. "Where you going?"

"New York City too."

"And what's your trip for?"

"Work."

They held each other's gaze for a moment, then the other cop nudged his partner, nodded ahead along the car. I turned my head to see a group of teens was up there, four of them looking guilty just for being alive. That's kinda the default for teenagers after all, poor bastards. Without another word to us, both cops moved off to harass the kids.

I caught the woman's eye. "Couple of assholes, huh?"

"Seriously."

"You know, I think anyone who wants to be a cop should be disqualified from the job. Same with politicians."

She laughed softly. "Nice idea. It'll never catch on."

"No, I guess not. You okay?"

"Sure, why not?"

She was masking it well, but I'd got her rattled again. I should have just left it, but it was a six-hour ride and I'm a curious person. "You seemed a little tense at first, that's all. Bad experience with cops before?"

"Has anyone ever had a good experience with them?"

I laughed. "I certainly haven't. I guess some people do, though."

"I guess. So why are you really going to New York?" she asked, turning everything around so fast I blinked.

"What do you mean?"

"I can read you way better than those cops. You're nervous."

"Seems we've been paying attention to each other. Maybe *we* should be the cops."

"Fuck that!" She shook her head. "Can't imagine a worse job."

"Well, by my philosophy, that makes you eminently qualified."

She shook her head again. "Uh-uh. No way. Not a politician either. But you're neatly avoiding the question. Why New York?"

She was good, I'll give her that. "Honestly, I have nowhere else to go. I'm at a kinda loose end, starting over. I know a guy there, that's all."

"Starting over? Sounds like maybe there's an interesting story behind that."

"Maybe. Tell me yours, I'll tell you mine." I wouldn't, but I could make something up.

She eyed me for a moment, lips pursed. Her eyes were soft, her lips full. She was smoking hot, and easily confident. Which I should have known could only mean trouble. "Okay," she said eventually. "Why not. I'll tell you something about me and we'll see what you think."

"What I think?"

"Sure, I'm interested. You look like a self-assured kinda guy, I'm wondering if you'll break the mold."

"Okay, now I'm intrigued. What mold?"

She took a breath, eyed me a moment longer. "I'm a professional gambler."

Not what I expected. "That right?"

"Yeah. A few years ago I answered a job ad in a newspaper for a Professional Gambler's Assistant."

"And you managed to work your way up from assistant to actual gambler?"

She smiled, even white teeth and a sudden warmth in her eyes. "You already broke the mold a little bit. Well done."

"I did?"

"Sure. Most guys simply can't see a woman as a gambler. They always think I mean I'm a croupier or something."

I was confused, and I frowned. "But you said you were a gambler."

"I did. The ad for an assistant turned out to have been placed by a genuine professional gambler. He wanted to train a team to play blackjack in casinos around the world and rake in the cash. He taught us strategy, how to count cards, how to beat the house every time. It's a kind of geeky and repetitive thing to do, and you have to play all day, every day, without mistakes, to turn a profit. But the upside is you get to travel the world. He took us all over. We played in casinos from New York to New Orleans, in England and Australia, Malaysia and Macau. My life was a series of casinos and hotels, piles of money counted up on different hotel room beds every night. Glamorous as hell, right?"

I was genuinely impressed, it sounded amazing. I wondered if she could teach me how to do it. Maybe that could be my new start. "Sure sounds it," I said.

She looked at me for a long moment, and then it seemed like I saw a decision made somewhere behind her eyes. "Yeah, well, not so much. Maybe for you it would be, but for a woman? Turns out we're not allowed to be cool."

"What do you mean?"

"This guy who employed us? His name is Jerry Slovak." She spoke quickly and easily, like a dam had broken. I figured maybe she'd been aching to tell this story for awhile and finally found a mark in me. I didn't mind that at all. "He chose a team of young woman because he was an ugly prick in his sixties and he wanted to fuck young women," she went on. "He got his way with a lot of them too, they were looking for something to lift them above the rest of us and thought the occasional fuck or blow job was worth it. Maybe it was, I don't know. I didn't take that route.

"We all lived and traveled together, and this sleazy-ass boss used us for jollies and profits. Women left all the time, but they were quickly replaced with replicas. It was easy for him, and the money was good. The excitement, the travel, for a while it was fun. But it got old real quick."

The glamor sure rubbed off her story quickly. "Yeah," I said. "Sounds like it would."

"And Jerry, he wasn't only creepy, but paranoid too. I mean, he was always carrying heaps of cash, so I get it, but it made him angry and volatile, you know?"

"I guess I can see that. But what do you mean, you weren't allowed to be cool?"

"Not me personally, but women. Whenever we'd have time off and try to chat up guys in bars, tell them what we did because it was cool as fuck, they would always start telling us how to play cards, like we hadn't just said we were actual professional gamblers. Like I said, you broke the mold already. I thought maybe you would. Most men are so insecure they can't imagine a woman in a role like ours. Honestly, I wanted to brag and be cool and get laid, but I couldn't."

"What the hell?"

She laughed. "Right? First off, men would be incapable of understanding what I'd said. Maybe after three or four times, they'd finally get that I was an actual gambler. Then they'd try to tell me how to gamble, and they would always, and I mean always, be so fucking wrong. It was exhausting. And then they'd tell us how dangerous our life was, like we didn't know. Like we couldn't handle it. So they missed out. Idiots. So many hot guys, so many idiots." She laughed again, but there was tiredness behind it.

"You surely can't have trouble getting laid though," I said. "I mean—"

She held up a hand. "Don't go there. Of course I can get laid. But only if I keep what I do to myself and act like a woman is supposed to."

"That's shitty."

"You don't need to tell me. I mean, some of these guys could have used my skills, you know? Maybe I'd have been willing to teach one of them. Maybe even steal Jerry's money as starter cash and go off with them. But they never even imagined the temptation because they couldn't imagine I was telling the truth. Like I said, women aren't allowed to be cool. It's a man's world."

I nodded, infuriated, but saw the truth of what she said. "If it's any consolation, I think you're cool as hell."

She looked down. "Mold-breaker," she said quietly.

We were quiet for a moment, then I realized something. "But if the boss was an asshole and you knew what you needed to know, why would you need another guy to go off with?"

"What do you mean?"

"You said maybe you could have taught one of those idiot men, stolen the boss's money and gone it alone. Why would you need one of those men? You could take your boss's money and have it all to yourself. You know all you need, so you only need yourself, right?"

"Well." She smiled, then looked away again. "I guess so."

Her bag was still on her lap and I saw her knuckles whiten again, and suddenly it all clicked into place.

"This is confessional," Sly said, appearing beside me in a cloud of fragrant smoke, echoing my thoughts perfectly. Or perhaps he was just a personification of my thoughts.

"It's why she was paranoid of the cops," Graney said. "And why she's so talkative all of a sudden. This is guilt-ridden."

The rat-faced dead cop was dead right. She saw me as a sounding board and probably someone she'd never need to see again once we got to Penn.

"Take her fucking bag, cocheese. You want a new start? If that bag holds all her boss's cash, there's your new start right there."

"She's awfully trusting," Michael said. "You gotta wonder why."

"What are you thinking about?" she said.

I jumped slightly, caught her eye again. "Sorry, I have a habit of drifting off like that. Just thinking over what you told me, that's all."

She smiled and it was full of ice-cold confidence. "I should point out that I'm armed. And not much scares me."

I returned the smile. "Except those cops." I nodded over my shoulder but the police had obviously grown bored of the teens and moved on.

"Well."

We were quiet again for a while, the world outside flashing by the window. Eventually I had to ask. "So why did you tell me all that?"

She smiled, nodded. She'd been waiting for me to come up with the question, I guess. "You said you were at a loose end and needing a fresh start. I'm quite capable of taking care of myself, but it would be nice to have another set of eyes. A back up. I have a meeting in New York, you see."

"And you think maybe I could be your bodyguard, that it?"

She shrugged. "Look at you. You're kinda intimidating. You can fight, I bet. You can look mean, right?" She smiled.

I wasn't sure if she was toying with me or not. "You don't know me at all. Maybe I'll take whatever you've got there and fuck off." I wouldn't, but she didn't know that.

She shook her head just a little. "No, you won't. I told you, I can read you better than those cops could. There's something about you, like you need to make good on a promise, maybe." She frowned. "No, I'm not explaining that right. But there's something..."

I guess she was right. And right then, I did need some direction. Anything to put off calling in that favor from Tony Moretto. It all felt a little fated, and I didn't like that, but I couldn't ignore it either.

"Take her fucking bag, cocheese."

Alvin was back and he agreed. "Why make life complicated? You've got some money but only a few grand. Imagine how much she might have in there. Look at those white knuckles."

Graney appeared, sitting right next to her, grinning across the narrow table at me. Sly was leaning up against the back of her seat, staring into nowhere while he enjoyed his ever-present joint. I think half the reason he smokes them constantly is to wind up Dwight, who wants some so badly but can't bring himself to ask a black man.

"Is this atonement?" Michael asked me. "Is this making good? Or is it falling back into old ways?"

I didn't answer him, because I didn't want the woman to think me mad. But he had a point. Truth is, I didn't know the answer.

"Well? You want to help me, big guy?"

"What's in it for me?"

"Adventure?"

I raised an eyebrow.

"How about adventure and five hundred dollars cash?"

"For one meeting when we get to New York?"

"Yeah."

"Make it a grand."

"Seven-fifty."

I shrug. "Okay, cool. Why not?"

She smiled and reached a slim hand across the table. "Bridget Carlson."

I shook. Her skin was warm and smooth. It felt somehow dangerous. "Eli Carver."

Chapter 25

Now

We push back into the restaurant, crunching over broken glass, stepping over pools of blood.

"How the fuck ain't you dead, cocheese?"

"You got some dark gods lookin' over you, white boy."

Graney, Alvin and Michael are there too, all of them pushing through the doorway behind us as we hurry back in.

"Fuck all y'all," I growl, and Bridget looks at me askance, but says nothing. I brush through the ghosts and see the chef has emerged from the kitchen and he's helping Lombardi up. The man has blood all down his left cheek from a head wound, one hand pressed to it as he grimaces. The only heavy not shot is helping his buddy up, that guy's suit jacket dark with blood all across his right shoulder.

"Clear the door," Lombardi says through gritted teeth. "Shut everything up."

He's right, the law will be here any time. I hope that door at the back does lead to another way out. I grab the leg of the first guy I shot, still lying on the sidewalk outside, and drag him in, then shut and bolt the doors. Seems pointless with all the glass blown out. I do my best to ignore the people shouting and coming to gawk. Cell phones will start filming through the smashed windows any second. These fucking idiots, there could be more gunfire any moment for all they know. Either way, I keep my face down and well out of any potential video.

"Let's move," I say, and gesture at the back. I grab my gym bag and Bridget's suitcase and start through the restaurant.

"Yes, go." Lombardi is on his feet, pushing the chef ahead of him. A teenager, face white as chalk, comes from the kitchen and opens the back door. We all pile through, into a short corridor, then a barred back door. The teenager then the chef, then Lombardi, me and Bridget right behind him. The two heavies come through on our six and then we're all in an alley that's dark and grim, stinking of refuse and piss.

"Go," Lombardi tells the chef. "Take Jacky with you. Lie low, I'll call."

The chef needs no more urging than that and he grabs the kid and hauls him away.

Lombardi turns to me. "Some shooting. You better get gone too."

"No way. We're staying with you."

"What?"

"We need info."

He stares at me for a moment and I see his eyes lose focus then find me again. The bullet that clipped his skull has left him mildly concussed is my guess. There's a shiny black Cadillac parked twenty feet up the alley and the heavies have already unlocked it. The wounded one is in the passenger seat and the other stands half in the driver's door. "Boss?" he says.

"Let's go," I tell Lombardi and he's smart enough to know what's most important.

He stumbles to the car and falls into the back seat, me and Bridget piling in the other side. My door clips a big metal dumpster as I pull it closed because the heavy has already peeled away. We hear distant sirens as the Caddy reaches the end of the alley and screeches left into a blare of horns and braking tires, then he floors it and we're away. I notice

Lombardi has the blood-soaked money Bridget gave him clutched in his free hand. Maybe not so concussed after all.

If I'm honest, this isn't quite the new start I'd envisioned, but it feels right somehow. I guess I shouldn't be surprised.

"Let me look at that," Bridget says, from the middle of the back seat next to Lombardi.

He takes his hand away, blood all down the inside of his wrist, soaking into his sleeve. Bridget checks the wound, lips pursed. Seems like maybe she knows what she's doing. "Got a handkerchief?" she asks.

The wounded guy in the front passenger seat reaches back with his good hand. "Here."

"Thank you, Johnny," Lombardi says.

Bridget moves the boss's hair aside, presses the folded handkerchief to the bullet graze there. It's bleeding like a son of a bitch, but looks fairly superficial to my eye.

"You should be grateful you have so much product in your hair," Bridget says. "It deflected the bullet."

Lombardi side-eyes her and she gives him a tight, humorless grin. I like this woman.

"Davey, head for the townhouse," Lombardi says.

The driver nods. "Yes, boss."

Davey and Johnny, good to know. And the boss is Paul Lombardi. I wonder how many are left in his crew after this night's work. The chef and his young helper are probably outsiders to the family. Could this be all Lombardi has left? Seems unlikely. I need to know more.

Lombardi leans his head back and closes his eyes, takes long deep breaths. "So why the fuck are you riding with me?"

It's a fair question. The sensible thing would be to get as far away from this albatross as possible. "That bag the gunman took," I tell him. "It had a lot of money in it. So I need to know who that was So I can go get it back."

Lombardi barks a short laugh. "You are some piece of fucking work. Good shooting back there too. I had six guys and they did nothing, you took out the shooters on your own." He tips his head toward me, opens one eye. "Who the fuck are you?"

"No one. Just a friend of Bridget."

"Sure. Well, I'm sorry about the money, but that's just collateral damage."

"The fuck it is!" Bridget shouts. "I put everything on the line here, I paid you back, and the rest of that money was for me to get away."

"Then I'm sorry you got caught in the middle of that. Really, I am. But what can I do about it?"

Bridget looks down at the money still clutched in Lombardi's other hand. She's shit out of luck there, but I know she'll ask.

"We could start by you giving me that money back."

Lombardi barks his laugh again. "Why would I do that?"

"Because you caused me to lose the rest."

"No, I didn't. These events are unconnected."

I catch Bridget's eye and shake my head. "Mr. Lombardi, I know Bridget is upset and she has every right to be. I know you don't owe her anything. Your business with her is done. The fact she got robbed by that asshole isn't your concern." She's scowling at me, but she's also smart enough to let me speak to this guy in his own language. "So while it's not your problem, as it happened on your turf, perhaps you could do us a small favor and tell me who the fuck it was. Then let me take care of our business."

Lombardi gives me that one-eyed look again. "You're something else."

"I'm just a guy."

"Sure."

Things are quiet for a minute and I let him think things over. I'm guessing his thoughts are sluggish right now, but he's a pro. He'll be considering every angle. And he'll want something for this favor, even though he already owes us. That's how these things work. Power builds on power, the more you have, the more you take, and that way you stay on top. I'm happy to play the game for now.

Davey heads into the Holland Tunnel. I'm glad we're leaving the city behind, it feels right. But I have a feeling I'll be back before too long.

"How much was in the bag?" Lombardi asks.

Bridget glances at me and I nod. At this stage, she might as well be honest. She sighs. "Eighty grand."

Shit a brick.

Lombardi smiles. "That's not small change."

He's right. It certainly isn't.

He looks back at me. "And who the fuck are you? Name?"

Oh well, if we're being honest. "Eli Carver."

His eyes widen slightly, Johnny twists from the passenger seat and narrows his eyes at me. Seems my reputation precedes me, even though I have no idea who these assholes are. Interesting. I don't think I like this feeling of notoriety.

"The Eli Carver?" Johnny asks. I notice he and Davey look a lot alike, and I figure them for brothers. Wide jaws, deep foreheads, broad shoulders, black hair and blue eyes.

"The only one I know," I tell him.

"Johnny, call Doc Brown," Lombardi says. "Tell him to meet us at the townhouse."

Johnny nods and turns back to face the front, aware the order is a veiled version of *Shut the fuck up and mind your business*. But he makes the call, muttering quietly as we drive. He's a hard fucker, given he's sitting there with a bullet wound in his shoulder, bleeding heavily.

"Okay, here's the deal," Lombardi says. "I'm in a compromised position right now, and I could use some help. Especially given the unfortunate loss of life back there. You need to get Bridget's money back, I understand that. So we're going to work something out. But for now I have a motherfucker of a headache, so everyone is gonna shut up until we get to the house and I get some painkillers and treatment." He leans his head back and closes his eyes again.

Bridget looks at me, her eyes searching mine. I nod. This is okay. We'll figure something out from here.

Chapter 26

Then

We made small talk for the rest of the train ride, but it was all superficial. I told her I was orphaned at five years old by a drunk driver, grew up angry. That much is true. I skirted the edges of where I went in life, but I guess she filled in the blanks enough. She told me she's the only daughter of an Irish-American father and a Japanese mother, her parents live in Florida now, and she had a brief stint as a nine-to-five wage slave until she answered that ad for a gambler's assistant. It's weird where lives go, random branches, fractal events leading to unknown destinations. I let my eye rove over the other passengers in the car and wondered at their stories. Everyone has one, everyone is the protagonist in their own personal drama. And every life story is interesting, even the most seemingly boring. In all honesty, a boring life is the most interesting thing there is to me, it's so different to my experience.

Even the ghosts went quiet, my festering five drifting off to wherever they go when they're not harassing me. It was a little after 10:00 p.m. when we got to Penn Station. "Is it too late for this meeting?" I asked Bridget.

"Nah, I told them when I was getting in. They're expecting me around 10:30."

She headed out, pulling her small suitcase by its handle behind her, the other bag over her shoulder and held tightly by its strap. I shouldered my bag and followed. She led us onto West 31st Street and turned left with confidence, then right onto 7th Avenue at the next light. She clutched the bag tighter to her chest.

"We gotta go far?" I asked.

"Yeah, but the walk will be good after sitting in that train for hours. About twenty blocks, toward the Village."

"Cool." She was right, the walking was good. I was glad we weren't taking the subway.

The streets still bustled, New York City never really sleeps. I'd switched automatically onto alert. It was a little shocking how easily the old habits came back. My eyes were everywhere, senses strung tighter than garroting wire, but on the outside I looked calm and casual. I just wished I had a gun. I didn't want to risk bringing one over the border, but I felt naked working without one. I'm a natural shooter, Vernon always used to say, and it's true. I can shoot better than anyone I know, but I've put in hours of training and practice too. Being a natural just makes the hard work easier. You still have to put the hard work in. I guess I can rely on my hand-to-hand fighting skills if I have to, I've put a lot of hard work in there too. But if we come up against bozos with guns, all the punches and kicks and chokeholds in the world might not be worth shit.

"Hey, Bridget, you said you were armed, right?"

"Got a thirty-eight in my bag."

Not much, but something. "You want I should hang onto that, in case?"

"In case what?"

"In case I need to actually be a bodyguard."

She smiled up at me and shook her head. "I'll hang onto it for now. Thanks though, for taking this seriously."

Cars crawled by, engines and impatient horns making most of the noise. Sometimes music blared from a diner or bar. "So talking of taking it seriously, tell me what's happening."

She glanced up at me again and nodded. "Fair enough, you deserve that, I guess. Okay, I'll give you the abridged version. Remember how you said why didn't I just go it alone? Well, I decided I was going to. But Jerry has this habit of noticing when his girls are getting itchy and he quickly starts cutting them off, making it difficult. He's a cunning fucker. So I couldn't let on that I was thinking of leaving. And the money was good, but he rationed it out, to stop any one of us from having too much all at once."

"Pretty controlling, huh?"

"To say the least. But we had time off, we had *some* money. Not retirement cash, but something. So I decided to build myself a private enterprise. I started going to smaller casinos when I wasn't working, places Jerry didn't bother with because he preferred higher stakes. I kept my head down, played well in those places and saved up. It was going well. Then I fucked up."

We stopped at an intersection, waiting with half a dozen other people for the light to change, so she clammed up. It was a companionable silence. As soon as we started walking again, she picked up where she left off.

"In one of these small places I heard about a high-stakes underground game."

"Oh, I can see where this is going." I felt bad for her, but if I was right, she was pretty dumb.

"Yeah, well, I guess I was a little naïve." That was just another word for dumb. She should have known better, but I kept that to myself.

She pursed her lips, maybe thinking the same as me. Then, "I got in on this game, and it was obviously rigged."

"And you can't count a rigged game."

She twisted her mouth into a wry expression. "Exactly. And I went into the hole a little before I figured it out. I should have run out, called it quits, but I was annoyed. I thought I could play myself out, figure out their fix and play it against them."

"Naivety and hubris? Dangerous combo."

She laughed softly. "Fuck you. Anyway, I said I was gonna give you the abridged version. I lost all my nest egg, and then some. I owed these cats a lot of money."

"How much?"

"Thirty grand."

"Shit, that is a lot of money."

"It sure is."

"So who is it you owe?"

"Mobster by the name of Paul Lombardi." She glanced up at me. "You know him?"

"No." And I wasn't lying. I'd crossed paths with many over the years, but Paul Lombardi wasn't a name I'd heard before.

She paused, checked the street signs. "Nearly there. Let's cut to the chase. I tell Lombardi I can get the money, I just need time. He says I can have thirty days, but then I'll owe forty grand. So fuck it, I have to pull the last chance gambit."

"You take all Jerry Slovak's money."

"Exactly. So I have the money I owe right here, and a decent cut on top. We go, I pay my debt, we leave. I give you your money and you fuck off. We never see each other again. I start over clean with a decent chunk of Jerry's money in my bag, you have a little more cash for your start over. Okay?"

"Sure. What about Jerry?"

"What about him?"

"Won't he be looking for you?"

"Of course, but he won't find me."

I wondered if she knew how hard it really is to disappear. "You sure?"

"We're here." She pointed to a restaurant on the corner of 7th and West 15th called Gino's, then gave me a tight smile. "Let's go."

Before I could say anything, she pushed open the door and strode inside.

And pretty soon it was a fucking bloodbath in there.

Chapter 27

Now

The townhouse is a three-story brown brick on the end of a row of similar residences on a quiet street on the outskirts of Bridgewater, New Jersey. There's a sign for Washington Valley Park at the end of the street. I try to remember the details for future reference. It's taken around an hour to make the drive and not a word was said by anyone the rest of the way. Lombardi is resting his head and I'm impressed with Johnny, stoically enduring his gunshot to the shoulder. I have no idea how bad it is, but his jacket is wet with blood and his face is pale as ash. He's a hard bastard, that's for sure. I'm guessing he's glad he called the doctor.

When Davey pulls up in the street outside, it's nearly 1:00 a.m. and everything is still, like only the suburbs can be in the middle of the night. In nature, the night is alive, but wherever people have taken over, they kill the life and everything goes into a kind of stasis when they sleep. It's the height of the unnatural. Uncanny.

As we climb out of the car, the front door opens and an ancient black man stands in the light pouring from the hall. His face is like a walnut, it's so deeply lined. His eyes are concerned as he steps back to let us in. He has a quick look over me and Bridget, but doesn't seem surprised to see strangers with the boss in the middle of the night. "Doc Brown is here," he says.

"Thank you, Alfie." Lombardi gives the man a smile, and it's genuinely warm.

I get the feeling these two go back a long way. Perhaps the old guy worked for Lombardi's dad before him or something, probably known the boss since he was a boy. But that's speculation, and that kind of guesswork can be dangerous. Better to wait and know, than think you already have knowledge that might come back to bite you. I mentally lodge the suppositions, anyway. I need to learn everything I can about these people.

We troop into a large front room and a middle-aged guy in shirtsleeves jumps up. Even though Johnny is clearly the more injured, he goes directly to Lombardi first. Johnny isn't surprised and Davey helps him into a chair, fussing quietly over his brother.

The doc works without questions, cleaning and dressing Lombardi's head, then gives him painkillers. Bridget was right, it's not too bad. "Just let me know if you feel any dizziness, nausea, blurred vision, stuff like that, okay?" the doc says.

Lombardi nods, then sits back and closes his eyes again. "See to Johnny," he says, but the doc is already over there, taking the man's jacket off.

As his shirt is peeled away the entry wound is obvious, a dark hole in the meat of his substantial deltoid muscle. The man winces but says nothing. The doc leans him forward, but there's no exit wound. "Bullet's still in there," he says. "This is gonna hurt."

"Already does," Johnny says.

They lay him on a heavy wooden table and the doc gives him drugs then gets to work. Johnny doesn't make a sound and after twenty minutes the slug is out and the wound stitched. Johnny sits back in the chair, arm in a sling, face still pale.

"The bone got clipped, but not broken," Doc Brown says. "You're pretty lucky. Just try to keep that still for a week or two."

Johnny nods, shuts his eyes.

"Okay, everyone to sleep," Lombardi says, getting groggily to his feet. "It's late and all business can wait until tomorrow, no arguments. Alfie, show Eli and Bridget to the guest rooms. Johnny, Davey, you two stay in the room down here." Without another word or glance, he leaves.

"Sir?" Alfie says, touching my shoulder. "Madam? If you'll follow me."

He leads us up two flights of stairs to the top floor where three doors surround a small landing. He points to the first two. "Take your pick. Each has a bathroom, and they're made up. Anything else I can get you?"

"No, thank you." I look at Bridget. "You gonna be okay?"

"Sure. But we're leaving it too long. That money has flown."

"Don't count on it. Plenty of options yet. Trust me."

She looks at the floor, her body sagging with fatigue. "This really isn't how I expected any of this to go down."

I shrug. "When the wind blows, you bend or break. We'll figure it out."

She puts a hand against my upper arm, squeezes. "Thank you. You know I don't have your seven-fifty anymore, right?"

"Yeah. And I might charge you a little more than that when we get your money back."

She laughs. "Fair enough."

Without another word she turns and goes into the first room. The door closes behind her, then a lock *snicks*. Alfie is still hovering. "Thanks," I tell him.

He nods and heads back downstairs.

I look at the other room he indicated, then glance at the third door. Call me paranoid. I open it to look in. It's a kind of study, a desk and chair, computer on it. Ornaments on the desk, the color scheme, the drapes, all make me think this is a woman's space. A large bookcase fills one wall and there are weird little carvings on it. Black wood with hectic, real-looking hair and grimacing faces, and strange metal geometric sculptures. A lot of the books look old, a few spines show titles like *Occult Science, The Black Arts, The Book of Smokeless Fire*, and there's stuff from Anton LaVey and Aleister Crowley. Among them are books on quantum physics, string theory, astrophysics. There's a Bible next to a Koran, and various volumes on wicca, voodoo, astrology, kabbalah and more. Quite the esoteric collection. I log it all for future consideration.

I go into the room next to the one Bridget took and it's simple but well-furnished. Fatigue crashes over me like a wave. I lock the door, go into the bathroom to piss, then fall onto the bed, fully clothed except for my boots. Darkness is quick to swallow me. As I go under, I wonder where the fuck my ghosts have got to.

Chapter 28

"Wake up, cocheese!"

Sleep drags at me like an anchor and I want to let it pull me back down, but that seems unwise.

"Don't miss all the fun, motherfucker." That's Alvin.

I open my eyes to watery early light and Michael nods from where he leans by the door. Dwight and Alvin prop themselves against the wall nearby.

"What fun?" My voice is like a wino's, thick and cracking.

"I don't give a fuck, someone is gonna bleed for this!"

Oh, that fun, perhaps. Lombardi's voice is pure rage, so I guess his head has cleared. He starts yelling again, voice fading as he heads downstairs.

Sly and Graney are sitting on the edge of the tub in my *en suite* bathroom, smoking a joint as they watch through the open door.

"You really wanna get into this?" Sly asks.

"Let him!" Graney says. "My boys will catch him more easily if he gets tangled up with a bunch of two-bit mobsters."

"What makes you think they're two-bit?" I ask him. "They could be high up for all we know."

"You ever heard of Paul fucking Lombardi before?"

Graney has a point.

"I've been out of the loop for two years. A lot can change in that time."

There's a rapid tapping at my door and when I look over at it, the ghosts have all gone. I get up and open it to see Bridget outside. Her eyes look haunted.

"Come in."

"What are we going to do?" she asks.

I wave her in and she shuts the door behind her.

"First, I'm gonna shower." The sight of her pink cheeks and wet hair has made me feel like the bottom of someone's shoe. "Then we go down and I talk to Lombardi."

"I've been thinking about it. Honestly, I've hardly slept and thought about nothing else. I need that money, Eli. I'm out to sea without it."

"I know. Don't worry. One way or another, we'll be okay."

"We?"

I smile, but try to make it friendly, not lascivious. I didn't mean it that way. "I have a habit of finding my way through circumstances. In fact, I pride myself on it. My whole adult life has been dealing with difficult situations. I had something of a slip a couple of years ago, but I'm back on keel now. I'll make sure you get your restart money. Somehow."

"Why?"

She asks a pertinent question right there. I have to think about it a moment or two, try to straighten up my thoughts. The five amigos are crammed in the bathroom, sniggering at me.

"Tell her why!" Dwight says, mock whisper. "Tell her what you want to do to her!"

And that is part of it. I'm a man with desires, and she is beautiful and smart and gutsy. All those things I like in a woman. But it's not that, not primarily. "I'll tell you why," I say, picking my words carefully. "I've been out of the game, out of *my* game, for a while, and I need a way back in. So I was planning to see this one guy, who's an asshole, but I might have found some work. So I might as well see if I can find work with *this* asshole instead. Plus, I have a new outlook on life. I have things to…atone for. So helping you pays forward the debt I'm carrying."

"You're a fucking superhero now?" Graney says, voice gravelly with disdain. "Jesus fucking Christ."

Bridget is looking at me hard, her earthy brown stare drilling deep into my soul. "Atone?" she says eventually.

"You know what a rōnin is?" I ask.

"Remember I told you my mother is Japanese?"

Oops. "Oh yeah, of course! Do you speak Japanese?" The question is out before I think to stop it, but I guess it's not offensive.

"Yes. But that's moving a long way from whatever fucking point you're trying to make here."

I can't help grinning. I like her fire. "Okay. So if a rōnin is a masterless samurai, I guess I'm kind of the mob equivalent of that. Which means I have to find work, but I have to find meaning too. I have to find purpose."

"You've thought a lot about this, huh?"

"While I was in Canada, yeah. And especially when I was preparing to leave. When I realized I had another chance." Her eyes narrow but she doesn't push for an explanation and I'm grateful. "I figure I need to keep atoning for the sins of my past. I can't fix them, but maybe I can balance the scales a bit now." And maybe these pain-in-the-ass ghosts will finally leave me alone, but I don't tell her that.

She purses her lips for a moment, then says, "You know, rōnin literally means 'wave man'. It's idiomatic, means wanderer or vagrant, someone without a home. It was adopted to mean masterless samurai later."

"Okay. But that doesn't change the principle, does it? It's still pretty accurate, I have no home."

Her eyes soften again. "I guess not. So okay, you're a modern American rōnin, with a need to do good."

I can't help the slight flush that creeps up my cheeks, smile ruefully. "If you say it like that, it sounds hokey as hell."

"It is hokey as hell, Eli!" She laughs then. "But you know what? I'll buy it. Why the fuck not? You have more self-awareness than ninety percent of the people I come across. But here's the thing. You want to do good. Helping me isn't doing good. I fleeced casinos, stole from my boss, got in debt with the mob."

"But you were led astray by your job, you tried to do the right thing, and you got caught in some literal crossfire."

"You're rationalizing there, drawing some pretty wavy lines between good and bad."

She's right, but there's no other way to do it. "I find I have to rationalize a lot. There is no good and bad, Bridge. Just varying shades of bullshit. All I can do is try to help the people I think are intrinsically decent at heart."

"Intrinsically decent at heart? Holy shit, Eli."

I smile, shrug.

"Just one thing," she says at last.

"What?"

"Don't ever call me Bridge."

Not what I expected, but okay. "Sure."

She waits in my room while I quickly shower, then put some fresh clothes on. I do it all in the bathroom with the door closed. Then we head downstairs. I'm immediately a little uncomfortable. Alfie is there again, hovering obsequiously, and there's a black woman, maybe in her fifties, bustling around the table in the large dining room, laying out eggs and bacon. She's even wearing an old-fashioned frilly apron. This is some racist bullshit I do not like. Bridget catches my eye and mouths, *What the fuck?* I can only nod and shrug.

Lombardi is still on the phone, listening with his brows creased. The bandage on his head remains, the skin around it discoloring yellow and brown with bruising. After a moment he barks, "Then make that happen. This is getting out of hand. And get Stanley back from Miami."

Without waiting for a reply he stabs the end call button then turns a thousand-watt smile to us. "Good morning."

He gestures to the table. We sit and the woman starts serving. I want to tell her I can do it myself, but the set-up doesn't allow self-service. "Thank you, ma'am," I say instead.

She gives me a broad grin and pats my shoulder, then serves Bridget. It smells amazing. Davey comes in and sits down, gets his breakfast served too. "Johnny's sleeping it off," he says and Lombardi nods.

"Thank you, Stella," Lombardi says to the woman serving, then a kind of uncomfortable silence falls.

"Anything else, sir?" Alfie asks.

"I'll ring." Lombardi's smile is plastic. I want to smack it off his face. He'll ring?

Alfie and Stella nod and literally back out of the room.

"Now that is how you set up your household," Dwight says, chewing tobacco as he sits in the broad windowsill across the room.

"Fuck you, man," Sly Barclay says. "You ain't worth the shit on their shoes."

"Them?" Dwight barks a laugh.

I catch movement from Michael nearby, nodding toward Lombardi. I turn and he's watching me closely. I must be frowning, showing some outward sign, as he has a half-smirk twisting his lips.

"Making some assumptions about my arrangements?"

I jab a thumb back toward the now closed door. "Pretty clear how this place works."

"Is it?"

I stare. I won't be drawn into his bullshit, he knows exactly how I feel. It would probably have been wise to keep it to myself, but my asshole ghosts giving me away has put paid to that. I let him sit under the weight of my gaze. I'm expecting him to tell me how those people have been with his family for generations or some shit, how everyone is equal and they're respected and enjoy their jobs. But when one person is waiting on another person, and then has to reverse from the room in silence, there's no kind of equality.

Lombardi's smirk stretches slightly wider, then he looks to his food and starts eating. He has confidence, I'll give him that. Which is interesting, considering he got shot to shit last night. Someone is putting the hammer on him, but he seems less bothered than I might have expected.

The food is amazing and I realize how hungry I am as I start into it. Bridget is quietly putting it away as well. We sit in silence but for the *tink* of cutlery for several minutes. Once the plates are mostly cleaned out, Lombardi sits back and sips coffee.

"So, we have a situation."

"We do," I agree.

"Now, the thing is, we actually have a couple of situations and I think we can scratch each other's backs."

Here it is. The *quid pro quo*. He won't simply accept that his war cost Bridget her money and do the right thing. He needs to leverage his own fuck up. These people are the worst. I worked for one long enough to know them inside out. Hopefully I know them well enough to leverage right back. "You want to lay these situations out for me?"

"I'll give you all you need to know. The details aren't relevant, but the results are."

The details mean he's in the shit and probably started all this, then. He doesn't want to embarrass himself. I'll let it go for now. "So long as I have enough to work with, I don't need details." I do, but I'll get them later.

"My family and another are at something of an impasse. They have my wife."

Okay, that I was not expecting. These stakes just skyrocketed. It's one thing to fight and shoot up a crew. It's another thing entirely to actually kidnap a capo's wife. And I have to assume this guy is the capo. "Who are they, Mr. Lombardi?"

"The Andretti family. They're strong, but they're arrogant. We've been in something of a tug of war for a while now, but when they took Cora, things changed. We hit them hard, several of them died, but Cora wasn't there. So now they've gone to ground and finding Cora is going to be harder than ever. Meanwhile, they're hitting us at random spots, as you saw last night."

I think it over for a moment before replying. He's given me the names, I could walk and investigate this Andretti family on my own from here and find Bridget's money. Fuck Lombardi and his missing wife and his idiot war. So there must be something else. I can't see the angle. "What do you want from me?"

He smiles, predatory, his canine teeth showing. "I need you to find my wife, Mr. Carver."

"Why should I?"

"You think you can go it alone, find the Andretti's, find your friend's money?"

I shrug, it's no secret. Anyone with half a brain would come to the same conclusion. "Sure. Why risk more of my neck?"

"Look out, fool," Officer Graney says from behind Lombardi, grinning as blood drips from his throat.

I tense, but I'm already too late. Lombardi nods and Davey is up from the table in a flash. He has a 9mm against Bridget's temple and his other arm locked around her shoulders in an instant.

She lets out a yelp of shock, then, "The fuck offa me!" She struggles and Davey cuffs her across the chin with the gun butt, not hard, but enough to stun.

"Chill the fuck out!" I shout, quickly assessing the room. The door opens and Johnny is there, his gun leveled at me. Lombardi smiles. My assessment is that we're fucked. Seems Lombardi and his boys made some early morning plans without us.

"You ever hear the saying that a caged animal is the most dangerous, Mr. Carver? I am something of a caged animal right now. My numbers are depleted, my business interests are at risk, and I want my wife back. After last night, I'm under greater pressure than ever. The problem is, all my men are known faces. You, on the other hand, are unknown right now. Which makes you useful."

Bridget is stiff in Davey's grip, breathing fast and shallow. Dwight and Alvin are laughing their asses off over by the window, Sly smoking nearby shaking his head. Graney, his police badge reflecting the morning sunlight, stands behind Lombardi, his hands resting on the capo's shoulder. He smiles and says, "Don't you just love the criminal underworld?"

Michael steps aside as Johnny comes into the room. He has his injured right arm still in a sling, but seems confident as hell with the gun in his left. Bridget's eyes are wide, flicking rapidly between me and Lombardi.

"What makes you think I'll do anything for you?" I ask. "Or her for that matter."

"I like to think I'm a pretty good judge of character."

Hell of a ballsy move, but I'm angry he's right. I won't let Bridget swing in the wind. Would he really kill her? He might put the hurt on her if I refuse. These guys have no morals, he'll hurt anyone in many bad ways to get what he wants. "Where do I go?"

His smile is thin, lips only, but it's wide and genuine. "I'm glad we have an understanding." He looks up to Davey. "Put her somewhere safe."

"Eli!" Bridget says. "What the fuck?"

"We don't have much choice right now," I tell her, then turn to Lombardi. "You keep her like a five-star fucking guest, you hear me? Not like a prisoner."

Lombardi nods once. "Davey will take her to another of our houses and she'll be well looked after, given every comfort. I'm not a monster, Mr. Carver."

Debatable.

He nods again to Davey and the two brothers muscle her out of the room. As she leaves, she casts me one last beseeching look. *Trust me*, I mouth at her. I hope her trust will be rewarded.

"I only have two leads left for the Andretti's," Lombardi says.

Chapter 29

The streets are busy and the day is getting warm. Springtime heading toward summer, but still cool enough to be comfortable in jeans and a jacket. Which is good, because that makes it easy to conceal the two Glock 17 9mm semiautomatics Lombardi gave me. Not my first choice of weapon, but a good pistol. One in a shoulder holster tucked under my left arm, and the other over my right boot in a calf holster. I finally feel dressed again. It's been a long time, but it feels right. That should probably concern me, but I decide not to let it.

Lombardi told me he has two townhouses no one else knows about, both in fake names, both completely off-grid. One is where we stayed last night, the other is at a location he plans to keep secret, and where Bridget has been taken. I pressed him for some details and didn't get much. I know Davey and Johnny will be staying at the other house with Bridget, but I got the vibe maybe some other people might be there as well. Or at least passing in and out. I really need to know where that place is. Finding out is high on my To Do list.

Lombardi called in some others right before I left and three mooks showed up, so there's at least six people in the Bridgewater house, counting Lombardi and his staff. When he says his numbers are thin, I wonder how thin. I'm clearly being sent in as the sacrificial lamb. He's hoping I'll get some intel, maybe even take out a few of his enemies, without him having to risk his own crew. Maybe it was dumb following him back last night, but we had little choice and what's done is done. It's clear he's desperate to risk a play like this. What Mr. Paul Lombardi maybe hasn't realized is that he's made me a caged animal now too.

I saw the car that took off from Gino's last night, so I might have a little more intel than Lombardi knows about. Maybe I can use that. It was a dark blue Lincoln SUV, and I got the license plate: PSN-336. Of course, I have zero contacts in the NYPD and all my old mob connections are fully *dis*connected, so what can I do with this info? Lombardi can maybe help there, but I don't want to play that card yet.

First things first. If I want to track down Lombardi's wife, I need to learn more about Andretti. The two leads he had left for the Andrettis are a restaurant in Greenwich Village they use for a lot of their business meetings—cliché as hell, but I guess you don't fix what isn't broken—and a place out in Newark, a warehouse of some kind. I'll go to Greenwich Village first.

The Falcon is a stupid name for an Italian restaurant, but I'm no marketing exec. It's just one storefront down from the intersection and diagonally across is a small green space. It's well into leaf and there are benches along one edge. I cross with the lights and take one of the benches. If I sit a little crooked, I can see The Falcon well enough. If this place is a bust, I'll look into the one in Newark tomorrow. I prefer to take my chances in a much more public location first.

Lombardi gave me a photo of his wife, Cora. She's quite something, a fierce-looking brunette with green eyes and a slim, graceful build. He also gave me photos of Furio Andretti, the capo up against him in this war, and about a dozen others. Andretti is a suave-looking bastard, square-jawed with a confident demeanor obvious even in this crappy photo.

All the pics are on a simple smartphone Lombardi also gave me. I don't like the things, never carry one if I don't have to. But it might come in handy, to take photos as well as store them. The only number in it is a burner phone for Lombardi, but we agreed I'd only use it in extremis.

Otherwise, I'll update him at the Bridgewater townhouse whenever I go back. I think he's going to dig in there like a tick for the foreseeable future. He's scared, and that makes him dangerous. It also makes him endangered.

A lot of this stakeout bullshit is sitting around getting bored, but I figure if this restaurant is the main Andretti front, someone in one of the pictures on this phone will show up eventually and that'll give me a person to follow.

Hours pass and I've seen two people from Lombardi's photos go into the place, but not come out again. They could be there for hours, maybe I should go to Newark after all. I'm about to give up when a blue Lincoln SUV pulls up to the curb, its hazard lights blinking as three people jump out. I stand up to see the license plate and smile. PSN-336. The same one the surviving gunman got rescued in last night. And sure enough, there he is. This is better luck than I'd hoped for.

I check the phone and match his photo: Tony Lebretta. The two other guys with him are hard to see from this far. A fat dude stretching every seam of his dark blue suit and a young guy in a track suit. They stand conversing with the driver for a moment, ignoring the horns and abuse from the traffic held up behind. Then there's waving and the SUV pulls away. The three of them go inside The Falcon.

Okay. It's not much, but I've got something. Like a single snag can unravel a whole rug, here might be the way for me to unravel this mystery. Nearly 4:00 p.m. That seems like a good time for a beer.

I smile and nod as I walk into The Falcon, ask the *maître d'* for a table for one. "Somewhere near the window?" I suggest.

It's a big place, tables spread across the wide black and white tiled floor. A bar runs half the length of one side, two sets of double doors in the rear wall swing back and forth in and out of the kitchen. It's half-full, quite busy seeing as it's not close to dinner time but well after lunch. The three from the SUV are tightly gathered around a table in the back, talking quietly. They have their backs to the wall, of course, and are only a short hop from one of the kitchen doors. Smart positioning. It's where I'd normally have asked to sit, but I need to stay as far from them as possible. The longer I'm anonymous, the better. I'm pretty sure Lebretta won't recognize me from last night. I'm in different clothes, and I finally shaved off that annoying beard before I left this morning. I looked like a child, staring back at myself in the mirror this morning, but it's a relief. My hair still hangs long. I'll get that cut later. Maybe. I kinda like it.

"Here, sir?"

The table is up against the large plate glass window, The Falcon Authentic Italian Cuisine visible backwards in cursive script. It'll do. "Thanks."

"The fuck are you planning to do?" Officer Graney is opposite me, smoking a cigarette as he leans back in the chair. Smoke curls out of the ragged wet hole in his throat. I ignore him.

"Yeah, cocheese. What exactly?"

Dwight, Alvin, and Sly take seats at the empty table beside mine. A gruesome collection of blood and bone, glistening in the afternoon sun through the big window. They lounge around, grinning at each other. I can't see Michael.

"You think you got any kind of handle on this?" Sly asks. He nods over at the table with Andretti's guys. "You can't hear them. If they leave and you follow, they'll make you. What's your plan?"

A waiter comes over with a menu and water. But I've already seen the specials board.

"I'll take the *osso buco*, thanks."

He nods and leaves, oblivious to my unwanted company.

"You're wasting time, dickhead," Alvin says.

They are all making valid points, but I'm in the wind here. Nothing else to go on, so I have to be patient.

An hour later, and one excellent *osso buco* heavier, the whole thing is a bust. Well, apart from the meal, that was worth the visit alone. But those three sat there talking, two others, one of them recognizable from Lombardi's rogue's gallery, came and then left again. And here I still sit, none the wiser. I won't say my ghosts were right, but maybe they have a point. These guys might sit here directing business until well into the night.

I head over to the bar and order a beer, intending to lean there and drink it, try to talk to the bartender. And from here, maybe I can overhear a little from Lebretta's table. I keep my back to them.

"Sir, please, let me have this delivered to your table." The *maître d'* is too damned efficient.

I put on my best smile. "I'm too full to sit down any longer. Okay if I have it here."

He's clearly uncomfortable about that, but what can he do?

"Certainly, sir."

He slings a pained looked at the bartender, then hustles away. That gives me an in.

"He always got a stick so far up his ass?"

The bartender grins. He's young, maybe early twenties at most. And here's me, a grizzled and world-weary 30-year-old. "He's okay," the kid says in a broad Bronx accent.

"You like working here?"

"Sure, why not? It's a nice place."

"Yeah, I guess it is. The food is great."

He puts the beer down and I take a long pull.

"You're not from around here."

I smile. "That obvious, huh? You're right. New Orleans born and raised." Not entirely true, but close enough. "So who owns this place? Some fancy celebrity chef?"

The bartender laughs. "You don't eat out much, huh? I mean, sure this place is nice, but it ain't some Michelin star establishment. Owner is Furio Andretti."

"He's not a fancy chef?"

"He ain't a chef at all, he's a businessman. The chef is a man called—" He breaks off, his eye caught by something.

I look over and the *maître d'* is at the other end of the bar, his face hard as granite. As soon as I turn, he switches on the creeping servitude again, but the message has been sent.

"I gotta go do...this," the bartender says and sidles away, tries to look busy doing nothing.

If I stick around or push any more, I'll be noticed. And I can't hear anything from Lebretta, anyway. I swallow down the beer and lift the glass. "Thanks!"

"You're welcome," the bartender says with a nervous smile.

I nod once to the *maître d'*, trying not to grind my teeth, and head out.

"You fucking loser, what a waste of time," Alvin says, laughing like a hyena.

"You're not really detective material, are ya, Carver?" Graney says.

"Is this what a rōnin would do?" Sly asks. He shakes his head in disdain, the shiny organs in his chest jiggling as he laughs.

But fuck them, I actually learned a lot. Nothing comes in quickly, nothing lands right in your lap. You have to put in the work. I don't know what I'll do with these tidbits of information, but it's all grist for the mill.

"You tell Furio I don't fucking care!"

The voice is angry and high. A woman with an incredible amount of blonde hair, tight leather pants and a short fur jacket climbs out of a yellow cab in front of The Falcon. I crouch, taking my time to tie my shoe, and listen.

She stands outside the restaurant, listening to her phone. Then, "He has no right to just brush me off like that! The time we've had together, does it mean nothing to him?" Another pause. "Busy man, my tight ass! Ever since he got wrapped up with Papa-whatever, he's been ignoring me! I'm at The Falcon now, I'll talk to Tony. And if he ain't here, I'm going straight to Charlie's Bar." She pauses again, shakes her head. "Yeah? We'll see about that!" She hangs up and slams her way into the restaurant, not even noticing me.

I head off up the sidewalk, make sure I'm not seen loitering. Maybe sometimes things do fall into my lap. Papa-whatever. Charlie's Bar. Not much, but more details all the same. I'll head back to the townhouse and see what Lombardi makes of all this.

Chapter 30

"I want to talk to Bridget."

Lombardi looks at me with one eyebrow raised. "You think you're in a position to negotiate?"

"Fuck you, we're in a business arrangement here. Cut it out with the *Goodfellas* bullshit. I have questions to ask you, but I want to talk to Bridget first, make sure you're keeping up your end."

"She's probably being raped and tortured by those big-ass twins!" Dwight says, dancing an awful, boney jig behind Lombardi. Alvin laughs, Graney raises his hands, as if to say, *He might be right.*

Sly is sharing a joint with Michael, both leaning against the mantlepiece at the back of this large and ostentatious lounge room in the Bridgewater house, away from the others.

"You should just walk away," Michael says.

I cock an eyebrow at him.

He shrugs. "She got herself in this mess. If you weren't there at Gino's she'd probably be dead by now, caught in the crossfire. All these assholes would be dead. Fuck 'em."

He has a point, but I have a code. If I'm going to rebuild myself, if I'm going to follow my new path as a rōnin, I need to accept what comes my way. I made a promise to Bridget. I need to try to be a better man.

"Alfie, the phone, please?"

The old man goes to a table not six feet from where Lombardi is sitting and picks up an old landline phone, carries it over. The boss nods as he takes it, then presses the buttons to dial a number. I try to watch and get them, but Michael stands behind Lombardi's chair and reads them out as he dials. I log it for future reference. I need to at least find that area code. That'll put me one step closer to where Bridget's being held.

"Davey, put the woman on." There's a pause, then, "Bridget? Your boyfriend wants a word."

I take the receiver. "You okay?"

"My boyfriend?"

"He's decided that, nothing to do with me."

"Hmm. Yeah, I'm okay, other than being held hostage. But it's comfortable here, they're giving me good food and letting me watch TV and shit like that. Could be worse."

"Nice place?" Come on, Bridget, give me a hint.

There's a scuffling at her end and a cough and she whispers something real quick. Then she says, "Sure, I guess."

"That'll do," Lombardi says, snatching the handset away from me.

Good girl. I think I heard her say Dorset Girls School. Hopefully she covered it enough that any goon with her didn't notice. Lombardi is dumb, he just hangs up, doesn't talk to his man anymore. Hopefully it'll all go unnoticed. Maybe Davey will tell him later that she said something. All life is risk. Again, for now I just log it away.

"So she's having the vacation of her life. Tell me what you know."

Lombardi is scared. He's rattled. I could go and find Bridget and get the hell out, but there's the problem of all that money. I need to play along. Alfie takes the phone and puts it back on the side table. Stella arrives and offers us iced tea from a silver tray. She looks at me and I see something I can't place in her eyes.

"What do you know about Charlie's Bar?" I ask.

Lombardi shrugs. "Nothing. I can look into it."

"Yeah, do that. I'll check it out tomorrow, might give me new leads. What about someone called Papa something?"

He frowns. "Papa something?"

"Yeah, but I don't know what."

"No idea, never heard of him."

"You see that?" Michael asks, leaning on the back of Lombardi's chair.

I don't say anything, or even nod, but I did see it. Stella flinched at the mention of that Papa character. Alfie is giving her hard eyes across the room and she scurries away. Interesting.

"I guess we need to find out something about Charlie's Bar then."

Lombardi sits back, face angry. "That's it? That's all you got from a whole day?"

I smile and sip my iced tea. It's really good.

Chapter 31

I don't know where Lombardi goes at night, but after dinner he's nowhere to be seen. I guess he has an office here somewhere, there are several closed doors I haven't seen behind. I head to bed early, around 10:00 p.m., and listen as the house goes still and quiet. The three guys Lombardi called in when I left earlier are still here, one in the room next to mine where Bridget was the night before. I hear him snoring through the wall. The other two are in rooms downstairs.

As I creep back down, careful to stay silent, I hear a TV playing quietly from one of those rooms, nothing from the other, but both doors are shut. I go into the kitchen and look across at two doors. One leads out into the small back yard of the house, the other is where Alfie and Stella go, so I figure it's their quarters. I wonder what their story is. The age difference is too much for them to be partners, but they could be father and daughter. There's a distinct family resemblance.

Standing in the kitchen, I wonder what to do to get their attention. I could just knock quietly and ask for something, see if I can get them talking from there. The door opens. I notice there's a camera above it. Well, that works too.

"Help you, sir?" Stella asks. She's in a housecoat and looks tired.

"I'm sorry, did I wake you?"

"No, not sleeping yet. You need something?"

"I got hungry, thought I'd make a sandwich, but I don't know where anything is."

"Let me make it for you."

I don't want her waiting on me, but I do need an excuse to keep her talking. I can't in good conscience let her serve me though. "Maybe just tell me where—"

"In the time it takes to explain I can make your sandwich, sir. What do you want on it?"

I guess I can't argue with that. "Ham and cheese okay? Maybe a little relish or something."

"Of course."

She gets to work and I hover nearby. "You like working here?"

She smiles. "I know how it looks."

"Oh yeah?"

"My uncle was here since he was a boy, used to help his daddy when Mr. Lombardi's grandfather owned the house. When my daddy died, his brother, he took me in. Mr. Lombardi looks after us both."

"Looks after you well?"

Stella glances at me, that indefinable look in her eyes again. "Better than he ever treats Cora."

Interesting. "He's rough with her?"

Stella looks at me a moment longer, her lips pursed. A tiny wince passes over her brow and she looks away again. I think she wants to tell me more but doesn't dare. I need to tread carefully, move around things. "Alfie is your uncle, huh?"

"Uh-huh."

"And your mother?"

"She was killed in a car accident when I was five, Daddy died when I was ten."

"Man, I'm sorry. That's awful."

"Uh-huh."

"Alfie have a wife?"

"No, sir, he never married. But he has good friends." She flicks a smile back over her shoulder and it's loaded with unspoken details. I wonder if she means his best friends are other guys.

"Can I ask you something?"

"You already did." She cuts the sandwich in half with a wicked sharp carving knife and puts it on a floral ceramic side plate.

"When I mentioned something to Lombardi earlier, it seems to me like you maybe recognized the name."

"You have everything you need now?" Alfie asks from the door. His eyes are hard. Stella's lips tighten and she presses them together. She smiles and hands me the plate.

"Thank you so much."

She nods, points at the fridge. "Milk in there if you want it, glasses up in that cupboard. I get you anything else?"

"No, that's great. Thanks."

She slips past Alfie back into the small unit beyond the door. It looks like they have a couple of rooms back there, maybe three, and a small bathroom at the end. There's a framed picture on the wall of the short hallway, all blacks and purples, like a scene from Hell. I can't figure out the tangle of limbs and bilious clouds represented there. Under it is a small table, and on that a kind of altar. Black candles, votive icons, beads and feathers hanging from the bottom of the picture frame.

"You need to be awful careful, Mr. Carver," Alfie says. He shuts the door before I can ask any more.

I take the sandwich back upstairs to eat, then go to bed. I don't know how to get better intel here, it's all proving to be stubborn. Sleep steals over me while I'm trying to see a way to use the tiny clues I have.

Chapter 32

The first thing I notice on waking is the noise in the house. Lots of raised voices. The second thing I notice when I sit up is a scrap of paper on the floor by the door, like it's been slipped underneath in the night. When I pick it up, I can't help smiling. In a neat, tight script is reads:

PAPA NIGHT – MAPLEWOOD

Thank you, Stella. At least, I assume that's who left this little breadcrumb for my trail. I have another lead. That's three things I plan to follow up on today.

But first I'd better check what the shouting is all about.

Turns out the Andrettis hit one of Lombardi's bars last night. At least, that's my assumption, the place shot up and the takings stolen. Their war continues. Lombardi tells me to focus on my part of things. The sooner I find his wife, the sooner he can go full auto and wipe the Andrettis off the map. That's how he puts it, but he's still a scared man posturing. I get the feeling he's all talk and he's fast losing this war.

Regardless, I'm happy to follow his suggestion. He tells me that he's found Charlie's Bar, a place in Newark where some of Andretti's people apparently hang out. He gives me the address.

"I need a car, I'm all about the suburbs today."

He frowns at me and I shrug.

"You can take the Oldsmobile out front."

He gives me some keys and I head out.

First off I only drive a couple of blocks then find a shady spot under some trees to park. Using the browser on the phone Lombardi gave me, I do some research. Papa Night comes up with no results.

So I look up Dorset Girls School. Nothing comes up. But scrolling through the almost hits I see a few entries for Dorset Hills School. That could be it, I misheard Bridget's rushed whisper. One of those Montessori places, it's on the edge of a country club not far from Morristown. I double check that with the area code I saw Lombardi dial and it checks out. Only about thirty minutes from here. I tap up the address into the phone's GPS and start driving.

Forty minutes later I've found the place, Davey's shiny black Cadillac parked on the driveway of a two-story square house, yellow brick underneath with pale blue siding on the top floor. That easy. Finally something goes my way. As soon as I spot Davey's car, the same one we all rode back in from the shoot-out at Gino's, I log the address and keep driving. Hopefully no one will be looking out the window the same moment I go by. I hang a left at the next intersection and head toward Newark.

That's one job of three covered. I know where they're holding Bridget. The temptation is to grab her now and just leave all this behind, but I need to find her money if I can. For now, the Papa Night lead is a bust, so I move onto job three.

It takes another thirty minutes to drive east to Newark and I find parking about two blocks from Charlie's Bar. I'm wearing a black hoodie and jeans, my two guns concealed like before. I slip the phone into my hip pocket, pull up the hood and walk. I'm a fairly big guy, but going unnoticed is more about attitude than physical presence. I learned long ago in the life that there are three types of people. I think of them as victims, assholes, and ciphers.

Victims are the kind of folk who expect the worst from the world, so they usually get it. They walk the streets terrified of being jumped, so they act and move scared and skittish. Even if they're big, they look like a victim. Someone on the prowl for a fight or a mugging isn't looking for a challenge, they're looking for a victim. They're looking for chumps like this, people who have defeated themselves already.

Then there are assholes, the kind of guys who strut and swagger everywhere. They act like their balls are so big they have to curve out their knees, and their backs are so broad they have to carry imaginary piglets under each arm. More often than not it's insecurity and these guys are scared, but they overcompensate the opposite way from the victims. Most guys fall into one or other of these categories, to varying degrees.

Then there are ciphers. Often if someone is described as a cipher, it means they have no agency, no power. They're used by other people. But it can also mean a person is indefinite. Indefinable. Ciphers are unknown quantities, but usually confident, which makes them dangerous. And the best of the ciphers are the sort of guys who don't even get noticed. Victims and assholes are spotted right away, everyone sees them. A cipher kind of guy can move around without raising too much attention, without being noticed at all.

I try to be a cipher.

In the two years I was laying low in Canada, I studied a lot. It's when I learned about rōnin and realized that's what I was now. That led me to study eastern culture and I learned a lot about samurai. One of my favorite books is by Miyamoto Musashi, called *Go Rin No Sho* or *A Book of Five Rings*. He also wrote another fantastic thing called *Dokkōdō* or *The Path of Aloneness*, which is just a list of twenty-one concepts, his philosophy for life. He wrote that only a week before he died back in 1645.

Everyone talks about Sun Tzu's *Art of War*, which *is* a great book, but *Five Rings* and *Aloneness* get overlooked. Musashi was a Japanese swordsman, philosopher, and rōnin. He became famous for his unique double-bladed swordsmanship. He was undefeated in sixty-one duels. He even founded his own style of swordsmanship, the Niten Ichi-Ryū School. He wrote *Five Rings* and *Aloneness*, and gave them both to a dude called Terao Magonojō, the best of his students. He lived to be sixty-one and then died of lung cancer, which is some bullshit for a guy like that. This universe sure does lack justice.

Anyway, his books really stuck with me. They helped me through those two years of exile. *Five Rings* has wisdom like "If you wish to control others you must first control yourself" and "All men are the same except for their belief in their own selves, regardless of what others may think of them". Now that last one, that hit me. It plays into my victim-asshole-cipher theory. What you think of yourself matters. Not the lies you tell yourself, but what you *really* think of yourself, in your heart. That's what comes out when the shit goes down. And it's how you ultimately present yourself to the world.

I know myself. I can fight, I'm a hell of a good shot—Vernon always called me a natural—but with shooting and fighting, I practice a lot. Aptitude is nothing without hard work. And I have a granite chin. No idea why, but I've always been hard to KO, which has saved my ass a few times now. So knowledge of those things gives me confidence, but I'm smart enough not to let my confidence show unless I choose to show it. I skim under the radar whenever I can. I cipher myself. That plays well into the realization that I'm rōnin now.

And that's the attitude I carry for two blocks, and then into Charlie's Bar.

The place is pretty busy, several of the tables surrounded by people drinking, another seven lined up on stools at the bar. A small group is gathered around a pool table at one end, talking too loud and overplaying themselves. Four guys and two girls, they look like they're heading toward quite the party later on. Five Finger Death Punch is pounding from the speakers, not super loud, but enough that everyone has to raise their voice a little to speak, so the whole place is buzzing. Glasses chink, pool balls clack, one woman laughs like a coyote in heat. For just after 11:00 a.m., this is quite the pumping place.

With my hood up and my face down to account for any CCTV, I head straight to the bar. There's a table in the back and four people sit around it, at least one of them was in The Falcon last night. I don't let my gaze linger. At least the intel was right that Andretti's guys use this place too. Now to see if I can pick up any further clues, anything to lead me closer to the boss.

"What'll it be?"

"Just a beer, thanks."

The bartender nods and pours for me. I pay him.

"The fuck are you thinking here, cocheese?"

"You can't call him that anymore, Dwight. He's a rōnin now!" Officer Graney's voice drips sarcasm.

He and Dwight sit on stools to one side of me, Alvin and Sly to the other. Michael is behind the bar like he works there, leaning back against the rear counter under a long double row of spirits. I ignore them and drink my beer.

"You planning to follow someone from here, Mr. Samurai?" Sly asks, joint smoke spilling from his nose and mouth while he talks. He passes the spliff to Alvin, who draws deep. I hear the cherry crackle, then a cloud of fragrant blue envelopes me. I blow gently, making sure not to inhale any. I need to stay sharp. I'm not even certain I can get stoned on ghost weed, but I'm taking no chances. It's happened before.

"What *are* you gonna do?" Michael asks me. "You got other ways to make money. Get out of this while you can."

I catch his eye, raise an eyebrow, but I don't plan to talk to these fools in a public place. Michael stares a moment longer, then tips his head to one side in warning. I look without turning my head and in my periphery see the mook from the restaurant yesterday. He comes and stands alongside me.

"Hey, Danny!"

The bartender looks up, comes over. "Yeah?"

"What time is he in?"

Danny checks his watch. "About a half hour?"

"Okay, cool. We'll take another round over there when you're ready."

"Sure thing."

Someone is coming in here about 11:30. Is that relevant to me? I jump when a heavy hand lands on my shoulder.

"You having a good day?" the guys says, friendly, but menacing.

I have no choice but to glance up at him. "Yeah." Keep it simple, not impolite, but make it clear I don't want to chat. If I plan to stay under the radar, I need to be the opposite of memorable. "Just enjoying a quiet beer." I offer a half-smile, then turn back to my beer.

"That right?" he asks. "A quiet beer, huh?"

If he thinks parroting me will draw me into conversation, he's wrong. But he's clearly trying to decide if I'm someone. Keeping my hood up to avoid cameras has probably made me more noticeable after all. So much for being a cipher today.

"Not cool," Michael says from over the bar. "Talk to the guy."

"He's made you," Graney says, with evident satisfaction. "He may not know why, but you've lit up his warning sign."

Fuck 'em, they're right. "You having a good day?" I ask, without looking up.

"I'm not sure yet." He slaps my shoulder once more, then looks over me. "Danny, those beers?"

"On their way."

The guy turns and walks away.

"Don't look up," Michael says. "The other three are all watching."

"You fucking idiot," Alvin says, cackling.

"What did you expect, coming into this place?" Sly asks, still smoking. "You know what it was like when you would hang in one of Vernon's places. Some random dude comes in off the street, you notice. When you notice, you prepare. Fuck me, it's why I died, and I was prepared."

"Yeah, but you weren't good enough, were you," I mutter.

"Sorry, what was that?" Danny is standing right in front of me, where Michael was before. I didn't even see them change places. Maybe Sly's damn ghost weed did get me a little wasted.

I grin up at the bartender. "Sorry, just talking to myself."

He laughs. "The only way you can guarantee intelligent conversation, am I right?"

Demonstrably, yeah. Well, shit. This has to change. I guess I need a little more practice at my rōnin act. What the fuck was I thinking? I've always been a hired gun, a muscle man. I was never some covert operative. Maybe I can be, but not yet, evidently. I guess we play this the old-fashioned way. "One must make the warrior walk his everyday walk" is something else Musashi said. I guess those guys have done that to me. So be it.

I could get up and leave, but I've learned nothing and those guys would follow me, anyway. Let's see if I can't force a little confrontation instead. Might as well play to my strengths. Four on one. I can manage that, if I manage it right. The thing about being outnumbered is that the group always overestimates their advantage.

I get up and head for the bathrooms. There's movement from the corner table, all four getting up to follow, like sheep. There's a short corridor leading away from the noise and bustle of the large bar area. I pass the women's bathroom on the left and head for the men's right at the end. That's a good distance away. As I push the door open and walk in I see my ghosts inside, gathered under a window at the back wall, ready for the show. Fucking ghouls.

The door opens inwards and I step around it as it swings closed. The four guys all pile right on in, no caution at all. Like I said, people overestimate their advantage all the time. The first guy is just slowing and turning to look around as the last of them comes in and the door starts to close. Another great line from *Five Rings* comes to me: "No fear, no hesitation, no surprise, no doubt." Not for me, anyway.

Let mayhem commence.

I bring the butt of my Glock down on the back of the last guy's head so hard I feel his skull crack and he drops like a sack of sand, blood pouring from his nose and the split in his scalp simultaneously. My knee is already coming up and I kick the next guy right over the top of the one who fell, driving hard and long, like I'm trying to kick down a door. My foot plants hard into his chest as he turns and the air rushes out of him like an explosion. He flies back into the one behind him, the guy I recognized from The Falcon. The one I kicked goes down gasping, the one he fell into is staggering for balance, grabbing at a sink, and the first one in finally gets a gun out.

I level mine right at him and there's a sudden stalemate. His gun is half raised, the one from The Falcon has caught his balance and has his hand inside his jacket, but he's smart enough to freeze there. The one I pistol-whipped won't be moving for some time, if he ever moves again, blood pooling quickly, dark around his head. The last of the four is still gasping, hands clutching his chest, face scrunched up in pain.

"Carlo, I fuckin' told you it was that same guy," the mook from The Falcon says.

Carlo is the one with his gun half up. "The fuck are you, guy? You're not one of that dickhead Lombardi's men."

"You at war with anyone else right now?"

He looks at me, eyes narrowed. "What's that supposed to mean?"

"I could be anyone." I smile at him, show I'm not at all threatened. My adrenaline is pumping like a fountain, but my hand remains steady and my aim true, thanks to long, deep breaths. Control your breathing, control your body. Up to a point, at least.

"Let's deal with this another way," Carlo says. "How about you tell us what the fuck you're doing here?"

I step over the bleeding guy on the floor and use my foot to shove him back hard against the door, make sure we're not disturbed. I don't take my eye off Carlo while I do it.

"You gonna die, cocheese!"

"No way you can contain these three," Alvin puts in.

I ignore them. Graney is frowning at me, and I wonder if there isn't even a tiny bit of respect creeping through. Although maybe that's just wishful thinking. And why the hell do I want the approval of some dead asshole cop?

"Watch that one," Michael says, nodding at the floor.

The one I kicked down has started to get his breathing under control and his hand is moving snail-slow around his back. He probably has a gun in the back of his waistband. He honestly seems to think I won't notice. Time to stamp my authority on this. I pull the trigger and Carlo's eyes go wide as a bright red hole appears between them and the back of his head blows out across the white tiles of the wall behind him. Dwight, Alvin, and Graney all cry out as they're sprayed with gore and dive aside. But the mark up the wall is uninterrupted. My gun is immediately between the guy on the floor and the one from The Falcon. Both know there's no way they can draw without getting shot. Maybe if they both drew simultaneously, one might survive, but neither wants to be the other one, so they both freeze. Two down, two remain.

Cold-blooded murder has a way of stamping control on a situation.

Carlo slumps to the floor, blood spreading around him like a shroud. I have to hope the noise of the bar and the distance to the bathrooms is enough that the sound of my shot goes unnoticed. It was loud as hell in here, my ears ringing with it. Just in case, I have to be quick.

The guy on the ground is staring, his face now white as the tiles. The one from The Falcon is muttering "Fuck fuck fuck" over and over.

"Shut up. What's your name?"

His face travels through a variety of expressions.

"Your name, fucker?"

"Terry."

"And you?"

The guy on the floor swallows, his trembling evident. "Sal."

"Okay, Terry and Sal. Answer me some questions and you live. First, take that fucking hand out of your jacket, real slow." Terry does as he's told. "Now sit on the floor next to your buddy here. Both of you, hands on your knees."

They do it, looking like a couple of ugly overgrown school kids. If they went to school in a sea of blood, that is. I need quick answers and a quicker exit. Still, at least I feel in my element now. Know your strengths.

"What does Lombardi want?" Terry asks. "Maybe we can help?"

"You think now is the time to negotiate?"

He looks up at me, shakes his head.

"Where's Andretti?"

"We can't tell you that!" Sal wails. "He'll kill us!"

"I'll kill you now if you don't."

They share a look, panicked.

Michael is beside me. "Hurry up, people in the bar are coming."

"Let 'em come," Dwight says. "Cocheese here can shoot all a'them too."

Terry and Sal sit trembling. I need to bombard them. "Who's Papa Night?"

Sal startles. "How do you know about him?"

"I'm asking, not answering. Talk!"

"He's a guy Furio knows, some freaky fucking voodoo asshole, I don't like him."

"I didn't ask what you like. What's Furio doing with him?"

"Don't know, him and Cora are planning something, have been for ages."

That gives me pause. "Him and Cora?"

"Yeah."

"She's working with him?"

Terry and Sal share another look, realize they've said something I didn't know and it compromises them. "Yeah," Terry says slowly.

"Cora is with Andretti willingly?" I'll give them a tidbit, to keep them talking. It won't matter in the long run. "Lombardi said Andretti kidnapped her."

They both bark a laugh. "Kidnapped?" Sal says. "Maybe that's what Lombardi prefers to believe. Cora went to him, she hates Lombardi. She knows strength, she can see which way the fucking wind is blowing."

"And what are they planning?"

"Don't know," Terry says. "They keep that shit private."

"Where's Andretti?"

They grimace, look away from me.

"Hurry up!" Michael says.

The bathroom door shifts the corpse pressed up against it, but doesn't open. Then there's banging as someone pounds a fist on it.

"Where's Papa Night?"

"We can't tell you this shit!" Terry wails.

I shoot him in the face, blood arcing back as he slams into the floor. Sal screams and scuttles aside, but I grab his shoulder and press the hot barrel against his temple. He starts blubbering, piss spreading in a dark cloud around his groin. He stares at the fallen form of Terry, glassy eyes gazing in disbelief at the ceiling.

"Hey! Open up!" The banging on the door increases, the shoving and rattling harder. The body against it starts shifting.

"You gonna get your ass handed to you, dickhead!" Alvin says, literally dancing a jig with glee.

I drag Sal around and heft him up on top of the dead guy, press his back against the door and lean into it, holding it closed.

"Where is he?" I yell, right up close into his face.

More fists bang on the door, it shakes in the frame.

I jam my gun into Sal's cheek, hard enough to grind the bone. "Where is he?"

"Inner Vision in Maplewood!"

Finally.

"Move it!" Michael yells.

"Die!" Dwight and Alvin shout together.

Sly is laughing, Graney shaking his head. "You're a fucking thug," he says.

I pull the trigger, Sal's blood and brains spray up the door behind him. The banging stops for a moment. I send two more slugs through the door, high enough I hope not to hit anyone, but that should keep them away a moment longer. I grab Terry and the other corpse and sling them like hay bales, all four stacked up against the door. Then I'm at the back wall, levering the window open. Please don't let it be bars outside.

It's not. The gap is way too small for me, but I haul myself up onto the ledge, put my feet against one side and drive my back against the window frame. I'm strong, hopefully strong enough. I hope the sound of smashing glass doesn't send people around to wherever this comes out. Hopefully the gunshots will keep them at bay. Using all my force, and a growl of effort, the window finally bends up in its metal frame, shattering at it does, and makes just enough space for me to squeeze through. I drop to the dirty asphalt below. Some stinking back alley, but there's a busy road at the end. I run for it.

Chapter 33

I dump the hoodie halfway back to the car, put my oversize T-shirt on top of the shoulder holster, and go around an extra block to make sure I'm not being tailed. Any CCTV in the bar won't have much to go on, so I should be in the clear. And the other advantage of wasting made men is that the cops usually don't give too much of a fuck. It's a public service for most of them and they're happy to avoid the paperwork. Unless they're the cops on the mob's payroll, but that's a whole other problem. There's blood on my boots and jeans though, which is a more immediate concern. It's not too obvious in dark jeans and black boots, but I stop in at the only store I can find, a sports place, and grab some baggy track pants and a pair of sneakers. It's easy enough to find another quiet alley, double check for cameras, then make a quick change, leaving the soiled jeans and boots pressed down deep in a dumpster full of rotting food and old packaging. It's all fairly cursory, but it should suffice. I'm in the car and driving away from Newark before I allow myself to think about what I've learned.

The five amigos are lined up in the impossibly large back seat if I look in the mirror, but I try to ignore them. They harangue me anyway. Michael won't be ignored. He leans forward between the seats, the hole in his ear dripping blood. Thankfully I can't see the right side of his face, where most of the flesh is missing, the exit wound an explosion of bone and meat that'll never heal.

"You gonna tell him?" Michael asks.

He means Lombardi. It's definitely a new spin on things, and I don't know how he'll react. If he knows Cora left him willingly, will he go apeshit and take the war to Andretti? How scared is Andretti, anyway? He's lying low, but it seems to me he's in a far better position than Lombardi. Although he is four soldiers down now, thanks to my work today. And if Lombardi loses the plot and goes medieval, how do I get Bridget's money back? It all comes back to that. We can't go on too well without funds. Shit, I can make money in other ways. So can she, for that matter. She's a professional gambler, we could find a small initial stake, head to some casino far away, and start rebuilding her fortune. But there's a principle at work here too. One of the twenty-one tenets in the *Dokkōdō*, Musashi's *Path of Aloneness*, is "You may abandon your own body but you must preserve your honor." This is a matter of honor. If I plan to live this code, I can't pick and choose.

So how do I move now? If I go back to Lombardi, things could spiral out of my control. I pull out the cell phone he gave me and hit the only number in it.

"This better be good." His voice is tight, concerned. He's scared.

"I got all kinds of things to follow up on, so just letting you know I'm on it. Don't be surprised if I'm quiet for a while."

"I ain't your fucking dad, asshole. Do what you gotta do."

He hangs up. So that went well.

"You're a fucking idiot," Graney says from the back. He accepts another joint from Sly, who deliberately reaches across Dwight to give it to him.

"Get outta my fucking face!" Dwight shouts, and they tumble back in yet another fistfight.

"Those two should just bone and get it over with, am I right?" Alvin says, grinning like a wolf as he takes the joint from Graney.

I have to pause at that thought. I wonder if he doesn't have a point there. Dwight is one racist asshole, but is there more to his fear than ignorance and hate?

"You wanna focus?" Michael asks, leaning in between the seats again.

"Shut the fuck up, all o'ya!" My voice is cracked with tension. These assholes bother me more the less centered I am. I concentrate on the road ahead and drive, making my way to Maplewood.

It's only a fifteen-minute drive and I park up out of the way again, trying to keep the car incognito. I spend a little while buying new boots, jeans and a jacket, because I feel like a heel in these joggers. Back in my preferred uniform, the shoulder holster back above a new T-shirt, I feel like myself again. My available cash is running low, so I hope I don't need to waste much more. I use some on a big lunch, from a pizzeria opposite a 7-Eleven service station. I figure I need the fuel, and that debacle back in the bar left me starving. Adrenaline dumps and murder always make me hungry.

While I'm there, I look up Inner Vision. In all the mayhem, I don't know what question Sal was answering—is this a place for Andretti or Papa Night? And who the fuck even is that? *Some freaky fucking voodoo asshole*, Sal called him. Andretti and Cora are working together with him, cooking something up.

"You don't wanna mess with shit," Sly Barclay says, sitting opposite me, looking over the empty, greasy pizza pan.

I cock an eyebrow at him.

"Not really my thing, but what I know, I don't like." When I keep looking, willing him to go on, he smiles. "First time you ever listened to me, huh? Voodoo is from Haiti, but Jamaica has a version. Called Obeah. There was an Obi-Man near me where I grew up and he was one freaky son of a bitch, man. I didn't like him. He did wrong stuff. It's as close as I got, but I learned one thing: You stay the fuck away from that shit."

"You really believe this ni—" Alvin's fist shuts Dwight up real fast. Seems like my resident racist is starting to alienate the rest of the crew too. They all had one thing in common before, and that was hatred of me for killing them. It makes me happy to see them starting to turn more and more on each other. Assuming this isn't all just my own psychosis, because if that's fighting itself, it says bad things about my state of mind.

Turns out Inner Vision is a new age shop. Sells incense and tie-dye and all that crap. So maybe Sal was answering about Papa Night, not Andretti. Then again, maybe it's an Andretti business front. And maybe it also belongs to Night. I guess there's only one way to find out.

Maplewood is a nice suburb, all leafy green streets and smart, two-story detached houses. It's not too busy with traffic, the shops and businesses are small and neat, nestled in between the homes on their squares of manicured lawn. Some of these houses must be worth big money, the place looks affluent to me. Then again, I'm no investor. Regardless, when I find Inner Vision, I'm surprised. It's a double storefront, two big plate glass windows either side of an ornate door with ironwork in strange patterns over the glass.

It's two stories high, the upper floor looks like apartments of some kind. A single-story building, a Peruvian restaurant, is attached on one side, and a narrow alley runs down the other. Next to the alley is another single-story building, a boutique clothing place. At the end of the alley are trees and healthy green grass, a few cars parked there. The back of Inner Vision is huge, like an old warehouse. From the street it looks sort of quaint and old-fashioned, creamy weatherboard and pointed gables above. At the back it becomes quickly industrial, the walls of the warehouse brick, with no windows.

Hanging in the windows of Inner Vision are dreamcatchers and T-shirts, hemp shoulder bags and sarongs. There's shelving with resin dragons and fairies and dolphins and skulls. The musky aroma of incense drifts out into the street. Inside, the place is jammed with row upon of row of new age paraphernalia. There's one shelf dedicated to tarot decks, there must be over a hundred different designs. Glass cases of jewelry stand around all over, another shelf dedicated to semi-precious gemstones in all their polished colors. The woman behind the counter is a waft of diaphanous silks and fire-engine red hair, her arms jingling with a hundred bangles. Her knuckles are mountain ranges of rings, silver spiders and turquoise and quartz.

"Can I help you?" she asks, singsong and soft.

"Just taking a look around." I smile, trying to be relaxed. I can't do much to cover my identity in here, wearing a jacket rather than a hoodie, but I have to take that chance. There are cameras in every corner, technological eyes looking over the superstitions of the past.

"This fucking place." Alvin sneers, crouching to look at a witch riding a broomstick in a snow globe.

"What about it?" Sly asks.

"Wall to wall bullshit!"

Sly shakes his head. He looks worried. "Don't discount this stuff. One thing we know for certain is that we don't know everything."

"That doesn't mean there really are witches and angels," Officer Graney says.

"This shit offends God," Dwight says, lip curled in general disgust.

"Assholes like you offend God," Sly says.

I walk away from them, sick of their bickering. What do I expect to find here? It's a hippy shop that may or may not be an Andretti front, but that's it.

"Here." Michael stands in a back corner, looking up at a poster on the wall.

It has a photo of a black man with a shaved head, his face made up in corpse paint to look like a skull. It reminds me of something I can't place for a minute, then I remember. The Baron Samedi character from that old Bond film, *Live and Let Die*. He had a face like this toward the end, only the guy in this poster has far more detail in his. It looks almost uncanny, like it's not really makeup. Maybe it's a digital effect in post, but it looks real enough. The poster advertises private meetings with Papa Night, but it doesn't say what for.

"You think you'd like an audience?"

I suppress the urge to jump at the wafting woman sneaking up behind me. She drifted from the counter without me noticing, which makes me nervous.

"Maybe she's a ghost!" Graney laughs at his lame joke.

I turn away from the poster, but it feels for a moment like the eyes in the picture follow my movement. I resist the urge to look back.

"I don't know," I tell her. "What's an audience for?"

"Isn't that the question?" She smiles enigmatically.

This is all some pretty bullshit. But at least I know Night has a connection to this place, and that might be the only lead I have to Andretti and Cora. I need to stake it out for a while.

"An audience is whatever you need it to be." The voice is deep, soft. It reminds me of mahogany. That's an association that makes no sense but there it is.

This time I can't suppress the slight jump at the unexpected appearance. These people are fucking ninjas. I turn slowly to see the man from the poster. He's tall, over my own 6'2" by a good couple of inches, and lean. He wears a beautifully tailored charcoal silk suit, with a pale blue shirt underneath and a purple tie. On the tie is a strange design of an eye, encircled by a series of lines and shapes that make me queasy to look at. As I tear my gaze away from it he's smiling broadly. Behind him one of the display cabinets has opened, a secret door revealing a small room beyond. I see the edge of a table and chairs, a candle burning. Incense drifts out, thick and cloying. That smile is disarming me, too wide. At least he's not wearing the corpse paint.

"Do not fuck with this guy," Sly says, and stalks away. The others stand around to watch, clearly interested. Michael has his eyes narrowed, distrust evident. I share his sentiment.

"Whatever I need it to be?" I ask. "What does that mean?"

"What *do* you need?" His smile, impossibly, widens. "What do you *seek*?"

"I'm always on the lookout for answers, but the questions change all the time."

He inclines his head in acceptance of that, his eyes never leaving mine. His irises are a strange color, dark but with an almost purple tinge. He must be wearing contact lenses, part of the act. I'm not impressed with this vaudeville shit. "But one question always stays," he says. "Doesn't i t?"

"And what question is that?"

The smile falls from his face, like water draining away. "Why are *they* always here? Trailing you, dogging you, what do they want?"

My heart races slightly, I'm wrong-footed by the comment. "Who?"

"I think you know."

I think I might, but how the hell can he? These haunts are not real, surely. Have I accepted them yet as either real or psychosis? It seems to be a question I constantly avoid, if I keep trying. I push it away again, ignoring the nag of it. I need to be away from here, away from this freaky guy. I've got all I need for now.

"I'm looking for a gift, actually. For my sister." I turn from Night back to the woman.

She nods. "Okay."

Night smiles and glides back into his chamber, the cabinet door swings silently shut. All that's left is the thick scent of incense.

Five minutes later and I have a stupid ceramic dragon in a bag marked with the Inner Vision name and logo, an eye in a pyramid in a kind of parody of the Illuminati. I carry it with me across the street and look up and down. Leafy suburban places like this are hard to hide in. Too open, too much neighborhood watch.

"What about that?" Michael points to one of those big two-story homes, diagonally opposite Inner Vision. It looks like all the rest, houses and no shops all along that side of the road. Only the color of the siding, the choice of plants in the front yard, really make it look individual.

"What about it?"

A woman jogging by, looking fit in Lycra, side-eyes me as I talk to myself.

Michael nods at the end of the driveway. "Look at the mailbox."

It's jammed with letters and flyers, mostly junk mail as far as I can tell, and a lot of it sticking out is weather-worn like it's been there a while. Looking over the house it seems dark inside, still. It sits there, waiting for something.

Before I draw curious eyes, I stroll on along the sidewalk, then make sure no one is paying direct attention. Seems I'm a non-entity right now, so I turn into the driveway and walk quickly down alongside the property, out of sight of the road. The grass in the large back yard is overgrown, not kept neat like the front. I get the feeling some real estate agent is keeping the place presentable to the public eye. Maybe it's in the middle of a sale, perhaps a deceased estate. Something like that. Regardless, it's currently empty and serves my purposes.

I find some tools in a small shed at the back of the yard and set about making this place mine for a short while. It almost certainly has an alarm system, but that's easier to deal with than most people think. I find the power box outside and use a hammer to crack off the small padlock holding it closed. I flip the breakers and any power to the house is gone. That includes the alarm system, but they often have a battery backup. The tools make quick work of picking the lock on the back door, and I hurry through the house and find the alarm panel is right beside the front door. It has a keypad to enter a pin, and a locked section below that. I don't need a key for plastic casing, the hammer takes care of that. I flip out the battery and that's it. Any sensors are disabled, with no backup power. Sometimes a security firm will respond to a power outage, but more often than not they don't. Power flickers on and off more than people realize and security companies get complacent. So far I haven't put a finger on anything except the hammer, but from here on I'll have to remember to wipe anything I touch.

"Add breaking and entering to multiple homicide," Graney says, standing there with his hands on his hips. "You've barely had a clean slate for five minutes, thanks to Carly, and here you are racking up the felonies again."

"I cannot help it, said the scorpion to the frog. It's my nature."

"What the fuck are you talking about?"

"You dumbass piece of shit cop," Dwight says. "Even I know the parable of the scorpion and the frog. Crossing the river?"

Graney shakes his head. "Fuck me, it's a sad day when this piece of shit knows something I don't."

The house is like a show home, furnished but clearly unlived in. Seems like it's sitting museum-like for some reason.

"Maybe the owners already moved and they're leaving an agent to sell," Michael says.

Sly shakes his head. "No For Sale sign out front."

"Doesn't matter," I say. "I don't plan to be here long."

An upstairs bedroom with a single bed and frilly-edged vanity has a window that gives me a clear view of the front of Inner Vision and the alleyway down the side. I can't see all the alley, but I can see over the small clothing boutique which gives me a view of most of the leafy parking lot behind the warehouse at the back of the store. Pretty good, I don't think I'll get a better spot than this.

Using tissues to open cupboards, so I don't leave prints, I discover the kitchen is entirely empty of food. I'll need some supplies. Thirty minutes later and I'm back, food and drink in hand. I even found a pair of leather driving gloves in the service station shop, so I can touch things without fear. I'll leave the power out, I don't plan on using any lights. Now it's a waiting game.

Chapter 34

I'm woken by a phone ringing about 7:00 a.m. and it takes me a few moments to figure out where the hell I am. The burner phone Lombardi gave me is buzzing on the small table beside where I lay fully dressed atop the bed. As I grab the phone, I see there's hardly any battery left. I don't have a charger for it, that'll be back at the Bridgewater house, I expect.

"Yeah?" My voice sounds like a 90-year-old man with emphysema.

"Where the hell are you?" Lombardi sounds more scared than ever.

"You told me to get on with the job. I'm getting on with the job."

"The party we're trying to find apparently lost four assets yesterday. You know anything about that?"

"Would it make a difference if I did? Or didn't?"

There's silence but for heavy breathing for a moment, Lombardi clearly trying to control anger. I recognize that sound from Vern. They're really quite alike considering how different they first appear. Except Vern is long dead, of course.

"It brought a world of pain down on me," Lombardi says.

"Retaliation?"

"Of course retaliation!"

What can I tell him? "There are casualties in war."

"You want maybe there should be another casualty? Maybe one you arrived with?"

If he thinks threatening Bridget will affect me, he's an idiot. He knows she's the only chip he's got to bargain with and I think he's reached a point where he genuinely needs me. If he lost more men yesterday, perhaps his numbers are growing thin. No wonder he sounds scared.

"You wanna make an omelet, etcetera."

He's quiet again. He gets the reference. Then, "You got anything to tell me?"

"I'm following a lead right now. Last night it was a bust." And that's an understatement. The shop had a total of three more customers all day, then the woman in all the silks and silver closed up and went down the alleyway to her car. Interesting she left through the front, but her car was parked out the back. I watched the place all evening, finally giving up about midnight when fatigue got the better of me. I didn't see Papa Night leave, so figure maybe he lives there. Perhaps the back is his domain.

"And if it's a bust again today?" Lombardi asks.

It might well be. "I plan to give it a little while, then force the issue."

"How long is a little while?"

"Is this situation suddenly time-sensitive?"

"How long?"

I suck in a breath, thinking. Honestly, anything happening at this front will likely be after business hours. Am I wasting my time? Movement out the front of the shop catches my eye. I think it's the woman shopkeeper at first, but it's too early for that. Then I start as the person lets themselves into the store with a key and I catch their face as they glance back before going in. Alfie. Lombardi's butler. What the fuck?

"Give me twenty-four hours," I tell Lombardi as Alfie disappears inside Inner Vision. "Tomorrow morning I'll come back there and fill you in on everything, and by then I expect to have plenty to tell you."

"Twenty-four hours!" Lombardi says, like he's imposing the deadline instead of simply agreeing to what I just told him.

"You got it."

I hang up and watch the shop intently. Alfie was carrying something in a canvas bag, I couldn't see what. But he had it pressed close to his chest like he didn't want it to be seen. No lights come on and I can't see inside, so I sit and grind my teeth. About ten minutes later, Alfie comes out again and locks up behind himself. He doesn't have the bag with him anymore. He heads off down the street and I can just make out a car on the next block. He gets in and drives away.

"Well, isn't that an interesting development," Michael says. "Alfie working for Andretti?"

"Or Papa Night," I say. "He's the only one we know is connected to this place so far. And that might explain how Stella knew to give me the name."

"Maybe Alfie gave it to you."

"Nah, he tried to warn me off. I think it was Stella, she seemed rattled. She's bothered by something." I glance up at Michael. "You're being more friendly and helpful than usual."

He grimaces. "Don't think you're forgiven, asshole. You shot me in the fucking head." He turns the ruin of the exit wound to make sure I get a clean view. It's a bit much to witness before breakfast, his broken teeth working wetly where his cheek should be, distended bone instead of an ear, pink brains pulsing slightly behind.

I look away. Sly leans against the wall, the massive shotgun hole in his torso glistening in the morning light, organs slick and shining. Dwight and Alvin have almost matching bullet holes between their eyes, the backs of their heads open in frozen bone explosions. They both turn to show me. Officer Graney leans forward to let blood drop from his torn open throat, the other two bullet holes staining his pale blue uniform shirt. Why the fuck are they all displaying like some kind of twisted floor show, a catwalk of mortal destruction.

"You lot got something you want to say to me?"

They gather around, dripping blood and sneering. I guess it's a display of hate, nothing more. They can't hurt me, can't affect me, if I don't let them into my mind.

"You piece of shit," Alvin says. "No warning, just boom!"

"Murdered me through a fucking door," Graney says. "I left a wife behind, two grown-up kids."

"People miss me too," Dwight says, and even the others find that hard to believe.

It gives me the break in tension I need and I laugh right in his face. "If I didn't shoot you, someone else surely would have before long. Nobody liked you, Ramsey. You're a grade-A asshole."

Sly laughs, stepping back. "That much is true. You deserved it."

"You all fucking deserved it!" I yell at them, and before they can protest, I add, "Just like I'll deserve it when my time comes."

"Live and die by the sword, huh?" Michael asks.

"Yes! As if it was ever any other way. We're not good men, any of us."

"I was a cop! I did the right thing by society."

I turn to Graney. "You know what, out of everyone here, you maybe have a genuine grievance against me. But tell me, were you truly virtuous? Did you never plant evidence? Did you never hurt someone for pleasure?"

"He killed a black man and called it self-defense," Sly says. "Like so many pig racist cops, you are not a nice guy, Officer Graney."

They stare hard at each other for several seconds, then Graney shrugs. "No point arguing now, I suppose."

I nod. I actually feel a little better about wasting the bastard now.

"Musashi says that 'to win any battle, you must fight as if you are already dead'," I tell them. "I've been doing that since even before Caitlyn and Scottie died. I was beginning to find a different way when Vern murdered them. So that set my path. You lot want to trail me like tattered flags in my wake, be my guest. Or fuck off. I won't lose any sleep over you or anyone else I killed. Musashi also said, 'Do not regret what you have done.' There's nothing I can do about what's already happened. All I can do now is walk the path of the rōnin and try to do good as I pass." Here I am, talking to my fucking self. I guess I'm trying to convince myself this is all true.

"You killed four men yesterday!" Graney says, his voice high with incredulity.

"I killed four mob assholes. That makes the world a better place."

"Sounds like you're going to be rationalizing a lot on this new path of yours," Michael says quietly.

I shrug. "Who isn't? Everybody does that every day, in ways small or large. We're all just well-dressed animals, remember? Fuck off, all of you."

I drag a chair up close to the window so they can't get in front of me and pull food from the sack by the bed for my breakfast. Stakeouts are long and boring, but I have the patience of Job when I need it.

Chapter 35

It's a long, boring day, but if nothing else, the five fuckwits are scarce and I'm left genuinely alone. I enjoy the peace and quiet, but I'm starting to think maybe staking this place out isn't the best use of my time. Perhaps I should be back at the Bridgewater house, putting the hard word on Alfie for intel, or trying to get Stella alone so she'll talk. Maybe there's a way to get her alone and pry information out. I'll give it a few hours after closing before I quit.

It's close to 8:00 p.m. and I'm eating the last of my supplies and about to give up when my patience finally pays off. A limo pulls up out the front of Inner Vision and a woman gets out. It's dark, but the streetlights are enough that I can see it's Cora, Lombardi's supposedly kidnapped wife. She seems entirely untroubled and free to move where she pleases. A large man climbs out behind her, dark skin, bald head. He's wearing a long black coat with iridescent feathers around the collar, his feet clad in shining leather black shoes with long pointed toes. Papa Night. How did he leave without me seeing? Maybe while I was sleeping last night?

"At the back," Michael says quietly. I hadn't noticed him reappear beside me. I assume the others are back too, but don't turn to check.

Another car has pulled up under a tree behind the warehouse and a few men climb out. It's harder to make out details for them, much gloomier out the back than in front where there are streetlights. They disappear out of view under the edge of the warehouse and don't emerge in the alley, so I can only assume they've gone in the back.

Papa Night produces keys and lets himself and Cora in the front of Inner Vision, and the limo they arrived in smoothly glides away from the curb. The door shuts behind them. Well, something is happening. I wonder if one of the others arriving around the back was Andretti. Whatever, I need to be closer. Time to move in and see if I can't spy something.

"You're a fucking thug, remember?" Graney says.

"You are certainly no ninja," Sly says, laughing. "And besides, I already told you not to mess with that badass Obeah shit or whatever that dude is into."

Michael catches my eye and offers half a smile. "Maybe today is a good day to die?"

"Fuck all y'all."

I sneak out the back of the house, making sure to take all my garbage with me. I don't expect to return. I move away from Inner Vision so I'm a good hundred yards past before I cross the street, dump the trash, then head around the block to come into the parking area behind the warehouse. At first I'll rely on the trees and the night to mask my presence. After that, I'll play it as it comes.

At the rear of the warehouse is a large metal roller door, closed, and beside it a regular door with a glass panel in the top half. The glass is frosted, light glows through it from inside. Several cars are parked nearby.

The night is dark and tree shadows allow me to get right up to within a few yards of the door, but I can't hear a thing. There's more light coming from the far side of the warehouse. Trees grow close to the building there, only a gap of a few feet between them and the wall. Orange glow paints the trunks next to a long window, a little higher than my eye level.

"You're gonna get shot to death, fucker!" Alvin sounds especially happy about it.

I can't help wondering if these assholes are simply going to hang around until I die a violent death. They're waiting for the ultimate matinee performance. So maybe I have them for life, however long or short that may be.

"You will certainly fuck up soon," Graney says.

We'll see. They'll have to wait a long time, if I have any say in the matter. But it is what it is. As far as I'm concerned, I've been on borrowed time since the bloodbath at Vern's when Caitlyn and Scottie died.

I sidle up near the warehouse under the shadows of the trees. The long window isn't frosted, but it's over my head height as it turns out. Double-checking I'm alone, I jump and grab the narrow sill, do a half chin-up to peek over the edge. The warehouse is huge and largely empty. Dozens of cardboard boxes of various size are stacked up along one wall, but the space is so big they hardly make a dent in it. There's some furniture around, tables and chairs, some kind of mechanical gear up in one corner I can't quite see. But in the middle of the open space are two stainless steel tables, like you'd see in a coroner's lab for autopsies. They stand only a few feet apart, naked metal gleaming under the high halogen lights up in the ceiling. What the fuck are they for? Several people are milling around, and I recognize Furio Andretti from Lombardi's photos. He's head-to-head with Cora and Papa Night, talking with serious faces. My arms start to tremble and I drop back down.

Something hard presses into the small of my back.

"You fuckwit!" Dwight howls, laughing.

"Who the fuck are you and what are you doing?" The voice has a strong New York accent.

I don't wait to assess the situation. Sometimes you have to move hard and fast. When people put a gun on you, they expect instant compliance. If they press it right against your body, they've given themselves away. Knowing exactly where the gun is, I spin on the spot, using my forearm to bat it aside. The mook's eyes are widening as my other hand arcs around and my hard fist cracks into the side of his head, right up against the temple. His eyes cross and he drops, but the gun booms, his finger twitching on the trigger despite my speed. Cement chips burst from the wall beside me where the bullet strikes. Damn it.

But that's the least of my problems. There's another dude a few yards farther away and his gun is rising.

"Finally dead!" Alvin shrieks.

Fuck that. I hit the deck and roll, snatching up the gun that was about to kill me as I do. The mook fires fast, dirt kicking up beside me, but I keep rolling. If he was smart, he'd track ahead of me. In the instant I hear a pause in his firing, which is almost certainly the moment he realizes he needs to fire at where I'll be not where I am, I stop and twist back the other way.

I'm a crack shot, but writhing on the ground like this I take no chances and aim for center mass. His weapon booms again as my bullet punches into his chest with a satisfying burst of blood and he staggers back. Full marks for tenacity, he doesn't go down and squeezes off again. Hot fire sears across my left forearm, but I ignore it and put a bullet between his eyes.

Blood trickles warm down over my wrist and hand, but I can tell the wound is superficial without looking. I have bigger concerns. Shouting and doors opening at the back of the warehouse. The guy I punched out is stirring, so I press his gun against his head and fire. Blood and bone spatter out across the dirt. I can't have him getting up again.

"Will you just fucking die already!" Alvin says, a distinct whine in his voice.

No, I will not.

If I try to run, I'll get shot in the back. Passing the mook's gun to my left hand, already slick with blood from my forearm, I draw my Glock from the shoulder holster and spin around just as men start pouring around the corner. The first reckless idiot gets hot lead in the brain and drops like the sack of shit he is.

"Hold back!" someone yells.

Another body starts around the wall, then leaps back as his friend falls at his feet. I squeeze a shot off anyway and hear a yelp, but don't know if it's from shock or injury.

"Who the fuck is out there?"

I don't know the voice and I don't plan to answer. I've bought enough time to run. I hurry back away from the corner, staying close to the trees, using their shadows for cover.

"Oh, finally!" Officer Graney says, grinning at something off to my right.

I have a half second to wonder what he means before I see Alfie step from behind a tree trunk beside me. He must have been there all along, in the shadows, and I backed up right to him. He's already swinging something long and heavy. A crowbar, I notice, as I instinctively duck, but too slow. It cracks across the top of my head and everything swims into darkness.

Chapter 36

I come to on the dirty ground, pain throbbing behind my eyes. It's only been a few seconds, but already several people are leaning on me, holding me down while I'm tied up. It's Hollywood bullshit that KOs last minutes or even hours. If a person is knocked unconscious for more than thirty or forty seconds, that's potentially serious brain damage, or death. Most knockouts are only a few seconds and even that means a few days of mild concussion at least.

But these guys are smart enough not to fall for movie nonsense and they have me trussed up like a Thanksgiving turkey already. The fact they haven't simply put a bullet in my brain is interesting, but my thoughts are sluggish, I feel nauseated and untethered from reality. I can't see straight, my vision blurry and doubling up in the low light.

Then everything is bright, too bright, and I realize I've been carried inside the warehouse. Something hard presses into me and more tugging and pain at my ankles, wrists, shoulders. Something presses hard against my chest. I phase in and out again and find I've been tied to a chair. Voices, smeared and slurring, come to me muffled, like I'm under water.

A sharp pain in my face as a hard, heavy palm slaps me. It helps straighten my vision and I suck in a long breath and force my eyes open, try to focus. Furio Andretti is leaning over me, hand drawn back ready to slap again.

"Oh, you see me now?" he asks, anger in his voice.

"I see you." My voice is slurred, like I've downed half a bottle of bourbon. My head feels like the morning after I've downed half a bottle of bourbon. I force myself to take long, slow, deep breaths. My equilibrium begins to return.

"Who the fuck are you? What are you doing here?"

Cora is standing behind Andretti as he yells at me, her face serious. Across the room I see Papa Night, sitting in an armchair with his hands pressed together as if in prayer. His lips move as he mutters rapidly. There's a thick, cloying smell, like incense but also like something else. I kind of recognize the odor but can't place it. At least a half-dozen others are in the room, all men in suits. All Andretti's crew, no doubt. I notice the shooter from Gino's, Lebretta, among them.

My five assholes are all lined up along the wall not far from where I'm tied. Alvin, Dwight, and Graney look expectant and excited. Sly is watching Papa Night, his brow creased in a frown. Michael stares at the floor. As I notice him, he looks up and shrugs. "Might as well come clean," he says in a defeated voice.

"You're obviously working for Lombardi," Andretti says. "Only he would be stupid enough to send someone so dumb. But how does he know about this place?"

Michael is right. Why should I hide anything now? "He doesn't know about this place. I found it."

"But he sent you?"

"He thinks you kidnapped Cora as part of your war."

"Yeah, well he was supposed to think that. Keep him on edge. But the coward piece of shit has gone to ground. You know where he is?"

I press my lips together. Do I need to flip here? I wish my head wasn't pounding so hard, it's difficult to think. Goddamn Alfie, cracking me with a crowbar. Sturdy old bastard.

"Furio," Cora says softly. "Time."

He raises one hand to silence her without taking his eyes off me. I catch the look of anger that triggers across her face.

"You tell me where Lombardi is, you get to live. How's that?"

"Oh, fuck off!" Alvin sounds like a wronged teenager.

"Just fucking kill the shithead," Dwight adds.

Graney shakes his head, face twisted in disgust.

Sly turns and catches my eye. "Some bad shit gonna go down here. Probably best you get shot now."

The smell in the room is increasing, a haze of smoke making the lights swim. My eyes are itchy and I can't help blinking rapidly. I wonder if my head not clearing isn't something to do with whatever this stuff is. The others present are rubbing their eyes and looking a little wasted.

"Furio, seriously," Cora says. "If we don't move now, we'll miss the window. Everything will be wasted."

He turns to her, a little unsteady on his feet. Everyone is getting wasted on this smoke.

"He'll keep until afterwards," Cora says. "He's not going anywhere."

Furio nods once. "Yeah. Okay. Let's do this." He gives her an indulgent smile and I notice a slight wince crease her eyes. Seems like Andretti thinks he's humoring her and that rankles.

His hands are shaking as he walks away from me. Papa Night is up out of the chair as soon as they move and he starts talking in a low voice. People hurry to comply with his instructions. Tall black candles are put all around the floor, Papa Night making tiny adjustments to their positions. The lights are all turned out, everything sinks into a fiery dim glow, the smoke drifting through the large space thickens. There is definitely more than a knock on the head affecting me now.

Papa Night raises his voice. It's deep, sonorous, as he chants something in a language I can't recognize. The words meld and slip, both jarring and mesmerizing. The others gather around the table, lit in flickering contrasts of shadow and orange candlelight. The half-a-dozen mobsters look at each other, all smirks and rolling eyes. They think this is bull-shit. Now a few others have arrived, all of them black, middle-aged or older, four men and two women, dressed in bright colors, faces made up with striking, uncanny designs. They approach each mobster, dabbing something onto their faces as Night's strident, deep voice chants on. Each suited mook stills, hands hanging limply, faces slack, they stand and stare. Then they're chanting too, but low and whispered. What just happened to them? They're led to form a circle just inside the stuttering black candles, one mook between each of the brightly-dressed others to form a large ring of people around the two autopsy tables.

My head swims, my eyes sting and blur as I repeatedly blink tears away. My hands strain at their bonds, I'm so desperate to rub my eyes, but I can't.

Papa Night moves into the center and stands between the metal tables. The group begins slowly circling, counterclockwise, my view of Night a slow flicker play in each gap as they pass. All the mobsters move wood-enly—zombified?—while the rest, Night's people, are animated, their faces alive. I see Stella in the group, she's crying, wet tears streaking her vibrant makeup. She glances over, but the moment she sees me looking she turns away.

Drums start from somewhere, a rolling, hypnotic cadence. I can't see drummers or their instruments, but the sound fills the air along with the swirling, thickening smoke.

Alfie steps forward beside Papa Night, who turns and I jump when I see his face made up in that incredibly detailed skull corpse paint, like the poster in the shop. Did I black out again? When could he have done that? He wasn't wearing it moments ago. It's not a mask, his face moves naturally as his deep chant continues.

The drums thrum and pound, my heart races, my vision swims.

Night has a white chicken in each hand. Held by the legs they flap and thrash upside down. Alfie steps up with a knife and neatly takes the head clean off the first of them. Night holds the twitching bird over one of the autopsy tables, letting blood pour and spatter from its neck onto the shining metal. He throws the bird's corpse aside, then turns. Alfie cuts again and Night repeats the act covering the other table with blood.

"This is no voodoo," Sly says from somewhere I can't see. "This is something else. Something far worse."

The circling people continue their slow but constant rotation, whispering as they go, the suits somnambulant, the others lively. The sounds of their whispers, Night's deep chanting, the thumping drums, it's all drilling into my ears, into my brain, like a wind blowing incessantly across my mind. My vision struggles in the low light, swims with the drugged air.

Papa Night throws the second dead chicken aside and raises his hands, his voice rising too. Andretti and Cora step into the circle. They're both naked but for sharp marks on their faces in charcoal or black face paint. Without instruction they each climb onto one of the autopsy tables and lay flat on their backs. Andretti is smirking too, like this is the craziest fun. He casts another indulgent look at Cora, then lays back. Her face is rigidly serious, her chest rises and falls rapidly with panting breath. She looks both elated and terrified.

Papa Night leans over Cora and she stares up at him, then nods once, decisively. He smiles. The circle of people keeps turning and whispering, but Night's chant stops suddenly. The drums pound on, getting faster.

My chest heaves as the smoke in the gloomy room increases. Night's people move to Andretti's table and fall on him. Four of them grab an arm or leg each and crouch down, using all their weight to pull him hard against the metal surface. Alfie and Stella stand by Andretti's head as the six mobsters continue their slow marching circle.

He cries out, tries to thrash free, but they have him held tight.

"Night, what the fuck?"

"Too late to change your mind now," Papa says, laughing.

The drums get faster still, the pulse against my temples and eyes strains to burst free.

"Cora, I went along with this bullshit ritual for you. You said it'd make me powerful! What's this shit?"

"Oh, it will!" Papa Night laughs.

Through the haze in my brain I realize Andretti thinks it's about him, thinks Cora is doing him a favor of some kind. One he was happy to play along with. But whatever is going on here is Cora's doing. She's set Andretti up. But more than that, she's going it alone, not doing Lombardi's bidding. He still thinks she's kidnapped. She's played them both, but to what end? Fuck, if only my brain worked properly.

She lays there, gasping rapidly.

Andretti is thrashing and yelling, but still held fast. Papa Night stands tall over Cora. He tips his head, inquisitive. She does that one decisive nod again, closes her eyes. Night raises a blade, shining in the candlelight. It's thick and gleams, wickedly sharp, a white bone hilt stark against his dark skin. Cora grabs the edges of the table and her knuckles whiten as she braces herself, her body rigid, teeth clenched, eyes squeezed shut.

Night starts his chant again, rapid and deep. The drums pound on, louder, faster. My heart is racing, thumping against my ribs, my head swims. Night brings the knife down, slamming it into Cora's sternum below her throat. What the hell? She arches up off the table, a scream ripping from her.

"The fuck?" Andretti yells, head twisted to one side, compelled to watch. "The fuck the fuck the fuck?" He thrashes but he's held fast by four grimacing people, his crew marching their slow circle, oblivious.

Night rocks the blade hard against Cora, carving through her sternum, then drives his other hand into her chest. With a wet sucking, he pulls it free and he's holding her fucking heart, letting her blood pour from it over his face, into his mouth. Cora falls still and Night turns to

Andretti. The drums reach a crescendo of speed and volume, the circling mooks are moving, moving, whispering loud and sharp.

Andretti is screaming senselessly now, animal noises of panic and terror. Night draws the blade down Andretti's chest, not deep, but opening the flesh from throat to stomach. Blood sluices out, Andretti screams higher still. Night raises Cora's heart and slams it down into the wound. It bursts like ripe fruit, an unnatural splatter, and Andretti bucks against the table like he's being electrocuted. His scream is like nothing I've ever heard before, and hope to never hear again.

I feel like space is opening around me, as if portals to some frozen void are howling through the huge room. I'm such an insignificant fucking speck. The candles flicker, other colors like lightning lance through the air. Everything wavers, reality rippling like water from a thrown rock. Whatever this smoke is, I'm tripping balls on it.

Night's chant and the whispering of the circle reaches a fever pitch, the drums an almost solid wall of noise. The four holding Andretti down grimace at the effort as he wails and bucks, Alfie and Stella now chanting loudly beside him. The candlelight flickers and dives, the smoke thicker than ever, my head pounds and pulses as my eyes focus and unfocus and I feel blackness swelling in at the edges of my consciousness.

Papa Night's voice rises in volume and pitch, an inhuman screech like a pterodactyl from a bad sci-fi movie. The drums are suddenly silent. The circling mooks stagger and drop to their knees, some fall flat on their face. The four holding Andretti down lose their grip, collapsing to the cement floor. Alfie and Stella sag, stagger back. Night's screech dies and everything falls into a heavy silence. Stillness, but for thick, swirling, sweetly acrid smoke.

Through the dense clouds I watch Papa Night look down at the inert Andretti. Alfie steps up next to him. For a moment everything is motionless, almost tranquil, and I feel my consciousness fleeing, like I'm falling backwards through a tunnel.

The last thing I see through the haze is Andretti sit up, blood pouring from his chest. A wide, white-toothed smile splits his face as he reaches out, takes hold of Papa Night's hand and Alfie's hand.

Then I'm swallowed by the dark.

Chapter 37

I have no idea how long I'm out, but sound comes back in pulses that match the pain in my head. It's lessened at least. I suck in a shuddering breath and try to wipe my eyes, but my hands are still tied behind the chair. My wrists are sore from the rope, my back complains, my forearm burns from the bullet graze.

"Welcome back." I can't see well, like there's a thick fog in the room, but blinking rapidly seems to clear it a little.

Furio Andretti is standing by me. His face is pale, but alive, his eyes glittering. They have a slightly purple hint in the low light. Behind him I see the six suited guys from his crew all sitting on the floor against the wall. Two are still out but the rest are rubbing their eyes and looking at each other in confusion. They share words and shrug. It looks like they have no idea what happened. I wonder if they remember any of it.

I can't see Papa Night or any of his people, except Alfie who lingers behind Andretti. The two metal tables are shining in the light, cleaned of blood. Cora's body is nowhere to be seen.

Andretti leans into my field of vision, and down the neck of his open shirt I see bright white dressings covering the long gash in his chest. No wonder he's pale, the amount of blood I watched him lose.

I try to speak, but my mouth is dryer than a dead camel's ass. Andretti smiles and gestures to Alfie, who scurries away. I take a moment to suck in another breath, my head still spinning. Some of the lights are on, the smoke is gone, the fucking drums have stopped, thankfully. Alfie returns with a glass of water and Andretti nods. The old man holds it to my lips and it's nectar. Ambrosia. I swallow it all down and Alfie moves away.

"How do you feel?" Andretti asks, his voice is smooth and deep, it reminds me of a late-night radio DJ. Not like the angry yelling from before.

"Hard to know, if I'm honest." It's the best I can do. I genuinely don't know how I feel.

"Your timing was most unfortunate, given how time-sensitive the ritual was."

"Why so time sensitive?"

Andretti smiles. "Too much to explain. Planets and alignments, numbers and seasons. The million spheres. The interplay is complicated, but on occasion, power is there for the taking."

A frown creases my brow. "That is some ambiguous bullshit."

"Nevertheless, it's all I'll tell you."

"So now what?"

Andretti smiles again and pulls up a chair, sits facing me. "Isn't that the question?"

I try to push aside the fog in my brain, remembering how Andretti was so angry and scared, how Cora seemed to be the one in charge, in cahoots with Night. Then the knife... Now Andretti is so calm and balanced. "You killed Cora," is all I manage to say. I want more water.

"Did I? It's hard for a woman in a man's world. I risked everything for power. Did it work? Now I'm a woman in a man. Should be easy rolling from here on. Yes?"

"You're... Cora?"

"Am I?" He grins, and it's disconcerting as hell. "Or am I just fucking with you and I murdered that bitch because Lombardi's an asshole? And I used a ritual to do it to give me more power. Or because it was fun. Did I humor Cora and she died for her nonsense? Or did Andretti humor me and he died for his hubris? Does it even matter? Why would you care?"

His eyes glitter and I stare. This is some messed up bullshit. All I actually need is money, Bridget's money. The rest of it can all go to hell. "Your guys hit Gino's a couple of nights ago." Andretti nods. "Okay, so I was there with an associate of mine."

"I know. You cost Andretti..." He smiles. "Cost *me* assets."

I let that pass. Honestly, what the actual fuck? "Yeah, well those assets were trying to murder everyone, so fuck you."

A genuine laugh escapes Andretti, then he winces and puts a hand gently against his torso. "Fair enough. And?"

"And one of them took my associate's bag, and in that bag was a lot of money that belongs to no one but her."

"Really? I'm wondering if maybe that kinda cash might have belonged to someone else before her. After all, it's unusual to carry around so much, no?"

"Regardless, it's not yours."

"It is now."

Everyone's an asshole. I stare at him, anger making my head pound more. I take a deep breath again to control myself. "My associate needs that money. It's all she has. The only reason I'm here at all is to get it back. I don't actually give a fuck about you or Lombardi or anything else. We just need our money."

Andretti nods, sits back, that hand still resting lightly against his chest. "I'm impressed you found me, honestly. Even more impressed you managed to stay alive until now."

"We're all fucking salty about that," Officer Graney says from somewhere off to my right. I ignore him, don't take my eyes from Andretti.

"But you'll get nothing from me." Andretti holds up his free hand to forestall my response. "Except, perhaps, your life."

I nod, but don't reply. I suppose I should have expected this. There's nothing to stop him wasting me right here. I'm nothing but excess baggage, after all.

"Lombardi needs to go," Andretti says.

"And you want to use me for that, huh?"

He raises his hands, palms up. "I don't know where he is. You do, I presume."

"I do."

"So go kill him for me and I'll let you live."

My brain is slowly clearing, the water helped. My body aches to move. "What's to stop me leaving once you set me free? I mean, I could tell you I was going to kill Lombardi, then just fuck off."

Andretti smiles. "But you won't. Because of…your associate. Besides, can you really not see how badly Lombardi needs to die?"

"That's your business, not mine. You stole from me, not him."

Anger flashes across Andretti's face. "You have any idea what he did to me? The depravities he enacted on me, while I was too weak to resist?"

My eyes narrow. "Cora?"

Andretti sniffs, sits up straighter. "He lives with his *staff* like some plantation owner asshole, he fucked around behind my back, he has less honor than a fucking cockroach. You'll do the world a favor taking him out."

"Wait a minute, his staff are your friends. Alfie right there, he knows exactly where Lombardi is. Fuck, he could get Stella to poison the fucker's food and you'd be done with it. And if you're really his fucking wife in there, you know exactly where he is, surely?"

"Are you fucking stupid?" Alvin hoots behind me.

"You signed your death warrant right there, cocheese!" Dwight says.

Andretti smiles. "It's true, of course. But I want to remain distant, keep my family distant. You are a cipher, Mr. Carver."

It surprises me to hear him use that word.

Andretti relaxes back into his chair again. "Besides, it pleases me to think of you taking him down and I agree you and your associate deserve some recompense. This will work out for all of us. I want to sic you onto my husband, Mr. Carver. He'll see me coming, I'm the enemy remember? He knows my crew. You can get close."

These assholes all using me as their performing monkey. This is a lot to take in. "Are you really Cora in there?"

Andretti shrugs. "Does it really matter to you?"

"I guess not."

"Tell you what, here's something to sweeten the deal. In Paul's office in the house in Bridgewater is a portrait. Of him, naturally. Big fucking ugly thing. But it swings out and there's a safe behind it. He always keeps a stash of clean cash in there. The code for the safe is 8-9-4-3-2."

I watch him, trying to force my foggy brain to think around all the angles. But I repeat the number in my head a few times. I'm good at remembering numbers.

"There's really nothing sinister going on here," Andretti says. "All that stuff you saw last night? You dreamed it all. The drugged air. It was a harmless ritual."

"Not for Cora Lombardi!"

"But that wasn't real either." I frown and Andretti gives a wide smile. "Honestly, all a dream. She's fine! And you'll get no money from me, giving back anything goes against my very DNA. But take Paul out, take the money, get your friend, then fuck off forever. Or get dead right here. Seems like an easy choice. Should you mess it up in any way, I can organize a clean-up later. You'll certainly make things easier for me, however far you get. And until it's all done, myself and my whole crew will be publicly far from Bridgewater, clearly not involved at all."

I'm over a barrel, really. If I want to get out alive, I have to agree. If I want to save Bridget and get her money, I have to do want Andretti wants. Whether it's Cora in there or not is pretty much irrelevant. I mean, maybe Alfie knows Lombardi's safe code and he told Andretti. It's not like only Cora could know that information. What do I care if she's dead, it's all part of their war. Already I can't be sure of what really happened last night, like a dream that fades on waking.

"Does it matter?" Michael is standing behind Andretti, looking over him at me. "I mean, any of it? Whether or not we're real, whether that's really Cora in Andretti's body, whether the fucking tooth fairy is actually saving up kid's teeth? I mean, what the fuck would a fairy want with millions of tiny teeth, anyway? You ever think about how fucking creepy that is? All this stuff is bullshit that doesn't matter in the real world. What matters is what you do. How you live. The choices you make."

"Okay," I tell Andretti.

He smiles. "Okay." He nods and someone unties my hands.

As I'm rubbing life back into my wrists, dried blood over my hand from the bullet graze that's already scabbing over, Alfie comes around the front and unties my legs, then the ropes across my chest.

"You better stay away from Bridgewater too," I tell him.

"We ain't ever going back anywhere near there," he says, and turns away. I hope he and Stella will at least be treated like equals here, like people.

Andretti stands, moving gingerly, and goes across the room. He comes back with the two Glocks Lombardi gave me and hands them over. I notice his crew have cleared their heads while we talked and they all stand at the ready. They look confused, and as if they're itching for a fight.

With a nod I holster both guns and leave the warehouse, my ghosts voicing their displeasure quite animatedly as I go.

Chapter 38

Dawn is painting the sky in shades of pink and peach as I head back toward the car. The air is cool, fresh, and I realize how much the warehouse still bore traces of the previous night's activities. Ritual? Hell, I don't really want to think about it. Already I can't be sure what I saw, can't be certain of what happened.

Musashi said, "Truth is not what you want it to be; it is what it is, and you must bend to its power or live a lie." I think there's a lot in that revelation, but there's also power in accepting some truths will persist whether we bend to them or not, and if it makes no difference, it's best to just ignore them. Musashi also said, "Do nothing which is of no use." I feel like dwelling on shit we can't really know is of no use. Whatever happened last night doesn't matter anymore. All that matters is what lies ahead. I get in the car and point it toward Morristown. Whatever else might happen, I have to get Bridget out first.

"He also said 'The path that leads to truth is littered with the bodies of the ignorant', you asshole." Graney is lined up with the others in the back seat, leering into the mirror as I drive.

Since when did he read *The Book of Five Rings*?

"And he also said, 'Accept everything just the way it is'," I tell him. "So fuck you."

Graney growls a laugh, shakes his head.

"I told you to steer clear of that guy," Sly says. "You should steer clear of *all* this."

"No. This situation is here, and I need to deal with it. I'm rōnin now, so I walk the path before me. Right now, I owe Bridget. If I have no code, I'm nothing. Besides, that fucker Paul Lombardi has this coming. If we trace it all the way back, he's the one who ripped off Bridget in the first place with a crooked game. That's the only reason we find ourselves at this current juncture."

"She was planning to rip *him* off by counting the game," Graney says. "If anything, she started it."

"Leave her in the wind," Michael says.

"No, cocheese, go get her. There's still a chance you might die that way."

"I'm getting her because it's the right thing to do," I growl.

"Rationalization of the highest order," Michael says.

"So what? After everything that's gone down, I'm ready for some fucking mayhem!" Perhaps I really haven't changed that much after all.

Dwight leans forward, blood trickling down his nose from the bullet hole between his eyes. "Control your anger. If you hold anger toward others, cocheese, they have control over you. Your opponent can dominate and defeat you if you allow him to get you irritated." He sits back, *hyucking* as he goes.

"Even you quoting Musashi at me now?" Honestly, this may be the biggest surprise of this whole debacle. "Fuck you all. Shut up and let me drive."

I pull into a fast food drive-thru and sate the hunger that's tearing at my gut, then head on again. The Glock 17s, as their name suggests, hold seventeen rounds as standard, and the two Lombardi gave me are as standard as they come. I try to search up a store using the smartphone but the battery is dead, the phone a useless brick. I wonder how long it's been out. But it's not long before I see what I need and stock up on ammo. Both pistols now have seventeen each, and I have two spare mags. Let's hope I don't need more than sixty-eight rounds.

There's nothing left to do but the job.

The house near Morristown, right by Dorset Hills School, is quiet as I drive by, Davey's limo still in the driveway. I keep going, head around the block out of sight, then walk back, coming up on the blind side of the house. I'm hoping the neighbors aren't paying attention as I slip along their driveway and hop a low fence into the back yard of the place where Bridget is being held. So far, so good. Crouching low in the shadows of some leafy shrubs, I case the back.

It looks real quiet.

My ghosts are wandering around the backyard, looking at the plants, a pond with goldfish in it. Michael strolls brazenly up to the kitchen window that looks out over the yard, cups his hands to peer in. Then he moves across to see in through some glass-paneled double doors.

He turns back to me and yells, "Place looks deserted."

I'm still going to have to go in and make sure. Where the fuck are they?

Graney comes strolling across the lawn. "Dude, quit skulking about. Ain't nobody here."

I want to trust them, but I still don't even know if they're real. And they all want me dead, so it would be a huge laugh for them to convince me to stand up into a firefight. Then again, the place looks and feels dead.

I don't chance it, but skirt the garden to sneak closer, then crouch under the kitchen windows and sidle along the wall. A quick peek shows inert dimness inside. The five assholes are standing around looking at me with smirks and derisive eyes as I scurry along to catch a glimpse in through the glass double doors.

"It's a bust, cocheese. What now, huh?"

They're right. I stand up, squint up to the windows of the first floor, half expecting someone to lean out and shoot me, but the place is deader than these five dickheads leering at me.

"Something there." Michael points through the window.

I go back and lean in closer for a look. There's a round pine breakfast table in the middle of the big kitchen and a piece of paper lies on it, stabbed into place with a bowie knife. That certainly is something.

Michael glances at me. "A trap?"

I shrug, past caring. Something is up here. The kitchen door has a window in the top half. I pick up a stone from the edge of the pond and launch it through, the crystalline rain onto the kitchen tiles starkly loud in the still morning. Reaching through I realize the door was already unlocked.

Graney barks another of his guttural laughs. "You're fucking losing it, kid."

He's right too. Well, half-right. I'm not losing it, but I'm still groggy from the drugged air last night, and mildly concussed from the blow Alfie gave me. I need to get my shit together. I pull the knife out of the soft wood of the table and slip it into my jacket pocket. Might come in handy. The paper has large blocky hand-written letters.

Message from Mr. Lombardi
Situation Changed
If you happen to find your-
self here turn on your fucking
phone

Lips pursed, I realize I missed the deadline. I promised I'd call in by 7:00 am. and it's nearly nine already. But what can I do about that?

"Here, fucker."

Sly is standing by the kitchen counter next to the stove and there's a selection of cables and chargers there. I find one that matches the phone

Lombardi gave me. I plug it in and wait while it sucks in a base charge then boots up. Immediately it pings with messages.

> *You gonna call?*

Then

> *I'm calling and you ain't answering. Not good for you.*

Then

> *You better call in, things have changed. The name Jerry Slovak mean anything to you?*

My peanut gallery is gathered behind me reading over my shoulder. Alvin and Dwight both hoot with glee, Graney chuckles low in his ruined throat. Sly and Michael both shake their heads, lips pressed into a thin line.

That name does ring a bell, but why? Then it hits me and my stomach lurches, a cold pulse rippling out along my arms. That's the name of the asshole Bridget worked for. The one she ripped off for over a hundred and twenty grand. Why the fuck does Lombardi know about him?

"Isn't it obvious, dickwad?" Graney asks.

"He's found her," Michael says.

Of course they're right. Shit. I hit the only number in the phone to dial Lombardi.

"So you finally got the fucking messages?"

I decide to play dumb, not let on that I'm at the Morristown house. "The phone ran out of battery, you didn't give me a charger. I just managed to find one."

"Sure, whatever. You need to be better."

"What's changed. Who's Jerry Slovak?"

Lombardi laughs. "You know damn well who that is, and he's only fucking my life up even more. Until you come in, I ain't letting Bridget go with him. So you'd better get here, and you'd better have some good news for me."

I don't want Lombardi to let Bridget go with Slovak at all. And I'm sure it's also the last thing she wants. "I have some news for you. I'll head back to Bridgewater now."

"No you won't, because that ain't where we are. You need to come to the Vesuvius Lounge." He gives me an address in Newark. "And no funny business, you walk right up to the front door, the rest of the place is locked up tight. This situation needs resolving."

Before I can say any more, he hangs up. Well, okay then. I get the feeling we're heading into some kind of endgame here. Whatever else happens, no way can I let Slovak leave with Bridget. Who knows what he'll do to her.

"You're on the back foot, cocheese."

"No shit."

Alvin dances stupidly. "You gonna get shot to shit in the Vesuvius Lounge!"

I shake my head. "Don't be an asshole. Lombardi wants to know what I've learned."

"He's in control now," Graney says, that self-satisfied grin glued in place. "What now, rōnin?"

Now I walk into the lion's den and take my chances, I guess.

It doesn't take long to drive to the address Lombardi gave me. I park across the street and walk right up to the doors, just like he said. Assuming there're cameras all around the joint, I keep my hands in plain sight and wait. The door opens and Davey is there, looking out with narrowed eyes.

"Inside." He tips his head like I wouldn't be able to work out the way otherwise and I sigh and step past him.

There's a small lobby, cash desk for patrons to pay entry, that leads directly into the wide-open space of the lounge. Clearly a place for pole dancers and asshole clientele, there's a runway stage right through the middle, with three gleaming chrome poles evenly spaced along it. The stage is encircled by tables and chairs, none of them currently occupied. We're obviously outside of business hours for the place. The lights are all on, giving the lounge that weird out-of-time feeling for a place designed to be seen with low lighting. There's too much detail, like an old hooker without her makeup on. A bar runs the full length of the room on my left as I walk in, shadowy booths take up the other long wall. Davey's hand lands on my shoulder. I stiffen, but pause, no doubt about to be frisked. Lombardi is standing farther in, about halfway along the elongated stage. There are seven more wise guys with him, all looking tense and twitchy. Lombardi's face is tight, eyes narrowed as he stares at me. So that's nine guys, but no sign of Bridget and Slovak.

Davey turns me and starts patting me down. He finds the two Glocks, the two spare mags, and the Bowie knife, puts them all on the end of the bar, then guides me in toward Lombardi. I stop halfway across the room, doing all I can to keep a lot of space around me.

"Where's Bridget?"

The boss looks at me like I'm entirely made of shit. "You don't get to ask any questions!"

"What, we're enemies now? I thought we were working together on this."

I see movement in one of the booths along the far wall. Michael is over there, pointing in. Bridget sits stiffly, lips pressed into a tense line.

Someone else is opposite her, but I only see knees in gray flannel pants. That must be Slovak.

"What news do you have for me?"

I have little advantage here, but I'm not giving up what I do have. "Let's just establish what the fuck is going on, shall we?"

"Shall we?" Lombardi's eyebrows shoot up.

Slovak stands up out of the booth, dragging Bridget with him. She cries out in pain at his hard grip on her upper arm, face twisted in the closest thing I've seen to hate in a long time. Slovak is a classic slime-ball, somewhere in his sixties, gray hair slicked back with product, gut stretching a yellow polo shirt. He has a thick gold chain around his neck and several oversized rings turning his ham fists into mini jewelry stores glistening with semi-precious stones.

"You think I couldn't find her?" he asks me, like I'm the reason she ran away. Even now the dude is entirely underestimating Bridget and assuming me, the only man unaccounted for in his little world, must have been in charge.

"How *did* you find her?" I ask. I'm interested, but it's also fun to watch Lombardi on the back foot as the situation slips from his control.

"She stole a lot of money from me, you think I'd let that go? I know people. I know everyone in the game. I ask around, show her picture, soon enough I start to track down the games she's been into without my okay. That quickly leads me to one of Lombardi's games, so I talk to people I know in Lombardi's crew. Easy as that." He grins, showing a gold tooth in his shit-eating face. He needed to tell me how easy it all was, to show what a big man he is. Thing is, if we hadn't been caught up in the hit at Gino's, the trail to Lombardi would be stone cold by now. Bridget would have cleared her debt and been long gone with the rest of Slovak's money. Her bad luck was his good fortune, it had nothing to do with his skills or contacts. It occurs to me that Bridget has been suffering a run of bad luck, like she's jinxed. She really deserves a break.

"Well, bully for you, motherfucker." I give Slovak a smile back. "But you're not leaving here with her."

"Oh, is that right?" Slovak starts dragging Bridget across the lounge.

"Hold it a fucking minute!" Lombardi says, his voice high with anger. "No one goes anywhere or does anything until *I* say so. Carver, where the fuck is my wife?"

He's trying to wrestle control of the situation, and who can blame him. But I plan to keep him off-center. "She's dead."

He actually steps back. I've never seen anyone physically taken aback before. "Dead?"

Whatever demands he expected, he never anticipated she'd be killed without any pressure. He clearly had no idea what was going on behind his back. But through all the haze and uncertainty about last night, one image is crystal clear. Papa Night slamming that knife into Cora's chest, pulling her heart out and letting it pour blood over his face. I don't want to speculate on anything else beyond the obvious. That woman is dead. "Yep. I saw her killed. Sorry about that."

Lombardi is shaking his head, staring hard at me. "No, that ain't it. That can't be it."

"You said I had to stay until this asshole came back," Slovak says, dragging Bridget again. "He's back, you two can sort out your own shit. I'm leaving, and Bridget's coming with me."

I catch Bridget's eye and she stares hard at me, shakes her head subtly. The message is clear, don't let him take me.

"Fine," Lombardi says. "Whatever. You two fuck off."

Slovak drags Bridget toward the door. Mayhem is imminent, but I can't figure how it's going to go down. I can't let them leave. Lombardi is standing with seven guys across the room from me. Davey has moved a few yards away and is leaning against the bar. Slovak and Bridget are nearly at the doors. Bridget catches my eye, looks at the end of the bar, then back at me, popping one eyebrow. I give one decisive nod, the side of my mouth quirking up slightly. Here we go.

Bridget moves with the speed and grace of a ballet dancer. She steps away from Slovak, spinning as she goes to break his grip, and snatches one of the Glocks from the bar. Still turning, she slings it toward me in a flat spin. Her own momentum carries her on and she completes a full three-sixty and brings her hand around to crack Slovak in the side of the head. It's a solid blow. He yelps and staggers, and I'm already moving.

I have no idea if she planned it this way, which would make her a hell of a pitcher, or if it was dumb luck, but the gun is flying a little forward and to the right of me. That works fine. I take two big strides then jump, turning in the air as I go. I snatch the Glock from the air as I come down onto the bar on one shoulder and slide across it. From my peripheral vision I see Bridget bring her knee up into Slovak's groin hard enough to lift him onto his toes. He squeals like a stuck pig, then my attention is drawn away as my eye targets.

Lombardi's crew are all going for weapons and I squeeze off two shots. One hits a mook dead center of his chest and he flies back over the narrow stage like someone yanked on a rope behind him. My second shot goes wide as the bar runs out below me and I drop behind it onto the hard floor. My brain automatically starts the count. Including Slovak, there's ten fuckers I need to kill. I shot one, and now there's fifteen rounds left in the Glock.

Nine fuckers and fifteen rounds is a little off one-point-five rounds per fucker. Tight, but feasible.

Breath rushes out of me as I land on my back but I don't pause, driving my heels against the ground to slide away from where I landed. Sure enough, Davey leans over pointing his own weapon at exactly where I was half a second before. As his eyes track up from there to where I am now, a couple of yards away and moving backwards, I put a bullet through his head. Blood sprays out behind him as he slumps out of sight.

Eight fuckers and fourteen rounds remaining.

I immediately switch one-eighty and start driving my heels to slide the way I came. Any of those guys seeing Davey drop will have pinpointed my position if they have any brains. I can only hope they'll assume I'm heading for the door. It would be the smart thing to do. But I need Bridget to head for the door. If nothing else comes of this except Bridget getting away before Slovak can swallow his balls back down, that'll be enough. She'll have to scratch around and start over, but she'll be free at least.

Slovak's high-pitched wails start to tail off and I can only hope he's still grounded, rocking in silent agony. Lombardi and his six remaining mooks are my main concern. I need to not be trapped behind this bar, I'm a fish in a barrel here. That means taking a chance.

Before any of them can get a look over, I roll over and hurry, hunched down, all the way to the other end, furthest from the doors I came in by. There's a closed office right near me, but no point going that way. I spring up, shoulder roll over the bar, Glock held out double-handed in front of me. Even as I turn, I'm scanning the room and see the crew have fanned out. Makes sense for them, and bad for me. I squeeze off three fast shots as I land on my feet and run for the end of the long stage for cover. One mook goes down, a new hole right through his cheek, teeth spinning into the air as he drops. Another takes a hit in the left shoulder and my third goes wide.

Seven fuckers, one wounded, and eleven rounds remaining.

As I drop down behind the stage, bullets crack and whine all around me, the crew letting fly. But I saw Lombardi heading for the doors, the chickenshit making a break for it. The stage is about four feet high, gives me plenty of cover as I move around it. I stay close and low, remembering the spread of the crew as best I can, then pop up for another volley. Three fast shots and three targets hit. For all their smarts, they didn't keep moving, and I'm warming into the game. One loses his face, another takes a hit dead center of his chest, and the third bends over a gut shot. He drops his gun as he gags and falls to his knees. The one I hit in the chest was the one with the shoulder wound.

Four fuckers left, eight rounds remaining. The odds are getting better.

But Lombardi is almost at the doors now. The gut-shot guy isn't dead, lowing like a cow giving birth as he writhes. I saw Slovak, face twisted in pain, dragging himself for the cover of the bar. Bridget was nowhere to be seen.

I hide behind the stage and double back, heading toward the bar. The two remaining crew are my main concern. As I round the end of the stage, I come face to face with one of them, running this way to cut me off. Damn it. His eyes pop wide and he fires just as I drop and sweep my leg around. Fire burns across my left shoulder, right along the shoulder blade from where I was hunched over, but I ignore it. My sweeping foot meets his ankles and he upends, sits hard on the cement floor with a crack of splitting tailbone. His face scrunches in pain, but already I've grabbed his head. I jam my gun under his chin and fire, leaning back from the spray as he jerks and arcs over.

Three fuckers, seven rounds remaining.

"Don't shoot!" That's Lombardi's voice, high and terrified.

I chance a glimpse over the stage and see Lombardi stopped by the doors, Bridget standing at the end of the bar with the other Glock leveled at him. Slovak is on the ground halfway between them, looking left and right, panicked. The last remaining mook glances back at his boss and that's all I need. I stand all the way up and fire, blowing out the back of his head. He pitches forward and rag-dolls to the ground.

Two fuckers left, Lombardi and Slovak, one grounded, the other under aim, and I still have six rounds. Nice work, Bridget. She didn't bolt after all, must have dived for cover at the bar after she dropped Slovak.

I level my gun at Lombardi. "Walk back toward me," I tell him. "Hands where I can see them." Craven piece of shit didn't even pull his weapon, just ran and left his boys to it. I wonder if this was all that remained of his family. Seems I did Andretti's dirty work for him after all.

Lombardi lifts his hands and walks slowly back into the open space halfway between me and Bridget. She nods at me and lowers her gun.

Before I can say any more, Slovak pulls himself into a sitting position. "Now let's talk about this," he says, looking wide-eyed up at Bridget.

She walks up to him and fires the Glock point blank at his face. His eyes and nose disintegrate and the back of his head explodes. He slams back into the deck.

"Holeeeee shit!" Dwight crows.

"I should have done that in the first place," Bridget says. She wipes the gun off with her shirt tail, then presses it into the hand of the nearest dead Lombardi crewmember.

"Eli, look out!" Michael's voice is tight and I look up to see Lombardi drawing. Seems like he finally found some balls when there were no other options, and I was distracted.

I yell in annoyance and drop, his shot whines over my head and I fire wildly from the ground. It hits him low in the gut and he doubles over, staggers back. Grimacing, he brings his weapon to bear again and fires rapidly. I logroll as fast as I can, cement chips spinning up from the floor. Then Bridget, weaponless, barrels into him with both arms outstretched.

He stumbles and goes down onto one knee, his free hand coming away from his belly, blood-soaked, to stop him face-planting. It's all I need, and I sit up and put two shots through the top of his head.

"Goddamnit," Graney says, looking around at the massacre. "You are *still* alive, you tenacious asshole."

"We need to get out of here," Bridget says. Her face is set, but her hands shake almost uncontrollably. This was probably her first gunfight. Honestly, she's handling it superbly.

I nod. "You're right." I wipe my gun down the way she did before and drop it near one of the dead bastards. As I stand up, I hear a groan. The guy I got in the belly. I forgot about him.

He's lying on his side, face white as the moon, a huge pool of blood spreading out from him in an expanding fan. He looks up at me with wild eyes. "I ain't gonna tell nobody shit," he says between hitched gasps.

Trouble is, he knows my name. He knows Bridget's name. In truth, he's already dead. Except a gut shot like that could take hours to finish him off. If someone showed up and got him medical aid, he might survive. If he survives, he might talk. The gun he dropped lies a foot or two from him. As my eyes move to it he shoots out a hand, remarkably fast considering his condition. He gets a grip on it, but I grab his hand and twist, turning the gun back on him. I scrunch his fingers so he squeezes the trigger and the round punches into his breastbone. He jerks and falls still.

I get up and join Bridget. "Come on. Let's get out of here."

Chapter 39

The back door of the Bridgewater house is easy enough to kick in, especially as I know no one is there and I don't need to be cautious. Going through the kitchen I find a note identical to the one at the Morristown house. I guess in case I came here first. We soon find the downstairs room Lombardi used for an office. Sure enough, above the desk is an oil painting of the dead fucker. Honestly, what kind of asshole sits underneath their own portrait? Wearing the driver's gloves I picked up, I pull against it and it opens like a door. There's a large wall safe behind.

"Seems like that much was true then," Bridget says.

I nod, remembering the number Andretti gave me: 8-9-4-3-2. It's entirely possible he knew that from Alfie, it doesn't prove it was Cora inside the suave-looking mob boss. I shake the thought away. I don't need to care about it. I tap the code into the keypad by the safe handle. Sure enough, the little red LED goes out and the green one next to it comes on

.

"Let's see then," I say. Inside the safe there're all kinds of stuff. A bunch of envelopes, some data discs, a few books, like old ledgers. None of that interests us. But there are also several stacks of cash.

"Jackpot," Bridget whispers. "How much is it?"

I pull all the wads out and we turn to count it on the desk. A variety of denominations in a variety of combinations, but it only takes us a minute to figure out it's just under one hundred grand.

Bridget looks at me, one eyebrow raised. "I know you don't really owe me shit. After all, you got in this mess entirely because you were kind enough to help me out." She's wondering if I'm going to share.

I put my hand between the piles and slide one lot over toward her. Eighty grand. The other eighteen and change can be for me.

"You sure?" Her eyes are wide.

"This whole thing is a confusing mess, but we seem to have come out on top. Lombardi cost you eighty grand. There it is paid back. You offered me seven hundred and fifty and I have eighteen large. Pretty good, right?"

She grins and it's a beautiful sight.

"You think you've won?" The voice is deep and startles us both. My hand is reaching for a gun that isn't there even as I realize it's Papa Night standing in the office doorway. He raises his hands, palms out. "Peace. I'm just here to check how things went down."

"You can tell Andretti he doesn't need to worry about Lombardi anymore."

Night tips his head to one side. "Andretti? Sure, okay."

We stand and stare at each other for a while. My ghosts are ranged about the room, all narrow-eyed as they watch him. Except Sly. He has reason not to like the guy, I suppose. He stands way off in the corner, staring at the ground. He's genuinely scared. Honestly, though, he's already dead. What the fuck can he have to fear?

"This guy freaks me the fuck out," Dwight says.

"He's not good for you!" Alvin adds.

"Don't listen to him," Officer Graney says. "He's a dangerous prick."

They all sound desperate. I like that. They're all scared of him. Could he be a threat to these dead fuckers?

Michael just looks from him to me and back again, his eyes tight.

Night stares hard at me, then around the room, nose tipped up almost as if he's trying to catch a scent. "Something lingers with you, hmmm?"

His voice resonates even when he speaks quietly like this. But he doesn't look directly at any one of my haunts. Seems he can't see them any more than anyone else. But I feel like he knows they're there. I guess in truth they're mine alone. Maybe they are just aspects of me. "Perhaps I can help?" Night says.

Perhaps he can, but I don't want anything to do with him. And not because Sly Barclay doesn't trust him, or because the others are so scared of him. It's because I saw him open a woman's chest and drink the blood right from her still-warm heart. At least, I think I did. It doesn't take a genius to know no good can come of associating with a man like that.

"No. Thanks."

He nods slowly. "Well. You know where to find me if you change your mind."

"Okay."

Papa Night turns and walks away and it feels like a full stop in this whole affair. Bridget picks up her money and stuffs it into a briefcase she's found near the desk. My own bag is still up in the room I used, so I head up and retrieve it, then cram my share inside while Bridget retrieves her small suitcase.

"What now?" Bridget asks.

I honestly don't know. I have a decent bit of start-up cash now, I guess, but a start up for what? I feel like New York isn't quite what I thought it might be. It would make sense to remove myself, for a little while at least.

As if reading my mind, Bridget says. "Fancy a trip to Vegas?"

"Oh, fuck me," Dwight says, face twisted in disgust. "After all that he's even gonna get laid."

Bridget's eyes are mischievous. "I could use a bodyguard, and I enjoy your company," she says, a little bit husky. She looks up through her lashes. "You look a lot better without the beard, by the way."

"Thanks."

"You know what I do." She hefts her bag. "And I have stake money."

"Vegas, huh?" I like the idea. I especially like the idea of spending time with Bridget.

"Sure," she says. "We get away from this house, find somewhere to patch up your wounds, we can be on our way before dark."

"What happened to being rōnin?" Michael asks, but a smile is twitching the unruined side his face.

Maybe this is being rōnin. After all, masterless samurai would take work where they could get it, so being a bodyguard fits the role. I guess I can always go back to a different way of life if it doesn't work out. I nod to Bridget, smile. "Vegas sounds like fun."

Part III

Ghost Recall

Chapter 40

Trouble finds me like flies find shit. Then again, I do like to see a motherfucker's tooth spinning through the air, his lip spraying blood like a split hose jetting water. Gonna have to get these knuckles cleaned up though. The germs people have in their mouth would make you sick to think about, and knuckles always get opened up by a motherfucker's teeth, and often end up infected. That's a concern for later though. I was aiming for his nose, but we can't always have what we want.

"Duck," Michael Privedi says.

I don't pause to think about why the ghost of my dead friend would say that, I simply comply. A piece of splintered two-by-four whistles over where my head was a fraction of a second before. I use my downward momentum to plant my hands and bring my leg around, sweeping the shithead's feet right out. He up-ends and hits the asphalt of the dirty alley on his back with a rush of escaping air and a *thock!* as the back of his head connects and he's out. Always an advantage of hard ground.

Burst Lip Asshole has regained his composure and found a new measure of anger, and his two mates are less surprised and more ready now. Four on one was tough going, now it's three on one and they're spread out wide across the alley, planning to paste me. Still tough going then.

"You are truly boned now, cocheese," the ghost of Dwight Ramsey says, blood trickling down his nose from the bullet hole between his eyes.

Oh, good. The gang's all here. Officer Graney, his throat ruined by the bullet I put through it and more scarlet blooms on the chest of his police shirt, is standing beside Dwight, ready to enjoy the show. Sylvester Barclay is leaning against the wall farther away, organs glistening where I blasted a shotgun shell through his chest, smoking his ubiquitous joint. Blue smoke curls out of his wide-open ribcage. Michael is somewhere behind me. Only Alvin Crake is missing, but I'm sure he's here somewhere. Ghosts of the bastards I killed. Well, five of the many. I still don't know why only these five. Now is not the time to think about it.

Michael strolls around behind the goons, the explosion of bone and brains where his ear used to be reflecting a streetlight at the end of the alley. He's the only kill I really regret, but he gave me no choice. "Better focus, dickhead," he says.

He's right.

"Gonna fucking kill you," Burst Lip Asshole says. Well, slurs.

They advance in a line, the other two fanning ahead and wide of Burst Lip, planning to flank me. I wish I had my guns on me, but I've got out of the habit of carrying them. Getting complacent. Now is not the time to think about that either.

Rule one of fighting multiple opponents: hit the leader first, to undermine the confidence of his lackeys. I assume Burst Lip Asshole is the boss here. Rule two of fighting multiple opponents: make space. Here I go, rules one and two together.

Instead of backing up like they expect, I rush Burst Lip. His hands are up, he thinks he's ready for me, but I sidestep at the last second and stiff-arm him, collecting one arm and his face as his punch finds only air. My forearm, hard as wood from a lot of training, slams him backwards. At the same moment I tuck my hip, lift my right knee and power out a kick into the ribs of the goon on that side. He folds up over my foot, crying out in pain, but I'm already planting that foot back on the ground and pivoting, bringing my other hand around in a tight hook that connects with beautiful solidity right behind Burst Lip's ear. He grunts and staggers forward, as good as out. His body just hasn't realized yet. The third goon, finding himself too far away, tries to close the distance and runs right into my front kick.

A good front kick is none of this snapping bullshit so many dojos try to teach. It's knee up high and drive out, the same as if you were trying to kick down a door. One of the most underrated techniques in any kind of fighting. I hear at least three of the dude's ribs snap under my foot and he clutches himself and collapses, howling in high-pitched agony, which is a strange noise when most of the breath has already left a body.

I turn one-eighty and punch the other goon back into the wall just as he's trying to stand up from my side kick and he drops like a sack of bolts.

Burst Lip Asshole has fallen to his knees, one hand pressed to the back of his head where I punched him. It must hurt because my knuckles are singing with pain. I hope my hand isn't broken, but it could be. You don't often get to hit some fucker's skull with all your strength and not break something. But my hands are pretty well conditioned to this type of activity, so I might be lucky.

"Ah, for fuck's sake," Dwight says, disappointed once again.

I walk around in front of Burst Lip Asshole and grab a fistful of his jacket, haul him up to look at me. "Why the fuck are you shitstains following me?"

"Lotta money on you," he says, sounding confused. He's punch-drunk, that weird state of not actually knocked out, but also not really conscious. His friends are starting to groan and I keep an eye on them, just in case anyone pulls a piece. I need to move along, this is a busy town and people are walking past the alley in droves. Someone will look in soon and it might be a cop.

"Cops are the least of your worries," Officer Graney says, voice harsh because he doesn't really have a throat to speak of. I don't understand how he talks at all, but then again, he is dead, so what rules should apply? Like Sly getting high with no lungs.

"That's it?" I ask. "Money?"

"Saw you cash out, leave the casino."

"That's my girlfriend's money. You think I'd just let you take it?" Bridget is a hell of a gambler, she's got Las Vegas twisted around her finger, playing all the casinos. Enough to get rich, but not enough to notice. Not yet. I cash up for her a couple of times a night, stash the money in a safe at our rented apartment. Every couple of days I take about half the winnings to the bank, but keep the rest loose. Avoid a little government attention, maybe. It's a good life, or it has been for the last few months. I think maybe we're both getting bored. Itchy feet.

"Didn't think you'd have a choice," Burst Lip says. "Four on one."

"Unlucky for you." I pop him, a short, fast jab across the point of the chin and he sags like an empty wineskin. I turn to leave, then pause. A quick search of the four turns up phones, about six hundred bucks in cash, and two 9mm automatics. Seems like poetic justice to me. I leave their cell phones, too much trouble to get rid of these days. Leave the guns too, who knows the history of those irons. Then I see a nice signet ring on Burst Lip's index finger. Thick and heavy, got to be a fair amount of gold in that. It has a black stone on top, maybe onyx, with a strange symbol carved into it. Whatever, the gold alone is probably worth more than the cash I took. His ring goes into my jeans pocket, the guns go into a dumpster, and I add the cash to Bridget's winnings to put in the safe for later. We've got a good amount put away. Maybe it's time we started thinking about a holiday.

Six months, she told me, to get cashed up. Then take a break and live large for a while. When the money starts running out, find a new casino and start over. Maybe Monaco, she said. Sounds pretty sweet. It's only been three months and we're already loaded. I can't see us hanging out here another three. But right now, as long as I get to hang out with her, I'm happy. The money is good, the lifestyle is enviable, and the sex is out of this world. And she's smart and funny and sassy. For the first time, the pain of the wound Caitlyn and Scotty left in me is a little bit dulled. It'll never go away, but with Bridget around it's easier to live with.

Given my life up until now, I guess I don't really deserve it, but I've been through a lot of shit. I'll take the win, for as long as it lasts. Nothing lasts forever, after all. But this? With Bridget? Feels like it might.

"Why the hell you tell him about the fucker what snuck up behind?" Dwight says.

"Yeah, why?" Alvin Crake says, bullet hole glistening in his forehead. So, there he is.

Of course, no matter how well things might be going, there're always these assholes. I turn off the main street, foot traffic thins considerably, and the five of them are walking with me like we're some kind of gang.

"Habit, I guess," Michael says.

"Would have been perfect if some fucking losers killed him in a dirty alley," Sly says, blowing out a cloud of bluish smoke. "He deserves an ignominious end."

"An igno what now?" Dwight says. "Speak fucking English."

Sly laughs, even I can't help cracking a smile at Dwight's racist ignorance. Then again, to be as hatefully racist as Dwight, you have to be dumb as a brick.

"Why *did* you save him?" Graney asks Michael. "It's been so quiet for so long, this was the first chance we've had in ages to let him get hurt."

It's true. Since we left New York, I've barely had a raised word with anyone. Come to think of it, just now is the first fight I've had since the gun battle at the Vesuvius Lounge in Newark. It's been the longest peaceful period of my life that I recall. Funny I hadn't even noticed. Even these ghosts have been more distant in that time, only showing up now and then to harass me for the sport of it.

"What do you think happens when he does?" Michael asks.

Graney frowns. "Does what?"

"Gets hurt. Or even dies. What then?"

I turn into our building, trot upstairs to the third floor and unlock the apartment. The ghosts are already inside, time and space seem a little more flexible to them than the living. They sit around the front room, staring at each other. Part of me knows what Michael's getting at. It's something I've thought about over the last few months. Seems tonight's fight has stirred it up in Michael too. Of course, what I think and what they think is the same, isn't it? Or not? That's something else I've been ruminating on since New York. I still can't be sure all our minds aren't just my mind, still fractured from grief and stress. But I doubt it more by the day. Now I'm inside, I chance talking to them.

"Papa Night, huh?"

They turn to stare at me. Michael nods. "It's something to consider," he says.

Duck.

How did I know to duck back there? Did I sense the guy sneaking up behind me and act on instinct, then just rationalize it by making it Michael's instruction? Recently I've done everything I can to ignore them. Even in New York I tried to disregard them throughout that whole debacle, tried to be just my living self. But they're still here. I'm not in any danger, I feel okay, but here they are.

"Don't talk about that fucker," Sly says. "He is bad news."

"Papa Night knew we were here," Michael says.

They all look uncomfortable. Honestly, I'm enjoying this. I can't help but agree with Michael. "He did. You shitheels should think about that."

They all turn to me. "Why?" Alvin Crake asks, his bullet hole leaking blood along his nose. "What do we care?"

"You're his friend," Officer Graney says, flapping a hand at Michael. "You don't think straight around him."

Michael's eyebrows rise and he turns his head to display the ruined mess where my bullet exited. "We were friends, but this changed things."

"Fuck you!" I say. "What would you have done? You crossed Vern, you were going to die one way or another. Either I did it and lived, or I refused and died as well. You were already dead, man. I was saving my own life. You shouldn't have double-crossed Vern."

Michael sighs and nods. "That is true. But let's at least say I'm conflicted about how I feel."

I've done my best not to think too hard about New York or anything else in the time we've been in Vegas. In my experience, dwelling on the past is usually fraught with side effects. But I need to readdress that for a minute. I head into the bathroom, find some hydrogen peroxide to clean out these split knuckles, hissing at the sharp sting of it. Of course, that's nothing to what Burst Lip Asshole will be feeling right now. My hand is swollen and bruised too, but flexing my fingers it feels like nothing is broken this time. Lucky.

Something lingers with you, hmmm? Perhaps I can help?

That's what Papa Night said to me right before we left. I wanted nothing to do with him and still don't, but help how? He knew my haunts were here. If these fuckers really are ghosts, could I exorcise them? I've done my damnedest to ignore a lot of weird shit, but if I'm honest, there's been a fair amount of less than natural stuff happening around me lately. Is it such a leap to think maybe I could find the right kind of person to get rid of these hateful fuckers? I mean, a sane person would suggest a good psychiatrist, though no brain doctor is getting the dirty on my life. That would be problematic to say the least. But maybe it's not a brain issue.

I head back into the front room, sticking a couple of Band-Aids over the worst of my torn-up knuckles, and realize they're all staring at me. They do usually know my thoughts, after all. "Scared, motherfuckers?" I ask.

Michael nods slowly, then turns his head to look meaningfully at each of the others. "What then?" he asks. "Where do you think we'd go?"

They're all really uncomfortable now. Where *would* they go? They were all nasty people in their lives, even the damn cop. Cops are usually the worst of all in my experience.

I let them stew on it while I put the money in the safe, keeping a few hundred aside for pocket cash. I've arranged to meet Bridget outside the Bellagio at 11:00 p.m., which is only just over an hour away. An hour to have a couple of beers somewhere. I feel like being among people. Living people.

"I'll leave you fuckwits to your committee meeting," I say as I leave. "Enjoy your existential crisis."

Chapter 41

While Vegas has been excellent for income, I have to admit that I kinda hate the place. It's a living monument to greed and the worst of humanity. Shoulder to shoulder are people with more money than they could possibly spend and people who've just gambled away their last buck, their house, their future. And the glitz and lights and noise and cars. It's like excess is a god and he's vomited here in the desert. The place appals me. Maybe that's part of the reason I have itchy feet. I need to talk to Bridget about leaving.

Leaving America for Monaco, or anywhere else really, is appealing right now for so many reasons. This country is going down the shithole fast. I don't know if anywhere else will be better, but I'd like to find out. Given how I feel about this town, I've found a few places here and there that are kinder on the eye and the ear. One is The Dali Room. It's only a few minutes' walk from our apartment, and ten minutes or so in a cab to go and meet Bridget later. It's a hole-in-the-wall place, with herringbone tiled floors and a wooden bar. It's dim inside and on a weeknight it's pretty calm.

I choose a stool at the bar and order a beer. I've only had one sip when Michael on the stool next to me says, "Heads up."

The rest of my ghosts are all loitering around behind the bar, but the bartender doesn't know that. He's idly staring at nothing. I glance sidelong at Michael, one eyebrow raised, and he nods back toward the door. Three men have entered. Two are gorillas, the kind of goon who's mostly muscle with a walnut for a brain. Lackeys. Mooks who follow orders. But the one in the middle is different. Small, wiry, with slicked-back black hair and a black goatee oiled to a point. His skin is a deep tan, but his eyes are piercing blue, standing out against his dark, neat suit. He slowly pans his gaze across the small bar like he's looking for someone, and as his eyes fall on me, I feel a deep stab of burning pain at my hip. A slight involuntary flinch makes me shift on the stool and the goatee asshole points one long finger at me.

What the hell hurt me? I'll have to think about that later, as those two gorillas are heading right over. I've beaten bigger and meaner dudes before, but two of them in this cramped space is a challenge. And two fights in one night after such a long spell of peace seems unfair. Then again, life is anything but fair.

I slide off the stool, keeping it between me and them. If they get too close, the first of them will be wearing it for a hat. But they stop about six feet away, standing far enough apart that I'd have trouble getting past them if I made a run for it, but not so far apart that I could easily slip between them. I'm not the kind of guy who runs, anyway.

Goatee smiles, anything but friendly, and wanders up. "What's your name?"

I frown and shake my head. "Not in the mood for company tonight. Fuck off."

His smile widens. "A tough guy? I'm Jose Santiago. I think we need to talk."

"We really don't, buddy."

"Careful, Eli," Michael says. "There's something weird about this guy."

"Yeah, he feels a little like that Papa Night fucker," Graney says.

"Watch yourself," Sly says.

The fuck are they all so concerned about all of a sudden? They always used to whoop and holler whenever I was in danger, excited to see me hurt. I've made a hobby of disappointing them. There has been a fundamental shift in their attitude here and I'm not sure I like it much. But right now, Jose Santiago is a more pressing concern.

He leans forward. "Yes. We do. This can be easy or hard. You have something that doesn't belong to you and I want it back. Give it to me and this is all finished."

"I don't have anything of yours, asshole."

The gorillas bristle, itching for a fight. Santiago raises one hand to stay them a moment. "Not mine," he says. "But not yours. That's the point."

"The ring," Michael says.

What fucking ring? Then I remember the stab of burning pain at my hip. The heavy gold and onyx signet ring I took off Burst Lip Asshole and stuffed into my pocket. I forgot all about it.

Santiago's smile widens again. "I see your brain has caught up with our conversation." He holds out one hand, palm up. His fingers are long and slim and impeccably manicured. That alone pisses me off. "Let me have it and we need never see each other again."

Now fancy hands or not, I don't like this guy. Some people are the human equivalent of a bad smell. No matter where the smell is from, you just don't like it. Take those fucking lilies they always have at funerals. Symbolic of the soul of the departed or some shit. They have such a strong perfume, and they're flowers, supposed to be beautiful. But I fucking hate them. Whether it's because I associate the smell with death or something, I don't know. The fact is, they may be a beautiful and calming flower, but I hate how they look, how they smell. Hell, I hate that they exist. And now and then we come across people like that. I hate that Santiago exists. For whatever reason, it doesn't matter. So, there's no way I'm giving him anything he wants.

I'm also a curious person. It gets me in trouble, because someone who goes through life never asking questions is usually happier. You ever notice how the happiest people are the most fucking stupid? If a person is smart enough to ask questions, they rarely get good enough answers, and that leads to discontent. It takes a real idiot to be happy all the time. Regardless, I have questions. Who the fuck is this smell of a person? How did he find me? How does he know I have the ring? Why did the thing burn me? *How* did it burn me? Why is he so desperate to get it back? Because he may be trying to act calm, but I can see the concern in his eyes.

See, that's a lot of questions. And the search for answers will only bring me unhappiness. But what can I say? I'm a man at the mercy of his nature.

"Eli!" Michael says in alarm, at the exact same moment as both Officer Graney and Sly Barclay say, "Oh shit."

But already the barstool is in my hand sweeping upwards. One leg of it cracks Santiago right in his oily beard and he yelps and staggers backwards. Then I have two hands gripping the seat and I stab the feet of it at the gorilla on the left. His hands are coming up, but too slow. Two out of four blunt points of wood drive hard into him. One in the eye, one in the throat. He makes an interesting noise as blood floods over his cheek, but I don't have time to enjoy it. Santiago is down on his side, groaning, but the other gorilla has had time to get moving.

I sweep the barstool hard to my right, but he has both hands up and the wood smashes to pieces across his meaty forearms.

"Hey, what the fuck?" the bartender yells, but I don't have time to converse.

Using the moment I bought with the barstool, I skip to my right, trying to get alongside the big fucker. Now the thing about big people is they carry a lot of weight, but their knees are just the same as yours and mine. Sure, if they're smart enough to not skip leg day their muscles are strong, but all joints have weak points. A big, heavy dude's knees especially. As the gorilla draws back a fist to clobber me, I lift my foot and stamp down hard on the side of his knee with my heel. There's a snap like a gunshot, probably his ACL or meniscus separating, or both, and he squeals like a pig as his leg folds up underneath him.

To his credit he still delivers the punch, but he's already dropping and I turn to catch it on the shoulder. His fist is like rock and my left arm goes instantly numb and weak. Thankfully, I have another one. Pivoting on the ball of my foot I bring a sweeping punch around right into his cheekbone. The impact is satisfyingly solid, but the repeat pain through my already bruised and torn-up knuckles less so. Not to worry, he grunts and goes floppy, tries to put his hands down, but manages to miss the floor and face-plants.

I'm already running, the bartender still yelling behind me, several people screaming or shouting encouragement. It's funny how different people respond to violence. The night is cool and fresh and I run to the corner and turn down the next street. Fortune smiles and there's a cab cruising toward me, light on. A wave and he stops. I jump in.

"Bellagio, thanks."

"You got it." The driver has a huge smile in a dark face. "Having a good night?" he asks.

As we drive back past the Dali Room, I see Santiago leaning on the door of the bar, one hand pressed to his chin, looking furious. "Actually, yeah," I tell the driver. "I'm having the best night in a long while."

"You're gonna regret that soon, I reckon," Alvin Crake says, twisting around from the front seat.

I flip him the bird and settle back, trying to ignore Michael, Sly, Dwight, and Graney all crowded into the back with me.

Chapter 42

I need time and space to think about everything that's happened tonight, but first I have to put this ring somewhere safe. Literally a safe is probably my best option, but that Santiago fucker managed to track me down somehow, so the one in our apartment is maybe not a good idea. How did he find me? Was it something mundane like CCTV? Seems unlikely. It feels like he was able to find the ring itself. And the way it burned me when he arrived... Not good. I have somewhere else nearby in mind.

I ask the cab driver to stop on Las Vegas Boulevard a little before the Bellagio. I tip him an extra five bucks and wish him a good night. As I get out of the cab, Sly says, "Silver."

Making sure no one is close enough to hear me talking to myself, I say, "What?"

"Put it in silver, man. He won't be able to trace it that way."

"How do you know that?"

Sly shrugs, lighting a fresh joint. Blood drips from his gaping chest wound but never reaches the sidewalk. "Just do. Seems I know a few things now I wasn't privy to in the land of the living."

"He's right," Michael says. "Silver should work."

"Gift shop over there." Graney points. "Find something there, maybe."

"Why are you assholes so helpful all of a sudden?"

"Yeah, what the fuck?" Dwight says, looking with a confused expression at his cohorts. "Fuck cocheese here, I wanna see him kilt!"

Michael shakes his head. "Trust you to be too stupid to get it."

"Hey, fuck you too!"

Michael ignores him, turns back to me. "Seriously, for now just make sure that Santiago weirdo can't follow you anymore. If you put that thing inside silver, it'll block him. Like lead with Superman's X-ray vision, yeah? There's a reason for all those legends about silver bullets and werewolves and vampires and shit. Silver disrupts certain energies. Trust us, okay?"

I find a small solid silver pill box in the gift shop. Not cheap, but I feel like there's little choice right now. Outside, I drop the ring inside and take a photo of it with my phone before I close the lid. I think I'm going to need to study the weird symbol carved into the black stone. My gaggle of ghosts are all visibly relieved the moment it's sealed away. Except Dwight. He still has no idea what's going on. I guess that's been a lifelong condition for him.

Then I call Stanley. He runs a little boutique café not far from Planet Hollywood and lives right there in the back. He can't afford another rent, understandably. We became friendly a couple of months ago when we got drunk together at Beer Park. I was waiting for Bridget, he was lamenting the wife who ran out on him with a dealer from Circus Circus Casino. "She ran away to the fucking circus, can you believe the irony?" he said to me through a haze of good single malt scotch. I know a little something about losing the love of your life, and I was feeling friendly, so I hung with him.

Stanley is a good guy, strangely out of place in the glitz of Vegas. Somewhere in his mid-forties, but he looks over fifty already. Plenty of hair, but all of it white, he's short, friendly, going a little soft around the middle. We've become buddies of a kind, and I eat at his place a lot now, we go out drinking sometimes. I think he'll do me a favor.

"You jonesing for a drink?" he says by way of answering the phone.

"Why, are you?"

He laughs. "Not gonna lie, I'm way ahead of you." His voice is a little slurred. "But I'm drinking at home and about ready to drop. Another time?"

"Actually, I just wanted to ask a favor. You got a good safe in your place?"

"Of course, why?"

"Can I leave something with you for a while?"

When he lets me in his eyes are red and wet, his shoulders hanging low like a suit jacket on a too-small clothes hanger. Sadness washes off him in waves. "This gonna get me in trouble?"

I smile. "Nah, it's nothing illegal. Just a secret from Bridget, so I can't keep it in our safe." The lie comes easily to me and I hope I'm right. If these haunts are right about the silver, Stan has nothing to worry about.

We go through the café, stools upended on tables, a smell of pine-fresh bleach in the air, and there's a small office before the main rooms he uses as an apartment. The safe is under the desk and he opens it up, I tuck the silver case.

"Pretty," Stan says. "Some kinda anniversary?"

"Not really. Just a surprise."

"I remember when I used to do shit like that for Keri. Just random acts of love and kindness, you know? I wonder why I bothered." He glances up at me, sways slightly. "Sorry, man. I hope it's different for you. But you never know, you know? Shit changes in an instant. I was happy until she said she was leaving me. Apparently she'd been unhappy for a long time. How did I not know?"

I see he's reached the melancholy stage of drunkenness. "Some things just aren't meant to work out, I guess." It's a lame thing to say, but what else is there? Suggest he wasn't good enough for her? I don't know their story.

"Have a drink with me, eh?" He heads through into his apartment.

He's doing me a favor, so I don't feel like I can just walk out, even though I want to. I follow him, sit on a sofa while he slumps in a well-worn armchair. Some game show is playing on the TV, the sound muted. He pours me a bourbon, pours himself another twice the size.

"To women, while we have the pleasure of their company," he says, raising his glass.

"I'll drink to that."

I stay for as long as I feel is polite, but only have the one drink. He's nodding in the armchair anyway, eyes hooded, and I excuse myself. I wish I could make his life better somehow, but maybe he just has to grieve for a while. I understand that.

I stroll back down the Boulevard toward the Bellagio. I feel lighter and realize I've had the sensation of someone watching me all night and now it's gone.

The fingers of my left arm are tingling, my shoulder still throbbing where that gorilla's punch landed, and my right hand aches like a son of a bitch. My knuckles have bled through the Band-Aids a little, but otherwise I'm in pretty good shape for someone who's had two street fights in one night. And honestly, I'm a little elated by it all. Plus, I feel like I have something to do. It's been great to hang out with Bridget, enjoy her ability to rake in the cash, plan for a future of beaches and high living. But I've been so damn passive throughout, I didn't realize how much I was missing a purpose. Being the boyfriend and bodyguard is good, but not entirely fulfilling on a personal level. Now I have my own focus, and I also feel like I shouldn't bring Bridget into it too much.

"Hiding things from the wife is the first sign of the end," Graney says with a wolfish cackle.

"Yeah, man," Alvin says. "You'll kill her passion in an instant if you start lying."

I ignore them. Like Alvin fucking Crake is any kind of relationship counselor. I need a long conversation with these assholes. Figure out this attitude change in them. Seems that existential crisis they had was more powerful than I thought. I also need to find someone like Papa Night, as I have some ideas circling, like sharks in dark water, ready to surge up and start taking bites. I don't think about it too hard, because I don't want the peanut gallery to think too hard on it either.

Bridget slings her arms around my neck and pulls herself up for a long kiss the moment she sees me. This woman fires me up inside, she's so beautiful and confident and downright amazing.

"Good night?" I ask.

She grins and hefts her bag. "Remember what you banked for me earlier? Twice as much again here. It's been a *very* good night. Let's take this home and celebrate."

I get butterflies immediately and ignore the groans and slurs from my ghosts. They hate it when I get laid, knowing they'll never enjoy anything like it again. They all make themselves scarce when it happens too, thankfully. I'd half-expect them to hang around and be the worst kind of voyeurs, but maybe it's too much for them.

"What happened here?" Bridget picks up my hand, looking at the Band-Aids.

I don't want to lie to her, but I do plan to omit a lot of what went down tonight. Once I have a better idea of what's happening, I'll tell her all about it. I ignore the scoffing ghosts around us and say, "Couple of idiots saw me leave with the cash earlier and jumped me."

"Eli!" Her face is shocked.

"Hey, it's fine, really. We had a dust-up, but they came off worse and the money is safe at home." I realize I still hadn't started carrying a gun again yet, and maybe I should.

She nods, but she's not happy. "I'm glad to hear that. But you need to be more careful. It's not like you to be seen. Followed."

A feel a flush of shame at that. She's right. I've been getting complacent these last few weeks. "It was a wake-up call, yeah. I'll pay more attention. But it's all good, I promise. Nothing to spoil our night."

She smiles crookedly. "Well let's get home and I'll kiss it better. Anywhere else get hurt?"

"I can think of a couple of places that might need kissing, yeah."

Chapter 43

Bridget sleeps deeply after sex, every time. I don't want to blow my own trumpet too much, but I feel like she gets exactly what she needs from me, and I'm happy with that. But I can't sleep. Even after all this time out of the life, I'm often on edge at night.

I'm sitting in the gloom of our living room, nothing but the dim glow of streetlights outside and the light of my phone as I look at the photo I took of the ring. The heavy gold weight of it is one thing, but that stone gets to me. When I got undressed earlier... Well, when Bridget undressed me, I saw a red mark on my hip where it had sat in my pocket when Santiago walked in. Thankfully Bridget didn't seem to notice, her eyes were elsewhere, so I didn't have to field any more questions, but it wasn't just a random sensation. The ring actually burned me. It's still tender to the touch.

"Santiago activated it." Sly is sitting opposite me on the couch, his internal organs glittering in the low light. I realize Graney is next to him, Michael leaning against the kitchen doorframe, Alvin in the other armchair, and Dwight is standing with his back to me, staring out the window, the lights of suburban Las Vegas a dim orange glow.

"Activated?"

Sly nods. "Bad shit, man. Leave it alone."

"You should listen," Graney says. "We told you Papa Night was bad news and look what happened there."

I flex my aching hand, stiffening up from the bruising, and stare at the symbol in the photo. The black stone is engraved with a kind of spiral, bisected by two converging lines. It's fine and beautiful work, at the same time intriguing and disquieting.

"You lot were crowing about the trouble I was in there. You're always disappointed when I survive. What's changed?"

They clam up, if anything they look a little contrite. I remember what Michael said earlier. *What then? Where do you think we'd go?*

"You really are all having some kind of existential crisis, huh?"

"Just leave this ring shit alone," Alvin Crake says. "Get on with your life. You got it good now, fuck ya."

"And you all hate that. But suddenly you don't want me dead anymore."

"I'd love to see you die, cocheese. It would be worth it, you ask me."

"Only because you're too stupid to consider the consequences," Sly says.

"Fuck you!" Dwight spits a bunch a racist expletives and dives over the couch, wrestling Sly to the ground. They trade punches, Sly's joint bursting in a cloud of sparks and smoke under Dwight's knuckles.

I ignore them, turn to Michael. "What did he mean, when he said Santiago activated the ring?"

"We feel energies where we are," Michael says. "Hard to explain, but it's like ripples in water, or wind pushing away smoke. There's shift and movement around us all the time, and when someone living manipulates something...supernatural, I guess, we see the eddies and ripples. We saw it when Santiago walked in and then the ring burned you. Seems some people have genuine supernatural powers."

"Like Papa Night?"

"Yeah."

This is too much to think about, but I have to follow it through. "You said 'where we are'. Where are you?"

"No idea."

"And that's what's got you scared?"

"I guess."

"I don't think scared is the right word," Graney says. "It has us confused."

"I'm fucking scared," Sly says. His eye is swollen shut and his lip is bleeding, but Dwight is nowhere to be seen. Sly grins. "I kick his ass every time, but he will not learn."

"You're not always around me," I say. "Where do you go then?"

They shrug, look around at each other.

"I guess it's kinda like being asleep," Michael says. "You're like this beacon in a foggy night, so we find you easy. The rest of the time we're in the fog, but I never really notice. Time is... Well, there isn't really time here."

"For nearly two years I was hiding out in Canada, things were pretty quiet, I hardly saw you. Now and then you'd crop up and go away again."

"Two years?" Michael shakes his head. "Might as well have been last week."

I think about it for a while. *What then? Where do you think we'd go?*

"So now you've been spooked by Papa Night, and the things that happened then, and you're thinking maybe if something happens to me, you won't be lingering around in the fog anymore. You'll end up somewhere else."

"Maybe."

"And you think it won't be such a nice place?" I can't help but grin.

"Fuck you, man," Graney says. "You think you'll go anywhere better?"

"I don't know. But I'm not dead yet. I'm trying to atone for my sins. Besides, I don't even know if I believe any of that Heaven and Hell shit. Maybe your brain just switches off and that's it. No one has any memory of before they were born, so why would it be any different after you're dead?"

"You just end and that's it?" Alvin asks. "Fuck, what's the damn point in that?"

I frown at him. "Why does there have to be a point?"

"Regardless," Michael says. "We've decided that maybe you should enjoy life a while and we'll all just get along."

"Fuck getting along," Alvin says.

"Yeah," Graney agrees. "I don't know about getting along. But just don't die yet. I hate you, but you should probably stay alive for now. While we think about this some more."

I can't help laughing. "I have never met a more conflicted bunch of idiots. You think you'll be able to do something about your situation? Plan a new ghostly future?"

"Screw you, man," Sly says.

"Help me then. Help me figure this out." I hold up my phone, the photo of the signet ring.

"Fuck you," Alvin says.

"Yeah," Graney agrees.

Michael shrugs, Sly lights another joint. Where the hell does he get them? Dwight is back, battered and bleeding, subdued in the corner. Graney scowls.

"What a waste of time you all are," I say. I'm starting to feel tired after all.

As I get up to head for the bathroom, Bridget appears at the bedroom door. "You talking to someone?" She's blurry with sleep.

I wave my phone, then drop it in my pocket. "Just Stanley. Drunk and melancholy again."

"Huh." She nods, eyes still mostly closed, and goes back to bed.

Chapter 44

"This is bullshit, man!" Alvin's face bears the same combination of disdain and fear as the rest of them.

"Yeah, don't mess with this stuff, man." Sly isn't smoking a joint, so he's really distracted as he stands half-visible in the bright morning sun.

I glance at Michael and he shrugs, his face resigned. Can ghosts get depressed? Just my luck to be haunted by ghosts with mental health issues. Then again, I still think maybe these assholes are *my* mental health issues. And in this day and age, it's hard to imagine anyone without some form of brain trauma.

Madame Yennifer, she sounds like a try-hard. Fortunes Read, Lost Loved Ones Contacted the sign says. Her small shop is all diaphanous drapery and soft music, and the cloying stink of incense burning as I walk in. A few shelves of trinkets—crystal balls, dream catchers, angel figurines. It's awful. Reminds me of the front of Papa Night's place, but th at *was* a front, to hide stuff far more sinister. This? I think it's all front.

"You are troubled."

Ugh. Her voice is like wind chimes. She moves like she's made of smoke. Kinda hot though, I expected an old woman, but she's barely thirty. She lifts aside the curtain she appeared through.

"Shall we?"

"You should just fuck this phony, cocheese. That's the only way you'll get anything out of her."

Graney chuckles as he walks beside me. "You're a dipshit, Carver. How did you not end up in jail before you were out of your teens?"

They're all suddenly relaxed and jovial again. "No ripples in the fog?" I ask Michael.

He's already in her chamber, the other side of a round table with a black velvet cloth over it. He shakes his head. "There's nothing for you here."

"Sorry, what did you say?" Yennifer's brow is creased.

"Just talking to myself."

She sits and gestures for me to sit opposite. When I take a seat, she places her hands on the table, fingers interlaced, and smiles softly. "What do you need?"

"A genuine medium would be a start."

The crease between her eyebrows flickers ever so briefly, but the smile stays. "I can help, if you'll allow it." She slips her palms over a crystal ball on a stand in the center of the table. "A reading, perhaps? Know your future? Or your past."

"She can tell the past!" Graney says with a bark of laughter. "Man, she *is* good."

The others laugh, even Michael.

"You see the dead around me?" I ask.

The smile slips away. "You suffer from grief?" she asks.

"Nah, I suffer from fucking ghosts. They tail me like tattered flags in my wake. You tell me if you see them and I'll know if you're genuine or not."

She sits back, lips pursed, eyes narrowed. Then she takes a deep breath and slips into an act. Her eyes close, she nods slightly, turns her face a little left, a little right. "I see a...a woman. And a child."

My heart stutters just slightly.

"Lucky guess," Alvin says. "Ask her to describe them."

"The woman is elderly, but kind."

"There you go, she's blown it already," Sly says. "She's a fake, man."

"Tell her to blow you, cocheese!"

"Michael, come here, please," I say.

Yennifer pops her eyes open, looks around. Michael is wearing a crooked smile, he's enjoying himself for once. He stands at my shoulder. I gesture up at him. "Describe this dead fucker right here."

Yennifer looks from me to the empty space beside me and back again. "I don't... I'm not sure we can really work together, Mr. Carver. Perhaps you should go."

Michael glances at me and there's something serious as hell in his eyes. He leans forward, puts his fingers against the crystal ball, and for a moment his concentration is intense, his face twisted like he's in pain. The other ghosts start yelling at him to stop, then Michael yelps as if he's been burned and the ball tips off the stand with a *thunk* and rolls into Yennifer's lap.

"You fucking idiot!" Alvin shouts.

Yennifer screams and leaps up, the ball dropping heavily to the floor as she backs away from it like it's alive. The other ghosts are furious. Except Michael. He's smiling a little, but looking at me with one eyebrow raised.

"His doubt was all we had!" Graney yells, blood spraying from his ruined throat. The low light glints off his police badge.

"You're really real," I say, almost a whisper. My heart is racing.

"Who do you think saved you at Vern's place with that wheelbarrow?"

"I thought maybe a cat, a bit of luck..."

"You denied it then, you denied it so hard throughout the whole thing in New York. No more."

"You are fucking crazy, man," Sly says, fading out.

"But if you lot won't help me, what difference does it make?" I ask Michael.

"Who are you talking to?" Yennifer wails, her voice high and panicked. She's looking all around the small room like she's about to be attacked. "Get out! Get out get out get out!"

The ghosts all vanish, their angry voices fading, so I turn to leave. Then turn back. Her hands come up like she needs to defend herself.

"Chill out, okay? I'm not going to hurt you, and I will leave. I just want to ask you one thing." My head is spinning, too much in flux right now, but I have this one thing to focus on. I pull up the photo of the ring on my phone, zoom in to the stone and the carved symbol. "This mean anything to you? You ever seen it before?"

She's trembling all over as she leans in for a look. "No. No idea. Now, please leave."

When I step out into the bright day, there's a guy on a bench across the sidewalk staring at me. He looks homeless, raggedy layers of clothing, gray stubble on his chin, wisps of gray hair curling out from under a wool cap full of holes. He raises a bottle in a brown paper bag in a kind of toast, smiles at me. What few teeth he has are yellow.

I return the smile, nod. No harm in being friendly, it might not be his fault he fell on hard times. Everyone has a story and some of them are tragic. Talking of tragic, my ghosts are nowhere to be seen.

The homeless guy tips his head to one side, eyes narrowed. "She didn't fool you, huh?" His voice is gravelly, thick with drink, probably smokes, though he isn't smoking now.

I jab a thumb back over my shoulder. "Madame Yennifer? She's a crook."

"I like to sit here and watch people come outta there. Some are cryin', you know, bawlin' their eyes out like they just met their dead gramma or something. Some look scared. I allas wunnered if she had the goods."

"Nah. She's got nothing."

"How do you know that? Yanno, for sure?"

"Inside information."

He cackles a wheezy laugh. "Have a good day, yeah?"

"Yeah, man. You too." I start to turn away, then stop. "You need a few bucks? Something to eat?"

"Fuck yeah."

I dig in my pocket and find a twenty, hand it over.

He takes it with a strangely gentle touch, then smiles softly. "Thank ya. Really."

"You're welcome."

As I start to walk away, he calls out. "There's another, across town."

"Another what?"

He waves a grubby hand at Madame Yennifer's place. "Another one a'these folks. Luxana, she goes by." He tells me an address I never heard of.

"How far is that?"

"Dozen blocks maybe."

"You think this Luxana is the real deal?"

He laughs. "You know that shit, man, not me. But I sometimes sit outside her place too."

"Thanks. I'll check her out." I wish my heart would settle. Feels like my world has tilted a little off-axis. They're real. They're really real.

He nods, gestures with the twenty by way of thanks, then sits back to drink from his bottle.

Chapter 45

As I'm heading down the street, I get a text from Bridget.

> Lunch?

It's early for that, so I guess she's had a good morning at the tables. I text back,

> Across town right now, running an errand. Rain check?

> What errand? What are you up to?

> Secret biz. You okay to skip lunch?

> Maybe I'll find a high roller, take him out.

> As long as you fleece him and don't fuck him.

She texts back a smiley face and I send a love heart. It's all so easy with Bridget, no pretense, no jealousy or suspicion. I feel bad for not telling her more about what's happening, but I'm honestly not sure how much she would take. The last thing I want to do is scare her away.

As I stride the blocks toward this Luxana's place, I make a decision. When I see her later, I'll show her the photo of the ring and explain all that happened there. See how much she believes. And then I'm coming clean too about the errand I'm on, because really, that's what I want. More info about this symbol, this group, the weird sensation I got from the ring in my pocket when that asshole found me. *How* that asshole found me. I know I'm doing all I can to not think too hard on the peanut gallery and what Michael did back there.

"Black limo on your left, don't look."

Talk of the dead, there he is, walking beside me.

"What about it?" I ask.

Michael sniffs, I see sunlight glint off the blood as it drops from his ruined head. "Been tailing you for about two blocks now."

"Where's the rest of the gang?"

Michael shrugs. "Around. They're mad at me."

"I saw that. Why did you do it?"

"No more pussyfooting around."

"That's not all though, right? You guys are scared."

"Maybe. Look out."

People like me, we exist like cats. It's ingrained. They say a cat never enters a room until it knows all the exits and dead ends. That's why they always pause in doorways. Fuck knows if that's true, but it tracks. You stay alive in a world like mine by thinking the same way. And these guys know it. The limo slides to a quick halt at the curb right in front of me and I know already I'm mid-block. There was a side street about fifty paces back, an alley another fifty paces ahead, and the next side street beyond that. Right now there's nothing but the road on my left and a solid wall with windows on my right. The doorway into the building is on the other side of the goons who pile out of the car.

"Three behind," Michael says. "Didn't see that car following too, but must have been."

I don't need to look to picture the second car, pulled up to the curb between me and that first side street. Well played, assholes. Classic pincer. How did they find me again?

Worry about that later. Three behind, and three from the limo. That's six. I can see the silhouette of the limo driver, sitting there ready. "The driver of the other car still in his seat?" I ask.

"No," Michael says. "That idiot is one of the three now on the sidewalk in a line."

He knows the score too, I can hear the amusement in his voice. He sees there's an out here and he knows I'm going to go for it. Just got to pick my moment. A moment of overconfidence by that driver behind me will hopefully be their undoing.

"You are a slippery customer," one of the three in front of me says and I realize it's Jose Santiago. His voice is a little clipped, talking without moving his mouth much. The goatee has been shaved off and there's a line of stitches under his chin. I did a good job with that barstool.

"Take it easy," Graney says. "I get the feeling these guys won't hesitate to murder in broad daylight."

"Thanks for your concern, cop."

He bristles, but clamps his lips. The traffic on the street is medium, but constant. A few people are walking the sidewalks, but no one within a hundred paces of us right at this moment. A young couple are on their way, though, and a lone guy talking into a cell phone right behind them.

"Group of women with shopping bags just crossing the side street behind us," Graney says.

I nod. That gives these guys maybe a minute tops before things are complicated by the arrival of Joe Public.

I gesture at my chin. "Suits you."

Santiago scowls. "Just give it to me!"

"How did you find me this time?" I'm genuinely interested, because the ring is nowhere near me. It also buys me time. They want it badly enough they won't just drop me in the street.

"I have many and varied skills, Mr. Carver."

"You found out my name too. Does that mean you have some idea of my body count? Might want to rethink hassling me." Sometimes bravado pays off, sometimes it doesn't. I can see Santiago doesn't care, but the two goons either side of him are nervous, I see it in their eyes. I'm guessing they heard about the two gorillas in the bar last night, and maybe learned some of my history from Santiago.

"Shoppers about forty feet behind the goons," Graney says.

The couple and cell phone guy are about the same distance behind Santiago.

"We know all about you and we are not scared of you, Mr. Carver. Let's make this simple. All previous transgressions forgiven if you simply give me the ring. We need never see each other again."

I don't believe that for a moment. He'll come for revenge, but the ring is clearly the first priority. And it's my leverage. His eyes flick past my shoulder then back to me. He's clocked the shoppers coming, he'll move any second.

"Just take him!" Santiago snaps, wincing as he inadvertently moves his jaw too much.

My hand is still aching from previous trauma, but I'm going to have to suck that up. Both Santiago and the three behind me think I haven't seen them, so it's time to drop a few surprises. I hope my swollen and aching hand doesn't affect my aim too much.

Moments like this, lots of stuff happens at once. Prioritizing is the key to survival. I drop and roll backwards, pulling the CZ 75 9mm from my waistband as I go. I'm not above murder in broad daylight either.

I've already made sure no cameras are looking this way. As sure I can be, anyway. I want to pop a bullet in Santiago, but he's less of a threat now, so I squeeze off one round to the heavy on his right and catch him center-chest. He drops. The other heavy is drawing as Santiago dives straight for the limo. I twist and come up running the other way, my back itching because I know that one heavy is drawing a bead on me, but there's three here. Sure enough, they all have guns in some stage of readiness. I fire three times, hoping to drop them all, but even my great shooting skills aren't up to that, not moving like I am. But I get the first right between the eyes, the second in the shoulder of his gun arm, and miss the third.

No time to worry, I drop again, straight into a forward roll this time. The screaming has started from the people on the street, some car tires screeching as people swerve or brake in a panic at the gunfire. The one heavy behind me squeezes off rapid shots, trying to track me, but I keep moving. My nerves are on fire, waiting for that punch of pain to let me know he got a hit but it doesn't come. The one left standing in front of me now is wide-eyed and open-mouthed as I come to my feet less than a foot from him and slam my gun butt up under his chin. The idiot should have abandoned shooting for brawling and he might have had me at such close quarters. More fool him.

He staggers back, dazed, and I duck around the one I shot in the shoulder. To his credit, he's grabbing for me, still trying to do his job, but that's his last mistake. I grab him instead and swing him around just as the heavy who'd been beside Santiago fires again. Except now I have a human shield. He bucks and jerks as his compatriot's bullets slam into his back and arm, then I'm dropping him and diving in through the open front passenger door of the car they arrived in. Here's my gamble. If the keys aren't in it, I'm in trouble.

I scramble across the passenger seat, cramming my long legs and large frame into the driver's seat and allow myself a smile to see not only are the keys in it, but they left it running. I slam it into gear and roar away from the curb, wincing at the screeching tires of cars trying to stop behind me.

"Damn, son," Graney says from the passenger seat. "Impressive."

Michael, Sly, Dwight and Alvin are lined up in the back seat whooping and hollering. The rear window shatters as one of the heavies gets a final shot away, and my ghosts only cheer louder.

"Acrobatic motherfucker!" Sly says, with something approaching respect.

These ghosts have truly changed their tune.

Michael nods once, gives me a soft smile.

"Once you're safely away, you might wanna look at that though," Graney says, pointing at my upper right arm.

It's soaked with blood and, as I notice it, the searing burn makes it to my brain. One of those fuckers shot me after all.

Chapter 46

After driving a few blocks and making sure the limo wasn't tailing me, I pull over to tend to the wound. It's superficial, thankfully. Burns like a son of a bitch, and bleeds a lot, but it's not too serious. It'll scab over in twenty-four hours. Someone left their jacket on the back seat, so I rip the cotton lining out of it and use that to strap up a bandage around my arm. It'll be sore for a while, but nothing to worry about as long as I keep it clean. I've suffered way worse and survived.

Now the adrenaline is settling down I feel a little nauseated, but that's normal. I'm also feeling a moment of regret. I should have shot Santiago after all. I was right in the fact that he wasn't a threat at that moment, being the only one unarmed. The way he dived for cover like the chickenshit he is proved that. But he is perhaps a bigger threat in the long run. How did he find me this time?

"Some kinda seer," Sly says from the back seat, wreathed again in joint smoke.

"Seer?"

Sly nods, passes the joint to Alvin and sits forward. "My grandma used to tell the tales, some people can scry. I don't really get it all, but perhaps he can go into a kind of trance and travel astrally, look around for you. He met you once, so he knows your aura. Like a dog with a scent, he can look for you that way. Once he gets close, they search the old-fashioned w ay."

It's the longest speech Sly has made in as long as I can remember, and it makes some kind of sense. And it only confirms my thought that I should have shot him just now when I had the chance. Still, no point in dwelling on the past. I was making decisions then to stay alive and it worked.

"So that means he can track me again any time?"

Sly shrugs, sits back.

"You have to assume so," Michael says. "But a big city this populated? Can't be too easy."

"Might have bought myself some time then."

"Maybe give up finding this Luxana bitch and deal with the problem at hand," Alvin says, passing the joint on to Graney.

The cop nods, takes a draw. Smoke curls out of his blood-soaked throat. "Yeah, he's right. Focus."

"Focus, cocheese." Dwight is strangely subdued, the usual manic demeanor suppressed.

These fuckers are truly uncomfortable. I have them on the ropes in a way and I'm reluctant to give that up. Besides, I need information. "I'm not a seer," I say. "I need to know who these bastards are and this Luxana might be my only lead. If that bothers you, maybe just fuck off. The real problem at hand is these assholes trying to kill me. And before you say, 'Just give the ring back' you know we're past that point now."

I pull the makeshift bandage tight around my arm and use the jacket to wipe down everything in the car that I touched. Then I climb out and walk away quickly along the sidewalk. I need to replace my shirt, the shoulder and arm of it are bright red with drying blood. And I need to not be so noticeable. The jacket comes in handy, so I keep it, slung casually over my shoulder to mask the injury. But it's out of place, a smart suit jacket with my jeans and T-shirt. A thrift store up ahead provides an option. It only takes a moment to find a short-sleeved button-up shirt that fits, plain black cotton, the sleeves long enough to cover my makeshift bandage. My arm throbs underneath it, but I do my best to ignore that. My bloodstained T-shirt and the mook's jacket get crammed in a garbage can on the sidewalk not far from the shop and I'm back in business. A little more urgent now though, seeing as Santiago can find me, regardless.

The drive made up a couple of extra blocks so it only takes me a few more minutes to walk to the address for Luxana the homeless guy gave me. It's a plain-looking apartment block in a residential area. As I frown up at the building, wondering if I've been led up the garden path by a drunk, the man himself strolls up to stand next to me.

"Took ya long enough."

"The fuck is this?" Dwight asks.

"More than he looks," Graney says.

No shit, collective Sherlocks. I guess I'm starting to get used to this weird stuff, because I'm not really surprised. "Had a little distraction on the way here," I tell him.

"No time for side quests, friend." He grins and gestures with the bottle. "Apartment 419, fourth floor. Tell her Elvis sent you."

"Elvis?"

"Uh huh huh." He grins and walks away.

I choose not to pursue that any further and head into the building. The doors are locked, with all the apartments and their call buttons on a panel outside. There's no name next to 419. I press the button and wait. A small lens, like a shark's eye, stares at me from above the buttons and I wonder if Luxana is using it. I'm reaching up to press the button again when a voice says, "Yes?"

"Is that Luxana?"

"Who's this?"

"My name is Eli. I need your help. Elvis sent me."

"Did he now?"

Even through the tinny speaker, her voice is low and soft, sultry in a way. I feel like she's not putting it on, like she really talks that way. Which is actually kind of weird. "Said you were the real deal."

"He's very kind. Well, I know I'm going to regret this, but come on up."

The door buzzes and clicks and I push it open, head to the elevators and press number four. When I come out of the elevator, a door halfway along the hallway is standing open, a middle-aged woman framed by it. She's quite striking to look at, sharp features, but not harsh, long brown hair held back in a loose ponytail, floral cotton dress and bare feet. She nods when she sees me and it looks almost like recognition.

"Come on in. Bring your friends with you."

I glance around and see the five fuckwits all gathered in the hallway nearby, all looking a little pensive. "This is better already, eh?"

Michael allows a half-smile, but Dwight, Alvin, Graney and Sly all grimace.

"Probably don't do this, man," Alvin says.

"Why not?"

"I don't trust her."

"Me either, cocheese. Unless you plan to simply rape her and run, there's nothing for you here."

"What the fuck is your fascination with rape, you disgusting fucking racist?" I ask him. "Seriously, you have a real problem."

"No one would ever fuck him, so it was the only action he ever got," Alvin says.

Even Graney and Sly looked appalled at that.

"Maybe no one wanted anything to do with him because he's such a fucking awful piece of shit," I suggest, and don't wait for an answer.

Inside, Luxana's apartment is small but homey. The door leads to a short hallway, bathroom on one side, bedroom on the other, then opens into a large living area with a kitchen in one corner and a big view of the city through a huge window.

"It's more than big enough for me," Luxana says, though I didn't offer an opinion. "After all, I don't ever plan to share it with anyone."

"That's a little defeatist, isn't it?" I ask. "I mean, there's always the chance—"

"I'm ace, Eli, so it's not an issue. And I enjoy solitude."

"Oh, sorry. I shouldn't presume."

"The fuck is ace?" Alvin says, twisting his features like he smelled something bad.

"It means asexual," Luxana says. "I lack any sexual attraction to other people."

It takes me a second to realize she just answered Alvin directly. She's even looking at him. With various yelps of "Fuck!" and "Holy shit!" my ghosts all blink out, but Luxana shoots a hand forward and closes her fist, like she's grabbing at the empty air.

"What the fuck, man?" Alvin is writhing on the spot, twisting left and right, looking down at his chest with an expression of pain and horror. The others have vanished.

"I assume you want me to help get rid of these bad spirits for you?" Luxana says, tightly gripping the air in front of her.

Alvin stills, gasping, terror in his eyes.

"Can you do that?" I ask.

"Of course." She makes a gesture with the other hand, says something under her breath as she closes her eyes for a moment. Then she pops her eyes open again, looking right at Alvin. A moment of concentration, of strenuous effort, passes her features.

"Wait a sec—," I start to say, but don't get it out before Alvin screams. He bursts apart like smoke hit with a sudden gust and his voice trails away into nothing. I feel a moment of emptiness in my chest, a sensation of drag, then it passes.

"He's gone," Luxana says with a smile. "I can pull the others back too, and do the same to them, but now you've seen the proof, we need to discuss payment."

"You killed him?" I ask stupidly. He's definitely gone. I don't know how I can tell, but I can. He's disappeared, forever and always. Shit, I almost miss him in a way. I guess I got used to the five of them.

"Killed him? He's been dead a long time, Eli. These spirits, they're hooked into you, tightly bound. You've carried this burden for a while, I can see that much. It's not a healthy way for you to live, especially bonds this strong. But the bonds can be broken."

Shit, he's really gone. I could be rid of them. All of them. But then other thoughts rattle through my mind.

Duck! Michael in the alley.

My grandma used to tell the tales, some people can scry. Sly telling me about seers.

Shoppers about forty feet behind the goons. Graney, helping me time my move earlier.

Michael pushing the crystal ball off its stand.

These assholes are useful. If they are real, and not just in my head, then they give me an edge. Information, extra eyes. I can use them. Especially if they know I can get rid of them, perhaps they'll be a little more cooperative. At least, the remaining four might be. Why the hell couldn't she have got rid of that racist fuck, Dwight? It's not like I'm a big fan of any of them, except Michael, I guess, but I would have picked Dwight in a hot second if she'd given me a choice. Maybe I could still have her get rid of him and just keep Michael, Sly and Graney. Then again, if I want their help, if I want some kind of accord with them, I need to be cautious. My mind is racing, spinning, this is too much.

Luxana smiles at me and it lights up her face. "Quite the dilemma, eh?"

"Yeah." I can't help but laugh. "This is a truly weird day."

"Well, I'm here if you decide to use my services. And seriously, it's not good for you in the long run to trail spirits behind you like this."

"What will happen?"

"Hard to know, there are various possibilities. Usually some form of psychosis settles in. Having said that, the ones around you are far more stable than usual."

I laugh again. "Stable? I don't know about that!"

"Not psychologically. More bonded to you, more readily apparent. You converse with them freely?"

"Pretty much."

"Hmm. Maybe you can live with them then. Your choice. But like I said, if you need me." She rubs thumb and fingers together in the universal gesture for 'Show me the money'.

"I need to pay you for the job you already did. I mean, I didn't ask for it or anything, but I guess it is a service provided."

"Consider it a free trial. I know you'll come back if you decide to...change your situation further."

"As it happens, you can help me right now, with something else. And I'll gladly pay for that." I pull out my cell phone, open up the picture of the signet ring and hand it over. "Do you recognize this?"

Luxana's body stiffens and the lightness of her smile vanishes. She hands the phone back immediately. "Why?"

"You clearly do recognize it."

"I want nothing to do with these people. Are they looking for you?"

My pause is all the information she needs.

"Get out, right now. Go far away. I'll meet you at Mario's Italian Restaurant in Spring Valley, tonight at eight. You make a reservation. Never come here again. I won't have them aware of my place." She pushes past me and hustles down the hall, opens the door.

Her urgency is clear despite the forced calm. I nod once. "Thank you."

I leave the apartment and take the stairs rather than wait for an elevator. When I reach the street, I jog away from the building, putting as much space between myself and Luxana as quickly as possible. I'm fairly confident she'll show up for the meeting, she strikes me as honorable. My thoughts are tumbling with all that's happened.

"What the actual fuck, man?" Sly is trotting alongside me.

I look to either side. There's Michael and Dwight on my left, Sly and Graney on the right. No sign of Alvin. "He's really gone, huh?" I ask.

"Jesus, dude, she ripped him to atoms," Michael says.

"Where did he go?"

"We don't know," Graney says. "But wherever it is, there's no coming back."

I laugh. "So I could do that to any of you. I could do it to all of you."

"Why the fuck couldn't she destroy this racist asshole?" Sly asks, pointing across me at Dwight. I sympathize.

They all look contrite, and more scared than ever. And angry. "Tell you what," I say. "I'll keep you all around if you agree to help me. Stop fucking with me and actually help."

I feel something passing between them, some reluctant agreement. They are pissed, but more than that they're terrified. This might not last, but right now I have them all on the ropes.

"Agreed?" I ask.

"Yeah," they all mutter.

I slow to a brisk walk and keep moving back toward the city. It feels like the start of a brand new day.

Chapter 47

I message Bridget and she agrees to meet up for a late lunch after all. The ghosts are conspicuous by their absence, no doubt licking their wounds. I can't get used to the idea that Alvin Crake is gone. The five of them have been hanging around me for a long time. And it makes me wonder again, why those five? I killed a lot of folks over the years, and more than a few would have considered their execution unjust. Maybe something to ask Luxana later. Is five the limit? Will a new one move in? You see, this is why I'm so discontented. Too many fucking questions. Another hovering around me like a bad smell is this: How long before Santiago tracks me down again? The first time he only brought two heavies, the second time he brought five. I can't help thinking he'll show up with an army next.

"You look serious."

I startle slightly, realize I was lost in my thoughts and didn't see Bridget come in. She sits opposite me in the booth and takes my hand over the table.

"You okay?" she asks.

I allow a crooked smile. "That obvious, huh?"

"What's happening?"

Man, how much do I tell her? How much will she accept? Will it drive her away? Again with all the questions. I wish I could just return the ring to Santiago and forget all about it, but he won't let it go now, not after losing so many of his men. And besides, I need to know. My curiosity puts cats to shame.

I take a deep breath, then, "Let's order some food, and then I have a lot to tell you."

Bridget keeps quiet while we order burgers and shakes, tells me about her day as we wait for them to arrive. "I'm doing great," she says. "I'll be ready to blow this place before long. Honestly, I think I have to, anyway. I'm getting noticed."

The food arrives and the waitress smiles as she puts it down, then turns away without a word.

"So, what is it?" Bridget says. "I feel like you're about to break up with me. You meet someone else?"

"Holy shit, no! I'm worried you'll quit me when I get through telling you some stuff."

"I'm sure it's not that bad, Eli."

I stare into her beautiful eyes for a moment and she looks right back, unperturbed. She's strong, confident, assured of herself. It's one of her most attractive features. And she's smart, another damned sexy trait. I guess I need to be as honest as I can.

"Okay, it's like this. Those guys I ran into the other night? I took something from one of them. A ring. No big deal. It was gold, looked valuable. I thought it might be worth something and I figured I'd earned it, you know?"

Bridget shrugs, nods, keeps chewing.

"Well, turns out the ring belongs to someone and it has some kind of... I don't know, this'll sound hokey, but it has some kind of magic about it and the people I took it from can track it."

Bridget laughs. "Magic? Computer chip, dummy."

My turn to shrug. "Maybe, but I don't think so. Anyway, the guy who came after it wasn't the guy I took it from, so there's a group at work here. I don't know any more than that."

"And you're disinclined to return the ring and be done with it?"

"I may have caused some collateral damage because they didn't ask nicely. So, I think we're past the return and forget stage."

Bridget stares at me, swallows, but doesn't take another bite. I cover my discomfort by eating some of my own lunch. "And you wanna know," Bridget says. It's not a question. "You're a little bored mooching around while I make the big bucks, you're used to a little action and mayhem, and you feel kinda like maybe you want to run up against these guys and have some fun. Am I close?"

I can't help laughing. "Pretty much a bullseye."

"Eli." She shakes her head, but a soft smile is tugging one side of her mouth. "Okay, so maybe hide the ring somewhere so they can't find you and learn a little more first."

She's good. "I did exactly that. Trouble is, they found me again even without the ring."

Her eyebrow pops up and then she frowns. "How?"

"I wish I knew."

"This is why you said magic? You really believe in that stuff?"

I swallow, mind racing. I love Bridget, I think I have to admit that. I want her around, and that means honesty. Relationships only work when there are no lies. I need to take a chance here. "Magic's not the right word. But supernatural, maybe? You believe in anything like that?"

Bridget nods. "Yeah, a little. There's a lot of bullshit out there, but there's also a lot of stuff we don't understand. It's arrogant to think we know everything. My grandma was a bit psychic, she'd get premonitions and stuff."

"Really?"

"Sure. There's this story that when my mom was a kid, maybe four years old, she was playing outside. The family had a house and garden, big fish pond at the end of a long backyard. My grandma is busy in the kitchen when she suddenly goes cold and yells, 'She's drowning!' and runs to the door. My grandfather was gardening, and Grandma comes running along yelling, 'She's drowning!' and they both start sprinting to the end of the yard, and there's my mom, drifting face down in the fish pond. She went in after a ball and slipped out of her depth. My grandfather hauled her out, managed to revive her. Another few minutes and she'd have been dead."

"Holy shit."

Bridget smiles. "Yeah. Neither of them could see her from where they were, but somehow Grandma knew. There's a bunch of stories like that about Grandma. And I'm pretty sure I saw a ghost once."

"Really?" Now I'm starting to relax. This might be easier than I thought.

"Yeah, haunted house out near Hollywood when I worked for Jerry. There was a private game there, we stayed a couple of nights. This old lady, all in white, used to walk the halls. I asked about her and the owner said she died there in eighteen hundred and something. Only a few people ever see her."

"Well, how about that?"

"So, you think there's something supernatural about this ring? Ghosts and premonitions are one thing, but what you're describing is a bit of a stretch."

I nod, chewing more burger. "Yeah, I get it. But there's something else. There's something supernatural about me."

"You?"

"Michael, you there?"

Bridget frowns at me, but stays quiet, patient.

I'm about to ask again when Michael says, "What's up?"

He's sitting right next to me in the booth, the blown-open side of his face not a foot from me, glistening with blood, dripping onto his shoulder, bone fragments stark white against the fluorescents of the diner. "That thing you did with the crystal ball?"

"Yeah?"

I gesture at the table in front of us.

Michael sighs. "You want to show her we're real now that *you* don't doubt us anymore, that it?"

"Yep."

"Who are you talking to?" Bridget says tightly. "You're freaking me out, Eli."

I smile at her. "I'm really sorry. But this is me and I love you and I need you to know."

She's a little open-mouthed at that, and maybe I shouldn't but I find it sexy as hell. Shocking her is fun. I glance at Michael, raise an eyebrow. Graney, Sly and Dwight are lined up behind the booth, looking over Bridget, scowling.

"You know, it's really hard to do this," Michael says. "And it hurts like hell when I do. I never feel anything anymore, except when I try to interact like this and that's agony." He looks up at the other three ghosts. "They can't do it at all, they say, but I don't know if they ever tried."

"Please?" I ask. "Just a little."

Bridget is seriously uncomfortable now, looking at me like I'm mad.

Michael sighs. He reaches out, his fingertips near my water glass.

I sit back, make sure my hands are far out of the way and say to Bridget, "Watch the glass."

Michael lets out a moan of pain through gritted teeth and the glass slides about six inches across the table toward Bridget. Michael fades out and Bridget gasps.

"What the fuck? Did you do that?"

"No. I have... There are a few ghosts who hang around me all the time, and one of them can do that. His name is Michael."

She stares at me, dumbfounded. Seems like she's been doing a lot of that since lunch started. She goes to speak a couple of times before she finds the words. "How long have they been with you?"

"Few years."

"And they're always there?"

"Kinda. They come and go a bit, but yeah."

"How many?"

"Four." Seems strange to say that now. No new number five yet, anyway.

"Always the same four?"

"Yep."

"Wow. Okay. Fuck me."

"Okay?"

Bridget laughs. "Well, what else is there? I mean, if they've always been around since I met you, and you're telling me now, but I haven't noticed before, then I guess not much really changes, right?"

The relief that washes through me is palpable. I don't know if this will last, but it's a better first stage than I anticipated. "I hope so. I really hope so, Bridget."

"You love me, huh?"

"That didn't slip by you then."

She smiles, super sultry. But she doesn't say it back. I can see the mischief in her eyes. I don't want her to say it if she doesn't mean it. After what I've just shown her, I don't blame her for staying a little reticent. "And why *are* you telling me now?" she asks.

"Well, mainly because I think you deserve to know. Honesty, yeah? But also because I think whatever this is I'm mixed up in, it has something unnatural about it."

"Supernatural."

"Yeah."

"Shit, Eli. Maybe we should just go. We can. I have enough. I was going to play a few more days, but we can call it early if you want."

"No, thanks. I want to learn more. I feel… I dunno, kinda compelled to see more of all this. And that's the other reason I told you about this stuff.

I found someone today who knows more. She's got crazy supernatural skills. Honestly, I was pretty shocked. And she's agreed to help me, so I'm meeting her later. The ring has a kind of symbol carved on it and she didn't like it at all, told me to get away from her place and meet her later. So that's what I'm doing at eight. Okay?"

"I guess. I have a game starting at nine, so no sweat there. She? Do I need to be concerned?"

I remember Luxana talking directly to Alvin before she wiped him out. *It means asexual. I lack any sexual attraction to other people.* And I wouldn't cheat on Bridget anyway, not for anything. "No, you definitely don't need to worry at all."

Bridget nods, eating her food and thinking. Eventually she looks up and says, "Okay, but a couple of caveats. One, you don't take unnecessary risks. Two, you get me and we run if things get too weird. Three, no more secrets, even by omission. We owe each other total transparency, yeah?"

"Yeah. Okay."

"I'll be honest, Eli, I don't like this. I want it on the record here and now that my preference is to pack up and leave. You're freaking me out more than a little."

"I get that, and I'm sorry. But even if I wanted to, I think maybe Santiago could track me anywhere now, so perhaps I *need* to see this through."

She sighs. "Damn it, Eli. Be careful, okay?"

"Always."

Chapter 48

Mario's Italian Restaurant is a nice place. Nothing fancy, but spacious, well-decorated. The smell as I walk in is fantastic. A *maître d'* meets me and asks my name.

"Corleone," I say. "Table for two, eight o'clock."

It's ten minutes to, but I wanted to be sure I was here before Luxana.

If the *maître d'* suspects my cheesy fake name, he doesn't show it. "Your table is ready. This way."

It's in the back of the wide space, a small square table up against the wall, chairs either side. A good spot. A candle burns in a glass bulb in the center, cutlery and napkins neatly laid out. The tablecloths are all deep red, the chairs dark wood, the walls an off-white. The net effect is one of soft privacy despite the open room. Good choice by Luxana. I order a drink and pretend to study the menu while I watch the door from the corner of my eye. I hope she shows. I wondered if maybe she wouldn't, but then again, if she didn't show up she can only expect me to go back to her place to find out why. Which I would do. And I know she doesn't want that. My other concern is that Santiago has been conspicuous by his absence. I feel like he might show up at any moment, and that bothers me.

Michael, Graney, Sly and Dwight are sitting around a table next to mine, lounging in the chairs, scowling at me. I raise an eyebrow at them.

"Thought we might see what this bitch had to say," Graney says.

"Not scared she'll..." I grab the air then flick my fingers open.

"Yeah, that's exactly what we're scared of, cocheese. But you made us a promise."

I suppose I did, but I won't sit here talking to myself where the other diners can see, so I just nod and smile.

"You better keep the promise, Eli," Michael says.

My turn to raise an eyebrow at him.

"Yeah, yeah, and we'll help whenever we can."

"We won't fucking like it," Graney says. "Don't expect too much or maybe we'll take our chances."

I offer a small shrug at that and they go back to scowling.

"This woman, she's way more than Papa Night," Sly says. "And you remember the crazy shit he got up to. Watch yourself with her."

I nod again and notice Luxana arrive at the door. She looks directly at me, then her eyes flick to the table with the ghosts and she frowns. There's a moment of conversation with the *maître d'* and she points at me. He smiles and walks her over. She ignores the ghosts completely, offers me a pleasant smile and sits down.

"Thanks for coming," I say. "I really appreciate it."

"Best way to keep you away from my place."

"Yeah, that's what I thought."

She casts a glance at the ghosts and then back to me. "Decided to live with them?"

"Yeah, for now. I know so much more already."

"Right. Well, in that case, you can use them."

"Okay."

A waiter comes over, so we order wine and food. I let her choose the wine, and she orders a carbonara while I pick spaghetti and meatballs.

When the waiter leaves again, she says, "Okay, ground rules. One, you pay for dinner and give me a thousand bucks flat payment, no negotiation. Can you afford that?"

"A thousand bucks? Fuck that bitch!" Dwight says.

She turns a glare to him and he blanches and pops out, just vanishes. The other three remain, but look scared.

"I think he forgot you can see us," Graney says. "Hear us."

"He has very little in this department," Sly says, tapping the side of his head with one index finger.

"I can afford it," I say, to bring us back to the important stuff.

Luxana looks back to me and nods. "Number two, after tonight, we're finished. You don't contact me again, for any reason. If you're involved with these people, I want nothing to do with you."

"I plan to get uninvolved."

"I don't think that's possible, but best of luck. I'll give you all the tools I can, but it won't be much."

"Okay."

She pours water for us both from the decanter on the table and sips from hers. Then she looks up. "You don't have that ring on you, right?"

"No. But they can still find me without it."

She nods, glances at the big windows of the restaurant. "They probably won't challenge you in here, but maybe when you leave."

"I thought the same. I'll leave first in case they're out there."

"Yes, you will."

"Who are they?"

"The Acolytes of Ur."

My brain spins for a moment as I try to process that. She lets me think. Eventually, I say, "Okay, so Ur was a Sumerian city? In Mesopotamia?" Yeah, I'm a well-read motherfucker, I know some stuff.

She smiles. "Still is a city. And yes, it was an important city-state, dates from about 3,800 BCE."

"And an acolyte assists a priest or something, right? That name doesn't really make sense."

"It does if you believe what these assholes believe. An acolyte can assist a priest in the modern sense, sure, but they can also be the hands on Earth

of a god. This group, they believe that Ur the city was founded by the
moon god Nanna. They think the moon *is* a god, or at least the corporeal
representation of the moon god for us on Earth. They believe the god
sent a piece of itself to Earth and it landed and became the city of Ur.
You've heard of the Ziggurat of Ur? They believe it's a temple built to
revere the moon good, Nanna. But all this is twisted mythology and kind
of irrelevant. The main point is that they claim to serve a moon god who
is in turn a gateway to cosmic powers beyond the ken of mortal beings
like us lowly humans. They are the acolytes of that force here."

"Acolytes of Ur," I say quietly. "I mean, I guess Acolytes of Nanna
would sound pretty lame."

Luxana laughs, and it's a high, pleasant sound. "Right? It's an unfortunate word in English, but don't let logic or anything like that get in
the way of religious beliefs." She becomes serious again. "Don't underestimate them." She gestures at my ghosts, and I notice Dwight is back,
loitering a bit farther away now. "You know these spirits are real," Luxana
says. "You saw what I did to one of them."

I nod.

"You miss him? Wish I hadn't done that?"

"He's not the one I would have picked if you'd given me a choice. But
I can get used to it."

"Good. So you know they're here and you know I'm the real deal,
so you should be open to anything I might tell you. So, listen when I
tell you this. However hokey the Acolytes of Ur might sound, they are
dangerous and genuinely powerful. They're a cabal, essentially, of some
of the most rich and powerful men and women in the country and they
do whatever they like. They get away with anything. And they do it for
power. Corruption in politics, pedophile rings, snuff movies, all that
horrible shit. They prey on people for shits and giggles. They simply
crave power. They gain favor through the moon god from the cosmic

entities beyond. It's real, it's powerful, and you should have fuck all to do with it."

"Too late for that, I think." What she just said only makes me want to hurt them more.

"Extricate yourself if you can. I suggest you return the ring somehow, and slip away. They'll be able to find the ring if you leave it somewhere accessible. Do that and leave town. Maybe leave the country, in fact. They might let you go." Her eyes narrow. "Why haven't they taken the ring back already?"

"I hid it in a silver case, tucked away safe."

"Okay, makes sense. How did you know to do that?"

I tip my head sideways at the gathered assholes, now all four sitting at the table again, watching intently. They're quiet and well-behaved, for the first time ever. I like this new compliance.

"Smart," Luxana says. "But I don't know how long that'll last. It masks well, but not forever. Not something that powerful."

I feel a moment of fear for Stanley and hope he's okay. That should be my next job. If the ring isn't really safe there, I need to get it away from him. He has enough of his own troubles. "How many are in this cabal?" I ask.

Luxana shakes her head. "I don't know. In Vegas, at least a dozen, maybe more. Across the country?" She shrugs. "Maybe hundreds. Who knows? Across the world, maybe more."

"But it's the ones here I need to worry about?"

"I guess. I have no idea how much they all talk to each other. Really, Eli, just get away from them all."

Our food arrives and we're quiet for a moment while the waiter offers us pepper and parmesan. We eat a little in silence once the waiter leaves again. The food is really good.

"I've never seen spirits as realized as yours," Luxana says suddenly.

"Really?"

"Getting rid of that one, breaking his bond, that was the hardest I've ever had to work."

"They came to me in a period of…" I run out of words. What the hell do I call the breakdown that happened after Caitlin and Scottie died?

"Must have been some extreme trauma," Luxana says. "Spirits tend to gain a hold when a person is both traumatically compromised and their mind is open to corruption. It's a fairly unique set of circumstances, and even then a person might get caught by one spirit, usually a weak bond. You had five and bonded like nothing I've ever seen before. And those four are still so strong."

"My situation was pretty unique back then." Something occurs to me. "So, I won't get any more?"

"Not likely, without a similar set of circumstances. But anything is possible in this world. These happened to be around you at the right time. I imagine you're stuck with those four alone, though. Unless you want me to—"

"Not right now, thanks. We've got an understanding." I feel like I've learned a lot, and there's some solace in understanding the situation a little better.

"In that case, you can use them to stop the cabal finding you. In the short term, at least." She glances at the ghosts. "If they agree?"

"They better," I say, looking over at them too. "That's part of our agreement."

"We'll do what we can," Michael says. The others look annoyed, but don't contradict him.

Luxana looks back to me. "Okay, so this is how it works. The Acolytes can find you because they've met you. Everyone has a kind of psychic signature, like a dog always knows another person's scent, yes?"

I nod. "Sly said something similar. Hi grandma called them seers."

"Good enough a name. A strong seer can always find another person's psychic resonance. It's a skill some people develop. It's not common, it's very hard to do, but some folks have got good at it. If they stopped being able to track you by the ring you showed me a picture of, they would start using that method instead assuming one of them had met you."

"Yeah, and I met him right back with a barstool. So that's how they found me again after I hid the ring."

"Exactly. But you can muddy the scent for them, because you have those spirits. You need to have one of them always ghosting you, always close. It won't be comfortable, I expect, but you need one of those four always pretty much on you."

"On me?"

"Yeah. Like a piggyback or something."

"Get fucked!" Dwight snaps, then blanches when Luxana looks at him.

"A piggyback?" Sly says.

Luxana grins. She's enjoying this. "You'll feel them there, but it won't really be a physical burden. I don't know how it'll feel, to be honest. But because they're dead, their psychic aura will be indistinct. And unknown to the cabal, of course. So it will kind of mess up yours. Another living person would be easily discerned, even lying on top of you, it would be two clear auras. A spirit isn't like that. It's not physically here, but energetically exists, understand?"

"I think so."

She grins again. "Imagine there's a nice-smelling rose, then someone puts a rancid old cheese under the table the rose is on. Right nearby but just out of sight. What are you gonna smell?"

"Rancid old cheese," I say, and grin too.

"Don't enjoy this too fucking much, asshole," Graney says.

"Shut up, rancid," I say, without looking at him.

I realize that in all this time, my ghosts have been around but not that close to me. Always at least a few feet away. I already know I'm not going to like their proximity, but if it works, I'll put up with it. For a little while anyway, until I've taken care of these Acolyte assholes. Despite Luxana's fears, I plan to hit them hard.

"Okay, thanks. I'll do that." I look at the ghosts. "Choose who goes first."

They make noises of annoyance and anger then start arguing among themselves.

Luxana nods at my plate. "Eat what more you want, then you have to leave. We're done here. I'll take my time finishing my dinner, in case they're waiting for you. But I don't want them to see us together. I've already taken more of a chance than I'm comfortable with. Don't forget to pay on your way out."

The finality in her tone brooks no argument. "What about the grand in payment you wanted?"

She flaps one hand. "I don't really need that. I was just testing how serious you were about knowledge."

"Oh. Thanks."

"Don't thank me. You're in a world of shit, Eli, and I don't think you'll get out. No one who fucks with the Acolytes of Ur gets out. Good luck, but this is probably goodbye."

I can't help a small laugh. "Thanks for the vote of confidence."

She smiles, but it's half-hearted and entirely humorless. "Sorry."

I cram another couple of forkfuls of food, then stand up. "Thanks, really. I appreciate it."

She nods and I feel her watching as I leave. I pay and the *maître d'* asks if everything is okay.

"All fine, thanks," I tell him. "Make sure my friend enjoys her dinner and gets any dessert or drinks she wants, okay?" I put another hundred on the counter. "And anything left over is for you."

The *maître d'* smiles and inclines his head. "Thank you, sir. You have a good night, now."

"You too."

I leave, but something tells me my night is not going to be good at all.

Chapter 49

As I step out the restaurant door, Michael says, "Hood up."

I don't second guess the request, just pull my cap low over my eyes and put my hood over it.

"Stop in that doorway," Graney says.

I glance toward the curb and see him pointing at a darkened shop entry just up the street.

"Quickly," Michael says.

Nice to see these assholes are taking their new helpful role seriously. Without any delay I duck into the shadows and press myself into the corner.

"Ride him like a fucking piggyback," Sly says. He's leaning on the wall just outside this recessed entry, sucking on a joint. Dwight is next to him and Sly even shares his joint with the racist. He truly is distracted.

"Who am I hiding from?" I ask.

"Santiago is just down the street," Michael says, pointing. "He didn't see you come out, but he knows you're here. I don't think he knows who with, probably doesn't care. He's waiting for you."

"One of his goons strolled by the restaurant while you were jawin' with Luxana," Sly says. "Clocked you in there and reported back. I think maybe they didn't expect you to leave so soon."

Hopefully that goon won't remember enough about Luxana to compromise her. I was just having dinner with a lady friend. "How many?" I ask.

"There are two cars up ahead," Michael says. "A black sedan and a white SUV, both with four people inside. So that's seven plus Santiago."

Graney nods back the other way. "Two more cars down there, a pair of Jeep Cherokees, with another eight people."

"Sixteen mooks this time." I can't help thinking that's more of a challenge.

"How much ammo you got, sucker?" Graney asks.

I always used to use a Glock 19. It's what Vern preferred and he was the one who brought me up in the life. And it's a good weapon. But I'm a fucking good shot, supernaturally good some people have said, but shooting is just something that always came naturally to me. Plus, I put in a shit ton of practice. Now recently, with Bridget at the tables so much, I've had time on my hands. So I've been down the range plenty, putting in more practice. A guy there introduced me to the CZ 75 9mm. Man, it's a sweet pistol. The guy at the range called it a Czechmate, seeing as it's made in the Czech Republic and it always wins. I've come to find it much more comfortable. Which is all a long way of saying, I have twenty rounds immediately accessible, ten in each mag of the two CZ 75s I have concealed. I have another two mags, one tucked in each pocket. Honestly, even someone as paranoid as me should think forty available rounds across two weapons would be plenty for general self-defense, right? But then, not many people get sixteen mooks sent after them.

"Plenty of ammo," I say. I should be able to drop sixteen assholes without needing my second mags if the situation was right. But it's not. A big group to either side, wide open sidewalk, a fairly busy road right beyond that and buildings all along this side, I'm pretty hemmed in. I just need to get away. If I can end Santiago during my exit, I will.

"They didn't see me come out?" I ask Michael. "You're sure?"

"Pretty sure. You weren't on the sidewalk more than two seconds."

"If they did see you, they're not doing anything about it," Graney says.

"What *is* happening?"

Graney shrugs. "Nothin'. They're sitting in their cars like idiots." He looks up the street each way, shrugs again.

"Okay," I say. "Here's where we all start working together. No point in trying out this thing Luxana suggested as they know I'm here. I need to get away, then start carrying one of you pricks around with me. Getting away is the key part. What can any of you do to help?"

"We cain't do jack shit, cocheese. Michael seems to be able to exert like about a mouse's fart of pressure in the world, but that's it. We can tell you shit, but about all I gotta tell ya is that you're about to fuckin' die."

"You're a fucking idiot," I say. Graney, Michael and Sly all say exactly the same thing. We even manage to share a laugh about that. Look at us all working as a team suddenly.

"Fuck all a'y'all!" Dwight says, and fades out.

"He's chucking a temper tantrum?" I say. "Guess we won't miss him."

"He'll be back," Sly says.

"You reckon Santiago is the seer?" I ask Sly. "He's the one tracking me down?"

"Yeah, must be. But that doesn't mean he's the only one. Who knows how many of these fuckers there are."

"Good point. But if I can take out Santiago, it'll level the field at least a little."

"Take him out?" Michael says. "From here?"

"You tell me which one he is, and yeah. Then I pop as many of the heavies as I can and fucking run. Honestly, I can't think of a better plan, really. They're going to jump me the moment they see me, right?"

"Almost certainly," Graney says.

"Okay, well as you lot are useless for anything physical, let's at least get some reconnaissance. I need to know what weapons they have, what else they have, maybe what they're talking about. And which one is Santiago."

They all stare at me.

"Well? You helping now or what? Scram. Get me info!"

"Fuck me," Graney says, and stomps away toward the Jeeps back down the street. Michael and Sly head for the cars farther up.

It's an anxious few minutes. I want so badly to stick my head out of the shadows, take a look, check the street. Anything other than just standing in the dark waiting. But this concealment is the only advantage I have.

"Santiago is in the front passenger seat of the second car up there, the black sedan," Michael says, suddenly right beside me in the shadows. "The SUV in front of his has four goons, two armed with semi-automatic pistols and two have a shotgun each. The sedan has a guy in the driver's seat with a 9mm, Santiago beside him, without a weapon I could see. In the back are two more with Glocks."

"Pretty much the same configuration in the Jeeps back there," Graney says, jerking a thumb back over his shoulder. Except one extra gun. From what I can see, six 9mm pistols, two shotguns."

"So that's four shotguns and eleven 9mms at least. Fucking hell, that's some pretty heavy firepower."

Graney raises an eyebrow at me. "For just little old you. Pretty impressive."

"I think there's a way to cause enough mayhem to get you away," Michael says. At my look, he continues. "In the SUV, one of the guys in the back seat has his shotgun resting across his lap, but it's pointing toward the front. If it went off, it would kill at least one, if not both the mooks in the front seats."

I smile. "Now we're talking, my friend. You think you could pull that trigger?"

"I think so. If I had to."

"And I could take out at least a couple from the sedan before they started moving. Maybe even Santiago too."

"Timing," Sly says.

"What?"

"You're taking a hell of a gamble. It's all down to timing. And those assholes in the Jeeps will be out and after you in moments."

I run it through my mind a couple of times, then say, "Okay, but they still think I'm in the restaurant. I can buy a few seconds by starting here and a few seconds is a long time in a gunfight. I'll get away from the two cars behind, toward the mayhem, before they can really get moving." I shift back in the shadows and try to see down the street to catch a glimpse of the cars. I can just see a black corner of a sedan without giving up my cover. I describe it.

"Yep, that's the one Santiago is in," Michael says.

I try to build the picture in my mind's eye, imagining the dimensions of the car, the positions of the occupants. If a shotgun goes off in the car ahead of Santiago, their attention will be that way and I can surely shoot at least a couple. Then I wing it.

"Okay, let's do this. Michael, you get in position, Sly you stand by that sedan so you can see Michael. Graney, you stay here on the sidewalk by me. When Michael is ready, Sly signals you, you signal me. I say go, you drop your hand, Sly drops his, Michael booms the shotgun. Same moment, I pop out and take out whoever I can, hopefully including Santiago. I'll run right for those cars while I do it. With any luck, by the time the guys behind us know anything is going down, I'll already be moving well beyond them. As soon as I can, I'll lose myself in the traffic and run for it."

"We're all gonna fucking die," Sly says.

"You're already dead. Let's go, before they decide to check on me again."

"One other thing," Michael says.

"What?"

"Santiago was talking when I checked on them before. He was saying to his goons to make sure you're good and dead. He said, 'No questions, no pause, just kill this motherfucker.' So they don't care about the ring anymore."

A chill goes through me at that thought, but I can't spare it any time right now. "Whatever. Let's go."

Michael fades out, Sly walks away. Graney stands on the sidewalk looking down toward the cars.

"And what do I do, cocheese?"

"Suck your own asshole, for all I care."

Graney raises a hand. I draw my CZ 75s and take a long, deep breath. The adrenaline starts to surge, and breathing is the only thing that helps to mitigate the effects. Here we go. "Ready," I say.

Graney drops his hand, there's a muffled boom from up ahead, but I'm already moving. I step out, legs apart, and start firing. A gun in each hand, barking in alternating rhythm. Two heads in the back of the sedan burst, scarlet spraying black in the night as the window shatters. I fire more, aiming hard for the front passenger seat in the hope of nailing Santiago, but it's mayhem already. I take off running as someone falls out of the rear passenger door of the first car and the driver's door of the second opens. Whoever stumbled from the SUV was too distracted by the horrors inside to even look down the street and I drop him with a couple of quick rounds. That's three out of eight up there, maybe one or two more from the shotgun thanks to Michael.

There's screaming and shouting from all around, tires are screeching as cars going by skid to a halt or try to peel away from the sudden gunfight. A crash and tinkle of broken glass from collisions right beside me. I can smell gasoline and gun oil and gunpowder. The driver of Santiago's car twists up in the gap between the car body and the door he opened, the glint of a muzzle in front of him. I dive to one side as the gun barks.

I glimpse the muzzle flash, but don't feel the burn of a bullet, then I'm tucking and rolling off the curb.

The goons are only about twenty paces away, and I have no idea if the eight from the Jeeps behind are tracking me yet, but I have to move. Gritting my teeth, bracing for impact, I roll onto my feet and bolt out into the road. There's a high screech of rubber and a bright red Corvette is coming right at me, fishtailing as it brakes. It won't quite stop in time, but that's okay. I jump, plant one boot on the long, smooth, shiny hood, feel it dent beneath my toes as I launch off and drop down the other side.

"What the fuck?" I hear through the open driver's window, but I have no time to explain.

I pop up, fire a few shots at random into the cars waiting for me. I catch a glimpse of Santiago in the passenger seat of the second one, face sprayed with blood, his mouth twisting in a grimace of agony. Clearly hurt, but he might not be dying.

I take an extra fraction of a second to line up, then squeeze off a shot and his head whips sideways and out of sight, a fountain of blood jetting up. Fuck you, buddy. Bullets ping off the Corvette and I hit the ground again. Those shots came from back near the Jeeps, so those boys are finally moving.

"Fucking run!" Graney screams at me, but strangely enough I was already thinking that.

Doubled over I scurry away from the Corvette and slip between two more cars, both stopped in the middle of the lane, wide-eyed drivers behind their windshields. More bullets fly and one of the drivers ducks away as their windshield shatters, then I'm past and around those cars too. I pump my arms, pump my legs, sprint hard. Every chance I get, I duck and weave, left and right, putting more vehicles between me and the goons. There's a side street off to my left and I run across into it.

"The Jeeps are giving chase," Michael says.

I sprint hard along the side street, then see a car pull up to the next intersection. Sorry about this, whoever you are. I pull open the driver's door and a young man, maybe twenty years old, looks up in shock.

"The hell, man?"

I drag him out and notice, thankfully, he has no other passengers. Against his protests, I jump in and power away, make a right at the next intersection.

"Those Jeeps just made the turn," Graney says. "They saw the kid sitting in the road, but they didn't see what car you got in."

I slow to a more normal driving speed and start heading back toward the city, watching my mirror hard. Eventually I say, "Looks like I lost them."

"Can't believe you got away with that," Graney says.

"All about surprise and timing," I say. "Never underestimate either in a fight." I turn to Michael, in the passenger seat. "Good work with the shotgun."

"Blew away the front passenger," Michael says.

Graney, Sly and Dwight are all lined up in the back.

"Killed by a dead guy," Sly says with a laugh. "How embarrassing."

"It's a useful skill you have there, Michael. Why can you do it?"

"I don't know. Just can."

I glance in the rearview mirror. "You three should practice or some shit. Would be good if you could all do it."

Chapter 50

I drive the poor guy's car about halfway back home, then park it neatly at the curb.

"Wish I could think of a way to get this back to him," I say, as I wipe all my prints off it.

The fob has only the car key and one other on it, probably his home. I lock up, drop the keys in a drain. He'll get the car back once he reports it missing. It'll get found soon enough. Hopefully he has spares. I set off in a brisk walk back toward the Strip.

"Now where?" Michael asks me.

"First, did you guys decide who rides first?"

"Ah, fuck, man!" Sly says. "You shot Santiago in the head."

"Yeah, but we don't know that he's the only seer. I'm not taking the chance. I'm hiding until I get these fuckers taken apart."

"Take Luxana's advice," Graney says. "Collect Bridget and get outta Dodge. Just leave the country."

I shake my head. "If they're as powerful as she says, you think they're going to ignore that I've killed a bunch of their gang? Particularly Santiago, he'd be high up. They'll come for me. I won't wait for it. Best defense is offense and all that."

"Take the chance, man!" Sly says. "They won't be organized enough to start tracking you again yet."

I flick a glance to him walking farthest away from me. "So you picked the short straw, huh?" Why else would he be so against the idea?

He grunts in annoyance. "Fucking rock, paper, god damned scissors."

"Climb aboard, big boy."

The look on his face is priceless. The other three are laughing, but I don't know what they're so happy about. They'll all get a turn.

"One hour!" Sly says. "Then we switch."

"I thought you guys had no concept of time."

Sly jabs a finger at me. "I'm talking to you! You set a timer. Every hour, you let us know and we switch."

"Okay." I set a timer on my phone, but I make it two hours. See if they notice.

"God damn it," Sly says.

He moves over behind me and as he gets close, I feel a slight chill. He puts his hands on my shoulders and I barely suppress a gasp, the touch is like ice. It's as though my T-shirt and hoodie aren't even there, like dead skin pressed right against my flesh. Sly makes noises of discomfort as he climbs onto my back, but I don't feel any physical movement, just sliding frost, thick and somehow oily. I'm tempted to cup my hands behind, like giving a piggyback to a kid, but there's no point, I can't touch him. Memories of carrying Scottie like this flash through my mind, and grief is a gut punch that takes my breath away. Clenching my teeth, I push the thoughts away. Sly's body presses up against my back and the cold, oily sensation intensifies. Like someone has draped a thick, damp, greasy blanket over my back, shoulders, head. Except it's both heavy and gossamer at the same time. I can't *feel* it with nerves, but I carry the burden, regardless. It feels terrible, makes me a little nauseated. Saliva gathers in my mouth like I'm going to puke and I have to gasp a few quick, deep breaths to push the compulsion down again.

"This ain't fucking natural," Sly says.

"No kidding," I mutter. "What about any of you is anything like natural?"

Michael, Graney, and Dwight are walking alongside, all half-laughing, half-appalled. It's like they're watching one of those gross-out horror movies, funny and disgusting at the same time.

There's a push-pull sensation happening, I feel like I'm about to stagger despite the lack of physical weight. The etheric weight is considerable.

"Will you fucking relax!" I hiss.

Sly grumbles some more, but I sense him taking metaphorical breaths. Despite the amount of weed he smokes, spirits don't actually breathe, do they? Everything starts to settle, Sly's presence becoming more like a mist around me than an oily cargo.

"Better," I say.

"You look different," Michael says, squinting.

Graney nods. "Not like you anymore. Like, I can see the physical you, but at the same time, you're unrecognizable. I feel like I have dementia or something."

"This is what the seer would see," Michael says. "The physical presence is there, but the ethereal is weird. Without laying actual eyes on you, you'd never be spotted."

"We need to all stay close," Graney says, face a grimace of something close to pain. "If we fade out too far, we might not find our way back to him."

"If you get lost, whoever's covering me at the time can get off for a while," I say. "But stay close in case."

"I don't like any of this," Dwight says.

I shrug. "And I don't like you, you piece of shit, but here we are."

Sly huffs a laugh right beside my ear and it's a horrible feeling. I do my best to ignore it. He's got his legs wrapped around my waist, one arm hooked around my neck. In the other is the ubiquitous joint and I smell the weed, see the bluish clouds drifting around my head.

"You be ready to lose that the moment I say," I tell him. "I can't have spirit smoke obscuring my vision if I get in trouble."

"Just say the word, man." Sly passes the joint along the line of assholes.

As we walk past a large shop window, I catch a glimpse of us, four walking in a line, the fifth riding me like some giant kid at the fairground. How fucking ridiculous. At least anyone else would only see me.

I move past Planet Hollywood and head toward Stanley's café. The cold I'm feeling now isn't anything to do with Sly on my back. And I know I'm taking a chance, but I have to know. This is probably my only opportunity before they regroup.

The café is closed. I know the passcode for the keypad by the door and press the buttons. Usually when we caught up here, I'd ring and Stanley would come to open the door, some semblance of normalcy. Sometimes the grief got too much for him, the melancholy making him eschew crowds, even the sight of the street. Like I said before, he was never really suited to Vegas. Those times I'd let myself in, and I'd usually arrive with an extra bottle.

I lock the door behind me and go through the dim interior. The lights are off, chairs on tables, smell of bleach and old coffee. I realize how familiar this place has become and my heart is racing when I go through into the back. It's quiet. Too quiet. I didn't even bother to ring first. When you know, you know.

I find him in the bedroom and my anger flares. Absolutely no one deserves this.

"Jesus fuck," Graney says, turning away.

"Oh," Michael says.

"That ain't something anyone deserves," Dwight says.

Sly is strangely silent. I feel like maybe he's simply not looking.

Stanley is hanging above his big king-sized bed. They've used a nail gun or something similar through his hands and arms, pinning him to the wall crucifix-style. Blood runs down the white paint in thin rivulets, making it look like he has gory wings. His head hangs, chin on his chest, eyes wide and blank, staring at the mess on the stark white sheets.

They've thrown all the pillows and covers off the bed, sliced him open and dragged his entrails out to spell ELI across the smooth expanse of the bed. The way his eyes are open, I can't help feeling like he was still alive, watching them do that before shock and blood loss finished him.

The safe is right here in his room and the door stands open, the contents gone. All his cash and papers. And their fucking ring.

"Stanley, I'm sorry," I whisper.

"Too late for sorry," Stanley says.

The gasps of my ghosts match my own as I spin around. Stanley is there in the doorway to his bedroom, looking in. I can see the living room right through him, he's more insubstantial than my peanut gallery. Is he my new number five? Then I remember Luxana's explanation, that I needed to be suffering real trauma for the haunts to bond so tightly. Appallingly, this doesn't traumatize me. Saddens me, sure. Angers the fuck out of me. But that's all.

"Stan," I manage.

He flaps a hand. "Fuck it, don't worry about it. My life was a misery, anyway. Fuck me, though, it hurt." He grimaces, looks away from the mess of his physical self and his gaze drilling directly into my eyes is more powerful than it ever was in life. "Just do one thing, Eli. Fucking get them for me."

"I will." And I mean it. "I most definitely will."

He nods once and turns away, walks out through his living room and fades away to nothing as he goes.

"He's gone," Michael says. "Like, permanently gone. That felt like a more gentle version of when Alvin was sent away."

I nod, turn back to the corpse. My name in pink and gray entrails makes me furious.

"This is some fucking message," Graney says.

It is. And it says a lot. Not least that they anticipated not catching me at the restaurant. Maybe they did this before Santiago tracked me down again. Regardless, it means they're taking no chances. They're telling me they know all they need to know. Then a new chill blasts through me.

Bridget!

Chapter 51

"What's happening, Eli? You sounded so stressed on the phone."

I can never hide anything from Bridget. The Lily Bar and Lounge at the Bellagio Hotel is busy and crowded, appearing more packed than it really is with all the mirrors around the walls. We're sitting on velour couches the color of sick Caucasian skin and I'm attracting a lot of frowns for my jeans, boots and hooded top. The dress code is apparently "upscale fashionable attire" but, honestly, I don't even know what the fuck that is. I'm being tolerated because I'm with Bridget and she's a high roller. But I don't think they'll put up with me for long. That's okay, I don't need long.

"Yeah, sorry about that. I'm glad you're okay, that's all." I can only assume because she's been at the tables all day, the Acolytes haven't had a chance to get to her yet. And that worked for me. Stanley wasn't so lucky.

"Why shouldn't I be okay?"

"I can only apologize in advance, but I think I've dragged you into something really dangerous. I didn't mean to, and if I thought it would go like this, I'd have backed out well before now."

Bridget tips her head to one side. "Would you though? Really?"

I can't help a short laugh. "Maybe not. I dunno. But I am genuinely sorry."

"So, it's time to go? Where are we off to?"

"It's time for *you* to go. I have to stay and wrap this up or it might follow us."

She purses her lips, seemingly equal parts concerned and angry. As she opens her mouth to say something, my phone starts trilling an annoying, repetitive tone. I silence it and look sidelong at the gang sitting around me. "Time to change it up."

"Fuck." Dwight gets up and comes over.

"Thank fuck for that," Sly says, sliding off me as Dwight climbs on. The transfer is uncomfortable. If darkness had a texture, it would feel like this. Dwight feels different to Sly which is strange. Just as cold, but a different kind of greasy. I try not to think on it too hard, just grit my teeth as the repellent changeover takes place. I can't suppress a shudder as Dwight settles in. Sly joins Graney and Michael on chairs opposite me and Bridget.

"The hell was that?" Bridget asks.

"Okay, full transparency. I'm going to tell you as much as I can. But I have to be quick and we need to talk while we're moving, yeah?"

"The apartment first. I can be packed in ten minutes."

"No, sorry, we're going directly to the airport."

"What?"

"They know everything."

"Eli, there's a fortune stashed at the apartment."

"I know, and a lot tucked away in the bank too. I'll get back the money if I can, but I think they've already got anything we left there."

Bridget's eyes flash rage. "I worked my ass off for that money, Eli."

"I know. I'm sorry. But you have your winnings from today, you have what's in the bank. I'll do all I can to recover as much as possible while I tidy this mess up. I'm sorry."

"Jesus, Eli, stop apologizing. I should have known being tied up with you would have risky side effects. If I'm honest, I did know that, and I thought it was kind of exciting. Fuck! Let's go."

I love the way she rolls with the punches.

We stay in plain sight, and stick to crowds as much as we can. If any of the Acolytes of Ur are watching us, I can't spot them. My ghosts don't see anyone either, but that doesn't mean they're not there. By the time we've got a cab and made it out to the airport, I've managed to fill Bridget in on most of what's happening. Enough that she's as keen as me to get the fuck out of Vegas. We find her a plane bound for Dallas leaving almost immediately, and I tell her to make a new flight from Dallas to somewhere well out of the US as quickly as she can. I don't want to know where. I'll contact her once I'm done with all this and find out where she went. Hopefully I'll live to get at least some of her money back to her. And hopefully she'll have me back again too, when this is over. She kisses me hard, hugs me tight while she does it. And it feels like goodbye.

My relief when she's taken off and safely in the air is physical. I told her to message me when she boards the next flight so I know she's away and safe. I won't make any moves until then. In truth, I don't know what my next move is. Somehow I have to find out a lot more about these Acolytes.

In the cab heading back to town, I try the simple approach and Google them. I'm surprised to get a bunch of hits for the name, then discover the Acolytes of Ur are a local heavy metal band. Seems a little on the nose, especially as their bass drum has the same sigil as the ring that started this whole mess.

"That's plausible deniability," Graney says.

"Is it?"

"Anyone hears about these assholes they can redirect enquiries. Tell people the Acolytes of Ur aren't real, just a dumb rock band."

"Thrash," Sly says

"What?"

"Thrash," Sly says again, nodding at my phone. "It's a style of heavy metal."

"Probably the best if you ask me," I say. I've always been a rock and blues guy, but I get down to old school thrash too. I wonder if these guys are any good.

"What the fuck ever." Graney points at the small screen. "But even so, it's a place to start. Someone connected to the band probably knows something."

"Unlikely to be the musicians though," Michael says. "My money's on their management."

Graney looks at Michael and taps his nose with one index finger, then points. "You are probably dead on there."

I really want to go to the apartment and check it out. I can only assume the Acolytes have been there already, but it would be good to know.

"Hang on," Michael says. It still freaks me out when they read my thoughts. He fades away, then a minute later he's back. "Yep, the place is gutted. They've emptied the safe and ripped through everything you own."

"Motherfuckers." Still, finding that out was easy. I have to get used to these dickheads being cooperative now. "You can just go anywhere you like?" I ask.

"Not anywhere. But you spent a lot of time in that apartment, there's a kind of resonance there. Like an echo, maybe? So, I can feel it and go there."

"Huh. Good to know."

My phone pings and I check it. Bridget has sent a text.

> *Leaving Dallas in 5. Leaving the US. Good luck.*
> *xxx*

Damn. Even though the relief that she's away is intense, I hate that she's gone. I miss her like hell already. But I'm on my own now, and that's good given the circumstances. At least, as alone as I ever am now. The ghosts have the decency not to catch my eye.

"It's nice without Dwight around, ain't it," Sly says after a moment.

I jump slightly, but quickly realize he's still there, riding me. I start to gesture at my back and Sly grins.

"I kinda drifted off when I was up there," he says. "When our spirit mingles with yours, it's a bit like a sedative, it seems. He's out cold. I was for a lot of the time too."

"Useful. Maybe I'll leave him up there a bit longer, then."

Chapter 52

In a stroke of good fortune, the Acolytes of Ur are playing right here in Vegas tonight, at a rock bar called Count's Vamp'd Rock Bar and Grill. Which is a weird name, but I'm just happy to keep moving forward. A net search helped me find out the band are on at 10:00 p.m., so I head into the place a little after nine. It's less than a dozen blocks from Las Vegas Boulevard, so I walked over, constantly on alert, with my hat and hoodie pulled low. I'm wearing a surprisingly convincing fake beard from a dress-up shop and a new hooded jacket and a new cap. Hopefully enough to distract a cursory eye. Hopefully the dimness of the evening and the gloom of a club will be enough to stop me being noticed if anyone there knows what I look like. But I seem to have slipped the radar for now. Too much to hope killing Santiago has somehow handicapped the whole group, but I bought a little time. I'll take what I can get. With any luck I'll learn enough quickly enough to hit them while they're reeling. This piggybacking my ghosts thing appears to be working. It's amazing how quickly I'm becoming used to the greasy presence over my head, neck and back. I feel like I need a shower, but I also know one wouldn't help. Graney is in place right now, and man, he made more fuss than the others about it. I have to admit, I'm enjoying their discomfort.

Count's Vamp'd is kinda cool. It's a decent-sized building standing by itself in a parking lot parallel to West Sahara Avenue. Single-story, a red brick corner entrance in otherwise white walls, with a big black semi-circle awning. A sign above declares the name in vamp-ish script.

Inside it's high and open, the ceiling painted black. It smells of greasy food and beer and sweat, Metallica hammering from the sound system. The stage is not huge, silver metal lighting rigs crisscrossing only a few feet above the heads of the musicians, but they've had some mega names here over the years. The walls are purple with cartoonish guitars and music notes and other décor mounted on them. At the bar end are tables with high chairs around them, and there are booths with cobweb designs pressed into the seats around the sides. The lights above the tables are made from drums hanging on chains. Around the walls are glass display cases full of skulls and instruments, clothing and memorabilia, even motorcycles. The cobweb motif is everywhere. I immediately like the p lace.

I find a table near a back corner where I can see the stage, the bar, and most of the open auditorium. The place is busy already, and filling up fast. I order a beer and, as I haven't eaten since the rushed half a plate of meatballs earlier, I order a steak and fries too.

As the crowd increases, I keep an eye out for anyone who looks like something other than a regular punter. There's a lot of long hair and denim and leather and tattoos, but a lot of slacks and polo shirts too. It's obvious there's a certain percentage who are here for the thrill of visiting an iconic location, even though they really aren't especially into the rock scene. But among them all, I can't pick out anyone who might be a genuine acolyte. Then again, what would one look like?

The food is good and beer goes down well, but I only have the one. I can't afford to dull my reaction time right now. The band takes the stage at 10:00 p.m. sharp, to a huge cheer from the crowd. Looks like they're local favorites.

I have to admit, they're pretty good. Fast and hard riffs, double-kick drums like machine-gun fire. The vocalist is angry but not overly aggressive, delivering songs with power and emotion. Some of the song titles make me think twice. Stuff like "Little People Eaten by the Moon" and "Power to the Powerful" might sound innocuous enough in a metal arena, but they ring of hubris given what I know. Or what I think I know.

That's the thing about narcissists and people with power. They simply can't help flaunting it. Someone like that will always tell you what they're going to do, because they have to boast. They might try to make it sound like a joke, or a passing comment they laugh off, but it's not. And while these guys might indeed be plausible deniability for the real bastards behind the scenes, I wonder if they're not a little more directly involved than I first suspected.

It's a solid gig and I'm thinking despite that, my visit is a bust, but as they announce their final song, I notice a middle-aged guy move over near one side of the stage. He looks bored, almost annoyed to be there. And he's watching the band with a strange intensity. As they start to play, he half-turns to watch the crowd. He thinks he's being subtle, but honestly, he stands out like the balls on a skinny dog. When someone isn't really into a scene, their presence is always obvious. Like the tourists here in polo shirts. That's why undercover cops are always so easy to spot.

The band starts their song and this one is a little different. It starts slow, a kind of hypnotic melody. The singer starts crooning, but the words are a weird language, a little guttural, a little staccato.

"Eli!"

I startle and Michael is in front of me, his face serious.

"What, man?"

"They're searching for you. They nearly found you."

Not looking up too obviously, I peer out from under my cap and sure enough that one guy is scanning the crowd with intense eyes. A woman I didn't notice before is at the other side of the stage, similarly focused.

"Are they seers?" I ask.

Michael nods. "They're kinda washing through the space with their minds. I can't really explain it, but it's not a pleasant sensation."

I feel Graney hunker down over me more tightly, Sly and Dwight are pressed up close to either side, and Michael is leaning over the table, like he's shielding me. I can see him and see through him at the same time, and those two assholes are looking hard. The crowd is swaying, mesmerized by the weird music.

"They must have anticipated you learning their name," Michael says. "They know you're here."

"No," I say. "They suspect I might be here. They can't know. I expect they're searching all kinds of places. But they won't find me. And now I have someone to follow."

"Risky," Sly says. "Following one of their seers? The people most likely to spot you?"

"Any other choices?"

The ghosts are resounding in their silence.

Simultaneously both goons quit their intense scrutiny of the crowd. The first one I saw subtly nods to the singer, who turns to his band. They give a one, two, three, four, then the drums hammer in and the guitars crunch into a blistering riff.

The crowd surges up out of their apathy, cheering and leaping, head-banging furiously, hands with fingers making horns thrust up into the air. The two who were searching move over to one side, leaning close to talk over the volume of the band. Holy hell, this is a good song. A shame they're connected to whatever these bastards are into, because this band is killer.

As the man and woman talk, hands raised to cup their ears, I see both are wearing a signet ring just like the one I grabbed that started all this. Why didn't I think of that before? A quick glance at the band and I see the singer has one too. Not the rest of the band, as far as I can tell. Interesting. So much for the connection being management.

The two seers frown at the noisy, crowded space and the woman gestures sideways with her head. They move toward the doorway. I want to follow, but they might spot me. I'm guessing they know what I look like, so if I get too close they might see through my dime-store disguise.

"Sit tight," Michael says. "I can't go far, but I'll tail them."

He walks away, dropping into pace behind the pair. Sly and Dwight stay pressed up close beside me. With Graney on my back I feel like I'm in a sludgy, cold puddle.

"Ain't no fucking picnic for us either," Graney growls over my shoulder.

"Too bad you have to shut the fuck up and keep me alive, isn't it?"

Sly looks up toward the door, then turns to me. "They're talking. Michael is listening, and I can hear him."

"Okay. What does—"

"Shut the fuck up, man! The woman is saying, '*He's definitely not here, no way someone could hide from both of us.*' The man says, '*So what do we do?*' She says, '*What can we do? Go home, wait for the full, then proceed as normal.*' The dude again, '*And if no one has tracked this prick down by then?*' Michael tells me the woman shrugged, looked uncomfortable, then an awkward silence. Then the guy says, '*Maybe he really did leave. He took his woman to the airport, maybe he slipped away after that.*' And she replies, '*Well, she certainly did. It sticks in my craw that maybe we really lost him. Never lost anyone before.*' He says, '*Only temporary. We'll find them both, eventually. For now, we need to concentrate on the full. I'll call you.*' Then Michael says they kinda tapped their signet rings together by way of a handshake or some shit. Says he saw a ripple through the ether when the rings touched, felt a wave of power. Now they're getting into separate cars."

"Follow one!"

Sly glances at me, then concentrates again. "Follow one. I dunno, dude, fucking eeny meeny miny moe."

"What did they mean by 'the full'?" I wonder aloud.

There's a sigh in my right ear and Graney says, "The moon, dickweed. The full moon is the night after tomorrow."

"That's relevant?"

"Jesus fuck," Graney spits. "Weren't you listening to that Luxana chick? She said, and I quote, 'they claim to serve a moon god who is in turn a gateway to cosmic powers beyond the ken of mortal beings like us lowly humans. They are the acolytes of that force here.' So I would think it stands to reason that the full moon is pretty special to them right? Like a monthly sabbath or some shit."

"Good memory," I say.

"It's a cop's ear for detail and retention of pertinent information. You should try it sometime."

"Sure. Or I could just rely on you." Over his grunt of annoyance, I say, "But this is interesting. If they're pissed, they can't find me but they need to concentrate on the full moon, it gives us two useful pieces of information."

"Which are?" Dwight says. He looks at the others, his face annoyed. "What?"

"Just felt like you had to get involved, huh?" Sly asks.

Graney chuckles from behind me. "Hush, racist, the grown-ups are talking."

"Fuck all a' y'all!"

"Which are," I say, to stop an argument breaking out. I need these guys close and together to keep me covered. "One, the group is going to be preoccupied with whatever they have to do on the full moon. And two, perhaps the night after tomorrow, they're all going to be in one place for whatever it is they have to do."

"Two days to figure it out and plan an attack?" Sly asks.

"Exactly so."

The Acolytes of Ur finish their set to rapturous applause and cheers. They bow and slap hands with people down the front. The lead singer is distracted, looking out over the crowd with a frown.

"Is he a seer?" I ask Sly, nodding at the young man. He looks like any rock star, denim and a black T-shirt, long brown hair, cheekbones sawing through his thin face like shark's fins.

Sly looks at him for a time, then shakes his head. "Don't think so. Doesn't look the same to me. I can see the aura around his ring, like the others had. But he seems regular otherwise."

I realize Michael is standing in front of me again, looking contrite. I raise an eyebrow at him. "Followed for a few hundred yards, then got wrenched back here," he says. "I think we can't stray too far from you, unless it's to go somewhere you've spent a lot of time. Even then, like while I was checking the apartment, I had to strain against the compulsion to come back. Felt like I was overstretching a big rubber band. I got the plates of both cars, though. Might be useful?"

"Might be. Meanwhile, we concentrate on him." I nod at the lead singer, now helping his band pack up their gear.

The PA is blaring again, playing Korn this time. People are still drinking and partying, though the crowd has thinned a little now the live music is over.

"Concentrate on him?" Michael asks.

"Yeah. I think it's time I met a rock star."

Chapter 53

It's definitely safer to follow someone who isn't able to spot my fucking aura or whatever it is those seers do, but following anyone, singling them out, is not easy. I need him alone, not with the rest of his band. They spend a while packing up and I get the ghosts to watch what happens after they leave the stage. There's a green room out the back and they go there, towel off, crack a few beers, congratulate each other on a kickass gig. I can't disagree with that, they have the chops for sure.

I order another beer while Michael watches the band, reporting back through Sly like before. Nice little arrangement I've got here, able to spy on people as long as they aren't more than a couple of hundred yards away. Better than the damn CIA.

"Michael says they're wheeling their gear out to a van," Sly says. "Bit of a groupie crowd around them, asking for selfies and autographs, but they're slowly getting organized."

I need a vehicle. "Time to go," I say, and slip out the front door.

I flick a glance at the van, parked around the side of the venue near the back. A gaggle of fans is there, obscuring the band members as they load out, but I don't have long.

"If you're going to boost something, do it quietly," Graney says.

"Yeah, yeah. Thanks for the concern, Dad."

He grunts a laugh. But he has a point.

There are cameras all over the place, perched on the corners of buildings like gargoyles. I can't easily boost anything around here without being noticed. A car glides to a stop at the curb of the highway and I see the little white Uber sticker in the back. Someone gets out waving to others near the club, as I jog over.

"Hey buddy, I don't have the app, but you wanna make a hundred bucks cash?"

The young man driving raises an eyebrow. "Maybe."

I respect his caution. "Okay, so I don't want to go into details but I need you to follow that van." I point at the band's black vehicle as it heads for the exit of the parking lot a hundred yards ahead of us. Thankfully it's plain, no bright decals declaring who they are. I guess I respect that caution too.

"What is this, you think you're in a cop movie? Wait, are you a cop?"

"I look like a fucking cop? Seriously, I just need to know where they go. I'm a private eye, but my car got beat up and I can't afford to lose this lead."

"What happens when they get to wherever they're going?"

"I give you a hundred bucks and you fuck off."

I climb in the car to press my case and he shrugs. "Okay, but if they go beyond the suburbs, or it takes more than half an hour, it's another hundred."

"I'll give you a hundred for every half hour it takes. Just keep a few cars between us and them."

He laughs. "I know how to tail someone, man."

"Yeah? Seen a few cop movies? Just be cautious."

My ghosts are lined up in the back seat, watching intently. I still can't get used to seeing only four of them, Alvin Crake conspicuous by his absence.

"We don't really miss him," Michael says with a half-smile. "Guy was kind of an asshole."

I don't bother suggesting that they're all assholes. I guess they already know.

The tail only takes twenty minutes or so. I can tell my driver is disappointed. I pay him and get out about a hundred yards from the apartment complex the band piled into. They locked up the van without unloading, but parked it in a marked space beside the building, so I'm guessing maybe they share a place here. There's four of them, so I hope it's a big apartment. Unless they're two couples or something.

"Now what?" Graney says, voice rasping too close to my ear. "You going in, guns blazing?"

"Not yet."

"Hey, how long have I been here?"

I smile, it's been hours. "Yeah, time to switch out boys."

Dwight moans and bitches as he swaps with Graney, the oily cold making me shudder as they slide over each other and me. I think they're fucking with him, I'm sure Dwight has been given the job twice as much as the others. As I realize, so does he and everyone laughs. Except Dwight who bitches some more.

"All of you shut the fuck up," I say quietly. "Hopefully won't be for much longer. Suck it up."

The apartments all have big balconies and the band appears on one about halfway up, laughing and drinking beers. I hunker in some shadows to watch. At least now I know which is their place, but I still don't want to go in too gung ho. Then I get a lucky break.

Michael appears on the balcony, listening in, reporting back through Sly. Within a minute or two he says, "The singer's name is Bartok, he's leaving. Doesn't live here. The other three do. Seems like he's the boss of the band and they're happy to do what he says. They have another gig tomorrow, but Bartok is heading home."

Sweet.

Moments later I'm tailing Bartok along the sidewalk. It's late, and even though this is the kind of city that never sleeps, these suburban outskirts are a lot quieter. All wide streets and sandy edges and palm trees.

The night is mild and dark outside the pools of orange light under the streetlamps.

I guess Bartok here doesn't live far away, as he strolls along the sidewalk, relaxed arms swinging. More fool him. I wait for a dim patch between lights, then run softly up behind him. He hears me at the last moment, turns, a look of mild shock on his face, but all too late. I shoot out a straight right, deliberately oblique, catching him a glancing blow behind the ear. He staggers and goes to one knee, crying out, but his voic e is muffled by the dizziness he's suddenly feeling. I grab him and drag him into the shadows, one hand pressed hard across his mouth. I sling him onto his back on the sandy ground, one hand pressed on his face, one holding his arm hard against the sand, my knee pressed into his hip. I'm taller and significantly heavier than he is, and have him pinned like a bu g.

"Stay quiet and don't struggle and you get out of this alive."

I honestly don't know right now if that's a lie or not, but I need him to comply.

His eyes are wide and bright in the darkness, but he nods vigorously against my hand. I slowly lift it away. "You yell out, you die."

"We're cool, man." His voice is rushed but muted, his breath fast and shallow. "We're all cool. I have money, you want money? Or what? You want something else? I can get you weed, coke, hey fucking hookers, what do you—"

"I want you to shut the fuck up."

He clams, lips pressed together.

"Take him up on the hookers, cocheese!"

"And the coke, too," Sly says. "When you take shit, we feel it. That's why we like it when you drink."

I roll my eyes at these fools, but don't dignify their nonsense with a response.

"Now, your name is Bartok and you're the lead singer for Acolytes of Ur," I say.

He smiles. "You recognized me, huh?"

Jesus, the hubris of fucking celebrities. "You're also connected to the Acolytes of Ur that aren't band members but a bunch of moon-worshipping fuckwits."

His face drains pale as the moon he bows to and his eyes go wide again. "Oh no, man, don't go there. You need to divert from this path right now, or you die."

"That so."

His wide eyes narrow. "Hey, you're him! The one who took a beacon. They were looking for you at our gig tonight."

Well, I guess the poor bastard doesn't survive this encounter after all. That unfortunate realization was his death warrant.

"Yep, can't leave any loose ends," Graney says.

Typical cop methodology there, but in this case he's right. Damn it, they're a good band.

"Too late for all that, Bartok. I need information."

"Nah nah nah, I can't. They'll kill me. Worse than that, they'll pass me through."

Interesting turn of phrase. "I know the full is the night after tomorrow, Bartok. Where's the meeting?"

"M-m-meeting?"

"You guys have a ritual every full moon, right?"

"How do you know all this stuff? Who the fuck *are* you?"

"I'm justice."

Graney barks a phlegmy laugh right beside me.

"You think you're fucking Batman now?" Sly says, guffawing.

"From ronin to superhero!" Michael says, laughing. Wow, even the one ghost who's supposedly still my friend is ragging on me.

Bartok is struggling against where I'm still holding him down and I realize it's his hand with the ring on it. Something tells me I can't risk that hand getting free. I sit more across his hips, lean hard into his wrist. He stops, eyes narrowing again.

"What do you want?" he asks again.

"Information. Just where to find these fuckers, that's all."

"And what do you plan to do when you get there?"

Suddenly he's all confidence. I don't like that.

"He has a point," Michael says.

"Yeah," Sly agrees. "I mean, say you find out where this moon meeting is, then what? You just storm it, guns blazing?"

I shrug. Honestly, that is pretty much it. It seems to work for me.

"Jesus fuck!" Graney snaps and strides away.

Bartok sighs and I see something shift in his demeanor. "I might as well tell you. I mean, it'll do you no good and I'm already done for. You're not going to let me go, are you? Because you know I'll tell them this happened. Even if I promise not to, you won't believe me."

"That doesn't mean you have to die," I tell him. "You guys are a killer band. Maybe you can just keep doing that. I will have to have you detained for a while. Tell me what I want to know and I'll lock you up safe and secure somewhere until after the full."

"But you won't survive the full, so who will ever let me out."

"How about I schedule a message to go to someone, one of your bandmates maybe? For the day after. If I don't survive the message still gets outs."

There's a part of me that wants to make this work. I've killed so many motherfuckers, it's just part of the job, but that doesn't mean I'm a mindless murderer. If I can avoid killing, that's good. I have no qualms about killing actual bad guys. All the fuckers who I've ended pretty much deserved it one way or another. But this kid feels different. Perhaps he's not deep into this cult yet and maybe he can survive. He can't be much over twenty years old. I don't want to be the bad guy all the time. Sometimes there's a choice.

It makes me think of old mythology. I've never liked the trope that vampires have to be invited in, for example. That's some "free will" religious bullshit that blames the victim. Anyone with half a brain knows damn well that evil just happens to people, no invite required. But we can try to exercise free will to avoid evil, to fight against it. If I can fuck up these Acolyte weirdoes without taking this kid down, I'll do it. Give him a second chance. I can find a storage unit or something, tie him up there. He'll have a miserable couple of days, then be let out. Either by me, or his friends. I can try to do the right thing, can't I?

"Going fucking soft," Graney growls.

"Soft in the damn head, cocheese."

"You mean it?" Bartok asks.

"Yeah. I do."

"Okay." He nods, takes a deep breath. "Yeah, okay." He gives me an address. "Penthouse, right at the top. You get there, you'll see wonders. But you won't get there."

I have to hope he's telling me the truth. As backup, I ask, "What about some names? Give me some high ups in the group."

Bartok laughs, reels off a few names. These are not little people. He's naming internationally known stars and politicians. "Won't do you any good, Batman."

He's fucking laughing at me now. "Come on then."

I move my knee, trying to think of where I might lock this guy up. Maybe a motel room with a Do Not Disturb sign on the door will do it for a couple of days if I tie and silence him well enough.

I'm wary, watching him as he stands, waiting to see if he'll bolt or fight, maybe go for a weapon. But he just brushes himself off. He looks up, eyes kind of sad. "You won't survive it," he says. He raises his hand to his head. The one with the signet ring on it.

He presses the ring against his temple and all my ghosts cry out, "No!" at the same moment as Bartok mutters something.

My ghosts reel and stagger back as if hit with a shockwave and Bartok's eyes roll up to show the whites. Blood runs from his ears and nostrils and he drops, dead.

"Get the fuck out of here," Michael says urgently. "That was like a fucking alarm bell ringing out for miles. They'll know exactly where this just happened."

But I'm already running.

Chapter 54

"Why do you care, man?" Sly asks from my back. It's too weird when they talk to me so close-up. And that cold, oily sensation won't go away.

Michael gestures at him, as if to say, *Well?*

I guess they have a point. Why do I care?

"Gonna get yourself good and dead," Graney says.

"You ain't fucking Batman, cocheese. What's the point?"

"Just leave," Michael says, but I hear a kind of resignation in his voice. He knows I won't quit. "Get outta town, wait for Bridget to call, meet her in fucking Macau or Manila or something."

I pace back and forth in the motel room on the edge of Seven Hills. I figure it's far enough out of town to be safe for now. I rented a small car with one of my fake IDs to get here. I'm glad I always keep that stuff with me, not left in the ransacked apartment. In recent months I've got in the habit of wearing one of those traveler's belts that goes on under your shirt. Call me paranoid, I don't care. I'm used to the slightly bulky discomfort of it, but it means I always have my alternate IDs, a chunk of cold, hard cash, and a few other bits with me. Means I can lie low like this without risking exposure.

I wish I could go back to the apartment, try to salvage some clothes and other stuff, but I can't risk it. I have the clothes on my back, my phone and wallet, and my two CZ 75s, that's it. I guess I need to go shopping.

"They'll find us," I say eventually, even as I'm wondering if that's true. But I think it is. "Either I hit them on my terms, or I'm constantly watching over my shoulder, running defense. The best defense is offense, remember?" I do actually believe that. It makes perfect sense. Only a fuckwit would wait for someone to hit them before fighting back. If you know someone means to hurt you, fucking destroy them instantly with extreme prejudice. You may never survive the first strike otherwise.

"You really think they give a shit about you?" Graney asks.

"I don't know for sure, but I hurt a bunch of their guys. And now the singer from that band. That really sucks, the band was good."

"They'll love that," Sly says in my ear. "The Acolytes of Ur—the band, I mean—suddenly have a whole lot of attention. The lead singer dead, they get loads of press, the evil group get to hide further behind the public profile of the band. Then the band audition for a new singer, they're back on stage in six months. Maybe less. You probably did them a favor, they can't buy publicity like that."

It's a grim assessment but he makes a kind of sense. Regardless, I still don't believe this group will let me get away with it, even if that aspect does work for them rather than against.

I'm about to say something else when I realize the ghosts are looking at each other with frowns. Dwight starts to speak then Michael, Sly and Graney all simultaneously tell him to shut up. Michael tips his head to one side, like he's listening.

A trickle of ice finds its way into my gut. Have they tracked us down again? Am I wearing ghosts like fucking backpacks for no reason?

"How did you find us?" Michael asks.

Shit.

"Oh, I suppose that makes sense," Michael says.

"What the fuck is happening?" I demand through gritted teeth.

"It's Luxana," Graney tells me, while Michael concentrates. "She found you because she could look for us. She's seen us, after all."

"She says the way of hiding from the Acolytes still works," Michael tells me, gesturing at Sly on my back.

"Enough of this," Michael's voice is suddenly strangely high. His entire expression changes, almost like he's morphing into someone else. Graney and Dwight stagger away from him, Sly on my back curses. "I'll talk to you directly."

I'm looking at Michael but hearing Luxana, I know that without a doubt. "Good to hear from you, I guess. Unless it's bad news?"

"Frankly, I'm amazed you're still alive. Well done."

"You told me how to hide from them."

"Well, yes, I theorized a possible method. I'm glad it worked."

"You didn't know?"

"Not for certain. This isn't an everyday situation, Eli."

I suppose I can't argue with that. "So why are you here?"

"I've been doing a bit of research and, as you are still alive and still in Las Vegas, I thought I'd share what I've learned."

"Tell him to leave!" Graney says.

"Yeah, lady!" Dwight says. "Tell this dickhole to get the fuck out."

Michael turns to face them but it's clearly Luxana who says, "Hush." They're a little offended and I can't help but laugh at that. Fucking children. She looks back to me. "These are bad and powerful people, Eli. You sure you want to tangle with them?"

"I don't think I have a choice. They'll hunt me, right?"

"I don't know. But it is a strong possibility."

"So I take it to them. That's my style."

Luxana sighs. "Okay then. Well, know this. They meet every month on the full moon, to do their twisted thing."

"Yeah, I learned that recently. And I know where the next meeting is, in two days."

Luxana raises Michael's eyebrows in surprise. "You have been busy. Your timing is good too, because this full moon is a special one. There are a whole bunch of things the moon gets saddled with, all the old monthly names like Wolf Moon, Buck Moon, Harvest Moon, Hunter's Moon, you know about those, right?"

"I've heard of them…"

"Okay, doesn't really matter. Mostly they're just in reference to the time of year. Hunter's Moon is the one in October because that's when the deer are fat from a whole summer of good eating, so it's the best time to hunt. In the northern hemisphere anyway. But there are other moons that are infrequent and therefore more powerful. A Blood Moon, for example."

"I know that one. Full lunar eclipse, right? When the Earth gets between the moon and the sun, so the only light the moon gets is from around the edges of the Earth and it looks red."

"Clever boy. Air molecules from Earth's atmosphere scatter out the majority of the blue light, so what's left reflects onto the Moon with a red glow. Now tell me what a Blue Moon is."

I have to stop and think about that, but I know I've read about it before.

"Two full moons in the same calendar month," Sly says from over my shoulder.

Michael's eyes flick up to him and back to me with a smile in them. She makes him look so different, it's freaky. "That's the common thought, but not actually correct. Each year, the moon finishes its last cycle about eleven days before Earth finishes its orbit around the sun, so there's an offset. Those days add up and there's an extra full moon every two and a half years or so. That's the original definition of a Blue Moon, the third full moon of a season containing four full moons instead of three."

"Okay, so what?" I say.

"So, imagine if a Blue Moon and a Blood Moon coincided," Michael-Luxana says.

"A Blueblood Moon," Graney says with a grin. "It's a fucking British monarch?"

Michael's glance of derision silences him and Luxana's gaze falls back on me. "This is a significant astronomical event, Eli. And the Acolytes of Ur lap that stuff up. The meeting this time isn't just the local chapter, but acolytes from around the country, even around the world, are going to be there. You hit them now, you'll hit about every major player in their sick cabal."

"Well, isn't that a nice coincidence?"

"Is it?" Luxana's eyes are serious in Michael's face. "Or is it why you're here? Are you the agent of something else, you and these spirits? Are you here because some powerful destiny wills it?"

I don't like the sound of that at all. I hate all the preordained destiny and fate bullshit. I'm with Sarah Connor, there is no fate but that which we make for ourselves. Also, and once again, so what? Does it matter why I'm here now? I am here, and I'm planning some mayhem. Let that be enough.

"Whatever," I say aloud. "Bad luck for those fuckers. A roomful of pedophiles, corrupt politicians, immoral business leaders, whatever else you said before? Sounds like my kind of shooting gallery."

Luxana's smile softens Michael's face. It's sad. "I don't think you'll even get close. But imagine if you did!"

"You didn't think I'd last this long, but here I am."

"Fair point. These people, Eli, they control through fear. Everything is driven by fear. Everyone is afraid of something. Find out what, and you control them. These are the kind of people who exploit that relentlessly, in media, in politics, in everyday life. And they enhance their power and influence enormously through the energy they absorb via some entity through the moon. They are not playing on a level field. The energy they exploit radiates off this entity, some intelligence, that exists so far outside our understanding we couldn't comprehend it if we tried. I'm not sure of their rituals, but the rituals are designed to expose them to that...radiation, for want of a better term. Honestly, I don't know if you even *can* fight something like that."

"Everyone has a weakness. Why would this godlike thing give these scumbags anything?"

"I imagine it has no idea. Their ritual simply opens a portal, focused through a full moon. They get the power by taking it without permission. If the entity knew, who knows what might happen? But how would it even notice? Like rain washing the dirt from a road, the cloud above isn't aware of the cleaning taking place. We are insignificant. The cosmos cares not for the dust."

"There truly is no resource the rich won't exploit," Sly says.

He's not wrong.

"Well, thank you, Luxana. I appreciate the information."

"If you are going against these bastards, I hope you succeed. I doubt you will, but good luck."

I nod, and then Michael blinks and his face shifts, his eyes darken. "Fuck that," he mutters.

"What did she feel like *inside* you?"

"Shut the fuck up, Dwight!" we all say at once.

Chapter 55

God bless America, the guns and ammo shop half a block from my motel is more than happy to stock me up against one of my fake IDs. Once I've got my gear, I'm planning to lie low a little longer, do some planning. I pick up two more CZ 75s and a shit-ton of ammo for them, in multiple spare clips. One of those lame-ass hunting jackets with all the pockets comes in useful. They even have it in black. I pick up two bowie knives and calf sheaths for those. A couple of mace sprays, the high velocity, extra spicy kind. Then I grab a good pump-action shotgun, a Benelli Nova in anodized matte black. Twelve gauge and 4+1 rounds, I make sure to get a couple of extra boxes of shells too. I may or may not have reload time, but best to be prepared.

I learned the joys of the shotgun off Vernon Sykes. He was the kind of sick bastard who would never kneecap a guy with a pistol if he could blow off a foot with a shotgun. He always said the Benelli Nova was the most reliable one out there. I've never had reason to doubt that assessment, even if I am glad Vernon is dead now.

The shotgun is good for close-up and wildfire work. Once I'm in, my marksmanship skills with handguns will be all I need. I hope.

"Jesus, buddy, planning a party, huh?" the shopkeeper says once it's all on the counter.

"This'll show up on a police scanner somewhere," Graney says from my back. "Or maybe this guy is a conscientious shop owner and will directly report you himself."

I don't give a shit. In a little over twenty-four hours I'll be in the thick of it, then I'll be dead or gone. They won't find me in that short time, not with the ID I'm using.

"It looks like a lot," I say aloud. "My house got broken into and robbed. They took our home defense stuff." I gesture at the CZ 75s and the shotgun. "I'm just replacing it. Lucky I wasn't home, or they'd have had firsthand experience with the ones they stole before they got close."

The gun seller grunts a laugh. "I hear that. Chickenshit thieves only ever slink around in the dark."

I lock the weaponry in the trunk of the rented car, then head over to a clothing store. I get a few sets of new clothes so I can finally change, and a long coat. I'll need to conceal the shotgun on my way in. I also buy a new sports bag for my clothes, and I can jury-rig the shoulder strap of that to hold the shotgun in a kind of cross-body harness. It'll hang inside the coat, leaving my hands free, but can be easily grabbed and swung into a firing position. After that, it's food and snacks, then I'm ready to camp and wait for tomorrow night.

Back in the motel room I'm getting all the gear organized when a text message comes through. I smile, expecting Bridget. She's the only one who knows this phone, we have one each just for ourselves. I already dumped my other one once I knew this cabal were after me. Like I said, call me paranoid if you like. It's not paranoia when they really are out to get you.

But it's not Bridget. It's a list of names, lots of people I recognize, including a couple of ex-presidents, some major Hollywood types, a handful of world-famous billionaires. At the end it says,

Thought you might like to have an idea who you're up against. Lux x

"How the fuck did she get this number?" I say.

"I gave it to her," Michael says. "She asked me."

"How do you know it?"

He gives me a look and I have to ignore that. The mind-reading, the shared thoughts, I can't tell where they start and finish, how much these fuckers know.

"I pay more attention than the other three," Michael says, maybe trying to make me feel better.

I like the way they're actively helping me now, but I'm not so keen on them freely communicating with the world at large. There are seismic shifts happening in my life, and I don't like that.

"High profile list," Graney says. "That won't go unnoticed if you wipe out any of these folks."

"Especially if you wipe out all of them," Sly says.

"He won't get past the front damn door," Dwight says.

"I'll be doing the world a favor. It'll be a better place without all these pricks."

"Even the billionaire entrepreneurs, cocheese? You resent their success that much?"

"Especially those fuckers! Being a billionaire is not a success, it's a massive moral failure."

"A *moral* failure?"

"Of course. No billionaire is made without colossal exploitation, then they sit on their fortune like a dragon on a hoard of gold, just keeping it for no reason at all. No fucker *needs* a billion dollars. To be a billionaire while people around the world starve and die of preventable sickness is an atrocity. To have the means to end poverty and choose not to? That's about the biggest fucking failure possible. Successful entrepreneurs, my ass."

"That is actually a fair point," Graney says with a laugh.

"No rich person—like, really hundreds of millions or more rich—ever got there without other people suffering for them. Even the brats who inherit the money, they're inheriting blood-stained riches. Fuck 'em all."

"You trying to rationalize your choice here, man?" Sly asks.

"What do you mean?"

"You could leave it all behind. I know you keep saying they'll hunt you down, but you're hiding now. Keep hiding, you don't have to die for these assholes."

"He's right," Michael says. "We'll keep you hidden, the heat will ease, we can start again elsewhere."

I smirk at them. "You're protecting your own asses. I have a mission here. Ever since the thing with Carly I've been atoning for my past. It's led me to this. I don't truck with all the fate bullshit, but there is cause and effect. Whatever occurred before has led me here and I plan to see it through. If I pull this off, I'm doing a massive service to all of humanity. Look at that list! I wipe all those fuckers out, just think of the knock-on effect. I'll take them down or die trying. Maybe that *is* why I've survived until now. Maybe it is fate. Who cares? It's a job worth doing and I plan to do it. You lot want to stick around longer, then fucking help me."

"Holy sheee-it," Dwight says. "You really think you are Batman. Gonna get us all kilt."

Chapter 56

Patience is a virtue in any walk of life, but especially the violent life. It seems like a contradiction, everyone thinks violence is fast and furious. It often is in final execution, but that's the end point. More people die and suffer from rushing in than anything else in fighting. There's an old adage I learned from a kung fu teacher, Sifu Richard, I trained with many years ago. I spent a lot of time studying all kinds of fighting systems, not just gunplay. I'm an all-rounder when it comes to fucking people up. Anyway, this guy, he was a real traditionalist and a real badass. Took that old-fashioned stuff and trained it properly, knew how to make it work like it was supposed to.

"So many people these days don't get it," I remember him saying, anger in his eyes. "And it gives the traditional arts a bad name. People reduce the knowledge to a bunch of flashy moves they don't understand and then they propagate bullshit. But the old arts are genuinely deadly when you understand the applications, and the proper way to train them. They used this shit on battlefields, for fuck's sake, and they killed motherfuckers. Just because assholes these days don't understand it, doesn't mean the arts are no good."

I liked Sifu Richard a lot, we got along well.

Anyway, the old adage. I don't remember the Chinese terminology, but I really internalized the principle. Sifu Richard would always talk about the four tenets of good fighting: patience, focus, accuracy, and passion.

The idea is that you wait patiently in the first instance. Don't rush in, take your time, assess a situation, feel an opponent out as much as you're able. But never lose focus. Then when the opportunity comes, be accurate, exploit the opening with dead-eyed precision, and with passion. With absolute, relentless intent. Patience, focus, accuracy, passion. I've always remembered that and it's never let me down. In the times when I've fucked up, it's usually because I let one of those key principles slide.

So, sitting back in the motel room waiting for the moment to strike was easy. That was the patience. The focus was easy too, I didn't let myself get distracted. I didn't do something else while I waited. I ordered in food, I trained as much as the space allowed, I kept my weapons in top condition. The patience and focus were there. The accuracy comes next, and that's easy too. I know exactly where I'm going. I went out once and did a couple of drive-bys to check the building. I can't know more about it until I get there. But that's the chaos. No matter how much you plan, in the end fighting is always responding to chaos. You never know for sure what your opponent is going to do. But that's okay. That's the fun of it all.

In terms of accuracy, I also got a bit more information from Luxana. I sent her a text.

> *As you have my number, want to let me know the exact moment of the full?*

She replied back not long after.

> *10:47 p.m. Penumbral Eclipse begins*

11:44 p.m. Partial Eclipse begins

1:11 a.m. Total Eclipse begins (completely red moon)

1:18 a.m. Maximum Eclipse (Moon is closest to the center of the shadow)

1:25 a.m. Total Eclipse ends

2:52 a.m. Partial Eclipse ends

3:49 a.m. Penumbral Eclipse ends

So if they draw power from the height of the astronomical event, they'll be focusing on 1:18 a.m. You get there after 1:25 a.m. and you'll probably have missed it.

Good luck!

That was a hell of a lot more information that I expected, or maybe even needed. But when it comes to accuracy, that covers it. I figure these assholes will be busiest about 1:00 a.m. onwards.

Patience, focus, accuracy, and passion. Thank you, Sifu Richard.

I've been patient, and focused. Accuracy has me walking up to the building in question at exactly 1:00 a.m. Now comes the fourth tenet of fighting. Passion. Absolute intent.

Let's rock'n'roll.

The moon is full and massive, right above us, already almost entirely obscured by the shadow of the Earth. The curved shadow on the moon surface feels heavy to look at. I lose sight of it as I get close to the building, a tower of condos, glass and cement with a slight wave shape to the design. I need the penthouse right at the top. The first challenge is getting in the front doors, but we have a plan for that. As I walk up, there's a concierge desk opposite the double glass entry and a security guard looks up. I wondered if there might be a bigger presence here, but I guess they don't expect me to come right to them. More hubris on their part. Then again, maybe this is suicide. We'll see.

The guard raises an eyebrow at the guy all in black wearing a long coat, standing calmly outside. I have a cap pulled low, a hood over it, thin gloves to mask my prints. What the guard doesn't see while he's taking me in is Michael, right there in the lobby, blood dripping from the craterous wound in the side of his head as he goes to the door and presses the button to exit. These buildings are designed to stop anyone without a pass or keycard getting in, but getting out is easy. One button, usually big and green. Michael's face twists in a grimace of pain, then the glass doors separate with a hiss and I stride in.

The security guard's laconically raised eyebrow is joined by its twin in a shocked look of surprise and he starts to stand up. I can't let him get the jump on me, but this guy is pretty innocent, so I try to go easy.

"Hold it, buddy," he says, raising a palm to me. His other hand is moving toward his hip.

I swing up the Benelli from under my coat and shake my head.

He freezes, frowns at the door. "How did you?"

Then I've rounded the desk even as he tries to scurry back, but I'm too fast, my fist whipping out across the point of his jaw. He grunts and drops like a sack of butter. I duck with him, shooting a hand under his head to stop him cracking his skull open on the glossy marble floor, then switch my grip to his collar and drag him behind me. We go around to the elevators and there's a door marked Emergency Exit. That'll be the stairs.

As he starts to moan and writhe gently, about to wake up, I pat him down and find the holy grail—his passkey. One of those electronic ones like a thick credit card. I don't know how far it'll get me, but it will hopefully at least let me operate the elevator and save me running up thirty-six flights of stairs.

I blip the stairwell door open then pocket the keycard and drag the poor fool through. He's starting to protest and struggle, but still hasn't got his wherewithal back and I bring out the zip ties, secure him easily, hands and feet, through the railings at the foot of the stairs. I rip out the front of his shirt, twist it into a gag, and tie that to muffle any screaming for help he might try.

"The fuck, man?" he manages, just before I wedge it in place.

"Sorry, pal. Just sit tight and be patient, yeah? This is all finished for you now if you mind your business. Someone will find you, in the morning at the latest." I pat his shoulder. "Be good, okay?"

Then I'm back in the lobby pressing the button for the elevator. When I go in, I press for the top floor, but even though the security guard's pass card made the green light on the panel light up, the button for the top floor won't operate. Frowning, I try the next floor down. That one works.

"Looks like even security doesn't get to the top," Graney says. "What makes you think you can?"

"I'll try the stairs."

It feels entirely surreal to be standing in an elevator, armed to the teeth, slowly ascending while soft Muzak plays. My ghosts are crammed in with me, all looking apprehensive.

"Think this is the end?" I ask.

Sly shakes his head, looks away. I can see the panel of elevator buttons through the gaping hole in his torso, bits of rib poking through here and there like broken teeth.

"Probably is the end," Graney growls, throat raw, wet, dripping red.

"You're a fucking fool, cocheese. Gonna die for these assholes." I can't see Dwight perched on my back, but I know his bullet hole, right between the eyes, always trickles rivulets of scarlet down his nose and into his stubbly cheeks.

"You can still turn around," Michael says. "This is your last chance."

I watch the blood drip from the atrocious exit wound from my bullet, spatter on his shoulder. All their blood, all their corrupted bodies, they focus me in a way. I can picture wounds like these appearing on my enemies up there, delivered with extreme prejudice.

"You know I'm not gonna quit," I say.

"Probably get stuck one floor too low anyway," Graney says. "That'd be pretty fucking funny."

The elevator pings, the doors slide open. I already have the shotgun up and leveled at the lobby outside, but it's empty of people. Nice dark blue carpeting, green plants in terracotta pots against the far wall. The lobby leads left and right to a few condos, the door to the stairway and emergency exit are opposite. I stride quickly across, tap the pass card and the panel above the door handle turns green. I step into the cool, cement-smelling stairs, fluorescent lights harsh after the soft orange glow in the hallway.

As the door clicks behind me, Michael says, "Last chance, Eli." But I ignore him and start up, shotgun at the ready.

"The penthouse is two levels," Sly says.

"What?"

"We came out here and counted, remember? Thirty-six stories. The top button on the elevator was thirty-five, but you had to get out on thirty-four. So now we're going up to thirty-five. Means the penthouse has two levels."

I pause for a moment, wondering if that matters. Whatever they're doing up there, will it be on the upper floor? Maybe they even have an exit to the roof and a veranda or something. I guess I'll have to assume that is the case and go in quietly if I can. I nod at Sly and start up again.

As I reach the door to the penthouse level, my ghosts are milling around me nervously. The cold, oily feeling of Dwight Ramsey riding me grows tighter, like he's hugging me for comfort. Man, I won't miss having one of these bastards on my back every second.

"Feels bad," Sly says.

"Yeah, horrible energy up there," Graney says, looking up like he can see through the floor.

I shrug. "I guess that's because they already started. But that's good, I want them busy. I need more help now. Can one of you go through, tell me what's on the other side of that door?"

Michael steps past me, pushes through. A moment later he's back. "The other side is a hallway, a few doors either side, all bedrooms, I think. Elevator at the end. It opens out into a large lounge area. I didn't see farther. There's someone standing right there." He points at the door.

"Standing guard, you mean?"

"I guess so. And there are some people in the lounge farther up, I couldn't see how many. I've never been there before so I could only go a little way from you before I got hauled back."

"Okay then." I reach up and tap lightly on the door, a polite knock. Nothing happens.

"You're knocking?" Graney asks.

I tap a little harder. A little more insistent, but not too loud. Hopefully only the guy right on the other side will hear. Come on, who can ignore a knock at the door. Especially one where no one is supposed to be.

There's a click and it cracks open halfway, a burly guy with dark hair and a neat, short beard looks out, frowning. "You got the wrong fl—"

He doesn't finish the sentence because one of my razor-honed bowie knives open his throat right back to his spine. I grab him with my free hand and twist my body, hauling him through to send him in a header down the stairs. He smears bright red against the pale cement as he tumbles down, managing a kind of burbling grunt as he rag-dolls, no doubt already dead, or close enough to it. I slip in and quietly close the door behind me, lean against it. The pale cream carpet is plush as hell, which is excellent for stealth. I stare along the hallway, some forty feet or more before it opens out into a living room, but it seems no one heard. No one is coming. I can see the edge of white leather sofas and armchairs, one pair of feet crossed at the ankle as someone sits back in one. Glimpses of glass-topped chrome tables and beyond all that a wall of glass looking out over the Las Vegas night. I hear a TV burbling, a low murmur of conversation. There's more than one guy in there and I need to stay quiet if I can. Seems unlikely though.

I creep along the hallway, looking into each room. There's three one side, two the other, then the elevator. The first two doors are ajar, darkened bedrooms beyond. Second on the left is a bathroom, massive and marble with a huge hot tub. The last door on either side is closed. I move up to the one on left and nod at Michael.

He leans his head through the door, then comes back. "A study or office. Dark, no one there."

I point at the last door on the right, moving a little closer. He looks in. "Big ass bedroom, got a four-fucking-poster bed in there. Lights are on, but no one there."

I slide along the wall until I'm close to the end of the hallway, tip my head at it.

Michael and Sly walk forward, Graney moves a little away from me. Not sure why they're spreading out. "Four guys in here," Michael says. "Stairs on the other side up to another level. Must be where the action is. These four look bored, like they're waiting."

It feels wrong, them just standing there talking in normal conversational tones. I know intellectually that no one else can see them or hear them, but would it hurt them to pretend to be cautious? Maybe whisper at least. Then a thought occurs to me. What if there's someone like Luxana here who *can* see them? I guess I'll find out soon enough.

I move back down the hallway, gesturing my ghosts to follow. I need to split these four up a little if I can, and I don't have much time before the eclipse reaches full. I push open the door to one of the farthest bedrooms, step into the shadows and then call out. "Hey! Little help?"

I hope to hell they don't all come.

"The fuck, Tony?" someone shouts.

Tony's dead, motherfucker. "Help me out here!" I call.

"Jesus fuck," there's more muttering and I hear movement.

My ghosts are in the hall and Sly says, "One guy coming, big, but more fat than muscle. No gun in sight."

"The fuck are you, Tony?"

"In here."

"You sound fucking weird, man, what the hell?"

He goes to the wrong door, the one opposite where I'm hiding. That's okay, I can work with it. I step briskly across the hall, slap a hand across his mouth and keep going, drive him forward into the room. My bowie knife slams in between his ribs, one, two, three times, the deep *chunk* of it muffled by his weight. He flinches and cries out against my palm, but I reach around and stab him again, this time hard in the chest, hugging tight to me. He slackens and I let him slide to the floor, keeping his mouth covered just in case.

He rolls onto his side, eyes wild, blood bubbling out around my palm. I can tell the fight has gone and I step back.

"The fuck?" he whispers, then his eyes glaze.

"What's happening down there?" a voice calls.

Graney is at the bedroom door. "Another one coming, skinny."

"Where are you two? You know how they feel about us going in any of the rooms. Guys?"

"He's pausing," Graney says. "Smarter, this one. He's suspicious. Okay, he's pulled a piece and he's coming slowly."

Oh well, I guess the stealth ends here. Two down, at least, that leaves only three downstairs. I unhook the shotgun, throw the strap away, and take a deep breath. Here we go.

A quick roll has me out of the door in a crouch, much lower down than this mook would expect. Even as his eyes lock on, the shotgun booms and his chest disintegrates as he flies back, spraying the clean, pale walls with blood. As voices burst out, I'm already up and striding, racking another shell. One guy appears at the end of the hall and I blow his head away, then I'm stepping into the main room. The last of the four is running the other way, heading for the far side. I quicken my pace, rack, and fire. He launches forward as his back blooms scarlet, slams into the wall and slides down it into a heap.

The view of the city from up here is epic, glass walls on both sides of the big room. The TV is showing some late-night chat show, a beautiful Hollywood star sharing some anecdote. A quick scan proves no one else is nearby so I keep moving, across the massive space. An entire floor of a building for three bedrooms, an office, and a living room. How the one percent live.

On the far side of the main living space is another small hallway, a room off to one side with linens, washer, dryer, other stuff. Opposite that are stairs going up, floating design with glass siding.

"This energy is bad, man," Sly says.

All the ghosts are wincing now, acting like they're caught in the winds of a powerful storm. I don't have time to care. Feet come hammering down the stairs, so I blow them away at the knee through the glass. Crystalline squares glitter and sparkle as they rain down, spattered red, and the screaming is high and panicked as the man hits the stairs and slides down. I round the end of the stairway, looking up to see another guy in a track suit just appearing at the top, automatic pistol in hand.

He starts to swing it toward me, but doesn't have time before I blow him backwards.

Angry shouting erupts upstairs as I drop the shotgun, no time to reload, and draw a brace of CZ 75s. I finish the guy whose knees I took out, then both hands are leveling barrels up the stairs. I start to climb.

"Anyone laying in wait?" I ask.

Michael, Sly, and Graney all look down from the landing above and shake their heads. "Not if you're quick," Michael says.

Seems like maybe all these guys so far were just waiting around for their bosses. The Acolytes really didn't expect me to come for them. I'm almost offended at their lack of concern.

But I hear more voices up there. I run and find myself in a wide lobby, neatly carpeted like downstairs, tables against the walls with expensive-looking vases and other ornaments.

In front of me is a short hallway, one door either side, and then dark wood double-doors at the end. I can hear chanting coming from beyond the double doors. My ghosts are grimacing, bracing to stand still, their spectral hair swimming in a static wind I can't feel or hear.

"Look out!" Michael manages through gritted teeth, just as both doors on either side swing open and four men lean out into the hallway. They're all armed and bullets fly.

I'm moving on autopilot. As soon as the doors opened, I went down and right. As the first face appeared, I put a bullet in it. It disappeared back as another on that side leveled his weapon and fired. Still moving I jerked backwards, my leg and lower back screaming at the sudden change in direction, muscles forcing bones to move in strange angles. The wall right beside my head explodes as the round hits it. That would have gone through my head first if I hadn't managed to shift.

The two from the opposite door start firing, but I hit the deck and roll around the corner of the hallway. I stand up, press my back to the wall, guns ready. Three of them there and at least one a damn good shot. Or maybe he was lucky. I'll err on the side of caution and consider him a marksman.

I dip a shoulder forward, revealing just an inch of myself for a fraction of a second before ducking back, and a hail of bullets tears up the wall. They're crouched and ready, tigers waiting to pounce.

"They're in the hallway," Graney says. "Three abreast, just standing there, weapons leveled."

"You're pinned down," Michael says.

"Now what?" Sly asks.

"Goddamnit, cocheese, you fucking had to be Batman."

"Hold tight!" I whisper, then roll, using my shoulder like a break-fall to keep my hands free, right across the mouth of the hallway to the other side. Bullets rain, but as I go, I rapid fire from both CZ 75s, peppering the area as widely as possible.

There are screams of pain, but I'm gritting my teeth against my own hurt. My body was low enough to catch them out, but one of them got a bullet into my leg as I went over, punching into the meat of my right calf about four inches below the back of my knee. Went right through, but it hurts like a motherfucker and it's bleeding hard. Fuck it.

I have to take a chance, I can't let that keep bleeding. I put my guns on the ground, sitting where I rolled, and shrug out of the long coat. I rip out a section of lining, fold it into as thick a bandage as possible and start to bind my leg tight. Not tourniquet-tight, but close to it. I have to be able to move, but I need to stop that bleed. The pain is high and electric, makes me breathe fast and shallow, agony whistling from my leg up just about every nerve ending I have. I try to breathe through it, use the hurt to focus. I am not getting dizzy. I am definitely not getting fucking dizzy.

"At least tell me I got one of 'em," I snarl through gritted teeth.

"Two, actually," Sly says. "One down, curled up around a gutshot. He's as good as finished. Another you clipped in the shoulder. He's hurt and switched his gun to his other hand."

"Might put off his aim, at least," I say.

"Third one coming around the corner any second though," Graney says urgently.

Fuck! I drag the knot tight and snatch up a pistol just as the guy steps around the wall. The only thing that saves me is his assumption I would have moved farther back. He's looking just over and past me as he rounds the wall, and at the moment, it takes his eyes and gun to track a little lower I pump three bullets, championship grouping, right in his chest. He's dead before he hits the ground.

Howling against the hurt through my calf, I stand and step into the hallway entrance, trusting the guy with the gun in his off-hand might be a fraction slower than me. It's all I need. And I get it. We fire simultaneously, but his first shot goes wide. Mine doesn't. He fires twice more, but so do I and mine all find their mark while his find the ceiling.

Double doors at the end of the short hallway are all that stand between me and whatever these bastards are up to. My ghosts stand in front of me, grimacing, their hair whipping around like they're standing in a gale. Which is weird, because it's still and silent except for the moaning of the gutshot mook and my own ragged breath.

I kick the mook hard, right under the chin, and he's out. Let him bleed slow and quiet now.

"What's beyond?" I ask, nodding at the doors, trying to ignore the searing pain in my calf.

They shake their heads.

"Can't tell," Michael says with a wince. He tries to walk forward, but it's like he's glued in place. "Whatever's happening, we can't get close."

"That's inconvenient," I say.

Oh well, nothing for it, I suppose. I hope they're busy in there, enough to give me a moment. I lift my good leg, balancing painfully on the injured one, and drive my foot into the middle of the doors. My guns are held level, one in each hand, ready.

The doors bang back and there's five...no six mooks all lined up, AR15s or something similar trained on me. Four men, two women, all hard-faced as hell. I could start firing, but I'd be mincemeat in seconds.

Well, fuck. I hoped to get farther than this.

"Well done, dick cheese," Graney says. "You killed all the bodyguards, all the little people, and the rich and corrupt are untouched. Again. You're just another cog in their fucking machine."

Why is no one firing? My fingers twitch on the triggers. Could I drop six people with automatics? I'm good, but at about ten feet range? No one's that good.

"I want him alive!" a voice yells. "I'll take my time with him when we're done here."

My gaze, until now entirely occupied with the bristling barrels of my imminent death, moves past the line of armed guards and I see the room beyond. It's large, like a lounge area with more of those white leather sofas and armchairs. A bar along one side, a massive TV screen taking up half a side wall. A couple of doors lead off the other side. But the room only takes up half the level. On the far side are glass bifold doors, all slid back so the entire wall is open to a massive rooftop patio. It's easily half the size of the entire floor, a pool at one end with a hard cover over it, lots of tables and chairs and sun loungers all pushed back to the sides. A glass railing wraps around the three sides not connected to the room, offering a massive view out across the city. But it's the naked people that really catch my eye.

There must be thirty or forty of them, various ages, men and women. Some are instantly recognizable, powerful politicians, ex-presidents, movie stars, TV anchors, business leaders. Others I have no idea who they are, but they seem equally at home in the crowd.

One man, easily late 60s, fat and balding, his penis almost lost in a thick tuft of gray pubic hair, points into the corner of the room near the bar. "Tie him up good." Then he turns back to the group. They're moving into a rough circle, taking up the vast majority of the huge patio, chanting, looking up. This whole venture, me making it this far, has taken less than fifteen minutes. A big digital clock on the wall reads 1:16 a.m. Two minutes until the full eclipse.

The armed guards move forward. The two women step aside to cover me while the men grab me and drag me into the room. Kinda sexist. The red moon, the Blood Moon which is also a Blue Moon, is massive and directly above the gathering circle outside. The guards strip me of weapons and drag a tubular steel chair out from the side of a dining table. In seconds I'm seated in it, back against the bar, hands and feet tied to the frame, a few loops of rope around my chest and the chair back. They're not gentle, and I'm not going anywhere any time soon. Damn it, I got so close. What a waste.

From where I'm tied, I can see about half of the moon under the edge of the roof. I can see the circle of naked cultists. About eight or nine of them are seated in a tight circle, holding hands, chanting. The bigger gathering is forming a circle around this smaller one.

I look for my ghosts and they're near the door, all four straining forward like they're walking into a hurricane. They've made it about six feet into the room so far.

"What's holding you up?" I ask, ignoring the confused looks of the bodyguards.

"Whatever they're doing," Sly says, struggling to raise a hand to point at the smaller, seated circle. "They been at that a while now."

"Whipping up an energetic storm," Michael says.

"Fucking burns!" Graney growls.

But still they're trying to get forward. I don't know why. Get to me? Just plain curiosity? I notice Dwight doesn't say anything, but his face is twisted in concentration and he's moving farther forward than the others. He stands a little taller, seems less affected. But I don't know what difference it'll make, what can any of them do now?

"He secure?" the fat man asks over his shoulder.

"Yes, sir," one of the armed guards says.

"Then get to it! We have one minute."

The guards have a quick conversation, then one of the women stays close to me and the other five walk out onto the patio and take up ready positions. Two stand to one side, the other three move out of my line of sight toward a back corner. The waiting two hold their weapons casually, but they watch the gathering intently. Are they there to shoot someone if...what? If someone does something wrong?

"Don't know shit about shit, do you," Graney says. "Idiot."

Graney, Sly and Michael are nearer to me now, not struggling any more but leaning hard against an invisible force, seemingly just to remain in place. Their hair still whips around and the edges of them seem to stretch and fracture, like they're TV images slightly out of tune. But Dwight is still driving ahead, and he's nearly made it to the patio.

"The hell is he doing?" I ask.

"What is that idiot ever doing?" Sly asks. "I don't think even he knows."

"Like a dog barking at a squirrel because it's there, he's pushing against this shit because he can," Michael says.

The group outside join hands and start a loud chant. My ghosts make noises of pain and discomfort as the group raise their linked arms to the sky.

"Those rings they wear are combining this power somehow," Michael says, bracing harder against the preternatural wind.

Dwight yowls in angry determination, pushing harder into it. He's a couple of steps onto the patio now, his form stretching and spiking, almost breaking apart at the edges.

There's a scream and the three guards are dragging a naked, and clearly very reluctant, woman across the patio.

"NOW!" the fat man yells.

They duck under the arms of the outer ring and lift her, drop her unceremoniously into the center of the smaller circle. That group release their grips on each other and snatch from the ground glittering silver knives I hadn't noticed before. The woman tries to roll over, struggling to get up and away, but she doesn't have a chance. Those knives plunge into her, rise up, fall again. She bucks and thrashes then collapses. The larger group is chanting furiously, the woman screams as she's stabbed again and again, then her screams cease as her blood floods across the flagstones.

Even I can feel the strange wind now, a hot static that whips in eddies and vortices all around. It smells of metal and blood and something else. Something entirely unnatural. The moon expands, the half I can see growing suddenly huge, more massive than it has any right to be. Swelling from ruddy to scarlet, like the woman's blood. It blinks open like an eye.

My mind rebels at the sight, the eye staring down on the group, its iris like fire writhing in an ocean of blood. And in the center of the fire is a pupil, unfathomably huge, blacker than night, and galaxies swirl in there.

"This can't be happening," I yell, my voice whipped away by the cosmic winds. "People everywhere would see! For miles around."

"It's only happening here, in this place," Michael says, face twisted in pain. "This is outside normal space. This is impossible."

Dwight Ramsey is out there, staring up, weak, stubbled chin hanging open in shocked awe. We can only see half of it, the roof partially obscuring our view, but he's there taking in the whole profane spectacle.

"What the fuck is it?" I shout.

"Only part of it," Graney says. "That's just...a door. A gateway to something beyond, something... Fuck!"

My ghosts are staggering, clearly in pain. Dwight is shaking all over, his entire form vibrating. The cultists are chanting rhythmically, faces upturned, and I can see waves of energy washing over them, bathing them. They soak it up, gasping, exhorting, bodies flexing as it enters them. They're crying out in pain and joy. Beyond all human privilege, they gain their luck and ability, their influence, through whatever that energy is.

Even I can sense something gargantuan beyond the eye of the moon now. Some impossible entity, partially revealed, like glimpsing a whale's fin above water, knowing there's so much more of the creature out of sight. And without any prior knowledge, it's impossible to know what the rest of it might be like. Despite the energies washing down, I sense its ice-cold ambivalence. We are nothing.

Like rain washing the dirt from a road, the cloud above isn't aware of the cleaning taking place. We are insignificant. The cosmos cares not for the dust.

Luxana's words, coming back to me.

"It's incredible!" Dwight yells, and I hear him despite the now howling cosmic hurricane slamming down.

"It is vast!" Dwight says. "I can *feel* it. I could almost *touch* it! My god, y'all, it is wonderful and it is terrifying!" And he's laughing maniacally, clearly losing whatever he might have retained of his mind.

I could almost touch *it!*

And I remember more of Luxana talking about this thing, what she said before.

I imagine it has no idea. Their ritual simply opens something, focused through a full moon. They get the power by taking it without permission. If the entity knew, who knows what might happen? But how would it even notice?

"Dwight!" I yell into the maelstrom. "Dwight, touch it!"

"The fuck are you doing?" Graney shouts.

"Help him!" I point to Dwight. "You four, you're outside this world, this space! Bridge the gap. Get its *attention!*"

The three of them look at me for a moment, eyes wide.

"We're dead anyway, right? Otherwise?"

The three of them turn their attention to Dwight, pushing their hands forward. Dwight bucks, glances back, mouth stretched in manic laughter, then he turns his face up again. His hands shoot into the air, palms up, fingers spread wide.

"Bridge whatever unnatural space you fuckers inhabit," I scream. "Call to it!"

And Dwight starts to scream. His voice cracking, a sound beyond anything a human should be able to make, he howls through the void, shrieks into the abyss. And I feel it when the abyss hears.

Briefly, the entity out there spares Dwight a moment's thought, momentarily notices the ritual taking place. The radiation of its attention is nuclear.

The woman guarding me runs forward in shock to look, then screams at whatever she sees. She reverses her weapon and eats the barrel of her rifle, the back of her head vaporizing in the air. I'm burned, agonized, by the flood of awareness and use all my strength to launch the chair over sideways. I drive my feet against the bar to slide farther under the roof, into the corner out of view. Still, I feel the unnatural searing burn of its gaze. My ghosts are screaming, their forms tattering like old rags in a gale, but still they reach, still they exhort.

But nothing overrides the screams of the gathered Acolytes of Ur. In the wash of that profane sight, they're corrupted. Thrashing and screaming, their bodies bulge and flex, they're melding into a singular mass of undulating flesh under the blasphemous awareness of whatever is out there. My ghosts are traumatized by it, but aren't physical and can't be hurt like that. Mortal flesh, it seems, has no such protection.

As the acolytes corrupt, collapsing into two rings of melded flesh, their portal ritual is interrupted. I imagine the eye of the moon snapping closed, the energies cut off. My ghosts collapse, flickering half in and half out of existence around me.

Everything seems dark and still. Looking across the floor from where I lay, I can see a massive conformation of broken flesh, weakly undulating. Dozens of people in agony, dying, but many parts not yet dead, all melted and merged, horrifically entwined. Eyes roll among hair, teeth chatter and snap, elbows and knees flex and twitch in huge rolls of skin and muscle. Moans and cries of piteous hurt and hate rise up. Coughs and mewls of horror and agony grow weaker, but don't cease.

Chapter 57

It takes Michael a painful hour to slowly unpick one knot at my wrist, then I can finally free myself from the rest. The whole time, that massive ring of heaving flesh moans and whimpers. The smaller circle inside is a puddle of molten skin and bone. The guards are recognizable by their clothing, but they're broken and corrupted too. Part of me wants to take my guns and end the hideous suffering, but where would I start? Are there brains behind those weakly rolling eyes? Are there organs beyond those chattering teeth? Bones poke stark and white through mounded flesh that might be one or three or ten acolytes combined. In places blood and ichor leaks across the flagstones.

Michael, Sly and Graney stay well back from it as I slowly limp around the mass. It's hideous and fascinating. Even if I could somehow end their suffering, maybe I wouldn't. Fuck these predatory assholes, every one of them. What the hell is going to happen here now? At some point, this will be found. Imagine trying to explain it. I expect it'll be covered up, an impossibility too weird to accept, so forget about it. There are a lot of victims though, the kind of people that will be missed. Not like the little people who vanish every day, who no one but their precious few really care about. It'll be interesting to see how any of the disappearances here are reported. There's not one recognizable face anywhere in this mess, so I doubt this will be realized as the final resting place of these big names, these influential people. These unnatural human predators.

Dwight is sitting cross-legged right where he was standing when it all went down. He's rocking gently, hands in his lap. As I finally come around to him, he looks up, eyes wide and manic, mouth split in a grin.

"Stronger than those fuckers, ain't I!" he says, gesturing back at the other three ghosts. "Guess maybe I might come in useful again, huh, cocheese? Better keep me around."

I can't help a laugh escaping. I guess he has a point. "You...okay?" I ask. It sounds lame.

"Fuck no, cocheese. But what choice do I have?"

I suppose that's a good point too. "Come on."

He staggers to his feet, stumbling weak but moving forward. I gather my stuff and we leave. "You two better figure out what you're good for," I say to Sly and Graney as we stumble down the stairs. "Give me good reason to keep you around as well."

Chapter 58

For a day or two after that horrible night I'm on edge, staying in the motel. But I don't have any of my ghosts riding on my back to hide me. No one comes after me.

Dwight is changed. It's hard to say how, exactly, but he's different. I guess time will tell just how different. If nothing else, he's quieter, which is a blessing for all of us. Even Sly is giving him a kind of side-eye of respect for what he pulled off. I guess even unrepentant, dumbass racists can grow if they're given a chance.

Back in the apartment I find most of our stuff scattered and broken, but my clothes are mostly undamaged. A few reports are coming in on the news, certain influential people missing, but it's all low key. I wonder who found what and what stories may or may not get told. I don't care, time to move on. I figure I probably won't come back to Vegas again any time soon, if at all.

My cell phone rings, the one only Bridget knows the number for. And Luxana, but I know it's not her. I already sent a text that said thanks. She was impressed, I could tell.

"Hey!" I say brightly, trying to mask the shock that still permeates me.

"Wow," Bridget says. "You're still alive." There's a palpable relief in her voice.

"Yep, against all odds, really."

"Is it over?"

"Yeah. Done. I can come to you. I don't want to be in Vegas a minute longer."

"Don't blame you. I'm not planning to come back there either."

There's a pause and I sense something in it. Some weight. My stomach sinks. "You okay?" I ask, to circle around the subject.

"I am, yeah. But Eli..." She sighs. "I'm sorry, Eli, I'm not going to tell you where I am."

Fuck. My ghosts are respectfully silent, though they watch with sad eyes. "I can't change your mind?" I ask.

"I love you, Eli. I really do. You're... Well, you're not like anyone I've ever known. I just can't deal with the weird stuff, you know? And the weird, well it's a big part of who you are, right?"

"I suppose I can't deny that. Whether I want it or not, it is."

"Yeah. I'm an earthy girl. I like the real world, I like to gamble and make money. I wish I could still do that with you, but there's more to a decision like that than I'm willing to take on."

"I get it." And I really do. I fucking hate it, but I get it. "I'm sorry, I didn't get your money back."

"I have plenty. I'm already making more. Open an account under one of your fake IDs and text me the details. I have a chunk of cash for you. You earned it, so you deserve it. I don't want to leave you struggling."

"Okay. Thanks."

"And you have this private cell number. Call if you need money or anything, yeah? Anything normal, I mean."

"I will. I love you too, Bridget. I'm sorry it had to go down this way."

"Me too. More than I can say. Take care, Eli. Try to stay out of trouble."

"You too."

There's another moment's pause, then she hangs up. I sit in stunned silence for a moment, then a text comes in.

> *I'm serious about the money. Please send me bank details.*

I already have a couple of fake ID accounts, so I copy details from one into a text and send it. A moment later she texts:

> *100k deposited. Take care. xxx*

Those kisses help me feel better more than the money does. Bridget is a good person, she really does deserve better than me. I text back my thanks and replicate the three kisses. Maybe one day we'll cross paths again. I hope so, but only on her terms.

With a sigh, I put the phone aside and start to redress the bullet wound in my calf. It's ugly, but my home stitching is holding. Not the first time I've patched myself up. It hurts like hell, but it's slowly getting better. As long as I don't get an infection, it should be fine.

The four ghosts are lined up along the sofa opposite me, watching in silence. I glance up at them. Michael with his head blown away on one side, Sly with his gaping chest wound, dripping blood, Graney with his throat torn open and scarlet blooms on his chest, Dwight with the pinpoint bullet hole between his newly crazed eyes. I can picture the massive exit wound that removed most of the back of his head. They look at me, half-concerned, half-expectant.

"Guess I'm on my own then," I say, with a smile. "Except for you fuckers. And all you have is me. Lucky us, eh?"

END

Acknowledgements

I get enormous pleasure writing Eli Carver stories, so huge thanks to L.C. Marino and L.P. Hernandez at Sobelo Books for bringing these novellas back into print in this omnibus edition. Thanks also to Tony and everyone at Grey Matter Press for taking a chance on these books the first time around. I am stunned and indebted to Paul Tremblay, Brian Keene and Laird Barron (legends all) for their kind words. And of course, thanks to everyone who's had a hand in these stories or any others along the way—you know who you are. Lastly, but far from least, thanks to the readers out there. Without you, we can't keep doing this, so I am forever grateful. And who knows, maybe now there can be some new Eli adventures. Never say never.

About Alan Baxter

Alan Baxter is a multi-award-winning British-Australian author of horror, supernatural thrillers and dark fantasy liberally mixed with crime, mystery and noir. *This Is Horror* podcast calls him "Australia's master of literary darkness" and the *Talking Scared* podcast dubbed him "The Lord of Weird Australia." He's also a martial artist, a whisky-soaked swear monkey, and dog lover. He writes his dark, weird stories deep in the valleys of southern Tasmania. Find him online a t www.alanbaxter.com.au